PRAISE ~~...~~ ~~Library~~

'*Maria in the Moon* is storytelling at its finest. Beech is a beguiling wordsmith. Prepare to be hooked' Amanda Prowse, author of *The Art of Hiding*

'Oh, Louise Beech, what have you done to me? Just finished *Maria in the Moon* and you've had me at the brink of tears. Beautifully constructed, laugh-out-loud funny in places, and achingly sad in others. It's such a beautifully told story of loss and gain. Equal parts Victoria Wood, Alan Bennett and John Irving, all rolled up into an emotive, heart-breaking story. I completely fell in love with it. Thank you' John Marrs, author of *The One*

'Beautiful, poignant, funny, heart-rending, dark – this psychological thriller had me feeling so many different emotions. I was totally enthralled by Catherine and intrigued to find out which memory she had blocked out. This book will stay with me for a very long time. I loved it. Louise Beech is one talented writer!' Claire Douglas, author of *Last Seen Alive*

'In this brave, unsettling book, Louise uses the devastating Hull floods of 2007 as a backdrop to a story of pain and love when horrors from the past rise up. Moving and real' Vanessa Lafaye, author of *At First Light*

'A powerful and moving story about facing buried and difficult memories we would rather forget. Louise Beech is not afraid to tackle challenging but important issues, giving a voice to those stories that are often silenced' Madeleine Black, author of *Unbroken*

'Heartfelt and wry, *Maria in the Moon* will transport you into a keenly observed world; secrets are hidden, people are flawed, but humanity endures' Ruth Dugdall, author of *My Sister and Other Liars*

'*Maria in the Moon* is bold, powerful and redemptive. Full of dark humour and poetry, it charts the story of the complex and compelling Catherine, a woman who is constantly helping others in crisis and yet who has no idea how to help herself. The book follows her as she is forced to face up to the truth of something that happened in her childhood – something so traumatic she can't even remember it. Beech's skill in depicting human flaws and complexities is evident in every page and the result is a gripping, poetic and beautifully observed story, with the kind of characters I will miss and will still be thinking about in months and years to come. A triumph' Katie Marsh, author of *This Beautiful Life*

'This is a story about how we forget in order to survive, and the price we pay. Catherine is prickly, truculent, and utterly believable. Horrible to her stepmother while yearning for love and approval, stumbling her way through life in a way that's both too painful to watch and impossible to look away from. It's not the buried memory that matters so much as the journey of discovery and the impact it has on everyone. This is real life, bruised, torn and coffee-stained, refusing to give up, and finding a way to heal despite all the obstacles. Louise Beech has written a story worth a dozen self-help books; this is showing, not telling' Su Bristow, author of *Sealskin*

'A captivating and haunting exploration of truth, loss and redemption, *Maria in the Moon* grabbed me from the first page and would not let me go' Louisa Treger, author of *The Lodger*

'This is a gorgeous, honest and incredibly moving account of one woman's journey into a lost and painful past. In prose that's both raw and lyrical, Louise Beech delicately unpicks her heroine's tangled history and creates a book I simply couldn't tear myself away from' Cassandra Parkin, author of *The Winter's Child*

'In elegant prose, and with a deep affection for her characters, Louise Beech tells a story for our times. Global weather change is the prism – human relations are the focus. *Maria and the Moon* is in turns tense and affecting ... a wonderful piece of storytelling' Michael J Malone, author of *A Suitable Lie*

'Louise Beech effortlessly captures the grind of real life and infuses it with flourishes of subtle poetry to create a wonderful story' Matt Wesolowski, author of *Six Stories*

'Reading a book by Louise is like a visit to the wrong side of the tracks with a friend to hold your hand. As you pick your way through an unfamiliar and unnerving landscape she is forever saying "look – here is beauty; look, there is goodness"' Richard Littledale, author of *The Journey*

'I love the emotional honesty and glorious imagery of Louise Beech's writing and both are in plentiful supply in this unusual and intriguing story. This is a psychologically complex tale that will provide food for thought long after you finish reading. Highly recommended!' Gill Paul, author of *The Secret Wife*

'Catherine-Maria Hope is a woman with many faces. A face reflected in a cracked mirror creating myriad versions: Catherine, Katrina, Pure Mary, Catherine-Maria; a woman on the edge, in a ripped red dress, circling her past (and the locked-up memory of her ninth year) like an inebriated woman on a dodgy night out. Catherine has been on a few of those. Her memory is pretty good for such occasions and she has the art of self-sabotage honed to within an inch of its life. It is only the year she was nine she can't remember. From the beginning, this new book from the immaculate Louise Beech has a far darker edge. The air of expectancy is freighted with an undercurrent of something unpleasant and deeply disturbing. Catherine's voice is fierce and weighted with words she can only half recall. *Maria in the Moon* is spot on in so many ways. It's a psychological thriller and a sideways love story. It is impossible not to love Catherine-Maria Hope. In the moon or feet on the ground, being sick in a sink or dancing in a red dress in the rain, she will catch you unawares. After you turn the last page you will still sense her, and the echo of yet another woman's story: a story of loss and courage and hope. A million stars to enhance the moon' Carol Lovekin, author of *Ghostbird*

'Catherine Hope, the heroine of Louise Beech's third novel, is a conundrum ... Truculent and defensive, yet desperate to be loved, her personality is as inconstant as the names she has taken over the years ... But who is Catherine really? She, more than anyone, wants to find the answer to this question, to come to terms with what has been long buried. A dark, wonderful novel of self-discovery, of the things we hide inside ourselves and the bravery it takes to face them' Melissa Bailey, author of *Beyond the Sea*

'*Maria in the Moon* is the third novel from Louise Beech and by far the best yet. A novel that will test your senses through to the very last page. A dark psychological thriller with complex and damaged characters. So beautifully written, this is a novel that will linger long after you have finished reading' The Last Word Review

'Louise Beech's writing is so very powerful, she evokes every emotion in her readers. Yet, despite the heartbreak and damage that Catherine and her family suffer, this author injects her own style of true Northern grit and humour, which is subtly and cleverly interwoven throughout the story. Catherine is not a whimsical, fanciful character; she's modern, down-to-earth and, as we say here in the North, a bit of a mardy mare. Her relationship and interactions with her mother are a joy to read; strangely familiar to me, and I guess, to many others. *Maria in the Moon* deals with dark issues that are uncomfortable but necessary. This is superb writing; a story that will stay with me for a long time and is extraordinarily written and presented. There are moments of unexpected beauty from richly complicated characters. It really is quite spellbinding' Random Things through My Letterbox

'I wanted to read this book slowly, to savour every moment, yet found myself racing ahead, just to see what had happened to Catherine in the past and what was going to happen to her next. The book is filled with surprises – some good, some bad and some that turned me into a total wreck. All of Louise Beech's books are different in subject and plot, yet they evoke the same emotions – or rather, all the emotions. I defy anyone to read her books without at least a tear in their eye, although it's more likely to be a trickle or maybe even a flood' Off the Shelf Books

'Wow! *The Mountain in My Shoe* has a gentle start but my goodness it packs a punch. I was in tears at the end ... a moving and powerful book' Jane Lythell, author of *Woman of the Hour*

'Louise Beech proves with this incredibly moving story that the success of her debut *How To Be Brave* – a 2015 *Guardian* Readers' Pick – was no flash in the pan ... A fabulous, exquisitely written novel which will stay with you for a long time after you turn the final page' David Young, author of *Stasi Child*

'This gripping story is the kind of book to put your life on hold for ... I was in floods of tears by the end and know that the characters will stay with me for a very long time. A worthy successor to the brilliant *How To Be Brave*' Katie Marsh, author of *A Life Without You*

'An exquisite novel. Darkly compelling, emotionally charged. And I LOVED it!' Jane Isaac, author of the DI Will Jackman Series

'With great compassion for all her characters, Louise Beech deftly creates a story of the survival of life's sorrows which, with a little help, can lead ultimately to joy' *The Irish Times*

'Beech employs a touch of magic ... [*How To Be Brave* is] ... a gentle book, full of emotion, suitable for young readers, and it's similar in tone to *The Book Thief*, a book that Rose reads with a torch under the bedclothes' *The Irish Times*

'*The Mountain in My Shoe* is cleverly laced with a chilling and gripping storyline about a controlling, possibly psychotic husband. I couldn't put it down. Louise Beech is an author who writers with her heart on her sleeve' Fleur Smithwick, author of *One Little Mistake*

'A fascinating page-turner that wrenches at your insides. It's dark, compelling and highly thought-provoking and left me with tears rolling down my cheeks' Off-the-Shelf Books, selecting *The Mountain in My Shoe* as one of the Top 15 Books of 2016

'It is a brilliantly creative work of fiction, and a beautiful thank-you letter to the magic of stories and storytelling' Anna James, We Love this Book

'It was the two beautifully developed characters that drew me in – I felt real warmth and affection for them' The Very Pink Notebook

'Louise Beech has the ability to make you care about characters you've only known for a few pages, or even paragraphs ... Don't miss this book' The Misstery

'Such a captivating book which had me completely involved in the characters' lives' Portobello Book Blog

'The whole book is perfect. A delicately dictated story which intertwines several threads ... I highly recommend that you get this bought and read as soon as possible!' Emma the Little Book Worm

'Louise Beech writes with such a grace and elegance ... It is hard not to be enchanted by her work' Reflections of a Reader

'*The Mountain in My Shoe* ... is poignant, profound and perfectly crafted ... an absolute must read.' Bloomin Brilliant Books

'Beech's writing is ... deeply readable, the kind of book that changes the reader' Blue Book Balloon

'In places I could not hold back the tears yet the strength found by the characters to move forward make this an uplifting read' Never Imitate

'*The Mountain in My Shoe* is a beautiful and emotive novel that will leave you wanting more' The Welsh Librarian

'*The Mountain in My Shoe* is just a truly wonderful novel that will melt any heart ... I literally could not tear myself away from the story' By The Letter Book Reviews

'An astonishing yet humbling book written with a sensitivity that cannot, and will not, fail to move you' Little Bookness Lane

'This is a beautifully written, imaginative and profound book ... Louise Beech has perfected the art of showing and not telling the reader what is happening' Short Book and Scribes

'Louise's work seems more like tapestry than fiction. Her characters stand out from the page ... Every word-stitch has made them more vivid, believable and engaging' The Preacher's Blog

'*The Mountain in My Shoe* ... was heartbreaking and tragic, but also beautiful. Beech writes of this emotive subject with a steady hand ... A must read' The Bandwagon

'This book is as close to perfection as you'll ever get ... definitely worthy of a 5* rating' The Book Magnet

'The author's writing and narration of Conor's story is elegant, delicately put across and I found it hauntingly beautiful' 27 Book Street

'For me this is a 5* book because of the brilliant way author Louise Beech has of taking the reader right into the heart of the main characters' Emma B Books

'*The Mountain in My Shoe* is beautifully told from the outset, the author's grip of language and hauntingly original metaphor immediately drawing the reader in' Humanity Hallows

'Louise Beech writes with an emotional honesty and bravery that elevates her work from the crowd ... very highly recommended' Mumbling About

'A very cleverly written book' Needing Escapism, selecting *The Mountain in My Shoe* as a Top 2016 read

'The author has an incredible skill of bringing the characters to life and ensuring the reader is truly captivated in every chapter' Compulsive Readers

'Simply beautiful. A moving and hopeful 5 stars' Jen Med's Book Reviews

'This book is going to be with me a long time coming!' Chapter in my Life

'A story that held drama, some mystery, suspense at the right times, and so much depth of emotions' Its Book Talk

'*The Mountain in My Shoe* is the type of book to bring many different readers together to connect over something so wonderful and magical' The Suspense is Thrilling Me

'*The Mountain In My Shoe* deserves all its hype and much more ... I will be recommending this book to everyone' The Book Review Café

'A stunning book. I found it incredibly refreshing to read something so beautifully written and emotive' The Book Whisperer

'Heart-wrenching at parts, makes you think you know what was going on, but has that twist to show you that you REALLY didn't know what was coming' Nutty Reads Reviews

'*The Mountain in My Shoe* explores who and what shapes us as people, it's a story about love in whatever form that may take. A beautiful book' Woman Reads Books

'Louise Beech is a fabulous storyteller with a real talent' If Only I Could Read Faster

'I cried, I smiled, I laughed, I was frightened, I felt sorry. I lived this story' Chocolate N Waffles

'There were twists and heartbreak but also friendship and love in another fantastic and heartwarming novel from Louise Beech' Steph's Book Blog

'If you wish to be moved deeply and taken on a gripping and beautiful exploration of love, loss and the power of emotional connection then I can suggest nothing better' Shaz's Book Blog

'It truly tugged at my heartstrings but all the while balancing that emotion with a promise of hope ... This stunning book will stay with me' My Chestnut Tree Reading

'Louise is such an emotive writer, you can't help but get wrapped up in the characters and their lives' Bibliophile Book Club

'It is intriguing, deftly crafted and captivating ... I have a feeling that I have not read this book for the last time' Richard Littledale, author of *The Littlest Star*

'An absolute joy to read ... Louise is a natural storyteller' My Reading Corner

Maria in the Moon

Louise Beech has been writing since she could physically hold a pen. She regularly writes travel pieces for the *Hull Daily Mail*, where she was a columnist for ten years. Her short fiction has won the Glass Woman Prize, the Eric Hoffer Award for Prose, and the Aesthetica Creative Works competition, as well as shortlisting twice for the Bridport Prize. Her debut novel, *How To Be Brave*, was a number one bestseller on Kindle in the UK and Australia, and a *Guardian*'s Readers' Pick in 2015. *The Mountain in My Shoe* was longlisted for the *Guardian* Not the Booker Prize. Louise is currently writing her fourth book. She lives with her husband and children on the outskirts of Hull – the UK's 2017 City of Culture – and loves her job as Front of House Usher at Hull Truck Theatre, where her first play was performed in 2012.

You can follow Louise on Twitter @LouiseWriter and on Facebook at www.facebook.com/louise.beech, or visit her website: www.louise-beech.co.uk.

Maria in the Moon

Louise Beech

**ORENDA
BOOKS**

Orenda Books
16 Carson Road
West Dulwich
London SE21 8HU
www.orendabooks.co.uk

First published in the UK in 2017 by Orenda Books

2

ISBN 978-1-910633-82-3
eISBN 978-1-910633-83-0

Typeset in Garamond by MacGuru Ltd
Printed and bound by CPI Group (UK) Ltd, Croydon CR0 4YY

SALES & DISTRIBUTION

In the UK and elsewhere in Europe:
Turnaround Publisher Services
Unit 3, Olympia Trading Estate
Coburg Road,
Wood Green
London
N22 6TZ
www.turnaround-uk.com

In the USA and Canada:
Trafalgar Square Publishing
Independent Publishers Group
814 North Franklin Street
Chicago, IL 60610
USA
www.ipgbook.com

In Australia and New Zealand:
Affirm Press
28 Thistlethwaite Street
South Melbourne VIC 3205
Australia
www.affirmpress.com.au

For details of other territories, please contact *info@orendabooks.co.uk*

This is dedicated to Grace, Claire and Colin.
I wrote this one first; and I loved you all first.

'Your memory is a monster; you forget – it doesn't. It simply files things away. It keeps things for you, or hides things from you – and summons them to your recall with a will of its own. You think you have a memory; but it has you.'

John Irving

'And love was a forgotten word. Remember?'

Marilyn Monroe

'Everyone in Hull has a story about that day.'

Suzanne Finn – Hull City of Culture volunteer

Pure Mary

Long ago my beloved Nanny Eve chose my name.

When she called me it in her sing-song voice, I felt as lovely as the shimmering Virgin Mary statue on the bureau in her hallway. When I went for Sunday lunch, I'd sneak away from the table while everyone ate lemon meringue pie and I'd stroke Mary's vibrant blue dress. Then, listening for adults approaching the door, I'd kiss her peeking-out feet – very carefully so that I didn't knock her over.

I didn't want to break her. Not because I knew my mother would send me to bed without supper. Not because I knew I'd be reminded of my clumsiness for weeks after. But because Nanny Eve was given Virgin Mary by her own mother, and she loved it dearly. She would whisper to me that 'virgin' meant 'pure'. Pure Mary. Some of the letters in Mary were like those in *my* middle name.

But that was all we shared.

She was perfect, whereas I was always in bother. I'd try to imagine how nice it would be to shine so brightly and to not have fingers that got smacked for messing up clean windows. I'd hiss in Pure Mary's ear that when I got older I'd have a statue in *my* house and polish her with a special cloth, just like Nanny Eve polished all her special ornaments.

After the Sunday lunch pots had been washed, I'd slip into the living room and sit at Nanny Eve's feet. She'd always hum the same tune, and I'd know that meant I made her happy. Patting my head, she would say my long, sing-song name, and then she'd get on with her knitting – hats for relatives and coats for my small dolls, and while she did it, she'd tell me about her friends and church and the poor. And then she'd sing again, and the sun would break through her lattice window and land on our two curly heads.

But one day she stopped singing.

She stopped calling me the long, pretty name she'd chosen when I arrived.

I try now to remember why, but I just can't.

I think it was winter; I think the sun no longer had the strength to kiss our heads.

I know I'd accidentally smashed the Virgin Mary.

Utterly unfixable, she had been replaced with a pink plastic lady whose long, spiky eyelashes and crimson lips didn't call to me. Nanny Eve never polished her.

But there was something else; something I couldn't remember. Something as black as feverish, temperature-fuelled nightmares. Something that couldn't be fixed or replaced. Something that stopped all the singing in our house for a long time. But when I try to think of it, all I can see are the shattered porcelain pieces of Pure Mary spread across the floor.

Now I'm the one who chooses the names. I give people longer, different and more quirky ones. Whatever they're really called doesn't matter to me. I'll shorten them, or lengthen them, sometimes switch the letters around, or add a Y. Change them altogether.

Anything that means I've taken the word apart and made it whole again. Anything that might help me remember why my name got smashed up with Pure Mary all those years ago.

An *i* causes chaos

'So which name will you choose?' he asked.

'Katrina,' I said.

'Katrina?'

I pointed at a faded newspaper on the coffee table – at the headline that read 'Hurricane Katrina Hits' and the picture of the devastation it had caused: black, white and grey chaos. The column alongside had a colour picture of Paris Hilton emerging from a car, her silver dress blinking in the flashlights and visible crotch discoloured by a ring of coffee.

'Good choice,' said Norman, his eyes still on the stain. 'Memorable. We're off to a great start, Katrina.'

In this airless room of telephones, notepads and mismatched chairs, Norman would decide if I could stay; if I could be a volunteer. I imagined other interviewees might feel possessive about their names, might argue that they couldn't answer to anything else. Our first names are the one constant in our lives, travelling with us wherever we go, stamped in black on our passports and credit cards and driving licences. But I liked the idea of choosing who I could be; of starting anew.

'We change them so we're unique,' Norman said. 'So we're easily identified for an urgent call.'

'Suits me,' I said, and wanted to add: *I rarely call people by their given name.*

I'd only known Norman's for fifteen minutes and wondered why he'd chosen one that evoked a psychotic serial killer. Perhaps his real name was in honour of a long-dead relative. He wore a red T-shirt with *Sesame Street*'s Bert and Ernie on the front; their faces creased when he reached for the file bearing the name everyone calls me. A photo of my sullen face was stapled to the top by my furrowed forehead.

'I'm the only Norman here so I got to keep my name,' he said.

So he hadn't picked it – his parents had, many years before.

'Some volunteers choose a relative or family pet's name. Some opt for a film star; although callers might not take a Joaquin too seriously.'

'Especially if they're speaking to a female,' I said.

'Quite.' He stirred his coffee and tapped the spoon on the rim of his mug before placing it on the desk, parallel to my folder. 'We don't want names to eclipse why we're here. Take you, Catherine. We already have a Cathryn but she doesn't have an *i* in her name. On paper we could differentiate between you, but on the phone – well, imagine the confusion!' Norman held his hands in the air to animate the chaos my name with its *i* might cause.

Behind him was a sash window, with one shutter hanging perilously by a single hinge and the other fastened across the glass, giving a half-view of the street: overgrown gardens dusted with snow; fat hedges and fir trees.

'We also have a Jane who's the only one,' he said. 'Chris number two we call Christopher. Sam is really Sam, but Paul is Al because we had another Paul who left after his leg never healed. You see?'

'Um, maybe,' I mumbled.

'Flood Crisis is about sacrifice,' he said. 'And it starts with our names.'

The area behind us looked popular: colourful chairs and beanbags surrounded a centrally placed, stubby Formica table. Much-thumbed magazines covered its scratched surface, and on top a Barbara Cartland novel lay face down, as though she was burying her head in shame at a bad review.

'So, were you flooded?' Norman asked. It was the question we all asked one another. It had replaced enquiring after health or families.

'Yes,' I said.

'Is that why you volunteered?'

'No.'

It wasn't, not really. It was because of a flyer; and a child's slipper. I'd been buying wine in a supermarket and found a tiny silver shoe in my trolley, utterly at odds with my other items. When I went to hand it in at the customer service desk, the Flood Crisis flyer fluttered into my trolley, landing next to the slipper. The young girl on the desk said, 'There's a sign from above if ever I saw one.'

I'd buried it at the bottom of my bag beneath tissues and tampons. But the image of the slipper had kept me awake and had somehow become intertwined with the flyer. Was some child crying for her favourite star-coloured shoe; was she in a strange bedroom after her family home had flooded? Did she wander the new place, one foot cold and bare? Only when I called the number on the Flood Crisis flyer and asked for an interview did I sleep properly again.

Now here I was, ready to volunteer, despite it being only months since I'd walked out of a similar crisis centre. I felt destined to be here; not because I'd been flooded or because I'd done similar work before, and not because of the slipper either; but because of the name-changing.

Norman stopped playing with my folder and put it on top of the others. His fingers tapped the desk. Hands fascinate me; his were as slender as an anorexic woman's. I looked at my own red-raw fingers and resisted scratching them.

'Tell me about when you were flooded.'

'It was crap.'

'Crap?' Norman stared at my chest a moment before snapping back to my face.

I should have offered more. I was going to be taking calls from those who'd endured the same downpour, but 'crap' was all I had.

None of us had expected the rain. One weather report called it a freak event. Some said it was biblical. Climate change. Punishment. Atonement. Whatever had caused it, at the end of June 2007 it rained for two days. Relentless, like someone had left the taps on full. Water filled gardens, cars and houses. Hull had been labelled the forgotten city. It received the least government help and featured in few headlines. But our people came together. We carried one another's sofas upstairs and shared sandbags, towels and stories.

'Crap' was an apt word.

'Shall I tell you more about us, then?' Norman asked.

'Yes, do,' I said.

I uncrossed my legs and put my bag under the plastic chair. Interviews always make me fidget. The movement knocked off a shoe and it landed near Norman's foot with a rude clomp. I'd borrowed some too-big red wedges from my flat-mate, Fern. I fumbled it back on.

'We started two months after the flood,' he explained. 'We were six volunteers, now we're thirty-odd. Not many compared with the big places, but we put the time in. Other helplines were swamped after the rain, so something devoted entirely to flood victims was urgently needed.'

I nodded at Norman several times and wondered if the walls were painted school-PE-shorts-blue to create calm. The shade was at odds with the paisley sofa, velvet chairs and orange cushions. Norman's voice droned on, as irritating as a wasp in a bedroom.

'The rain caused all sorts of problems.' He slurped his coffee. 'People clearing out their ruined belongings remembered things long buried: affairs, given-up babies, secret abortions. We hear these stories every day.'

The Flood Crisis sign above the window seemed unnecessary. Someone had agreed with me – they'd made an O into a lake and drawn a headless, drowning stickman. Next to his body they'd written, 'I've eaten my own head.'

'It's like the water stripped the victims of their inhibitions,' Norman went on. 'The floodgates have opened and everything is being washed out.'

'Like my drawer,' I said.

'Your drawer?'

'There are two drawers in my kitchen,' I explained, moving my hand as though opening one. 'They meet at a corner. When one is open, I can't open the other. They can never *both* be open. No, wait, that's the opposite of the flood bringing old hurts to the surface. Sorry. It was a stupid metaphor.'

Norman stared at me until I looked down at the black skirt I'd thought suitable for a crisis-line interview and the streaky fake tan I'd hastily applied because my only tights were laddered.

'We're here to do the clean-up,' said Norman.

A steam trains calendar hung above his desk. November belonged to a burgundy one with gold lettering. It would be Jane's birthday in two weeks, the day after mine. Then Ed would celebrate forty, but, judging by the sad face drawn there, he wasn't excited about it.

Dates stay in my head, stuck like superglued post-it notes. I've a curious knack for remembering birthdays. Friends tell me theirs just once and I remember long after they've departed my life. I wake in a morning and look at the date and think of Barry or Anna or Rebecca.

'How did you feel when your home was destroyed?' Norman asked.

I returned my attention to him. 'Pissed off,' I said. 'I'd just had Marilyn Monroe's face painted on my living-room wall. Looks like Billy Idol now.'

Norman ran his skinny fingers through his hair. 'You really think this is the place for you?'

'I used to love volunteering.'

'You did?'

I knew I didn't appear the best applicant for a role that involved compassion. My mother regularly begged me to stop scowling, especially since I was nearly thirty-one and time was apparently no longer on my side. 'Wrinkles love frowners,' she often said, 'but men don't.'

'Yes,' I offered, more gently. 'I loved Crisis Care more than anything I've ever done. I was there five months.' I picked at the eczema between my fingers. 'I never missed a shift, never arrived late. I covered for other people, turned up when I was ill.'

Norman opened my folder. 'Can I ask why you left?'

He could ask, but I wasn't sure of the answer. It was easier asking questions. It occurred to me that that might be the attraction. Why

I was here again, hoping to answer the phones. Perhaps listening to others struggling with their issues meant I could ignore my own.

Norman's phone flashed, saving me. 'I'll let the machine get it,' he said. 'We're not open for twenty minutes. But Jane and Christopher will be here soon so we'd best crack on. Where was I?'

'Telling me about Flood Crisis,' I said.

He drained his coffee. 'We need people who've already worked on a crisis line. We don't have the funding for weeks of training and we don't know how long we'll be here.'

'And what do you offer callers?' I asked.

'Some of them call to talk about the rain. Others tell us things they'd never dream of sharing with Crisis Care; I think they find it easier because we're not officially a depression helpline.'

I glanced at the corner where two glass and plywood booths with pink inner walls looked like wombs; placenta wires snaked along the desks to black telephones that waited for life. I'd answered such phones before. I'd filled notepads with doodles and exclamation marks and words I'd never say to anyone else.

'Which days can you do?'

'Monday and Wednesday,' I said.

'We're open five days. Sex Addicts R Us use the place on Monday, and there are two Slim & Trim sessions on Friday. Would you be interested?'

'No thanks,' I said. 'Throwing up is easier.'

Norman scribbled something in my folder.

'I was joking,' I said.

'So you can do Wednesday?' he asked without looking up.

'Maybe an occasional Sunday.' I almost added 'unless I get any better offers' but played with the frayed stitching on my bag instead. The silver nail polish Fern had applied three days ago was chipped.

'There's no training?' I asked.

'We brush up on skills and active listening. Why do you do it?'

I wondered for a moment if Norman was referring to my picking at the seam on the bag.

'Why helplines?' He stopped writing. 'There are easier ways to help others. Standing behind the counter in a charity shop or filling an envelope with your loose change. Handing out leaflets dressed up as a teddy bear...'

'Teddy bear suits make me itch,' I said.

Norman studied me. His eyes were grey, like ash.

I searched for answers. 'These are real people. It's not like watching a TV show. The callers' troubles make mine less, somehow.'

'And how do you handle yours?' Norman put his pen into a red cup with a host of others and swivelled the chair to face me, his knee only inches from mine.

'I don't have any,' I said.

A bit of rubbish blew against the windowpane and stuck there for a moment. Someone's letter. Only the words 'FINAL CHANCE' were visible; then it blew away.

'We all have problems,' said Norman softly. 'They must have asked you about them in your Crisis Care interview – I needed a stiff drink after mine, I can tell you. We all cope in some way.'

'I have sex with strangers,' I said, immediately regretting it.

'You make jokes,' said Norman. 'It's a common coping mechanism.'

An ambulance wailed in the distance. Like an echo. Then the door-bell chimed.

'That'll be the next shift.' Norman stretched. 'Christopher and Jane are here until ten.' He pressed a buzzer and on the TV monitor above the door I saw a tall man push a bike into the hallway. 'We buzz each other in if we're here. Otherwise there's a door code, so remind me in case I let you go without it."

On the black-and-white screen, I watched the tall man shove his bike into a gap between the stairs and the wall, remove a rucksack from the basket, hang his jacket up and head for our door. He looked just as two-coloured when he walked into the full-colour reality of the room, his black hair cut short at the sides, but with a longer, floppy fringe, grey T-shirt and dark jeans.

'Hi Christopher,' said Norman. 'Must've been bloody cold on your bike.'

'Never noticed,' he said. 'Music.' A wire and earpiece still dangled around his neck like a miniature noose.

'This is Katrina. She'll be starting soon.'

For a second I wondered whom he was referring to. And then I remembered my new name; Katrina. I smiled. Wanted to whisper it aloud, test it.

'Hey Katrina.' Christopher plonked the rucksack by Norman's desk and untangled his wire.

'You're the *Christopher* Chris then,' I said.

He smiled and his face changed, like he'd taken Prozac and it had just kicked in. No longer black and white, his blue eyes crinkled with the laugh. 'Only my mum calls me Christopher; actually she calls *everyone* Christopher.'

I wondered if he had a middle name that no one called him.

'Katrina,' he said. 'Like the hurricane.'

The buzzer sounded again and a dainty woman came in, perhaps late thirties, with two carrier bags, a box of biscuits and a packet of crisps. Her hair had been cut into a sharp red bob that clashed with her green eye shadow; her hands were like porcelain. I eyed them with envy.

'You staying for the week?' Christopher asked her.

She hung her tasselled jacket on a chair. 'Another bus route cancelled. Travellers should be informed before they leave home, via that Twitter thing or text. This is the modern age after all.'

'This is Jane.' Christopher rolled up his headphone wire.

'You must be Jane who's really Jane,' I said.

She didn't look at me; she loaded the food onto the coffee table shelf, her many bracelets jangling like coins. I would call her Jangly Jane. Not to her face. Jangly Jane – to help me remember her name.

'We'll get out of your way.' Norman pushed his chair under the desk. 'It was a busy night shift – it's all in the logbook. The sleet unnerved people; they were worried it'd melt and cause floods again.' Norman picked up a case and locked a drawer. 'Shall I turn the phones on?'

'Go for it,' said Christopher.

They began ringing immediately, out of sync, urgent. It seemed like only yesterday that I'd heard the sound. Christopher and Jangly Jane went straight into the cubicles. Jane hunched over the desk and spoke softly. Christopher said, 'Hello, Flood Crisis, can I help?' and stretched until almost reclined.

I followed Norman into the hallway and got my coat and scarf. I'd been too nervous earlier to notice more than the stench of damp clothes and old paper. Now I saw a mustard-tiled kitchen, the fire exit and an open toilet door. All crisis places were the same; their cheerless walls oozed depression and addiction.

Norman fiddled with the main door's latch. 'I'll call you about our brushing-up-on-skills day. Warn whomever you live with that I'll call you Katrina. You can imagine the chaos it causes when we ring with a new name!' He threw his emaciated hands in the air again.

I fastened my coat. 'So that's it – I'm Katrina now?'

'Whenever you're here.'

He opened the door and the outside light blinded me. The temperature had plummeted since I'd entered the building an hour before. Having been cocooned in its airless confines I now shivered. Everything was white, like sleep. I took my time going down the steps; my borrowed shoes were as hazardous as the ice.

'You're Catherine again now,' Norman called after me. 'But only until you come back.'

The words 'Catherine' and 'come back' followed me down the path, along the street and onto the bus. They haunted me until I slept that night, after tossing and turning for five hours.

3

Everything can be replaced

Teatime traffic meant a long bus ride home. Though long past now, the floods continued their disruption; a circus of caravans and makeshift canopies lined the streets and slowed commuters, driveways packed with cement bags and industrial machines the sideshows. Snow fell on it all like glitter dust on a final act. In front of me a girl breathed on the glass and drew a clown in her mist.

'Can't believe they've changed the route again,' said the woman beside me, jabbing her finger at the window. 'That skip could be moved into a garden. Blocking a main bus route like that – should be ashamed.'

I guessed she hadn't been flooded; one of the lucky few.

'I need my kitchen doing,' she continued, to a bald man across the aisle, 'and I can't get a bloody builder for love or money. They're all doing flood houses, so I'll be stuck with shit worktops till next year.'

The man shoved his newspaper under her nose and said, 'They've landed on their feet and all they do is complain.' He pointed out an article squashed between Fern Fielding's 'Wholly Matrimony' column and a picture of John Prescott with a super-sized marrow. 'Chap here got fifty grand from his insurance company. He'll be in Majorca by next Tuesday, mark my words.'

A conversation about a woman who'd claimed for a conservatory she never had, using pictures of the neighbour's lean-to, drifted my way. When the bus stopped and they all got off by the cemetery I was glad.

The little girl in front wiped her clown off the glass and stuck her tongue out at me.

'Don't be rude,' hissed her mother.

I got off by the street where I'd lived until the rain came; near the house I'd seen ruined that long, wet day. I wanted to walk away, to return when it was rebuilt, when there were walls again, new carpets, doors that weren't black with mould and a toilet that wasn't blocked.

But my feet always made the decision and led me there.

Number two was empty; they'd gone to live by the coast. Number four was staying with relatives. A caravan sat on number six's drive, anchored by piles of bricks. Number eight was mine.

I closed my eyes. Remembered. Snow landed on my cheeks now as rain had that day. *That Day*. We all called it 'That Day'. That Day I'd opened the gate, causing a small wave. That Day I'd paused when brown, thigh-high water wet my underwear. That Day waves had lapped at the windowsill, splashed tears against glass. It spilled into airbricks, entered through every hole and crack, uninvited, intrusive. It ruined all that I'd built, all that I had.

That Day.

Now I unlocked the door, forced it open with my foot and stepped inside. No matter how I tried to prepare, the rotten smell always made me nauseous. Wires poked out between the ripped-up floorboards like weeds.

At least the great, alien-like dryers had gone now they'd done their job; my official certificate had come from the drying company a week ago. Dry certificates were the must-have item, like a new games console on Christmas Day. Neighbours called from one caravan to another when they got one. It meant the rebuild could begin. The flood had not won.

Letters fell from the flap when I closed the door: what I'd come for. Still, I couldn't leave without looking the place over. In the kitchen and living room the lower walls were stripped to brick. The garden beyond the patio doors was overgrown with damp rubbish. Birds pecked for discarded scraps.

I hated to look at the Marilyn Monroe wall, her face dissolved, chin and hair faded. Soon she'd be ripped out and replaced too.

Upstairs, the furniture I'd managed to save was stacked like boxed cadavers awaiting inspection. Sally-next-door had helped me carry stuff up and I'd done the same for her. We'd removed our shoes and walked barefoot through the water. Dog shit and leaves had swirled into our hallways. Those ruined shoes still hung in the cupboard under the stairs, streaked with salt stains. My mother had said I should claim for them. They were from Clarks and cost fifty quid, she'd said. Fifty quid is fifty quid, she said. Everything can be replaced, she said.

Time to leave.

On my way to the flat I bought a supermarket meal for one, a bottle of half-price wine and the local paper. By the time I climbed the rusting metal stairs at the back of the Happy House takeaway my gloveless fingers were blue.

A mostly naked Fern greeted me. 'Can't decide what to wear.' She took a bottle of vodka out of the freezer.

'I wish you would.' I plonked my bag on the tiny granite surface that our landlord, and the Happy House owner, Victor, called a kitchen worktop. The only other storage was a noisy fridge covered in rusting magnets, a double cupboard with no handles and the two drawers that couldn't be opened at the same time.

'I'm meeting Greg,' said Fern.

'Like that?'

'He's taking me to that new Thai place on Chants Ave.'

I put my wine in the fridge.

She poured vodka into a tumbler and added ice. 'He looks a bit like Princess Diana, but what the hell. Why'd you buy those crappy micro-wave meals when Victor will give you chicken madras for a quid?' She poked my frozen meal with a carefully painted red nail.

'Victor gives you cheap food because you flirt with him,' I said. 'For God's sake put some clothes on, woman, I want to eat.'

'You got a newspaper?' Fern headed to the bedroom.

'What's it about this week?' I called.

'DIY,' she said, and slammed the door.

Fern had written the 'Wholly Matrimony' column for our local paper for two years. She hadn't got around to telling her editor she was no longer actually married. Now separated from Sean for four months, she put as much effort into single life as she did her chatty marital column. Sean often threatened to tell her editor it was a sham. I'd suggested she offer them a singleton column, but apparently Mick Mars wrote one on a Thursday.

I found Fern on page ten. A grainy picture painted her as wifely: hair smooth, a shy smile and an egg whisk in hand; 'Wholly Matrimony – Dilemmas and Delights of Modern Marriage, with Fern Fielding'.

I put my curry in the microwave and read a few lines:

'After a calamitous weekend of lawnmower shopping, cake making and DIY, Sean and I found ourselves needing a frothy bubble bath and champagne on Sunday evening. He always sits near the taps, tells me I look lovely in candlelight and massages my thigh with his soapy foot. What more can a woman ask?'

'How *do* you think it up?' I opened the wine and poured a generous amount into a pink plastic cup. 'Will you still write it when you're officially divorced?'

Fern opened the bedroom door a crack and said, 'I'm just deciding between the red take-me-now dress and the silver I-have-class blouse.'

Her separation from Sean had come at a convenient time for me. After the flood, I'd needed refuge, and Fern was looking for somewhere to stay while they sold the house and split the money. Rental property was limited. There weren't enough places for all those the disaster had left temporarily homeless. Still, most families had turned down our tiny flat overlooking a urine-soaked yard. We'd snapped it up, however; it was close to everywhere, and it was cheap. Fern won the coin toss for the one bedroom, so I slept on the lounge sofa, my clothes stuffed in suitcases under her bed. She might as well have a comfortable bed – I rarely slept for more than five hours a night.

I took my meal to the sofa and turned on the TV. Simon Cowell was telling a man he sounded like a choirboy. While I'd done little to make the place home, Fern had marked her territory with clothes, hair accoutrements and lipstick, spreading all of it over the floor. I hated the mess she created. At home my things had been stored in alphabetical order: books, DVDs, even food. I moved Fern's pyjamas, put my feet on the coffee table and picked at the chicken and rice.

'This look OK?'

Fern wore a white dress with thin straps. She'd moisturised her shoulders; they shimmered in the soft lamplight.

'Not the red take-me-now, then?' I said.

'No, I'm starving and want to eat first.'

'You look pretty,' I said. 'He's not coming back here, is he?'

'You think he'll want to?'

'Unfortunately, yes.' I washed down the tasteless curry with wine. 'I don't need to hear what you get up to.'

'You've listened to worse stuff on those crisis lines.'

'I could hang up when they did *that*.'

'Why are you doing it again?' Fern looked into the broken mirror above the oven, fluffing her hair and blending her lipstick. She stopped, a finger still on her lip like a cheap glamour model, and looked at me. 'You left last time. The calls made you depressed for days.'

'Someone has to do it,' I said.

'Doesn't have to be you.'

'I want to.' No longer hungry, I dumped the half-empty carton of food on the coffee table. On TV, a man in purple leggings sang Celine Dion.

'Did the interview go OK?' Fern asked.

I wasn't sure. 'If they ring they'll ask for Katrina,' I said in reply. 'I had to change my name. There's already a Cathryn but without an *i* – or a personality by the sound of it.'

'Nearly forgot. Billy ... sorry, *Will* rang.'

The radiator clunked noisily into action. Fern rambled on about me listening to people whining about the flood, how I'd get sick of it and leave. Water chugged into the radiator pipes. How I hated the sound of it now. I turned to ask what Will had wanted but Fern was already gone, bills and receipts flying from the kitchen worktop in her wake.

I put them in the drawer that only opened when the other was shut. Outside a gang of kids ate takeaway food near the phone box and mocked an old woman who'd dropped her bags. On TV, the audience cheered a guy who looked like Rod Stewart. The phone rang.

'It's me,' said Will.

I knew the Manchester accent. I remembered the gentle tone he'd used with me when I hadn't irritated him. But, right now, I couldn't think of a thing to say. I could only think of the things we *had* said. The words we'd shared when we were Crisis Care volunteers together. The words we'd listened to on the phones and made into our foreplay.

'I saw Fern,' he said after a pause. 'She gave me this number. Said you're volunteering again, you had an interview. I was concerned.'

'Don't be,' I said.

'Why are you being like this?'

I emptied the rest of the wine into my glass. I was sorry for being abrupt but I didn't say it.

'I'm just surprised,' he went on.

'It's a flood-crisis line. I was flooded. It makes sense.'

'I know,' he said softly. 'I remember.'

He'd offered me his place when mine went under. I could have moved into his spacious, city-centre apartment rent free, for as long as I needed it; forever he'd said. But since I'd left Crisis Care, a few months before the flood, I had been working up the courage to leave Will, too. We broke up shortly after I rejected his offer of sanctuary.

'Haven't seen you in ages,' he said. 'How are you?'

'Great. We *love* it here.' I didn't tell him I was restless, my eczema had flared up again, and I often had insomnia. 'Why are you ringing?'

'I didn't want you to hear from anyone else...'

'Hear what?'

Two women in gold cat suits sang the theme song to *Beauty and the Beast*. Simon Cowell put his head in his hands.

'I'm getting married,' said Will.

Everything can be replaced, my mother had said of shoes.

'Congratulations.' I swigged my wine. 'Is she pregnant?'

'No. We've been together three months, and it's good. She's a great girl: reliable, kind. She doesn't mess me around.'

'So does she have a name?'

'Miranda,' he said.

Everything could be replaced, I thought again. 'I'm happy for you,' I said, and I was. I just wasn't sure why I needed to know about it, though. 'I bet your mum's glad. She never liked me, which is understandable – if I had a son I wouldn't want him dating me.'

Will laughed. 'Remember the time she took us to that place in Cottingham and the waiter heard you saying he looked like a rent boy and you were embarrassed and my mother wanted to know what you'd said and the waiter told her?' I could tell he was smiling. 'You always made me laugh, Catherine.'

I watched a guy in an advert hold up a wipe with all the dirt he'd cleaned out of his pores.

'Do you remember that caller at Crisis Care?' he asked. 'That guy who cut bits out of himself with a razor. Frank. Had a lisp. Said that by removing those chunks he could disappear. That when he was invisible he might have the power to confront his mother. She'd locked him under the stairs, tied him up, burnt him and bit him.'

'I remember.' I pressed my glass to my cheek.

'He still calls,' said Will. 'He took his mother to Home Farm and told her while she ate a prawn cocktail starter that she'd hurt him. He doesn't cut anymore.'

'That's good,' I whispered.

'Why did you leave?'

'I couldn't do anything for those people,' I said.

'I meant why did you leave me?'

I shifted the receiver from one ear to the other. It was a habit formed in my days at Crisis Care. It sometimes helped at two in the morning when I'd been on the phone for hours and my ear throbbed and my neck ached and my heart hurt.

'I know why you left Crisis Care,' said Will. 'But why did you leave *me*? Didn't I put up with more than anyone normal would?'

'Will...' I said, gently.

'You're still calling me that?' He paused and I thought he'd hung up. 'No one calls me Will.'

'It's just a name,' I said.

'Bullshit. All that crap about you calling me Will to make me feel special. It's to make *you* feel special.'

A car alarm shrieked outside; I jumped and knocked the wine glass over. 'Dammit.' I tried to catch the liquid as it dripped from the coffee table.

'What do you mean dammit? It's true.'

'Not you,' I said. 'I spilt my wine.'

'Enjoy it, Catherine,' he said.

'Enjoy your girlfriend.' I slammed the phone down.

Oh, the times I'd wanted to do that at Crisis Care. The times I'd listened to a teenage girl crying because she was on a bridge, staring at the water and thinking of jumping. The times I'd wondered why my face was wet when a middle-aged guy confessed to fantasising about his fourteen-year-old nephew. The times I could have walked out. And yet I'd lasted.

Until the nightmares began.

After shifts, when I finally fell asleep, I used to dream of a room at the end of a long, shadowy corridor. Reaching its door, I'd want to turn and run. Sometimes I'd touch the tarnished handle, my mouth as dry as splintered wood. Sometimes I'd sink to the floor, cover my ears and cry like a nine-year-old. But I'd never open the door.

Sometimes when I awoke there was a man. Just for a split second. At the end of my bed. Bushy-haired. Gone the moment I registered him.

I could never go back to sleep then.

The dreams and the strange man had both disappeared when I left Crisis Care.

Everything can be replaced, my mother had said after the flood. But even though the water had receded, leaving murky stains on walls, I knew the rain could return any time. Dreams could too.

4

Another seventy candles

When nightmares rolled in, Nanny Eve's image always anchored me to a familiar shore. I'd wake, sticky and hot, and hear that sing-song voice as though she were calling me to breakfast from downstairs. There was no downstairs now. It had been washed away by the rain. My bed was a sofa she'd never sit on to talk about fairies in the garden or to ask if I wanted rice pudding with cream.

But I could close my eyes any time and see her.

Nanny Eve's birthday was one week after mine. We often saved the candles from my cake to put on hers. She turned seventy-seven after I was seven, seventy-eight after I was eight. We'd stick my seven or eight candles in her sponge and say we'd just imagine the other seventy years.

'Pretend it's only twenty,' she'd whisper in my ear, her skin as papery as tissue wrapping.

I remember the time I forgot her birthday. So strange to remember forgetting. But that moment is as clear to me now as our garden pond was on a still day. When my nightmares about the room grew worse after the Crisis Care shifts, memories of that day dawned brighter in my recollection.

Nanny Eve was celebrating eighty-one so I'd have just turned eleven. It would be her last birthday. I hadn't meant to forget; I woke that morning with all kinds of plans in my head to make her day special: ideas for handmade cards and made-up birthday songs and chocolate-cornflake cakes. Nothing would get in my way. Not homework, not the TV, not helping Mother with the flowerpots.

But then Rebecca Houghton rang. She was the most popular girl in our class and had *never* called my house. Mother called me, covering the mouthpiece and saying, 'It's that lovely girl, Rebecca. I know her mum. She's big with the church ladies. Invite her over. She'd make a lovely friend.'

Mother didn't like my current best friend, Barry Hudson. He was in the special-needs class and his trousers were always just too short. I used to think it was his smell my mother disliked; a mixture of cabbage and unwashed hair was how she described it. But really it was that he was different. I loved that I could just be *me* when I was with him. I didn't have to brush my unruly hair or pretend to swoon over some pop star. We'd collect stones and rubbish along the river's edge, and climb the chalky cliffs in the country park to look for birds' nests, and fight using tree branches as swords. I favoured Barry's wild play over gossipy, already-lip-gloss-wearing girls. Or rather those girls favoured each other over me. My hair and moods and eczema didn't make me very appealing.

Rebecca Houghton was calling that day to see if I wanted to go ice-skating and then for a burger. All the kids in our class were going. Her dad had got the tickets free because he worked for the council. Of course I wanted to go. My Saturdays usually involved hanging around at home and getting into trouble for being in the way, or calling for Barry and going to the country park on the foreshore. Suddenly I wanted to be a girl instead of hanging from some tree.

I spent a good while selecting something pretty to wear. Mostly I wore jeans or shorts. But now I picked the lace dress Nanny Eve had bought for my birthday, and put on my birthstone necklace.

On my way out of the door Mother gave me a pound and said to buy Nanny Eve a nice card afterwards. 'Don't forget,' she said. *Don't forget*.

Of course, I forgot.

I got wrapped up in doing pirouettes on the ice and impressing Rebecca Houghton by being the only one brave enough to try the splits. The girls said they loved the creamy lace of my dress. We all skated in a line, like they do on TV. I could hardly eat my burger for smiling.

On the way home I had a head full of friendly girls' laughter and giggly secrets. Anna – who'd been my friend through junior school but abandoned me when Barry came on the scene – promised we'd have sleepovers again. It had been the best day. I forgot about Barry and his conkers.

I went straight to my room when I got home and curled up on the bed to cherish my sudden popularity. I didn't feel lanky and boyish. On the ice my usually clumsy hands had made star shapes and swirls above my head.

But Mother's voice jolted me out of happiness. 'Catherine, come down here right now!'

There was never any sing-song in her voice. It ordered and instructed and criticised. In the lounge Nanny Eve sat by the French doors with her knitting. She looked up with soft, questioning eyes as we entered, me behind Mother like a lace shadow.

Mother pushed me in front of Nanny Eve. 'Catherine,' she said, 'the selfish girl that she is, forgot your birthday.'

My hands flew to my face. Suddenly they were clumsy again. In all the excitement of showing off and being praised I had forgotten Nanny Eve's special day. In all the chaos of imagining new friends at school on Monday and selfishly planning to ignore Barry, I'd hurt my beloved nanny. The pound still sat in my left pocket, and I knew the queen on it was probably smiling.

I went straight to Nanny Eve, sat on the floor at her knees. 'I didn't mean to,' I said. 'I really didn't. I had all kinds of—'

Mother interrupted with, 'How difficult is it to go and buy a card?'

Nanny Eve patted my head and said softly that there was no need to fuss. Things were easily forgotten. Mother said I was a stupid, gormless girl and if I loved Nanny Eve I'd have remembered. Then she went and made shepherd's pie.

I cried. She was right. I couldn't have loved Nanny Eve enough. Surely love shouldn't be eclipsed by a fun day out. Surely love remembered. Perhaps this was when Nanny Eve stopped calling me by my pretty, sing-song name. But still she stroked my hair as I cried. Stroked and said that she *knew* I loved her.

It might have been around this time that I broke the Virgin Mary, but I'm not sure. I think perhaps she was already smashed and Nanny Eve had the plastic, red-lipped one. And I'm sure Nanny Eve had already stopped singing her mysterious songs. My memories come like playing cards picked from the deck. I never know which ones I'll get and most aren't the ones I want.

When they lowered Nanny Eve's coffin into snowy ground three months later I whispered that I would never forget her birthday again. And I never have. I light a candle every year for her.

Now I remember all the birthdays. Every time someone tells me their date of birth, I file it. Their numbers mount up like piles of revision notes in a student's bedroom. I can't forget. I won't forget.

Love always remembers.

Nanny, I'd think on each of her birthdays. *I hope you see the candles. Let's pretend there are another seventy.*

5

Memory with no rhythm

I waited ten minutes before ringing the Flood Crisis doorbell. I wasn't sure why.

Norman came down to open the door himself. 'Katrina, welcome back,' he said, and I knew I was supposed to be there.

The hallway yawned wide behind him, its muggy breath as familiar as if I'd been there twenty times. The days since Saturday's interview seemed part of another life; days spent with Fern and working nights at the care home. Now I entered the tall building with ivy clinging to brick like gangrene, ready to become Katrina.

Norman said, 'Let me give you the door code for next week.'

He glanced down at my feet as I stamped snow from them. I'd picked shoes that fit this time: knee-length boots with a zip that always got stuck halfway, but at least they kept my legs warm. I took out my phone and put the door code into my contacts list, under C for Code.

Today, Norman wore a black T-shirt with Che Guevara on the front and had a pink Support Breast Cancer rubber band around his wrist. 'Thank you for coming at such short notice,' he said.

I followed him into the lounge. The shutter had been fixed, so wintry light pooled in the centre of the room, where a young girl sat on the velvet armchair reading *What Car?* magazine, feet tucked beneath her. Her charcoal-shaded eyes viewed me frostily. She wore a shimmery top with a hood and gloves at the end of the sleeves.

'You're the last one.' Norman touched my back.

Perched on the sofa opposite Charcoal Eyes, a birdlike woman held a bag on her lap with her talons. Her lips chanted some mantra that perhaps prepared her for the calls ahead; her stick legs protruded from a long plaid skirt. Opposite the circle of chairs, a pinstripe-suited woman leaned against the desk where I'd been interviewed. Her buttocks creased our folders. She had bruised knees, as if she'd been gardening in shorts. I wondered why she hadn't worn trousers.

'This is Katrina.' Norman closed the door behind us.

Charcoal Eyes smiled but only with her mouth. Bird Woman looked up, nodded and quickly returned her attention to the bag. Bruised Knees came forward and shook my hand, her cool fingers soothing my raw skin.

She held my palms up. 'Can you not get cream for that?'

'I have some.' I pulled them away. 'It's the extremes – cold outside, warm indoors.'

'I'm Claudia Kent,' said Bruised Knees. 'I'll be doing the session. Have you met Lindsey O'Malley, Kath Grimshaw?'

I shook my head.

'Lindsey used to volunteer for Youth Voice. And Kath has years of experience with Crisis Care, and with Post-Menopausal & Proud.'

Kath nodded, opened her bag and extracted two knitting needles and a thick ball of magenta wool. 'Do you mind if I knit?' It was a soft voice that might require good ears from a would-be-suicidal. 'It calms me when I'm nervous.'

'Not at all,' said Claudia. 'I can't live without cigarettes.' She described how she had been the secretary for Crisis Care in London, a team leader in Manchester and ran a Permanent Pelvic-Floor Postnatal Class here.

She touched my shoulder. 'Katrina volunteered with Crisis Care for five months. Come and sit down, Katrina.'

I wondered if Lindsey was really Lindsey, Kath really Kath, Claudia really Claudia. There could have been eight names between four of us.

I sat next to Kath and watched her hands working the knitting needles with gusto. The click-click-click as they met was soothing; it reminded me of sitting at Nanny Eve's feet while she made miniature coats for my Barbie doll, fascinated by the magic those two silvery sticks created, in awe of her patience when I'd tried to do it myself many times and been sent to my room for calling a needle a bastard.

'It's a coat for my baby granddaughter,' Kath said.

'Lucky her.' I hoped she suited purple.

Norman made drinks and Claudia sank into the large beanbag. After a few efforts to plump it up, she resigned herself to being lower than us and pulled her skirt down, unable to hide the clover-shaped bruises.

'Today we'll brush up on the skills you already have,' she said. 'If a subject makes anyone uncomfortable at any point, they're free to step outside.'

Lindsey looked at me as though trying to ascertain if I'd be a quitter. Kath continued the click-click-clicking.

'Let's break the ice, shall we?' Claudia clapped her hands as though announcing pass-the-parcel. 'How about a game? Can each of you describe a memory from when you were nine? I'll start.'

'Why nine?' asked Lindsey.

'It's old enough for you to recall, young enough to contrast with now.'

'Wouldn't it be better to just talk about who we are now?' I suggested.

Norman kicked the door open and held it ajar while balancing four steaming mugs on a tray commemorating the 1981 marriage of Prince Charles and Lady Diana.

'Our history makes us.' Claudia took a metallic mug from the tray and sipped it, leaving a brown lipstick mark on the rim. 'My favourite memory from that age was getting a rabbit,' she said. 'I loved him: Stig. He used to eat chocolate out of my hand. My Aunty Marg gave him to me because I'd been brave when I broke my arm ... Kath?'

Kath stopped knitting and picked up her drink. 'I can't remember as far back as nine,' she said. 'How about fifty-four? I bought my niece a rabbit called Petal; it savaged my niece's cat.'

Claudia smiled; only her top lip still had lipstick on. 'Lindsey?' she asked.

'Does it have to be a rabbit story?'

'No. Just what you remember about being nine.'

'My Aunt Bessie used to irritate me.' Lindsey fiddled with her left sleeve's glove. 'She'd come over to watch TV and then go to the toilet for hours with the newspaper. When she came back she'd ask, "Did I miss anything?" I used to think, "Well, if I tell you what you missed we'll miss the next half-hour, and who's gonna tell us what we missed in *that* part?"'

I began to like Lindsey.

'Katrina, how about you?'

I thought about it. 'I can't remember anything about being nine.' I shrugged, ruining the game.

'There must be something,' smiled Claudia, the one glossed lip taut.

'Nothing.' I scratched the red in between my fingers.

'Nothing?'

'Nothing,' I repeated.

'Can't she just talk about her rabbit?' asked Kath.

'How do you know she had one?' Lindsey laughed.

'Did you, dear?' asked Kath.

'You can't remember anything from a whole year?' said Claudia. 'It's fascinating. How about your birthday? Christmas?'

I shook my head. I could remember my eighth and tenth birthdays. I could remember forgetting Nanny Eve's. But nine was blank. Not just the birthday, but Christmas, the whole year. As though it was a chapter that had been torn out of a children's book.

Claudia stared at me like I'd forgotten to put clothes on.

My memory had never been perfect. Relatives would talk about some uncle throwing up in the punch bowl at a wedding, or a car trip when someone's grandad got drunk and showed his bottom to the other motorists. I'd laugh because it was funny, but not because I recalled it happening. I wondered now if my knack for remembering birthdays was not only because of Nanny Eve but to compensate for lacking memories elsewhere.

'I don't remember,' I said.

'How about a holiday? A death? A pet?'

My hands were on fire. 'If I was a caller and was interrogated like this I'd hang up.'

'I'm sorry,' said Claudia. 'Let's move onto confidentiality. I'm sure you've all signed one of these forms before, but I'll sum up anyway.'

While she rambled on I tried to recall something from when I was nine. The click-click-click of needles hurried me. I remembered clearly listening to that sound at Nanny Eve's feet. How old was I then? Maybe six. Click-click-click. My memory had no such rhythm. Click-click-no-memory-click-no-memory-click.

'What we hear in those booths stays inside this building,' Claudia was saying. 'Share your feelings with a fellow volunteer but don't take it home. Each new starter is appointed a buddy for the first few shifts: an experienced volunteer they can talk to.'

'How soon do we go on the phones?' Lindsey glanced at them. 'At Youth Voice, I listened to other volunteers for five sessions because I was terrified about picking them up.'

The first call at a crisis centre is like losing your virginity: you never forget it. I'd needed two hours of foreplay at Crisis Care. I'd intended to sit through three sessions, observing others without picking up the phone. But I'd realised that I didn't want to go home and worry how it would be, so I'd answered on my first shift.

I'd said, 'Crisis Care, can I help?' in a voice that wasn't mine. I'd learned well on the course; I was non-judgemental, patient, gentle. My first caller was a fifty-year-old man who'd been married for thirty years but had always been desperately in love with his friend Jim.

'What should I do?' he'd asked.

It wasn't for me to tell him, only to listen, ask the right questions, and let him figure out his own feelings. I was shaking when the call ended but felt empowered.

I looked over at the phones and wondered what my first call might be this time.

'We prefer you get straight on the phones,' said Claudia. 'Crisis Care and Youth Voice have prompts in the phone booths, so you'll be familiar with those. We're less rigid about sticking with emotions here – if a caller needs to whine about a ruined chaise longue then so be it.'

'What about advice?' Kath paused mid click.

'There are website addresses to give out. Some callers need to talk about personal things, though; and there's a slim chance some could be suicidal.'

'What are your policies on that?' I asked.

At Crisis Care the policy was that it is an individual's right to die. It was a shock at first when I learned that we might have to listen to someone breathe their last breath and not intervene, unless they specifically requested help and gave an address. The leaders warned us it was unlikely to happen. Less than one percent of calls would be that desperate.

In my five months there that should have meant my chances of such a call were slim; I figured I took around seven calls in a three-hour session and covered five sessions a month. So, after five months I'd answered perhaps 175 calls. One percent predicted I should handle two suicide attempts. Unlucky with coins and dice, I was doomed with helplines too; I talked to nine people who had overdosed. Nine; the year I couldn't remember. Nine; the number of suicide calls I couldn't forget.

'We respect an individual's choice,' said Claudia.

I was tired. Looking at my raw hands, I remembered how it felt after a Crisis Care night shift, one where call after call came, waves from an angry sea onto our flimsy pier. I remembered a long conversation with a thirty-year-old woman who had four children and only months to live. Then straightaway having to put my emotions to one side because the phone rang again and the other volunteer was on a call. There was only me. Only me, and I was tired.

'Whatever you've learnt,' said Claudia, gently, 'is your foundation. But this is a *temporary* helpline, so while you need to treat callers with respect, we've no time to set an official agenda.'

Norman coughed and said, 'More drinks and a break, people?'

Kath wrapped wool around her needles and put them away. Lindsey stretched, her knee clicking. Claudia suggested we resume in ten with some practice scenarios and went outside for a cigarette. With her puffs of smoke passing the window every few seconds, and Norman in the kitchen clattering between drawers and cupboards, we fell quiet. The clock measured our uneasy silence. Lindsey stared at the magazines as though willing one to open so she could pretend to read it. I counted the carpet flecks.

'Were you flooded?' Kath asked me.

'Yes,' I said. 'You?'

'No. But I've been lonely since Hector died. My daughter lives miles away and my son's abroad.'

'Were you?' I asked Lindsey.

'Yes.' She sat up. 'We're staying in a caravan outside our house. It's driving me mad sharing a bed with my sister. She snores like a horse. I'd leave but can't afford to; I'm studying.'

'What subject?' I asked.

'I'm doing a BSc in Psychology and Counselling.'

'Is that why you volunteer?'

Norman dropped something heavy in the kitchen.

'Yeah,' said Lindsey. 'It'll look good on my CV. What do you do?'

'I just work in a care home; night shifts mainly.' I hated that I always added the word *just*. I *just* care for the elderly. I *just* don't find something better.

'Why do *you* volunteer?' asked Lindsey.

I used to think I did it to help humanity, but the human race is impersonal, vast, faceless. It doesn't call a helpline. I used to think I did it to make a difference. But people rang back time after time, no less depressed, no better at coping. So perhaps it was because I was addicted to the extreme stories, the tragedy, the truth. And apart from anything, meeting Will at Crisis Care had been an incentive to turn up. We'd flirt and eye one another between calls. Exchange quips when it grew dark outside and the phone calls became more intense.

Lindsey was staring at me.

'Gotta get my kicks somewhere,' I said.

'The worst part of the floods was afterwards,' said Lindsey.

I pictured my ruined shoes hanging in the cupboard.

'The mess,' said Lindsey. 'I slept at a friend's the night it happened. My mother called me the next day and said, "Don't come home." She wanted to clean up before I saw it. She was crying. "It's like the house has been raped," she said.'

Norman walked in with four more drinks, and Claudia entered just after, cigarette odour following her like a free-radical ghost.

'Scenarios,' she said. 'Norman will take on the role of a caller, you'll be listeners, and I'll assess.'

Norman proved a versatile actor. He was a suicidal teen with an abusive brother, a self-harming single parent and a man who couldn't sleep when it rained. Kath was adamant she should be allowed to knit while taking calls. Claudia suggested that clicking needles might be distracting to the caller; Kath argued that at Crisis Care she had improvised a needle silencer from a condom. I'd forever see her as Condom Kath.

It began snowing outside. Like new sheets on an old mattress, it hid weeds and mud and path. It was four o'clock and almost dark. I realised I was hungry. A text from Fern asked if I wanted a takeaway for tea.

'Great work,' said Claudia, as we concluded. 'Any questions?'

'You're not open twenty-four hours, so how do we get off the phones?' I said. I could tell she'd hoped no one would ask anything and was irritated. 'With no one to hand over to, what if you're in the middle of a difficult call?'

'With as much sensitivity as possible, wind it up.' Claudia made a circular motion with her hand.

'Also you don't have to answer the phone in the fifteen minutes leading up to the end of your shift,' said Norman.

'But if a caller's taken loads of paracetamol and doesn't want an ambulance, how can we wind it up?' I'd read the rota, seen how scattered and few the shifts were.

'We've not had any suicide attempts,' said Norman. 'Most people want to talk about the floods'

It didn't comfort me. *Give them time*, I thought. *Give them time.*

'I'm afraid,' said Norman, 'that if you're talking to someone who's made the decision to die and it clashes with you leaving you'll have to stay.'

'That's why I bring knitting,' said Condom Kath.

'I'm sure we all have homes to go to,' said Claudia. 'Here are the contact details for the volunteer who'll be your buddy.'

I took a sheet from Claudia. I was to begin the following Wednesday; my buddy was Christopher. Above my next four shifts was his address and mobile number, presumably in case I needed him before then.

'That's it,' said Claudia. 'Next time you come, you're on the phones. How do you feel?'

'Ready, I think,' said Lindsey.

'I need to buy more wool,' said Condom Kath.

I looked at the telephones, sensed a thousand callers waiting. It felt like I was backstage, watching the curtain rise before stepping into the spotlight's glare. I might have learned my lines, I might have done it 175 times before, but I was as sick as if I were being pushed in front of an audience for the first time.

I wanted to get it done.

To answer now.

But it was time to leave.

6

The first phone call

As I walked to the bus stop, the last call I'd taken at Crisis Care came to me. Will had been off sick; I'd felt relieved because our relationship had deteriorated by that point. I'd wanted to end Crisis Care on a high, perhaps make someone realise that life *is* wonderful and people *do* care. Rick was a regular caller who relayed a catalogue of miseries each time: a drunk, manic-depressive, ex-heroin-addict human.

'Are you *still* here?' he'd asked that last day.

Not for long, I'd thought.

'Why the fuck do you bother?' he'd demanded.

I'd spouted the usual response; it wasn't about me it was about *him*, about his feelings. He asked me again at the end of the call: 'Why the fuck do you bother?' I had no answer. I didn't know *why* I was drawn to these crisis places.

Maybe at Flood Crisis I would finally find out.

The bus was late; probably because of more roadworks following the floods. I shivered, stamped my feet and thanked God I wasn't working tonight and could stay in. I frowned: had I made sure my new shifts didn't clash with my care home hours? I went through my bag but couldn't find the sheet Claudia had given me only half an hour before. I swore; I knew exactly where I'd left it: on top of Barbara Cartland.

I looked back towards the street where Flood Crisis was. Would anyone still be there? I abandoned the bus stop and hurried back. How different it looked now, dark against the starry sky, the climbing ivy now an inky spillage down the wall. The lights were out. I was too late.

No I wasn't: I had the door code now.

But should I go in?

I climbed the steps, found the number on my phone and entered the digits into the metal square on the wall. The door opened with a soft creak. In the blackness, the smell was overpowering: damp tea towels, old carpets, shut-in air. I felt along the wall, knowing the lounge door was on my right. Once inside I flicked the light switch.

The strangest feeling washed over me with the sudden brightness; I felt for a moment that this was exactly where I was supposed to be. That my forgotten sheet had been more than an accident. I picked it up from the table and scanned the information. Then I looked around at the empty chairs, recalling our memory game earlier. Claudia's obvious shock at my memory-gap of a whole year made me now sit heavily in the velvet chair.

Why nine? What on earth had happened when I was nine?

Two of the telephones began ringing.

I dropped the sheet in surprise. Weren't they supposed to be switched off? I stood up, heart hammering wildly. They continued ringing, just out of sync enough so that one followed the other like an echo. I put a clenched fist to my mouth, as though to stem any words. What should I do? *Ignore them*, said my head. *Answer them,* said my instinct. This could be my chance to get that terrifying first call over with, and no one here to listen in.

It all came back to me: my time as a volunteer.

I went to one of the booths and picked up the phone.

'Do I have to give my name, dear?' he said.

I didn't respond for a few seconds because it took me a while to understand what he'd said. I wondered if he was drunk. No, that didn't seem to be it; the slur of his words was too consistent. It sounded like his tongue was too heavy for his mouth.

'You don't have to do anything you don't want to,' I said. The words came naturally to me.

'I know I'm difficult to understand.' He spoke slowly. 'I had a stroke so I'll try to speak as clearly as I can.'

'Take all the time you need.'

I sat in the chair, looked at the empty notepad in front of me. I could not record this call. I wasn't supposed to be here. Panic rose in my chest; should I tell Norman that I'd picked up the phone or never mention it? But I couldn't think about that now. This had to be about the caller.

'I've forgotten where I left my glasses,' said the slow-speaking man.

I smiled. At least I might be able to help him remember.

'When did you last have them?'

He ignored the question. 'I write things down for people, you know,' he said. 'Luckily it's my left arm that's paralysed – I'm right-handed, you see. Of course you wouldn't be able to see my words if I wrote them, so that's silly.'

I said, 'I understand you fine.'

'I know you're a flood place but I wasn't flooded. My friends were, though. I miss them.' It took him perhaps half a minute to say these two sentences. 'I'm Sid.' I knew he'd made it up. Our own names slip out easily, but he'd paused in a different way to the effort between his previous words, as though to think between 'I'm' and 'Sid'.

I opened my mouth, said, 'I'm Cath—' And then I remembered I wasn't – not here. 'I'm Katrina,' I said.

'That's nice. It's good to hear a voice. I get lonely.'

'That must be difficult,' I said.

'I live on my own. Some days I don't see a soul. My flat's on the second floor. But my friends were on the ground floor, so they've had to move away. There's just me and Arthur Dunn up here; but he can't hear too well, so we're ill suited – his hearing aid makes me even more difficult to understand. What a Laurel and Hardy we are. Do you mind if I just put the phone down a second to make some tea?'

I heard him pour water and stir a spoon around a cup.

'Takes me ages to make tea,' he said. '"Cripple" is what they call folks with useless legs, but I don't know what the word should be when one arm is useless.'

'Does no one come round and help?' I asked.

'Everyone's wrapped up in the floods. I don't mind. At least I've got my roof. Dora from flat three is sharing a caravan with friends. Am I painting a pathetic picture of myself, grumbling here when others are worse off?'

'No,' I said. 'You're just talking.'

Clumsily, he described how people in the supermarket laughed when he talked, and told me how, the day before, the cashier had asked if he was drunk. She said if he wanted alcohol, she'd fetch the manager. 'I only wanted a dozen eggs,' said Sid.

The image made my throat ache. He was perhaps the age my father would have been if he'd lived; I felt a pang of affection. Though we were warned at Crisis Care not to get attached to callers, I always had a soft spot for men that age.

'My memory is terrible,' Sid said carefully. 'I call folks "thingy". But you're Katrina, right?'

'Right,' I said.

'I've got to go and start cooking my tea. It's late, so I'll maybe warm some soup. Thank you for listening.'

And he was gone.

I sat for a while with the phone warm in my hand. If I replaced the handset it might ring again, but I couldn't stay here all night.

Go home, popped into my head. *Go home now before you get into this again. Go home before you need more than two shifts a week, before you count the hours until your next one. Go home before the nightmares begin. Go home before you wake and, just for a split second there's the strange, bushy-haired man at the foot of your bed. Go home.*

But this had been such a gentle start: no suicide or death or addiction. Just an old man who'd lost his glasses.

Yet, that night, for the first time in months – for the first time since I'd left Crisis Care – I dreamt of the room.

And saw the man.

7

Enduring trifle and peas

My mother shoved a hand inside the back end of a large chicken, pushing garlic-and-herb stuffing into its bowels, and only interrupting her efforts to stir the gravy with a wooden spoon and comment upon my attire as I entered the kitchen.

'You shouldn't wear red,' she said. 'It makes you look washed out and at least thirty-nine years old.'

Hanging my offending scarlet coat in the cupboard, I ignored the criticism and looked in the fridge for wine. A bottle lurked behind the peach smoothie and liver pate.

'Don't slam the door,' she snapped, as I did.

I took a sturdy tumbler from the cupboard and poured an endure-Sunday-lunch-at-Mother's-sized measure.

'I'm late putting it in,' she said.

'Putting what in?' I asked.

'The stuffing. Dinner will be ready in half an hour, but the stuffing might be a bit undercooked. I can't believe I forgot. I never have in all these years.' She stopped stirring the gravy and pushed some white strands of hair behind her ear. Tiny pearl earrings dangled from her lobes, a reminder of her elegance amidst the steam. 'Lady in Red' played on the radio. I smoothed my eyebrows with my index finger; she'd notice they needed plucking before the day was done.

'Not straightening your hair anymore?' She had a knack for seeing without even looking at me.

I touched my chaotic locks. 'Who's here, then?'

'Graham's reading the paper in the lounge.' She gave the lump of stuffing a firm pat. 'Celine's coming after the gym. Mark can't, he's showing some viewers the house.'

Graham was Mother's second husband; Celine was his daughter. I loved him and tolerated her. He'd moved in when I was thirteen. Fortunately, Celine had lived with her own mother and her brother, Stephen, so I only endured her at family functions and Christmas, or when someone died. Mark was her husband.

I'd always known Mother wasn't my biological mum. I asked her once why she'd never had children with my dad or Graham. 'You were enough,' she'd said, and not in a way that suggested I brought the joy of ten.

'Don't disappear, you can help me.' She opened the oven door again and rotated roast potatoes with a fork, obsessive about an even browning. New potatoes simmered in a pan on top. Peas, carrots and broccoli cooked in a haze of vapour.

'Why do I have to help?' It never took long for me to assume my role of whining daughter, my mother providing the boundaries every parenting book says should be created, if only to be kicked against. I was a rigorous kicker.

'I worked until five this morning,' I said. 'Only got four hours' sleep. Bet Sharleen won't help.'

'Don't start with the "Sharleen"; you know she's *Celine*,' Mother sighed. 'You've only been here five minutes.'

'I'll burn everything. I'm crap at kitchen stuff.'

'Go and see Graham then!' she said.

I moved before she changed her mind, fast as a ten-year-old who's been given the freedom to go and play for another twenty minutes. But I didn't go to the lounge at the back of the house, overlooking the acre of garden; I went to the study.

Once inside I closed the door and leaned against its cool surface. The study was a graveyard, the sheet-covered furniture looking like tombstones. I moved through the dust particles that drifted through the air like ghosts, pulled a sheet free and unveiled a chair – my dad's favourite. Its discoloured arms and scratched legs hinted at its years of use, at my many stolen moments curled up there. I sat down near it, by the lattice window, where I could see the naked lilac tree.

'Hi Dad,' I whispered.

A picture of us in a frame dull with age sat on the windowsill next to his golf trophies. The image was as familiar as my hand's creases. Dad and I rested on a rock, frothy sea behind us, wind buffeting my yellow dress, our smiles identical. The picture was imprinted on my mind, but where we'd been before and what we'd done after was blank. Because she also loved him, my mother permitted this altar to my dad's memory.

I had one too – to my biological mum; but I kept it inside me. She was Mum, a name no one could change. A mysterious angel I'd never known, since she'd died giving birth to me. Mother met Dad when I was already six months old. She took us both on: him through love, me perhaps through necessity. I was her only chance at any sort of child.

Next to the picture of Dad was a Peter Rabbit figurine. Dad liked rabbits; he'd grown up on a farm and had had millions running and leaping about the yard. He had promised one day to get me one. 'When you're nine,' he had said. 'You'll not want to do all the cleaning and feeding and brushing before that.' I'd insisted I was grown up enough and would look after it perfectly.

'When you're nine,' he'd insisted. *When you're nine.*

He died when I was eight.

I touched the picture's glass. A call I'd taken at Crisis Care came to me: from a woman whose father had died after a long fight with cancer. She'd cradled him for six hours before ringing anyone. She cried for two before telling me this. Said she couldn't bring herself to call anyone for all that time because when they came and took him he'd never be hers again.

'I look for him everywhere,' she'd said. 'In the pub, the kitchen, in the eyes of every new boyfriend.'

I was there when my mum died, on a labour ward; but, of course, being only minutes old, I can't recall it. I wasn't there when my dad died. I don't remember who told me, what time it was or where I was. I know it was a heart attack. And I know he died in his favourite chair. I sat in it afterwards, trying to keep his cushion warm, because if it got cold he'd have no reason to return.

Did I sit there during my forgotten ninth year?

Did the woman at Crisis Care still seek her father?

'Catherine! Where are you?'

I dropped the cushion. 'I'm coming, Mother.'

They were all in the dining room. Like actors in a weekly soap opera they'd assumed the usual positions: Mother at the top near the walnut cabinet that displayed her pottery creations, me next to Celine, Graham opposite us with his back against the wall where the Constable print hung. The best blue-and-white swirly china was being given its weekly outing, and a silk cloth hid the plain table. I smiled; Fern had stolen some fancy napkins from a restaurant and we used them for our TV dinners, eating boil-in-the-bag fish on the cream fabric.

Celine smelt of fruity shampoo and expensive shower gel, and looked like she'd barely work up a sweat at the gym. Her blonde hair was teased into careful curls.

'You OK, Graham?' I put my wine glass on a coaster to avoid staining the cloth.

'Yes; you?'

'Don't let it get cold,' said Mother.

The vegetables and carved meat steamed in trays, and extra stuffing sat in a silver bowl. I helped myself to copious amounts. Fern and I were no chefs and a decent meal was a rarity.

'I just read your friend's column,' said Graham. His face was a map of laughter; lines that always led to a smile. 'I love how she paralleled a badly put-up shelf with marriage.'

'What are you reading *that* for?' asked Mother. 'She's pretending to be married and running around with every man who looks her way.'

'I tell everyone her column is fake.' Celine ate her peas two at a time, chewing until she must have been eating her tongue.

'Like your breasts,' I said.

'Catherine! Can we not have breasts at Sunday dinner?' said Mother.

'She's talented,' said Graham. 'Wish I could write like that.'

'Dad, you'd not have made the money you have if you'd been a writer,' said Celine.

I wanted to say that she'd not have her new nose either, but refrained. Graham had made his money the old-fashioned way: hard work. He owned six double-glazing shops in the area.

'When do you start the voluntary work?' he asked.

'Wednesday.' My glass was empty. 'Any more wine?'

'You know where it is,' said my mother. 'Though I think you've had enough.'

I brought a bottle in from the kitchen, poured myself and Graham a glass each.

'I don't know why you have to do that suicide stuff.' My mother dabbed the corner of her mouth with a napkin. 'Why can't you find a decent man like Celine has and settle down? You'll be thirty-one next week. Why couldn't you make a go of it with Billy? He had a home, a job and that beautiful face; could have been your chance at beautiful children.'

'Where's Mark?' I asked Celine.

'In Scotland,' she said.

'Sleeping around with teenagers again?' I asked.

'Catherine,' scolded my mother. 'Those rumours were jealous tittle-tattle between bored women. Mark is a *marvellous* husband.'

I bit my fork.

'How's your house coming along, Cath?' asked Graham.

'The insurance company says work starts on the twentieth. Should take six weeks. I'll not be back in for Christmas, but soon after.'

'So you'll get all new carpets, furniture, wallpaper?' Celine pushed her plate away; it was still half full. 'Doesn't seem fair when some have to work hard for nice things. Your house was rundown *before* it was flooded, and now you'll get a brand-new kitchen and stylish furniture.'

'I'd happily have kept my shithole,' I said through a mouthful of potato.

'Can we not have shithole at the table,' sighed my mother.

'It's what Sharleen meant. She just didn't say it.'

'Because she has manners; and she's not Sharleen. Why do you have to be so crude?' My mother cut her chicken with vigour, the action at odds with her even tone. 'I thought you'd have grown out of it by now.'

'You're lucky to have that house.' Celine didn't even look at me.

'What's that supposed to mean?' I dropped my cutlery onto the plate; I no longer felt hungry.

'If your dad hadn't left you money you'd never have property. I don't know anyone who works in a care home and is single and has their own house.'

'What does my inheritance have to do with *you*? My dad worked hard for his money, and what he left me was mine to do with as I wished.'

'Maybe if you'd used it to go to university you'd have a better job now, dear.' Mother's face assumed a helpful, serene smile.

'Why is *my* money up for discussion?' I demanded. 'No one discusses what Sharleen does with money. Dad would be *glad* I bought my own place. He'd turn in his grave if I was still living here!'

I stormed out in true teenage style, went to the bathroom and sat on the toilet lid for ten minutes. The grout between the peach tiles was almost black and the shower curtain stank of mildew. As a child I used to hide in here to escape guests, family, nagging. Mother said I had a morbid fascination with places with locked doors.

'One of these days you'll get stuck,' she'd preached, 'and then what will you do?'

Now, I took a tube of cream from my pocket and coated my inflamed hands. Why did I so often feel the urge to hide? When had it begun?

Back in the dining room Celine eyed me through blue mascara. Only Graham was still eating.

'Where did we go on holiday when I was nine?' I asked after a while.

'Goodness me, I don't remember,' sighed Mother. 'How would I remember that?'

'Because you were there, maybe?'

'What year was it?' Then to herself: 'Who was I going out with?'

'Lots of people,' I said.

'Catherine! Don't be rude. In between your father and Graham' – she touched his hand – 'there was only Gary. Honestly, can't we have a Sunday dinner without rudeness?'

'And breasts? I'll try.'

'Menorca,' said my mother.

'Menorca what?' I asked.

'We went to Menorca the summer you were nine. Lovely hotel, lousy weather. You cut yourself in a rock pool. Bled for hours and ruined my beach towels.'

'I don't remember.' Despite covering my hands in cream, they still burned; I longed to scratch them. 'What else happened when I was nine?'

'You probably annoyed me,' she sighed.

'Specifically?'

'Specifically?' She grabbed the wine, turned her glass upright and poured. 'You were a moody so-and-so.'

'When I was nine Dad bought me a horse,' said Celine.

Graham smiled and nodded.

'Mabel I called her. Beautiful dappled coat she had.'

'We stopped calling you Catherine-Maria.' Mother seemed pleased that she had a snippet of memory to give me. Perhaps it would shut me up.

Nanny Eve had always called me Catherine-Maria when I was small; I already knew that. I loved to hear her words in that musical Irish voice. She said Maria with the same reverence as she spoke the Hail Mary. It was beautiful, she said: Italian for Mary. She'd picked it when I was born. But until now, I'd had no recollection of *when* everyone stopped using it. Nanny Eve died when I was eleven and I'd thought the name just died with her.

'When I was nine?' Second-hand memory was frustrating.

'Yes. I remember writing your tenth birthday card and I just put

Catherine. I'm sure that was the first time.' My mother had already finished half her wine; a sign she was edgy. I took pleasure in irritating her.

'Why?' I asked.

'It seemed childish – a mouthful. You were ten, after all.'

'But Nanny Eve loved it.' Suddenly I felt my identity had been stolen and wanted a culprit to pin the blame on. I'd always known the name had died, but now I knew it had happened when I was nine – my blackout year – and I desperately needed to know why.

'Why are you so snappy? Why do you care about us changing your name?'

'Because you said I was *nine*.' I wrapped my hands around the cool crystal tumbler.

'Who wants dessert?' she asked.

'Oh, me,' cried Celine. 'I only ate two potatoes and eighteen peas, so I can.'

My mother scraped the uneaten food into a pile on one plate.

'What is it today, dear?' Graham lit a cigarette, inhaled and leaned back in the chair.

'Trifle,' she said.

I thought of the *Friends* episode in which Rachel made a trifle with peas and carrots and meat because the page in the recipe book was stuck to the one for shepherd's pie. Everyone rubbed their bellies and pretended to like it so they wouldn't hurt her feelings. We all endure trifle and peas in some way.

'Just a small portion for me,' I said. The wine had made me lightheaded and I didn't want to ruin the high.

Mother carried the trifle in like she was presenting a winning sculpture.

'Just thought of another line from Fern's column,' smiled Graham. 'She said a husband with a power drill was as happy as a wife on a weekend with the girls.' Graham had a mild crush on Fern; it only made him more endearing.

'I really don't like that girl,' snapped Mother. 'Why would you want to live above a takeaway with her? And that owner is a pervert. I don't like his ears. He has devious ears.' She touched her earrings.

'Don't talk that way about Fern,' I said. 'I don't diss your tanned-to-within-an-inch-of-her-life friend Barbara. Fern is just having fun. Fun! Anyone remember *that*?'

I jumped up and in my haste caught the cloth, sending wine and trifle flying like white-and-red fireworks. Celine screamed; I turned to see her lap fill with jelly and custard, her white trousers massacred. Mother gasped and ran for a cloth.

I headed for the garden and sat on the bench near the steps, where a wall protected me from the eyes inside the house. My jeans didn't protect me from the cold metal and so I shifted from one buttock to the other. Traffic hummed beyond the fir trees: life; escape. When gravelly footsteps sounded behind me I knew it would be Graham, though I didn't expect him to be wearing my red coat.

'Does it suit me?' He grinned. 'It was the only one in the cupboard.'

'Apparently it doesn't suit *me*,' I said.

'You know how she is.' Graham perched on the wall, took out a pack of cigarettes and offered me one. I considered, but declined. I didn't need to give that bad habit up again.

'Let's not have the monthly you-know-how-she-is talk,' I said. 'What have I done so wrong?'

Graham exhaled smoke with a shrug. Reflected in the frozen pond were the leaves on the evergreen trees. I thought of a man up my street who had lost his carp in the flood. Flushed out of their pond, they'd swum wild in the temporary garden lake. He couldn't catch them, so when the water subsided they drowned. I'd watched him drop six fish into the bin; each dead-weight thud haunted me for weeks after.

'Nothing,' said Graham.

'I get on with my life, ask for nothing.' My voice broke. 'I'm not doing too badly for nearly thirty-one.'

'I think it's great that you do crisis-line stuff.' Graham ground the cigarette out with his foot and put the tab end in one of my mother's plant pots. We shared a knowing smile. If she ever looked in the tub, there would be at least a year's worth of Graham's smokes. 'I think you'll make a great listener. They're lucky to have you, Catherine.'

'Why can't she say that? It's not difficult, is it?'

'No.'

'Graham, where are you?' Mother's voice came from the kitchen window; his smoke rings must have given him away. I knew all the best hiding places in the house and this wasn't one of them. The cupboard under the stairs was a good one, and behind the shed. Not inside it though; I'd never liked the darkness there as a child.

'Will you drive Celine home?' called Mother. 'She's not feeling well.'

'Duty calls.' Graham headed inside, the sleeves of my red coat just too short, his shoes crunching on the gravel.

I didn't want to go in yet. I'd always preferred my own company, even as a child. That much I *could* remember – because it hadn't changed, I supposed. I used to hide in alcoves and cupboards, behind curtains and under beds. I hid in my dad's study once during one of my birthday parties, long after he'd died.

Images flashed randomly before my mind's eye, like a computer slide show. Balloons stuck to a banister, one floating free. A banner draped from a curtain rail. Ten candles blazing on a pink-and-white cake. So I was ten. I was in Dad's chair clutching a stuffed bunny I'd won at pass-the-parcel. I saw the rabbit as if I held it now. White and soft, with plastic whiskers that tickled my cheek when I kissed it.

Someone disturbed me – it might have been Mother or maybe Nanny Eve. I wasn't sure. Then the image dissolved, like a word on the tip of your tongue: just within reach, but the letters liquefy as you try to arrange them.

'Catherine!'

My hands wrapped around the stuffed rabbit I no longer had. Fisted fingers clutching at the memory.

'Catherine, you'll get pneumonia,' called my mother from the kitchen. Two birds departed the fir tree in a flap of startled wings. 'Graham's back and said he'll take you home. For goodness sake, come inside and stop behaving like a child.'

I went inside with hands that were on fire and a memory as frozen as the garden pond.

8

Dad's protective cloak

Exhausted after Mother's house, before Fern had come home, I fell asleep on the sofa with *Songs of Praise* still on. I dreamt about Dad. It must have been because I'd sat in his study armchair earlier. When I woke again, a memory came vividly to me.

After he died, Dad's study was one of the many places I would hide. In there I was clever and loved and safe. In there my hands didn't itch or knock things over. In there he smoothed my hair and it stayed down.

In the memory, I was looking for an answer. Dad was who I'd always gone to for answers. No matter how many questions I asked, he had some sort of reply. Whether he looked it up, invented it, or happened to know the answer already didn't matter. I'd sit in the green chair in his study and wait for him to come home from work, my head full of queries.

Mrs Willis, my English teacher, had set us a piece of homework: we were to answer the question 'What do you want to be when you grow up?', and then ask a member of our family what they had wanted to be. I'd known Mother would shoo me away and send me to ask Dad. Nanny Eve would say that in her day women dreamt more of children and marriage than of fancy careers or exciting adventures. But Dad would come up with something special. I had already written my answer. I wanted to help people. I wasn't sure how. I had written in blue biro that I wanted to help old people walk up the street and sad people become happy. Whatever job that was, I wanted to do it.

I curled up in Dad's chair and waited for him. He entered with a briefcase in one hand and a coat over his arm, smelling of the outside and work. Whiffs of Mother's chicken casserole drifted in from the kitchen. We wouldn't have long before she'd be calling us for tea.

'What's up, sweetie?' he asked. 'Have we got spellings to practise?'

'What did you want to be when you grew up?' I asked him.

He put his coat around my shoulders, like the magical protection cloak a superhero might wear. Peter Rabbit sat on the windowsill. His blue jacket was chipped and his stone feet were dusty. I wriggled my toes and pulled the coat tight. One day, much later, I would look for Dad's protective cloak. Mother would say it had gone to the charity shop. I'd wonder if it still had its powers on a different body. I'd spend a long time trying on the other coats in the house, looking for that safe feeling, but never finding it.

'I wanted to be an astronaut,' Dad said. 'Or a rock star.'

'Not you,' I giggled, pointing to his smart shoes and plain tie.

'Not me?' he teased. 'I'm cool. I could be.'

'Yeah, right!'

Then, because it was just us and I knew Mother could not hear, I asked, 'And what about Mum? What did she want to be?'

Dad looked sad. He was always sad when I mentioned her. 'She wanted to be a nurse,' he said after a while. 'And that's what she almost was. She had just finished her training when ... when you came.'

Mother called then that our food was on the table and we shouldn't let it get cold. Dad started for the study door and then stopped. He came back, face serious, and bent down so his eyes were level with mine. The chair's leather felt warm on my bare legs. Branches tapped on the glass like kids playing knock down ginger.

'I only wanted one thing when I grew up,' he said very softly, so that goose pimples spread over my arms. 'I wanted a daughter. Most men want sons, you know, to carry on their names, and do "guy" stuff with. But girls are *way* cooler.'

I think that moment was the last time I was absolutely happy. It wasn't long after this that he died. That happiness faded like his photographs. Now I don't even fully recall *how* it felt to be that happy.

Mother called us again, slightly louder. Dad ruffled my hair and we went to eat with her.

Now I tried to cling to the memory. To him. I imagined Dad stroking my hair and kissing my nose and saying he'd got everything he wanted and nothing bad would ever happen.

9

Losing with four aces

It was the day of my first Flood Crisis shift. I'd not slept more than a few hours. Fern stood next to the sofa, silhouetted in the dawn's half-light. Face shadowy but white shirt luminous, she leaned close to my cheek and said, 'I'm freaked out. He had me pretend to be a psychiatric nurse and wash him and shine a light in his eyes and put him in a strait jacket; we made one from a sheet!'

'Who the hell are you talking about?' I pulled the pillow over my head.

'Paul.' She sat on the sofa and handed me a coffee. 'He was surprisingly seductive last night. Sexy in an intellectual way. When we kissed, he suggested shock-treatment role play – even that I could have gone with if he hadn't wanted me to say, "Bite down on this strap, big boy."'

I spat my coffee out. 'This *cannot* start my first day at Flood Crisis.'

'I think it's the best start – fake shock treatment to suicide.' Fern unclipped her hair. 'Anyway, I have a column to write.'

She disappeared and I had a shower. The phone rang as I dried my hair. John, the man in charge of the builders renovating my house, said there were some serious problems with my wiring. He needed to meet me to discuss it before the floor went down. Could I meet him later, he asked. I said I had a commitment. He said that this was important stuff. Wires were life-changing. We agreed to meet at the house the next morning.

My mother rang straight after, asking if I was going to visit on Sunday, because if so she would bake a cake and maybe buy a balloon or two for my birthday. My birthday always reminded me of Nanny Eve, hers being a week later. How old would she have been? Did she see that I never forgot hers now?

When the phone rang a third time, I ignored it.

I'd soon be answering them non-stop.

At one I left for the bus. I like to be early for a first shift anywhere, and with so many streets blocked by caravans and renovations the buses were irregular. I put playing cards, a book, an apple, some crisps and my key into a bag.

Outside, puddles from the previous night's sleet had frozen. Grey clouds drifted by like old sheep, and stiff trees lined the street. Ten minutes' shivering in a graffiti-covered shelter later, the bus arrived; I dropped the correct money into the driver's tray and turned and looked straight at Will. His lips parted slightly as though anticipating a kiss. Had he seen me in the bus shelter, watched me climb on the bus, stupid and unknowing? His being there was as strange as if a horse sat cross-legged in the front seat wearing a tutu.

A woman with a baby on her hip and a buggy in her hand pushed me and said, 'Come on love, you're blocking the bloody aisle.'

'Sorry.' I was shoved closer to Will.

'My car's in the garage,' he said. 'They think it's the alternator.'

Long hair curled about ears I'd once stroked and whispered encouragement into. Two shirt buttons had popped open, freeing the fine chain his grandma had left him when she died. I realised he held a hand; a hand adorned with a silver bracelet from which dangled charms. A hand I imagined would resist being tied to a bedpost.

'This is Miranda,' he said of the hand.

I clung to the overhead railing as the bus lurched from one stop to the next. Miranda was beautiful; like Audrey Hepburn. Black hair framed a creamy complexion. She was purity on a dirty bus, with a lace blouse and long eyelashes, not stubby, uncurlable ones like mine. I loved her hands; they made me want to cry.

An old man with a plaid shopping trolley got up from the seat adjacent to theirs and shuffled to the doors. It would have been silly not to take his place, so I put my scruffy bag over my ravaged, unladylike hands and sat.

'This is Catherine,' said Will, and Miranda nodded.

Had they discussed me in detail? Had he described my many moods and oddities?

'We're going to meet the estate agent. Last-minute things to arrange. I sold the flat last week – got the asking price too. We're moving away.'

I wished he would stop telling me things I hadn't asked to hear; things that invited questions I was too stubborn to ask.

'Where are you going?' I had to ask that.

'Glasgow,' she said, and the accent told me it was her home.

'Lovely.' I couldn't think of anything else to say. 'When?'

'A week on Friday.' She smiled, showing perfect teeth.

'Lovely.' My palms felt like a million ants were crawling over them.

'Where are you going?' asked Will.

'My first shift at Flood Crisis.'

'You're going through with it, then?' he asked.

'Yes,' I said.

His free hand fingered his brown belt, and I remembered the time he suggested we tie one another up: only with scarves that could easily be undone, only for fun and only if I wanted to. I was nervous and felt self-conscious at first. But then I'd insisted he tie me so I couldn't pull free. It was so much easier to be fastened to his brass bedpost and have my neck bitten and his hands inside me than to consider whether I loved him. If he tied me, I couldn't leave. If he'd gagged me too, we might still have been together.

'Will you volunteer for Crisis Care in Glasgow?' I asked him.

'No. This is a good time to leave the place – new doors and all that.'

He'd loved it at Crisis Care, so I wondered if Miranda had influenced the decision. I studied his mouth – he bit his lower lip like he always did when nervous. He'd done it when he first said he loved me. I'd told him he didn't. He'd insisted he'd never loved anyone like this, and I said that even if he did, I'd probably only ruin it. He never said it again.

And I ruined it.

'I've given Crisis Care two years,' he said. 'It's time to move on.'

That's how I'd felt about our relationship; it only lasted five months but it was the longest I'd had. It wasn't that I didn't love him – I might have done. It wasn't that he was unattractive – quite the opposite. It was that I preferred it when he hurt me. Or when I hurt him and we argued and then made up. When we were at Crisis Care more than away from it, that's when I felt alive.

I'd often heard a line in my head and was never sure if someone had once said it to me or if I'd read it somewhere: *It's not love unless it hurts.* I said it aloud once to Will, and he'd asked what I meant. I wasn't sure but now I thought it might just be true.

'I bet you have a pack of cards in your bag.' He motioned to my lap.

'Why would she?' Miranda's charms tinkled as she laughed.

I opened my bag and took them out. They had Marilyn Monroe on them; she wore a different swimming costume for each suit. My favourite was the hearts: she wore a green bikini and still had mousy hair; was looking over her shoulder with a big smile.

'You never beat me,' said Will. 'You could have four aces and still lose. Remember – I took all your fruit pastilles and you still wanted to play? When you find another bad player, that'll be your soul mate.' He fidgeted with his belt again.

'You know I don't believe in that soul-mate stuff,' I said.

'We should play cards, sweetheart,' said Miranda.

'Catherine and me used to play at Crisis Care.' Will touched her cheek and she nuzzled against him; I looked out the window. 'They were long nights and we had to stay awake somehow.'

He didn't tell her what else we did when it was just the two of us and the nights were long and the phones mercifully silent. I wondered if he ever thought about when I undid his jeans and straddled him in the worn, corduroy chair. The phone had disturbed us halfway. Will had pulled my hair as I withdrew, saying, 'Just leave it,' and I'd said, 'We can't, we *can't.*' I answered the telephone with my shirt undone, whispering the line I'd said a hundred times, 'Crisis Care, can I help you?'

She said her baby was stillborn. She was Gina. Gina had taken two bottles of paracetamol. Only sixteen and didn't want an ambulance.

I had talked to her until my breathing synchronised and sympathised with hers. The words slowed too. Words like 'cold' and 'beautiful'. I listened. Questions would have intruded, so I only spoke to remind her I was there. When she'd been silent for fifteen minutes Will took the phone from me and put it back in its cradle. I didn't cry. I asked him to take me back to the chair. As Will pulled me back onto him my breaths were as erratic as Gina's.

My search for release came faster.

Will looked at me as the bus bounced over a speed bump, and I hid my blush with a sleeve. Miranda played with her charms, studying me.

'I prefer to read cards than play with them,' I said.

'I remember. We could never have a game without you telling volunteers they'd come into money next week or they'd be redundant by Tuesday.'

One of the charms on Miranda's bracelet was a silver rabbit with tiny diamond eyes. It winked at me in the weak light. She stroked Will's hand and the rabbit jiggled. I'd loved his hands. I wondered if she also enjoyed them scratching her thighs until they drew blood.

'Will your house be ready soon?' he asked.

'After Christmas.'

'Christmas. Where has the year gone?'

'I love Christmas,' said Miranda. 'I'll be putting the decorations up as soon as we get to Scotland, and they won't come down until the twelfth of January. Will loves it all too.'

He nodded, but I knew different. We met just before Christmas and one of the things we had in common was our loathing of all things festive, agreeing that we should just stay in bed from Christmas Eve to Boxing Day.

The bus passed the football stadium and trundled up the flyover.

'My stop's next,' I said. 'Nice to meet you, Miranda. Congratulations on the move.'

'Enjoy volunteering.' She barely looked at me.

'Enjoy Scotland,' I said to Will.

He held my gaze as I fumbled for my bag, dropping it and spilling keys and cards on the floor. One card fluttered free and landed near Will's foot; Marilyn smiled at me from the back. He bent down and turned it over, like a player taking his last chance: the two of spades.

'What does that mean?' He handed it to me. Our fingers touched for a moment – his beautiful, mine cracked.

'Separate ways,' I said.

The bus stopped, and he let go of the card.

Dizzy from suddenly standing, passengers swam before my eyes. 'Later, Will.'

As the name left my mouth I recalled that it irritated him. I started to apologise but he shook his head gently. For a second his lips parted, and I thought he would kiss me goodbye, that when he raised his hand he was reaching for my face. But he just turned away.

'You want this stop?' demanded the driver.

I stepped onto the path and watched the bus disappear, spitting stones and icy water from its wheels. Even if Will hadn't said he was moving to Scotland, even if Miranda hadn't held his hand so tightly, and even if I hadn't dropped the two of spades, I knew I'd never see him again. I knew it like I knew my mother would insist I was a fool for letting him go. I knew it like I knew Fern would say that there were plenty more fish in the sea.

When my house had flooded and the carpets were saturated with sewage water and the wallpaper came away like old skin, I was helpless. This time it was not water or weather. I had nothing to blame but myself. I could have tried harder with Will. I'd likely never meet anyone with a kinder heart than his, with more tolerance.

But even with four aces, I always chose to lose.

10

The weight of words

A woman in a man's coat at least three sizes too big pushed a trolley full of dog food up the street, mumbling about mobile phones and cancer. I watched for a moment before returning my attention to the Flood Crisis building.

I had already used the door code, but I couldn't remember if I'd stored it on my phone under F for Flood Crisis, V for Voluntary Stuff or D for Depression. Climbing the stairs to the front door, I scrolled through numbers. Misjudging the last step, I fell heavily against the concrete, grabbing a railing that wasn't there. The edge of the step cut me just below the knee. Blood dripped onto the ice.

I found the five-digit code under C for Code, bloodying my phone and then the door as I tapped it in. My DNA stained everything – handles, bricks, wall.

In the mustard-tiled kitchen I searched for kitchen roll, bleeding onto the lino. None. In the windowless toilet I groped for tissue, marking the tiles crimson. I tried to wrap the cheap toilet roll around my knee.

A sound.

I turned. In the hall was a person by the door. I screamed in surprise. Christopher – holding an armful of gold tinsel. His black hair was wet, as if he'd just washed it.

'I'm hurt,' I said.

'What happened?'

'I fell up the step,' I said.

'*Up* the step?'

'Yes.' I imagined the magnified plop of my blood hitting the floor.

'We should check that. Let me see.' He put the gold tinsel on the radiator, took off his coat, bent down and looked at my leg.

'It's fine.' I felt uncomfortable with him being there. 'What's with the tinsel? Are you a Christmas fairy in your spare time?'

'You should tie something tight around to stop the flow and elevate your leg.' He glanced at the tinsel, dangling festively. 'We need decorations – those are my mother's cast-offs.'

He went into the kitchen and returned with a damp 'Thirty-Five Years of *Coronation Street*' tea towel. Ripping Deidre Barlow in two, he put the strips over his arm and invited me into the lounge, calling me Hurricane Katrina. I considered telling him my real name but decided I liked the storm-inspired one more. It was a gift I had given myself. No one could ruin it. So I said nothing; I followed him into the lounge and sat in one of the velvet chairs.

'Put your leg on the coffee table,' he said.

'I don't want to bleed on Barbara Cartland.'

He laughed. 'She only wants your tears.' He dabbed my leg with the damp tea towel.

'I can do that.' I reached for the cloth, pulling my skirt lower and wishing I'd shaved my legs more recently. My mother would hang her head in shame.

'You think a man of the world like me hasn't bandaged a woman up before? This is going to be tight. There. Now, keep it up for a while.' He wrapped the strip twice around my leg and tied it in a knot. Deirdre Barlow's bespectacled eye stared at me. I felt foolish and awkward. My coppery hands burned and I scratched the palm. Christopher looked at them but didn't say anything.

'You certainly know how to make an entrance,' he said. 'Tea?'

Listening to him clinking cups and teaspoons in the kitchen, I stared at the two pink booths. I'd never let go of the rope that tied me to these phones. I thought I'd let it slip away when I left Crisis Care, but, after the flood, moving house, the night shifts and the end of a relationship,

I found it kept surfacing. Now it tightened, bound me again. It was why I was back here; I couldn't cut it.

The door opened. It was Jane who was really Jane. Jangly Jane. She took biscuits and crisps from her bag and put them on the shelf under the table. Her earrings, tasselled skirt and bangles jangled like wind chimes in a storm.

'It's you,' she said. There was no response to that. She searched on Norman's desk for something. 'What happened to your knee?' she asked. 'Did you record the injury in the Accident Book?'

I insisted I was OK, that I'd just fallen up the step.

'We have to follow procedure. Did you bang your head?'

Christopher kicked the door open and brought in two mugs, the gold tinsel wrapped around his neck. He put a drink next to me and dropped the garland into a box labelled 'Xmas Decos'.

'Did she bang her head?' Jangly asked him. 'If she gets concussion and falls on the way home she could sue us. We'd best cover ourselves.'

Christopher touched her arm, insisting it was just a flesh wound and that I was unlikely to sue a temporary crisis service.

'Best get the phones on,' he said, slurping tea. 'Do you want to wait before answering them?' He looked at me.

He didn't know that I already had. I wondered if I should say anything, and wasn't sure why I felt guilty.

'I'd like to answer them,' I said.

'Should give your leg another half-hour before you move,' he suggested.

Jangly Jane activated the phones at the main switchboard, and I expected the shrill siren of desperation to start immediately. Nothing. Disappointment uncurled in my stomach. Or maybe it was relief.

'There was a fault with them the other night,' she said.

'What do you mean?' asked Christopher.

He pinned back a shutter, letting buttery light penetrate the room. Jane grabbed a copy of *Horse & Hound* magazine and sat on the paisley sofa. Her bracelets tinkled as she flicked through the pages.

'They were ringing all night when no one was on shift.' She looked up from the page. 'We had loads of complaints when no one answered.'

I avoided her eyes.

The telephone rang in cubicle one. It was a sound I often heard in my sleep, in shrieking car tyres on a wet road, on a speeding train, in thunder. I sat up, alert.

'I'll get it,' said Christopher. He took his drink into the cubicle and picked the phone up on its fourth ring. At Crisis Care we were supposed to answer by the third if we could. If it was to keep the caller from waiting it was senseless. Someone who had waited twenty years to talk about something was unlikely to think us cruel for adding another few seconds and hang up in a sulk.

'Flood Crisis, can I help?' said Christopher.

The second phone started and Jane reached it before the fourth ring. I listened to the one-sided conversations and sipped my tea. Questions like, 'Tell me more about flood day?' and 'How did it make you feel?' are never indicative of the level of distress being discussed. They form only half the picture, the white not the black. I wondered if I'd be able to help these callers. Would I get them to feel; would they get *me* to feel; would they pull me in?

The rope tightened.

Christopher returned after a fifteen-minute conversation, and I said I'd answer the next call. I took my leg off the table to show I meant business, knocking Barbara Cartland to the floor.

'You lost my page,' smiled Christopher.

The phone rang. I stood and shrugged to show I wasn't daunted. It should have felt like the first time I'd walked towards a ringing phone almost a year before. Then I'd felt like a prisoner on death row, legs shackled, heading for that last room, inevitability as heavy as the chains. But not this time: this was my second call.

I picked it up on the fifth ring.

'Can you tell me it'll never rain again,' a woman's voice demanded.

I hadn't had a chance to say my greeting or grab the pen and pad. My mind was blank. This might be my second call, but officially it was my first. How should I respond? What was I to say?

'Tell me why you fear the rain,' I said finally, and wrote the date on the top of the sheet.

'Why do you think?' she snapped.

I knew the obvious response but I'd learned never to presume. Questions from callers were best ignored. We had no idea what answer they sought and no right to offer judgement anyway.

'Were you flooded?' I asked – the obligatory question.

'Yes.'

I heard the *Coronation Street* omnibus on TV and fingered Deirdre Barlow's all-seeing eye, which still encircled my knee.

'I can't sleep when it rains. I go to the window when I hear it on the roof and wait for it to stop. My husband sleeps in the kids' room. He can't stand my restlessness. I don't know when we last had sex. Do you think it'll happen again?'

Did she mean the rain or the sex?

'I can't answer that.' I spoke softly.

I was Katrina; Hurricane Katrina. I supposed I had been Katrina all through Crisis Care. I just hadn't had a name for her then. The rope did not pull. It loosened; *I* loosened.

'Tell me more about being flooded,' I said.

'I was at work,' she said. 'My son Evan rang to say the water was at the step and he was scared it was going to come in. The house three doors along was already flooded. They're an American family. She has some beautiful handbags. I wanted to go home but my boss said Margaret had gone early with diarrhoea, so I couldn't.'

I nodded, knowing she couldn't see, and remembered the rain. I'd been on a rare day shift at the care home when it came and I'd left at lunchtime, despite protests from the boss. I'd told her it was easy to be dismissive when your luxury home was on top of a hill. I'd called a taxi, afraid the buses would be cancelled.

I was too late. The water had invaded. But I'd refused to admit defeat. My neighbour, Sally, helped me carry things upstairs. 'They'll dry,' I'd said. They'll dry. And they did. But they were never the same.

'I went home, anyway,' said the caller. 'The water was up to my knees. Some bloke in a rowing boat was handing out bricks so people could raise their furniture out of the water. Frig knows where he got it.'

'How did you feel when you saw your house?' I asked.

She paused. I hadn't written any notes. This was familiar territory.

'It wasn't home anymore,' she said. 'When you can't see your carpet and your kids' toys are floating around I don't think a house can ever be home again, can it? We're living upstairs. Can you imagine it – with all the work going on downstairs? I often want to go to the door and scream "Cunts!" into the street.'

I wanted to tell her to do it. Say she might feel better. But that was instruction, and though Norman had said we could offer flood-related advice, I imagined telling a caller to swear in the garden was not what he meant.

'Does it help to talk?' I asked.

'I feel less agitated. You're a nice girl. Oh shit, he's back. Harry, my husband. Best go; he hates me ringing anyone.'

The phone died. I replaced the receiver and looked at the blank sheet of notepaper, sensing that the flood was the least of her worries.

I returned to the lounge area. Jane was still in the other booth; Christopher was reading *Good Housekeeping* magazine on the paisley sofa.

'How did it go?' he asked.

'It's like I never left the phones,' I said.

'And is that good?'

'I don't know.' I searched in my bag for an apple.

Christopher spotted the cards. 'Cool,' he said, pointing. 'Shall we play?'

Jangly Jane came back and dropped onto the huge cushion.

'Card-playing detracts from concentration,' she said.

'Lighten up, Jane,' insisted Christopher. 'Let's play to lose.'

'Oh, I'm good at that,' I said.

We settled into a polite, new-marriage-like, give-and-take routine, alternating turns with callers. A half-hearted game of gin rummy was side-tracked – a shame because I had a nine, ten, jack, queen and king of hearts, and I'd seen that Jane had nothing of value. But after I'd taken a call from a man who'd had constipation since the floods and Christopher had spoken to a regular caller, we couldn't remember whose cards were whose. So I worked out that Jane's jack of diamonds and three of spades meant a dark-haired man was cheating on her but refrained from saying so.

I took a few calls from people who immediately hung up and one from a man who shouted 'Whore!' and then sang 'I Get a Kick Out of You'. My notepad remained empty, awaiting someone's sadness, the weight of words.

'You never called me.' Christopher handed me a third cup of tea.

It had grown dark outside and the streetlights had come on, like a row of orange stars. Jane pulled the shutter across and it was just us and the wailing of another ambulance heading for tragedy in the city.

'I'm your buddy,' he said. 'You're supposed to call before your first shift. Talk about leaving a man hanging.'

The phone rang. I was glad. It was my turn.

'Hello, Flood Crisis, can I help you?' I settled into the still-warm leatherette recliner in booth two. Silence. I picked up the pen and read one of the wall prompts: 'Give your caller time, even if the silence lasts ten minutes.' I waited.

'I met Marcus because of the floods,' she said eventually. Well spoken but nervous. No background noise, nothing to give her life away. 'Where should I start?'

'Wherever you would like to; whatever comes to you first.'

'I was having sign-language evening classes at Eastfield School,' she said. 'It got flooded, so I had to swap class. I was rather miffed. I'd been enjoying the course. So I started child psychology at another site and Marcus was my tutor. All I remember about that first day, other than his eyes studying me when I walked in, was how the fir trees near the classroom window were broken and looked sad, like they had down-turned mouths.'

She became silent again. The phone rang in the other booth. I chewed the pen end.

'Tell me more about Marcus,' I said.

'I love him,' she said.

I couldn't think of a single word. I read the prompts and none of them fit. Love was something I understood so little, I should have been overflowing with questions about it; yet I couldn't think of one. Instead I drew a heart in the top corner of the pad; and then I scribbled it out.

'The sex is amazing.' She giggled. 'Am I allowed to say that? I'm nervous. It's just ... very sexual. He gives me better marks when I ... well, when I give him reason. Last night he rang me while he was marking the work ... he got me to ... I'm embarrassed...'

'I'm not here to judge in any way.'

'He got me to, you know, play with myself while he talked,' she said. 'He told me exactly what to do. It was so arousing. He's teaching me but says I'm teaching him too, that even though he's my tutor we're both adults. It's wrong, isn't it?'

'Why do you feel that?' I asked.

Who could define wrong? I wrote the word on the paper. There had been nothing right about my last relationship.

'He makes me feel like a child. I'm twenty-nine but he's so persuasive. I know he's abusing his power. I tried to end it last week, and we ended up making love in the cupboard, me pressed against the door in case someone came in. I can't walk away from him.'

'How do you feel now?' I asked.

'I keep thinking about my acting lessons,' she said.

'You're having those too?'

'No. I used to.' Her voice changed, became childlike, and then she was silent again.

I moved the phone away from my ear, assessing its weight. I thought of Will, because it was evening, and turned off the cubicle light. I liked to listen in the shadows. Blind, I relied on my instinct and though it had let me down when climbing the steps earlier, it rarely let me down here.

'I'm Helen,' she said.

'Katrina,' I said.

She began to cry.

'If it feels difficult, just take as long as you need,' I said.

'I had acting lessons when I was eleven,' she whispered.

My throat felt tight and I scratched my fingers. I remembered the sense I'd get during a call when something seemingly innocuous was said that changed the direction of the conversation, so subtle, a casual observer would never know. But I knew. I knew that this was what the call was *really* about: acting lessons.

'If I were to ring back another time would you be here?' she asked.

I didn't know what to say. At Crisis Care we weren't allowed to give out our shifts. I felt I might lose her if I gave her the option of calling back.

'I'll be in again next Wednesday,' I said. 'But why don't you—'

The phone died. I didn't replace the receiver for a few minutes, refusing to believe she'd gone. It was frustrating when you made a connection with someone and they hung up. We weren't supposed to get attached, but I'm human and her words pulled at me.

After a while I went back into the lounge. Jane was still in cubicle one. Christopher was playing patience. I noticed the beginnings of a tattoo under his T-shirt sleeve. He had lean arms, sturdy hands. He looked up.

'OK?' he asked.

'Yeah.' I was tired. It was eight-fifteen and there were eleven different cups on the coffee table, some empty, some half full.

'We don't have to answer any more.' He looked at the clock.

I nodded and sat opposite him on a velvet chair.

'How's the cut?' he asked.

I had forgotten about it. Now remembered, it throbbed. Was it better to sometimes forget? Did cuts heal better ignored? I looked under the tea towel; the blood had congealed.

Christopher said I'd have to wash and stitch the tea towel back together.

Jane flopped onto the cushion. 'The girl I just talked to is addicted to sleep. She goes to bed at eight and sleeps all night. Then she takes the kids to school, goes back to bed, sleeps until midday, gets up for lunch, goes back, gets up when the kids come in and still sleeps all night. Said if she sleeps it won't rain.'

Christopher turned the phones off and stretched. We were done. It was over. My first shift. Jane carried half the cups to the kitchen and I followed with the rest. Then I got my coat from the back of the sofa and looked at the now-silent phones; I had no regrets about returning to them. Fern once read in some paranormal book that if you open the portal to the spirit world you can never close it, even with an exorcist or a priest. This was my spirit world.

In the hallway Christopher fastened his jacket, unlocked his bike from the banister and asked how I was getting home. The bus, I told him.

'Will you be OK?'

'It's a bus. I'll be fine.' I regretted my flippant tone but I hate people fussing over me.

'Don't fall up the step.' He carried his bike onto the path.

I wanted to go home, but remembered that it was ruined. That I had a lumpy sofa and the smell of old chicken to look forward to. I turned to say goodbye properly, but Christopher had gone. So I hobbled into the night with a leg wrapped in a stained tea towel and hands aflame.

That night I dreamt again of the room.

This time it occupied a house with furry walls that pulsated as though they breathed. Will was there. Miranda too. They talked in a sign language I couldn't understand, but I felt the weight of their words and knew they were discussing me. She laughed. Her silvery rabbit charm flashed a warning.

Then it appeared – the door to the room. I asked them to stay with me, but they signed something and shook their heads. Will's mouth was sewn up. And then they were gone. I couldn't look at the door. I couldn't think about the room beyond. Flies buzzed around the door handle, and I closed my eyes and began to cry.

Someone whispered, 'Don't cry.'

I awoke on the lumpy sofa with the sheet tangled around my leg. My cut knee throbbed. The DVD player displayed 3.04. A shadow. A *man*. The bushy-haired man in the room. My heart hammered. No, *Fern*. Just Fern at my feet, her face green in the digital glow. Relief. I wondered if I was still dreaming.

'You were crying.' She touched my cheek and I wiped it roughly. 'What were you dreaming about?'

'Can't remember.'

She scrutinised me. 'Bad calls today?'

'Are you alone?' I asked, closing my eyes.

'Yes. No crazy men tonight.'

'Good,' I said.

'Do you want me to sit here until you fall asleep?' she asked.

I whispered that I'd be fine and she should go back to bed. I don't know if she went or if she stayed, but I like to think she sat with me until I faded away again.

11

Girl in a red dress

John, the head workman rebuilding my house, pulled plaster off the Marilyn wall and looked satisfied when her nose crumbled and hit the remaining floorboards.

Marilyn was my Virgin Mary. When John ruined her face all I could see were the shattered pieces of blue porcelain on Nanny Eve's hallway floor. I wanted to kneel and gather up the pieces of plaster, as I had the porcelain back then. I found it quite easy to recall the bad things, like knocked-over statues. So perhaps my ninth year had been a *good* one. Perhaps no single unpleasant event distinguished it from the others. Perhaps I had nothing *to* remember.

'It's worse than we thought,' said John. 'You'll need a full rewire, a new boiler and the copper pipes ripping out before we start renovating. I guess this isn't what you want to hear.'

It wasn't, and on my birthday. The annual celebration was bad enough without finding out the one thing I'd invested my father's inheritance in had been completely wrecked by the floods. Having to get up at eight on my day off hadn't helped my mood either, and my hands were so itchy today, I'd drawn blood between the fingers.

'Would you stop doing that?' I frowned as John picked at the remains of Marilyn's forehead.

He stopped, but dead skin fell anyway; fleshy brick snow.

'Whoever did your house originally was a cowboy,' John added with relish. 'Even without the flood this place was on its last legs. Not seen wiring this old since they condemned my grandmother's place after she croaked last year.'

His trusty sidekick loitered where the fireplace had once been, one foot on a rare floorboard and the other against the wall. Fern would probably think John's apprentice nice, but his boyish face irritated rather than interested me. An aggressive woman had probably never yanked his floppy hair. He took a pack of cigarettes from his overall pocket and lit one.

'Do you mind?' I said.

'Oh, you want one?'

'No! Put it out. I know this place has no walls but it *is* my home.'

He stubbed it out on the brick.

I explained to them that the insurance company was paying the rent on my flat, but I didn't know how long for. 'So do you have any idea how long the rebuild will take?'

'You're looking at another eight weeks,' John said.

'The end of *January*?' I couldn't believe it. I'd imagined being home for Christmas. 'Can we arrange a date?'

John laughed. 'I'm married, love,' he said. 'But matey-boy here is single.'

Matey-boy – or, as I saw him, Robin to John's Batman – raised his eyebrows. When I didn't laugh or agree to a date, John suggested they'd start a week on Tuesday and said their plumber, Brian, would give me a call to arrange things.

I picked up the letters where they lay near the front door and waited for the two men to leave before locking up. Matey-boy Robin lit a cigarette by the gate and flicked ash into my front garden, not meeting my challenging eyes.

A green car pulled up at the muddy verge as they departed and my neighbour Sally got out with an armful of kitchen brochures.

'Catherine.' She locked the car. 'How are you?'

'Oh, you know. Where have you been? I haven't seen you since...'

We both knew since what. I was sure she pictured the day of the flood as often as I did. I hadn't seen her since I'd helped carry their huge plasma TV upstairs and we'd sat on her bed drinking juice because there was no electricity for coffee. We'd stared out of the window in silence, unable to do any more than save our items and wait for the rain to stop.

Now Sally admitted she'd not been to the house in five months. She didn't want to go in today. Her husband, Rick, returned weekly for the post and other necessities but was sick today, so she had no choice but to step inside her shell of a home. She asked if mine was dry.

'A few weeks back,' I said. 'Yours?'

'Last Tuesday. The drying-out is the longest bit.'

From three doors along came the monotonous hum of a dryer. We both looked towards the sound. Sally was probably glad I'd delayed her unlocking the door. She started to speak but couldn't seem to decide what to say. Eventually she asked where I was staying.

'Sharing a flat with Fern,' I said.

'And how's that lovely Billy?'

'Oh.' I pushed my unruly hair behind my ear. 'We split up.'

'Why?' She seemed surprised.

I had no answer. We had all struggled for words after the flood. We still did now. I considered offering her words that would satisfy: his job had taken him to Siberia, for example; or ones that would justify a break-up: he'd slept with my best friend, perhaps. 'It just wasn't working,' I said instead.

She touched my arm. 'I thought you two were great together. When you came the night Rick made that god-awful green curry I couldn't get over the chemistry. When you and Rick were looking at the car, Billy told me he'd never felt about anyone the way he felt about you.'

It began to snow again. White flakes landed like dandruff in Sally's dark hair.

'I bet he was drunk,' I said.

Sally finally looked at her house; newspapers had blown into her porch and flakes of roof tile surrounded the stiff rose bush like petals. I offered to go in with her, but she pulled her scarf tightly about her neck and said she'd be fine. It's what we all said. I'll be fine. Fine is a lousy word.

Sally approached the house the same way I'd faced mine the first time; slowly, warily. I watched her unlock the door and step inside, sure that if I called out and asked her how she felt seeing the inside again she'd have said 'fine'.

At the flat Fern was waiting for me in the kitchen, thankfully wearing her white dressing gown, and thankfully alone.

'Happy birthday!' She produced a bottle of champagne from the fridge.

I warmed my hands on the clinking radiator. Nanny Eve always used to tell me not to, that I'd get chilblains. I did it anyway. Stupid, with eczema. I told Fern champagne was for special birthdays like forty or a hundred.

'Don't be ageist – all birthdays are equal.' She popped the cork and it hit the roof and bounced into the sink. Fizzy liquid filled two mismatched plastic cocktail glasses. 'Where did you go so early this morning?'

I told her about the builders and said I couldn't drink champagne at this time of day. Fern smiled, saying builders were all muscle and sweat.

'No muscles today, only sweat. So where are we going tonight?'

'Town. Kate's coming too. Read my column, it's a special one. I'll get dressed. Read it out, so I can hear.'

She went to the bedroom, leaving the door ajar, and I picked up the newspaper, turned to page ten, took a sip of champagne and assumed the posh voice I used when reading her work aloud:

'"No underwear – whether lacy, silk or satin – feels quite as sensual on your skin as the fabric of your husband's shirt after an afternoon session of love-making, especially when you know you ironed it for him. And so I found myself—"'

'No, the last paragraph,' she called from her room.

I skimmed the words and resumed:

'"I wish my best friend, Catherine, happy birthday – who knows, she may be married too this time next year if the new man she's flaunting has any sense. Then he, she, Sean and I can enjoy life as a cosy four-some."' I shut the paper with an indignant crunch. 'You can't write that! What new man? She might deny it but my mother reads this. She'll be on my back saying I'm hiding some eligible suitor from her. Why do you have to *lie?*'

'Don't you like the message?' Fern pouted in the doorway.

'Don't make that face; I'm not some guy.'

'Stop being grumpy. It's your birthday.'

I felt bad. She'd meant well. I wasn't sure why it bothered me so much. She could write what she wanted. Maybe it was my lack of memory. Maybe it was someone adding further to my confusion, mud-dying what I knew for sure with fiction. I flopped on the sofa and asked her to save my champagne while I had a nap.

When I woke at three the flat was empty. The drip-drip-drip of the leaky tap greeted me. At night I had to tie one cloth around it and put another beneath the flow so the sound wouldn't disturb me. Noises rose now from the kitchen below: Victor and his Happy House staff preparing for a busy Saturday night. Using the last of the cheese, I made a sandwich and ate it while reading Fern's column again.

It still irritated me. Did it mock the life I had? Or maybe the life I didn't. But Fern wouldn't do that. Perhaps it just reminded me of my inability to sustain a normal relationship. Of Will and Miranda travel-ling happily to Scotland. Of my losing, even with four aces.

I'd finished showering and was drying my hair in the cracked mirror above the oven when Fern returned at four.

'Kate isn't coming,' she said, dumping a Debenhams bag on the sofa.

I asked why over the blast of hairdryer.

'She went out last night and she's too hungover. Bloody weakling.'

I switched the dryer off and unplugged it. 'What's in the bag?'

She fumbled around and pulled out a crimson dress, waving it like a matador teasing a bull. Frilled, with a slash-split thigh and thin straps that barely supported the soft fabric; designer tags still dangled from the hem.

'You'll look stunning,' I said.

'It's not for me – it's for you.'

I opened my mouth but, like so often these days, couldn't think of anything to say. Eventually words about it being too beautiful and me being too big and her being too kind spilled out.

'Try it on.'

I fingered the fabric as if it might disappear at my touch. Fern pushed me into the bathroom with it. 'Don't make me come in there,' she called after me.

Steam misted the mirror, softening my lines. I opened the window and chicken-curry odours wafted in. Reality. Dropping the towel, I slid the dress over my body. Chill air stiffened my nipples; the fabric was alien on my skin, like the hands of a new lover. I held my breath to zip it up. Anticipation. Shoulder straps straightened, I wiped mist from the mirror. The person staring back didn't look like me. If red aged me then I was better with age.

Fern demanded that I come out for inspection, and I opened the door, scratching and stretching my raw hands.

'You should wear red more often,' she said. 'You're stunning. Don't mess with the straps, they're fine.'

We finished the bubbly while Fern styled my hair, promising a night of debauchery. She knew the best places, she said, slipping into tight black trousers and a silver top. She insisted we pose for a photo to remember. I hated photos, dreading that I might look back at them one day and not recall the details.

A taxi arrived at eight and dropped us off near a pub so popular its inhabitants spilled down the steps and onto the street. Inside people jostled for space at the bar to buy overpriced cocktails. Fern flashed her most seductive smile at a man near the front and he bought us both a cosmopolitan.

'We're going where he goes,' she said. 'He's sexy in a scholarly way. Looks like he could teach me some new tricks.'

'If you don't know them all already, what hope is there for the rest of us?' I said.

We moved from one over-lit bar to the next, hands groping and pushing us through the throng, music louder in every venue. Fern acquired drinks from new contacts and old, had favourite songs played by DJs and found every fashionable spot in every busy corner.

In a bathroom my reflection surprised me; I had forgotten I was new. Red silk met pink flesh, crimson lipstick finished the newness. I liked how little like me I looked. A small blonde girl said the dress was sexy, and I thought about making a derogatory remark about my figure but resisted. It was nice to be the girl in the sexy dress. Nice to be sexy. I smiled at my alter ego.

Perhaps this was Katrina. Katrina stepped away from the phones and into the world, into the dress. '*Katrina*,' I whispered.

I found Fern near a fake bronze Narcissus statue. Eyes bright, she suggested a club next, but I wasn't sure I wanted to. I liked being in the bar where I was Katrina in a sexy dress.

'I know one,' she said. 'Drinks are cheap and women get in free.'

It was packed. Sleazy, dark and stinking of sweat, it tainted my dress. Most of the occupants barely looked eighteen; I felt old. But warmed by compliments and cocktails, I ordered more drinks. The barman looked about ten. He asked something I couldn't hear over the music; I nodded anyway.

I knew the song. I started to sing, but it was just a sample over pounding bass and screaming lyrics. The original had been cleverly rearranged for the younger generation; same name, different dress.

Fern returned from the bar, grumbling that she'd lost her necklace. Stupidly, I asked where, my question lost in the noise. The dance floor disappeared; I didn't know if it was the fog emanating from a smoke machine or if it was the effect of the cocktails. The crowd appeared to be dancing without legs, a collective of waving arms and heads.

'If you pass out I'll never find you,' I said into Fern's ear.

She ordered a vodka, drank it in one and demanded we dance. I didn't think I could – my legs no longer felt attached to my body either. I wanted to curl up on a sofa in a dark corner and people-watch.

'It's your birthday,' cried Fern.

'Happy birthday to me.' I downed another drink. It meant Nanny Eve's would be next week. *Happy birthday, Nanny Eve.*

Fern kissed me and was swiftly swallowed by the smoke on the dance floor. I got another cocktail and looked around.

Sofas scattered randomly under an archway sagged with the weight of kissy, gropey couples. I found a vacant one near the cigarette machine. A girl was arguing with her boyfriend near the stairs, waving animated hands in his face and shaking her head, incensed by his lack of response. When he walked away she cried on a friend's shoulder. Fern didn't return. I was beginning to think I could escape, when a man in a cream shirt dropped into the seat next to me.

'I was in your house today,' he shouted.

'What?' Then I recognised the irritating, floppy hair. 'You're Robin.'

'What?'

'Robin,' I yelled. 'John-the-builder's apprentice.'

'Who the hell is Robin? I'm Stan.'

'I'll stick with Robin.'

'What?'

'Doesn't matter.'

It was the perfect conversation: the music was so loud we couldn't hear each other, so I could say anything I wanted.

'Nice dress.' That I heard. Also: 'Can I buy you a drink?'

He reminded me of the men I'd had in my early twenties – young, eager, wanting to please. Promiscuous years of picking them up, sleeping with them and then calling them a cab afterwards. No names, no promises, no feelings.

'If you want to,' I shouted.

A drink was a drink. I barely had my taxi fare home now. At the bar Robin slid a wallet out of his pocket with hands too graceful to tear houses down.

I've always loved hands, marvelling at how one pair could create the *Mona Lisa* while another might steer an aeroplane into the World Trade Center. What might Robin's do to me? Ten years ago I'd have taken him home. I'd have enjoyed the rush of his attention, his eyes on my body. I'd have devoured him in the dark. But I'd have cried the next day.

Robin turned now and smiled at me, reminding me of a man once upon a time, whose name I'd never requested. No name meant no confusion. We'd fucked in an alley. He'd pulled up my dress, undid his zip, and entered me against the bins. It had rained halfway through, disguising my tears. Regret didn't always wait until I'd called them a taxi.

'Do you come here often?' Robin resumed his place on the sagging sofa and handed me a blue drink.

'Are you really asking me that?'

'I thought it was cute today when you told me off for lighting up.'

'Just how old are you?' I asked.

'Twenty-four.'

'Isn't there some eighteen-year-old you could talk to?'

'What?'

I shook my head again.

'Older women are hot,' he shouted.

'How old do you think I am?' So much for all birthdays being equal.

'Thirty. Are you wearing anything under that dress?'

'Under this dress I'm actually a man,' I said.

'What?'

'Nothing,' I yelled.

He grinned and put his hand on my thigh.

'I meant that I *said* nothing.' I moved his hand back to his own jean-clad thigh. 'Look,' I said into his ear. 'You're probably what normal people would call cute, but I'm with a friend and it's my birthday and I'm not after a shag.'

'There are so many other things we can do.' He grinned.

I studied him. He had his own teeth and they were clean, had hazel eyes, a good nose and soft hair. What was wrong with me? Why couldn't I enjoy the attention without overanalysing his intentions, my misgivings, the what-might-happens?

A song with a sample of a ringing phone played. The dancers cheered. I thought of helplines, that maybe the appeal of callers' stories was their distance. Distant drama, safe danger. No names, no attachment.

'Why don't you have a girlfriend, Robin?'

'How do you know I don't? And I'm Stan.'

'So do you?'

'No.' He spoke into my ear, hand firmly on his own leg. 'I've been away from home for three months, working here on flood houses. No time for a girlfriend.'

'Make sure you build me a good house.' I finished my drink.

'What's in it for me?'

I shook my head even though he was teasing and looked out at the dance floor; I couldn't see Fern.

'I need a cigarette. You coming outside?'

It was exactly what I wanted. We sheltered under an archway. Lights winked at themselves in frozen puddles. I inhaled fumes from my first cigarette in a long time. The nicotine rushed to my head, and I sagged against the wall.

'Easy.' Robin touched my waist. 'Long time?'

'Yes.'

I didn't want it to end. When it did, he kissed me and I let him. Our lips met clumsily, as strangers' mouths often do. I bit his tongue. My head span from the nicotine and the cocktails and the cold. I thought of Will. Of how he'd tied me up, restrained me, and I pressed into Robin, enjoying his muffled groan into my mouth.

'You're so sexy.' He nibbled my neck.

'Do that again,' I said.

He pulled me into him and bit my exposed shoulder. In the street a girl shrieked that she loved to party. I moved my hands up inside Robin's shirt and scratched his back. He kissed me harder, tugging my hair and pressing me to the wall. The sensation of cold brick behind and hot body in front thrilled me. I was the girl in the red dress; Katrina.

'Come back to my hotel.' His voice was urgent, breathy.

'You're staying in a hotel?'

'We all are.'

'I'm not going to an orgy, am I?' I snapped my head back.

'No.' He laughed and touched my collarbone. 'Other builders are staying in the same hotel. Come back to my room, it'll be just you and me. How good would that be?'

One of the club's bouncers threw a man into the road and told him not to come back. He staggered towards a takeaway. I asked if Robin had more cigarettes; his 'yes' had me getting into one of the taxis by the club's doors.

As we pulled away, the driver changed radio stations. Robin kissed me again and put a hand on my thigh, just beneath my dress's frill. The leatherette seat chafed. I touched his tongue with mine, expecting him to move his hand higher, hoping the driver might see. But he put it on my back. I rubbed his crotch and whispered, 'Put your hands inside me.'

He stroked my nipple through the silky red fabric and moved it lower. 'You're so hot, you tiger.'

I froze, not sure why.

'What did you call me?' I whispered.

'Tiger.'

Tiger: it was the word.

I shoved his hand away and moved my leg. Tiger. I felt like there was a hand at my throat.

'Don't call me that.'

I didn't know why the word so affected me. The driver looked at us in his mirror. I needed air. The car was too stuffy.

'What – *tiger*?' He leaned close to my ear again. 'But you *are* a sexy tiger.'

'Stop it. Get your fucking hands off me.'

He moved away and I did too. Outside, more snow fell. On the radio a woman sang about saying her name. What was my name? Did Katrina pull away or did Catherine? I tugged my dress down, tearing the frill. The dress. Ruined. The driver eyed me in the mirror and I told him to look at the bloody road when he was driving.

'What's wrong?' whispered Robin. 'It's just a word.'

'Don't say it,' I hissed.

'I won't. Sorry.'

He looked confused and I felt stupid. How could I explain to him why the word 'tiger' had had such an intense effect on me when I didn't know myself? Muscles in my stomach that had contracted with pleasure only moments before now just caused shame.

I told the driver to pull over.

'You're going?' Robin looked out of the window as the car stopped at the kerb, and then back at me. 'Let me walk you home.'

'No, it's not far.'

As I got out of the car my torn frill swung like discarded Christmas tinsel. I threw a fiver at Robin and slammed the door. He watched from the back window as it pulled away, streetlights shading his face in random colours.

I got home at one-thirty. Happy House had shut and the flat was cold because the heating clicked off at ten. I threw up in the bathroom sink. Cherry liquid splashed the tiles. Expecting more, I sat on the edge of the bath – but nothing else came.

I looked in the mirror; the word 'tiger' appeared above my head in a cartoon bubble. Tiger. It was just a harmless word I'd heard and used many times. Now it sounded sharp, dangerous. I squinted and it dissolved.

Then a rabbit lolloped along the bath behind me. I spun around. Nothing. Of *course,* nothing. Had I expected to see a bunny in the bathroom?

I thought of my dad. He'd loved rabbits. He used to do this card trick where he'd ask me to pick one from the deck and tell him what it was. Every time I'd ask why, and he'd say that it was part of the magic. I'd tell him and slide the card back among the others and he'd say, 'I bet I know what your card was.' Fooled me into telling him every time.

I yanked the strap and the dress fell to my feet, a pool of fabric blood.

Tiger.

My dad had never called me that, only 'Angel'. I kicked the dress to the corner of the room. I'd not been an angel since I was eight and believed his words. I'd only been clumsy and foul-mouthed and raw-handed and difficult. The last time he'd played his trick the card had been the joker, which means a surprise, the unknown. I'd kept it under my pillow until the joker's face faded.

Now I climbed under the duvet on the sofa but didn't think I would ever get warm or find sleep. I did. Mercifully it was dreamless.

12

Sweet milk gone sour

Mother never told me I was beautiful.

But she told me *she* was. Heads turned, she said. Boys wanted to be near her; girls wanted to know her, she said. So, when I was very small I'd look at my mother as though I had a mirror in my hand. I'd pretend her face was mine, that my eyes weren't ice blue but chocolate brown, and my skin wasn't white but olive, and my bluntly cut hair flowed like her silky mane. The only pictures I had of my real mum were too faded and out-of-focus to mimic. Though Dad brought her to life for me during our chats, I could not follow her, watch her, try to be her.

Before Dad died my mother took time with her make-up and wore perfume and beads; afterwards she devoted that time to baking. She was still pretty. Pearl earrings still complemented her elegant neck and a simple twist of her hand had her hair in an upward-sweeping style.

I remember following her around, aged perhaps four, trying to mimic her swinging walk. I couldn't. I clomped like a boy. Like your father, she said. Clomp, clomp, clomp. And though she loved him and said it fondly, no daughter wants to imitate her father's style. She wants to be her mum – and if her mum isn't there, then her mother.

Dad said I was an angel but I wanted my mother to think so too.

There came a time – and I'm not sure when it was – that I fell out of love with her. Maybe it was after Dad died. She changed. But so did I. Where she had treated me well (if a little coolly) during his lifetime, she now grew impatient, was less willing to talk. Perhaps it was during my forgotten ninth year that I stopped trying to please her and no longer wanted to copy her elegant style. Instead, I did all I could do to oppose and annoy and argue.

When I later tried putting all my memories together – like a child making a scrapbook from remnants – some stood out more than others. Forgetting Nanny Eve's birthday was one. Asking Dad what he'd wanted to be when he grew up was another. And a clifftop slap from my mother had never faded either. It was the first time she had raised a hand to me.

She met Graham when I was twelve, and a year later he moved into our large home, filling the cavernous space left empty by the deaths of Nanny Eve and Dad. Our first holiday was to Devon. We all went – Celine and her brother Stephen came too. I sulked because Celine got the better bedroom at the cottage, one with oak beams, a white bunk bed and a window that looked out over the sea. I slept in a box room full of stuffed otters and owls.

Every morning I woke early, long before Celine or Stephen, and took off along the beach. It was all mine at that time. Perhaps there would be an old man walking a dog, or a lady sitting on a rock, reading, but no crowds. Just me and sea and sky. I'd put bits of shell and unusually shaped stones in a bucket. I thought they might look pretty on my windowsill or make a nice gift for Anna.

Anna and I had been friends again since the day out skating with Rebecca Houghton and the whole class. We'd bonded over shared troubles at home and would swap magazines. At the same time – perhaps coinciding with us going up to high school – Barry Hudson realised it wasn't cool to hang around with a girl. It eased my guilt a little at having dropped him so fickly.

On our fifth morning at the Devon cottage everyone got up early so I had no secret time on the sand, looking for treasures. Alone I was calm and sweet and happy; when surrounded by the family – especially my mother and Celine – I soured. That was the best way to describe it. I went off like milk. Curdled. Became grumpy and awkward and sweary. I didn't know why, or how long I'd been that way, and I sometimes tried not to be but I just couldn't seem to help it.

So, when the whole gang joined me at seven with plans for a clifftop breakfast picnic and then a boat trip, I stomped around the kitchen and growled.

'Get out of bed the wrong side?' joked Graham, ruffling my hair.

'Ignore the grumpy madam,' said my mother.

They packed this and that, and we set off for the overgrown path that took you up the cliff. Wind buffeted the foliage. Celine skipped and twirled, and my mother laughed and chased her. Their dresses billowed like multi-coloured clouds. I hissed words I knew Mother would admonish, but quietly so I'd not have to go to bed early. One word I always got into trouble for saying was 'Sharleen'. But I just couldn't bring myself to say Celine. It hurt my mouth. My mother had once talked about a 'common' woman at number nineteen who had cheated at the Loveliest Garden competition. Her name was Sharleen. And I thought it suited Celine.

When we reached the top of the cliff Stephen helped his dad lay breakfast out on a checked blanket. There were cold sausages and hard-boiled eggs, bread and jam, and flasks of tea. The sun hung low in the sky and I thought it looked like it was bored. I was bored too. Small talk about Celine's upcoming dancing competition always sent me looking for something else to do. But here there were no cupboards to escape to. No bathrooms to lock the door in.

'I'm off to explore,' I said.

'Must you?' sighed my mother. 'We're having a lovely time. Why do you have to ruin it?'

How was I ruining it? By not being there I probably made it better. They could all talk endlessly about frilly frocks and bastard ponies, I thought.

I headed higher up the path. Stephen watched me, perhaps a little envious that I had the courage to go.

'Stay away from the edge,' called Graham, eyes darkened with concern.

I climbed, higher and higher. The sun rose with me. Burned my cheeks. I looked down at the frothing water. Stones fell into its whirlpool. A little lower, on a craggy ledge, something shimmered. Something silver. Perhaps diamond. Had someone fallen and lost it on the way down? Had someone dropped it on the path for the wind to steal? Was someone now looking for their precious gem? If I retrieved it, I would take all the attention away from Celine.

I looked back; my family were small dots now. Sod them. That was what my Aunty Hairy (really Mary) said about sales people who called: 'Sod them.' I wanted that shiny treasure. Not for myself, but to give back to the owner. And the danger excited me. Stephen would be impressed. And Graham. And my dad, if he'd been there.

And my mum if I'd known her.

I crawled on my front through the long grass to the cliff-edge. Then I turned, and worked my way down backwards. My feet reached tentatively for any rock or protruding twig, hoping it would support my weight. I was skinny and this probably saved me. My hands gripped clumps of grass or prominent stones. A few times I felt my feet go and panicked, clinging on tighter.

I looked down. The nearer I got, the further away the glittering prize seemed. I had underestimated the distance. I had also forgotten that I would have to climb back up. And I was very high above the water where it crashed against the rocks. I was suddenly and unexpectedly scared. Really scared. I didn't think I could make it to the ledge where the gem waited, or back up to where I'd started.

I don't know how long I clung to the cliff-face in the same position. The sun burned my back. Nearby, birds sitting on ledges pecked at discarded food. Below, water waited. No one came looking for me. I desperately wanted them to. The idea of my mother's voice calling my name – *any* of my names – now seemed wonderful. Seeing her, I would be sorry for all my behaviour. I'd be a good girl and go quietly on the boat trip and call Celine her proper name. I would be all my mother wanted me to be and she might call me beautiful and I might fall in love with her again.

But no one came. Hunger began to gnaw at my insides. Thirst dried my lips. I needed a wee. I thought of being safe, in Dad's study.

I thought of running on the beach every morning. But that just made this the loneliest place in the world.

And then I heard them, far away at first; Graham calling my name. Then Stephen's voice. And then my mother. She used my full name. Catherine-Maria. No one had called me it in forever. It floated down the cliff: 'Catherine-Maria...?' She must have missed me.

'Catherine-Maria...?'

'Here!' I shrieked, and my voice was a dry croak. 'Here!'

Their faces peered over the top like puppets above a box. Graham. Mother. Then, just as I had hours ago, he climbed down. I feared for him. He was heavy. Twigs might snap, sending him crashing and smashing to the bottom. How terrible I would feel then. I began to cry.

In no time Graham was at my side.

'The view is great from here,' he joked.

But I couldn't stop crying.

'I don't want you to die,' I sobbed.

'No one's going to die,' he said gently. 'Now, you're going to slowly climb up ahead of me. I'll be just here. Right behind.'

So we climbed. It was easier than I'd imagined. Just being with Graham gave me confidence. At the top Stephen helped pull me over the edge. Now I could joke, as Graham had. Now it all seemed so silly – my hanging there, my fears.

'Bet I had you all worried,' I said.

Mother marched over; her face was wet. I thought she might hug me. Maybe kiss me.

But she slapped my face. Twice. I recoiled.

'Worried?!' she cried. 'You stupid, selfish, horrible girl. You're always thinking of yourself. Always going off and causing trouble. Why can't you be more like Celine? Why can't you just be ... be ... *pleasant*. I never should have taken you on. God, if I'd known!'

Graham put an arm around her, tried to interrupt, but she shrugged him off.

'Believe me I've thought about that,' she said. 'Many times. Thought how lucky you are I stood in for your real mother – and this is my reward!'

She turned and ran off down the path, her words floating in her wake. She had resented being the stand-in for my mum. All this time.

Graham touched my cheek, said she'd just been frightened and was in shock. She didn't mean any of it. But he hadn't heard the truth. My real name; her real feelings.

I looked down at the silvery treasure. Someone else would claim it. Today was not my day of bravery or reward. Today was a day of truth.

My mother never told me I was beautiful but she did tell me she regretted standing in for my real mum.

I no longer tried – to be beautiful, or to be a worthy daughter.

13

All birthdays are not equal

'Look at this one, Catherine; you're about twelve. Until then I really thought you might turn out to be a late bloomer, but it never happened.' Mother held up a photo of me perched on the edge of a boat, skinny legs dangling in the water and too many ribs sticking out between the top and bottom of a lilac polka-dot bikini.

Of course, I remembered this picture being taken: the Devon holiday. After the clifftop slap, we had still gone on the boat trip, drifting past pretty banks and lush meadows, Celine pointing out certain flowers. I'd not spoken all day. And neither my mother nor I ever mentioned the cliff adventure again. To this day, I don't know if my mother remembered her cruel words to me.

'Christ on a bike, I look like a piece of string,' I said.

'Why would Christ be on a bike?' My mother put the picture back in the shoebox with the others and rummaged for another.

'The question is why would I want to look at old photos on my birthday? I'm not ninety-eight and dying of cancer.'

'Catherine, it's thoughtful of Aunty Mary to bring them for us.'

'I was having a big clear-out,' said my aunt, as if it justified the collection of faded memories I had to endure. She rifled through the snaps with fat hands.

Mary was Dad's only sister, and I'd always called her Aunty Hairy because she had a black moustache and chin stubble; as a child I hated having to kiss her when she visited. But I never said it to her face; at least, not after I'd been sent to bed for saying it once during tea.

'Martin said I have too much stuff,' she sighed. 'So I filled ten boxes with clothes and books and souvenirs, gave them to Help the Aged up the street.'

'Graham, look at this one!' cried my mother. 'Remember the feather hat? Goodness me, you did look a fool.'

'I think I look rather debonair.' He winked at me.

'Where on earth did you get it?' Aunty Hairy squinted at the image.

'I won it for him,' I said. 'At that funfair on the seafront. Can we have some cake now? I've got a screaming headache.'

The box of photographs seemed to be taking precedence over the gifts and food on the table; forgotten and remembered images were spilling all over my birthday treats. As promised, my mother had made a cake. It was perfect – square, white, a single candle and blue lettering that said 'Happy Birthday'. No name, no fuss. I wished the day were as simple.

'I'll get the matches,' said my mother, but Graham offered his lighter.

'I'm not ten,' I said. 'I don't need you to sing. My head's pounding. Can we just cut it so I can go home to bed?'

'Up to no good last night?' Aunty Hairy's chuckle made her three chins wobble.

I picked at a sausage roll, wondering if eating it would make me feel better. Arranged with precision on Mother's best cloth were two plates of egg-mayonnaise sandwiches, a ham quiche, seafood sticks, a bowl of salad and various dressings. The smell was dreadful.

'She was with Fern last night.' Mother put paper napkins on each plate. 'You know – that raucous thing with red hair who writes that disgusting column? I bet Catherine was with this mysterious man she doesn't deem fit to bring home to meet us.'

'There is no man,' I snapped.

Mother lit the candle with Graham's lighter and the flame flickered like a woman swaying in a fiery dress. Robin's confused expression came back to me in a crimson flash, and I tried not to think of the word. I would not think of him whispering it while stroking my nipple.

I shoved a whole sausage roll in my mouth.

'So what's that about you and a new man in her column, then?' demanded my mother.

'Just her idea of fun.'

'Lying is not fun. Isn't it enough that she makes a mockery of the sacred institute that is marriage?'

I rubbed my aching head.

'You should've drunk a pint of water before bed,' chided Graham.

'Let's sing.' Aunty Hairy kissed my cheek, tickling it with her stubble. 'Come on, sing to the lovely Catherine. "Happy birthday to you / happy birthday to you..."'

I endured the half-hearted song, glad there were only four of us and that my mother sang in a hushed, deferential tone as though it were a hymn.

'Make a wish,' said my aunt.

'Fuck, I don't do wishes.'

'Catherine, do we have to have fuck on your birthday?' My mother's hand floated near her throat, and I wondered if she wanted to strangle herself; I certainly did.

'My birthday was yesterday.'

'Just make a wish,' she said. 'It'll make Aunty Mary happy.'

I closed my eyes, pretended to be wishing, and blew out the candle.

'Didn't work,' I said. 'You're all still here.'

Graham laughed; my mother shook her head. She cut the square cake into even fingers. Aunty Hairy helped herself to sandwiches and sat at the table near the walnut cabinet. Graham piled a plate with food and joined her. I couldn't decide if I felt better or worse for eating.

'What about your gifts?' said Mother.

I'd ignored the small pile at the end of the table. There would be no surprises. That said, I liked the predictability, this equality of birthdays. There'd be perfume I'd never wear from Mother, a high-street voucher from Aunty Hairy that I'd pass onto someone at Christmas, maybe something of interest from Graham. One parcel was wrapped in red foil, at odds with the rest. I felt the cool fabric of last night's red dress on my heated skin and closed my eyes.

Fern had found it in the corner of the bathroom earlier. She'd held it up so the sun shone through the cocktail stains, highlighting the rip, and asked what the hell had happened to it. I'd buried my face in the pillow.

'There was a fight in the club, it got yanked,' I'd said.

'Must have missed that. I was too busy fighting off some fool called Carl who thought four drinks entitled him to grope me near the fire exit. I'd only been talking to him for ten minutes!'

'Sorry about the dress,' I'd said. 'I'll sew it up.'

Making me feel even guiltier, she'd told me not to worry and asked how my night went. I told her I'd bumped into the builder from my house and regretted it immediately. She smiled and sat on my feet.

'Did you two get it on, then?' she'd asked.

'No,' I'd lied. 'He was dull; I came home alone.'

Now my mother's voice chided me again to open my gifts. I looked at Aunty Hairy's anticipatory smile and picked up a blue flowered present. I feigned delight at the chocolates and Argos voucher.

'Buy a little something when your house is finished,' she said.

It would be a very little something with a five-pound voucher. But I thanked her and opened mother's gift, which was a slight surprise – face cream.

'Because you'll never stop frowning,' she said.

Graham's gift was the red one. Inside the folds, protected by white tissue paper, sat a topaz brooch with a tiny silver rabbit in the centre.

'Do you remember?' Graham asked me. The question was one I often asked myself, one heavy with obligation.

'I do,' I said.

I'd seen it at a craft fair in the town hall about four months before, held to raise money for those who'd been flooded but had no insurance and so couldn't replace their things. I hadn't so much liked the brooch as been fascinated by the intricate rabbit, the detail in the silver, the whiskers and the winking eye. Now I liked it because Graham had given it to me.

But unwanted words whispered all around it. I wouldn't listen.

'Thank you,' I said.

'You're so generous,' my mother said to him.

I pinned it to my collar and polished the surface.

'Suits your eyes,' said Graham.

'Brings out the red you mean.'

'Anyone else for crab sticks?' asked Mother.

She went out to make tea, bringing in the white pot with matching cups and saucers and milk jug. I forced myself to eat an egg-mayonnaise sandwich and some salad. I didn't want wine. I didn't want alcohol for a long time.

'Since we're all gathered for the occasion,' said Aunty Hairy with a huge sigh, 'I have something to tell you.'

She pushed her empty plate away and folded her polyester-sheathed arms in front of her large bosom, the static from the material threatening to set the table alight. Mother stopped pouring tea mid-flow. Graham lit a cigarette and I watched the smoke uncurl. I thought of the one I'd had last night beneath the archway, and my stomach knotted.

'Is it bad news?' asked my mother, the teapot still above my cup.

'Not necessarily,' said Aunty Hairy.

'Can't it wait? We're celebrating.'

'I do feel bad for interrupting Catherine's joyous day, but no, it really can't.'

'Nothing can be worse than a birthday,' I said.

'I have bowel cancer,' said Aunty Hairy.

You win, I wanted to say. All birthdays are not equal.

'What do you mean, you have bowel cancer?' My mother plonked the pot down and dropped into her seat. 'Did you get a second opinion? When did you find out? Why didn't you tell us?'

'Jean, stop fussing. I'm past the second-opinion part. I've had all the tests at the hospital – most uncomfortable and such a sensitive area too. You can't imagine.' She looked at me but I didn't want to think about her being probed with instruments. I dropped my lump of lettuce back in the bowl. 'The good news is that it hasn't spread,' she continued. 'So I'll have surgery and a course of chemo- and radiotherapy. If I'm lucky

I might lose weight.' She laughed weakly. 'Unfortunately I may lose my hair.'

I thought of Aunty Hairy losing her curls and the coarse moustache that had scraped me during many a forced kiss, and it was too much.

I laughed.

I covered my mouth immediately with regret. How cruel had I been?

'Catherine!' cried my mother. 'How can you be so insensitive?'

'It's OK,' said Aunty Hairy, patting my ravaged hand with her swollen one. 'It's a nervous reaction.'

'I'll never know how you do that crisis-line stuff.' My mother banged her hand on the table, knocking a teacup over with a clatter. 'Do you say fuck to everyone there, and Christ on a scooter, and do you laugh when people confide in you that they are dying?'

'No need to write me off yet,' said Aunty Hairy.

'I didn't mean you.' My mother got more flustered.

'It's Christ on a *bike*,' I corrected. I couldn't help myself. I knew what an idiot I was being, but my mother brought out the worst in me.

Mother put her head in her hands. Graham stubbed out his cigarette and went and rubbed her shoulders, whispering in her ear. I'd always been left out of the shouldery hugs and the secret whispers. I wished I was ten again so I could go and hide under the stairs or behind a curtain somewhere.

'The tea'll be getting cold,' Aunty Hairy said, poured four cups of tea and passed them around.

I added milk to mine and sipped it, placing the cup in the saucer with a soft, respectful tinkle. I pulled sugary topping off the cake and ate it, remembering when I'd had period pain for the first time and my mother had said I was just exaggerating so I could stay home from school. She'd said I wouldn't know pain until I'd given birth, like that was supposed to ease my cramps; I'd spat back that she couldn't possibly know what *that* was like since she'd got me without childbirth.

'Lucky me,' she'd sighed. 'Your arrival caused me no pain at all.'

Aunty Hairy had pressed me to her pendulous breasts and told my mother it was tough being fourteen. She persuaded Mother to let me stay home and we watched *Gone with the Wind* under the duvet on the sofa, eating icing off fairy buns. She was scratchy and hairy but she eased my pain that day, and now I'd laughed at hers.

I couldn't swallow any more cake.

'When do you have the surgery?' asked my mother.

'Haven't got the date yet; probably in the next few weeks.'

'You never told us you were ill,' said my mother.

'I didn't really know I was. I thought I was just anaemic, tired.'

I looked again at the picture of me dangling my legs from the boat. I hadn't noticed before that my hair was uneven. One side fell to my shoulder but the other had a great chunk missing. I picked it up to examine it more closely.

'Yes, *you* did that,' said my mother. She leaned over and tapped the picture. 'You were forever cutting your hair off or shredding your clothes. I despaired at you, really, I did. What person deserves such a child?'

I couldn't recall cutting my hair. But there I was, hair all mis-cut. I put the picture back in the box and closed the lid, then held the box out to Aunty Hairy. I tried to say I was sorry about her cancer, but the words stuck in my throat.

'I know you are.' She patted my hand, as if I'd actually spoken. 'But the pictures are for you, Catherine. There are some in there of your dad; I thought you might like them.'

'I can't take them.' I pushed them back at her.

'Of course you can.'

'Thank you.' I really didn't want them. In pictures I look uncomfortable, strange, out of place, and it didn't help that I often viewed them with no recollection of when or where they'd been taken.

'Jean,' said Aunty Hairy, softly. 'I wondered if I really should contact Henry about my cancer...'

My mother's head snapped up. The mood in the room darkened as though the sun had set too early. I studied her face for signs of why; then Aunty Hairy's to see a clue there.

When my mother spoke it was as though she was addressing small children. 'There's no need for that, is there?' she said. 'You said you're not dying.'

'It was just, you know, a thought. He was m—'

'Not now,' hissed my mother.

'Who's Henry?' I asked.

Aunty Hairy didn't look at me.

'Nobody important.' Mother smiled and busied herself with cups. 'More tea anyone?'

'Well now I think he *must* be important,' I said. 'You never smile at me.'

'He's no one.' Her tone silenced me.

So I said I couldn't give a damn who he was anyway and got up. I had a night shift at the care home later and needed sleep before I went.

'Want me to drop you off?' asked Graham.

'No, I'd rather walk. Thanks for the ... thing ... everyone.'

'Take care, sweetie.' Aunty Hairy kissed my cheek with an affectionate scratch. If she lost her hair, I would miss it. I wanted to tell her but didn't know how.

'Don't forget your things,' she said.

She put the box of pictures and the gifts and four slithers of cake into a carrier bag. My mother had gone into the kitchen and I heard the clatter of the dishwasher being loaded. She was ignoring me. Graham walked me to the door.

'How was your first shift at Flood Crisis?' he asked.

'Interesting.' No one else had asked. 'Thanks again for the brooch.' I kissed his cheek. 'Say goodbye to Mother for me.'

I got back to the flat as Victor was dropping two bulging bin bags behind the takeaway. He called out that it was chilly again, but I mounted the stairs two at a time, not in the mood for small talk. The kind of night where you wanted to be wrapped up in bed, he said.

Fern was typing something on her laptop, her glistening, rigid bare legs wide open. She warned me not to touch her, clicked 'save' and reached for a coffee mug without moving either leg.

'Fake tan,' she said. 'How was today?'

'I got a pot of anti-wrinkle-pro-something-super-strong face cream, a box of photographs – and my Aunty Hairy has cancer.'

'What?' Fern turned, still not moving her legs. 'Is it bad?'

'The cancer or the cream?' I turned the kettle on, opened the drawer for a spoon and was irritated when I couldn't look in the other one for a tea bag at the same time. I couldn't believe I had to go to work. 'Do you think family cancer is a good enough excuse to ring in sick?'

While the tea bag stewed in a cup, I put the box of photographs under her bed with my other belongings. When my house was complete I'd probably transfer them to the top of my wardrobe with all the other stuff I couldn't quite part from but didn't want to see.

The telephone rang. Fern answered. 'I think you've got the wrong number, honey,' she said. 'There's no Katrina here. Will I do instead?'

'It's for me.' I held out my hand. 'Flood Crisis.'

A male voice said, 'It's Christopher.'

I couldn't think of a response apart from 'oh'. He and Katrina and Flood Crisis were another life – a dream; a place that had nothing to do with this flat and Fern's legs and unequal birthdays and going to work.

'The good buddy that I am,' he said, 'I'm checking you're fine about your next shift, that you haven't hanged yourself with Christmas tinsel over having to work with me again ... OK, now the truth: Norman was pissed off that I forgot to get you to call him after last Wednesday's shift.'

'Why do I have to call Norman?' I wondered if he knew I'd taken that call the night I'd gone back to Flood Crisis alone. Would I be in trouble for it?

'It's just protocol after a first shift,' Christopher said. 'So it's all good? I can tell Norman I'm the perfect mentor and we're both ticking all the required boxes?'

As I often did on crisis-line calls, I listened for any background noise that might give Christopher's world away. It was silent, his life secret.

'Seriously,' he said, tone gentle. 'No problems so far?'

I wondered how he would react if I admitted that it was never a problem for me to listen to calls where people cut themselves or abused others or tried to die, but that I had a major problem remembering things. That I could not soothe my raw hands, that I reacted violently to random words and never slept without waking again and again and again.

'No problems,' I said softly.

'Good. See you Wednesday. Will I need to bring a surgeon?'

'A surgeon?'

'Your leg.'

I laughed; the cut was already a fading scar.

I hung up.

Knowing I'd never sleep before work, I ran a bath. A spark of silver demanded attention in the mirror: my new brooch. Its smooth surface cooled my fingertips. I loved Graham for noticing my interest in it, for going back and getting it, but hated how the rabbit looked at me. Like it knew things I wouldn't like. The clasp proved awkward to unfasten and the pin pierced my thumb.

I tossed it onto the side of the bath. Maybe I would just wear it when Graham was around.

Unexpectedly, I fell asleep in the bubbles. When I woke, it was if the rabbit had been watching me, sleepy, silver, sly. Feeling exposed, I put the flannel over my chest and covered the rest of my body with bubbles. Even with my eyes closed again I knew the rabbit was studying me. I turned it upside down. Still, I imagined its ears pricked up and its nose wrinkled. Still I tried to hide my body from its gaze.

It wasn't enough. I got out of the bath and went to work.

14

Never about the trees

Under the weight of snow, the tallest tree in the Flood Crisis garden bent like an old man. Trees had me thinking of John Denver on a poorly tuned radio, of being driven through Scotland by Dad, sitting in the back seat and being too small to see all the woods. Perhaps three, I'd pretended the treetops were witches.

Now, as I paused on the third Flood Crisis step, a similar tune drifted down the path. I turned to see Christopher dismount his bike and yank headphones out of his ears. The rhythm of my childhood anthem slowed. Christopher switched it off and said they'd ordered a stair-lift for me.

'Ha ha,' I said.

My new boots with extra calf-protecting length made me no less cautious. I stepped carefully over each ice patch on the steps.

'I also brought an amputation kit in case.' He tapped in the entry code and let me through before carrying his cycle into the hall and shoving it into the nook between banister and wall.

'You should be a comedian,' I said.

The lounge was oppressively hot; a plant on the windowsill wilted like a fainting woman in the Barbara Cartland novel that still sat on the coffee table. I tore off my scarf and jacket, and opened the shutter.

'Heating plays up all the time.' Christopher hit the radiator with the copy of *Horse & Hound*. 'It wouldn't go off on Sunday. Me and Lindsey nearly stripped off and answered the phones naked.'

I signed in on the wall chart. 'Doesn't Lindsey have her own buddy?'

'John was ill. I covered.'

Christopher opened his rucksack and took out two strings of pink tinsel and a silver foil star. He dropped them in the 'Xmas Decos' box, where tired trimmings waited to die. It was early yet – twenty minutes until we had to switch on the phones. I curled up on the sofa and read a five-year-old *What Caravan?* magazine while Christopher made tea. When the door opened again it was Jangly Jane.

'Oh, it's you again.' She dumped two carrier bags on the coffee table and threw her jacket over the back of the sofa, the sleeve barely missing my cheek.

'Apparently.' I could think of no other response.

'You should read the logbook if you've nothing else to do – catch up on calls from the last few days.' She went into the kitchen.

When Christopher returned with our drinks I was reading the logbook.

'Jane,' he said, 'she's a stickler for rules. Been known to take that thing home and type it up for her own reference. She can quote the Equality Act, missives from the Commission for Racial Equality, your disability rights. I should know, I've tested her. They say "shit", she jumps on the shovel.'

'Hasn't she heard of the Offensive Body Attire Commission?' I asked.

Like two school kids, we tried not to laugh when she returned.

'It's two-thirty,' she said. 'I'll turn the phones on.'

She sat in the velvet armchair holding an 'I Love X-Factor' mug, fanned herself with a newspaper and studied me. 'Do you know what's good for eczema?'

I looked at my hands, inflamed from the room's heat after the chill outside. 'I know what isn't: cheap jewellery.'

The phone rang in booth two. I was glad to escape her scrutiny and beaded earrings. The leatherette chair cooled the skin between my boot and skirt as I picked up the receiver on its third ring. Illegible scribbling covered the top page of the notepad. I tore it off and wrote the date.

His name was Arthur, though he said most people called him

Art. Only his wife had called him Arthur, and he'd loved her for it. I thought how I'd likely call him something else altogether if I knew him. Tempted to write 'Arthur' on the pad, I found I couldn't.

He said he was living in a caravan and it was so cold he wore gloves in bed. Eighty-five and coughing all night and having to wear scratchy, itchy gloves, which he had to wash in the sink, having no machine. I imagined what his hands were like and looked at mine.

Then I wrote 'lonely' at the top of the page and circled it twice.

The only photos he had of his wife, Irene, were ruined in the flood. All he had now were memories and he said they were fading. The harder he tried to catch them, the further they flew away.

I knew all about that.

I wrote 'remember' and added a question mark, and then scribbled it out. Arthur hung up suddenly, mid-sentence.

The phone rang in booth one and Christopher got up to take it. He wore faded blue jeans and there was a pen stain on the back pocket. I put the phone down and returned to the sofas. Jangly Jane pointed out that I'd not asked many questions.

I finished my tea and watched snow fall from the fir tree outside the window, like icing sugar onto a cake.

'Poor guy,' said Christopher when he returned. 'That was Malcolm. He rings every week to report the stages of his house rebuild. The builders have pulled out for the third time.'

I thought of my builders, of Robin, seeing his face as he'd watched me get out of the taxi on Saturday night.

'Did you bring cards this week?' asked Christopher.

'I forgot.'

'Admit it – you're scared of winning,' he said. 'Guess we'll have to play I spy instead.'

'Game-playing distracts from calls,' said Jangly Jane through a calamitous chorus of clanking. I wondered what she'd say if I described some of the games Will and I had played while waiting for the phone to ring. Then the one in cubicle two rang and she disappeared into the booth.

'I wonder what she does for kicks,' I said.

'Something arty?'

'I was thinking something more outdoorsy.'

'What do you do for kicks?' he asked me.

'I try and figure out what other people do for kicks.'

'What about me, then?' he asked.

I pretended to study him. Jangly Jane asked a caller why they felt it necessary to buy so many tins of beans, her tone better suited for talking to a four-year-old. Outside the trees bent in the rising wind and traffic was starting to clog the road.

'No idea,' I admitted.

'Where would you be right now if you didn't have to be here?' he asked.

'We *don't* have to be here,' I said.

I watched the queue of cars waiting for the lights to change. It was easy to be flippant, but something drew us all here; something made us come and answer the phones without being paid to, without having to.

'But what would you be doing if you weren't?'

I admitted that I'd probably just be watching *CSI*; he asked which one. I couldn't recall which it was, only that it had Horatio in it, the sexy-but-arrogant detective.

'I'm more of a Grissom man,' joked Christopher. 'I like a full beard, especially with that hint of grey.'

'Don't you find that the culprit is usually the second person you write off as the killer?' I shifted in my seat, wanting to get as comfortable in it as he made me feel.

Jane came back into the lounge. She dropped into a chair and asked what we were talking about.

'Beards,' we said at the same time.

The phone rang. I didn't want to go but it was my turn. Standing, I tried to free my mind of beards and mockery, but mainly of Jane. I said the greeting, already without thinking, and drew invisible circles on the pad until the ink came down and the pen worked.

'Is that Katrina?'

I sat up. 'Yes, it is,' I said.

'It's Helen. Do you remember me?'

'I do.' Some things I never forgot. It was the woman who'd talked of acting lessons and then gone. 'How are you today?'

'Sad,' she said, and after a long pause, 'I'm sorry I hung up on you last time.'

'It's fine,' I said. 'It's hard talking to a stranger about topics that are so difficult.'

'I'm still nervous,' she admitted.

'Take all the time you need.' I tried to write, but the pen had dried up again, so I scribbled until the ink returned. I wrote 'Helen'.

'I'm still with Marcus. You remember Marcus?'

'Yes, I do.'

I remembered all the calls. While my memory discarded my own history, it had no trouble with people who needed me to remember. But, like Arthur earlier, the more I reached for my own memories, the faster they flew away.

'Did I tell you he's my tutor? I'm trying to stop my affair with him. It's going to be harder than I thought to leave him. I woke up yesterday thinking I'd end it, that I'd tell him he isn't good for me, but I slept with him instead. Do you think I'm weak?'

'It doesn't matter what I think.' I knew how clinical it sounded. 'It only matters what *you* think.'

'I think I'm pathetic.'

I didn't write the word. No one who calls a crisis line could be described that way; only the bravest dare to pick up a phone.

'Why do you think it's so difficult to leave him?' I asked.

'At first I thought it had something to do with meeting him after the floods. Like he'd been sent to rescue me. Is that terribly silly?'

'I don't think so.'

It was a mistake to answer her, but I'm human and sometimes forgot how I was supposed to be. I wrote down 'rescue' because the word helped me detach and stay focused on the object of this call.

'Tell me more about what made you think of him as rescue?' I asked Helen.

'He was like something wonderful that happened after that rain. I deserved to be rescued from my pain. And maybe he is wonderful. Maybe the problem is me and I'm analysing too much. Do you do that?'

I didn't answer. Our opinions and emotions only counted when determining the next question and how we could bring the subject back around to their feelings, to them. 'What do you think makes you overanalyse?'

'When I had acting lessons it was drummed into me.' Her voice was suddenly childlike again. 'When assuming a role one must consider why the character acts a certain way, how they might respond to a particular situation, what compels them.' She seemed to be quoting someone, imitating their haughty tone. 'Even trees,' she said.

'Trees?' I asked.

'I had to pretend I was a tree,' she said. 'I didn't want to be a fucking tree. I didn't want to stretch my torso into a gnarled trunk or my arms into willowy branches. I didn't care if the snow froze my limbs or the sun warmed my bark. Trees don't have feelings. Who gives a fuck about trees?'

I tried to piece the fragments together. So many callers talked about a whining mother or a neighbour who stole sunlight from a garden with an overgrown tree, but we had to listen for what they were really saying.

It was never about the trees.

'Was this when you had acting lessons as a child?' I asked.

A sigh heavy with torment filled my ear. 'Yes. I don't know why it matters now.'

'How do you feel when you think about those lessons?'

'Anxious,' she said. 'My mother made me go. I wanted to please her so much, make her smile – she so rarely did. She loved that I was the best tree in the group, but it hurt to reach my branches in her direction.'

I knew how it felt to try to please a mother.

'I wasn't very good at acting,' she said. 'And I didn't like Marcus. I didn't like him teaching me how to be a tree.'

'Marcus?' I was confused. 'Was he your acting tutor too?'

'No,' she cried. 'Why would I say that? Marcus is who I'm with now!'

Her panic was contagious; the hairs on my back bristled. I wanted to take her back to the trees.

'I'm sorry if I misunderstood. Who was your acting tutor?' I said.

'I don't want to talk about him.'

'Shall we talk about something else for now?'

'I'm sorry; goodbye.'

'Don't go.' It was the wrong response; I wasn't respecting her right to withdraw. The phone went silent – she had gone.

I pressed the warm receiver against my cheek and remained in the booth for a minute or so because Christopher was on a call in the next one and I couldn't face Jane and her dingly-dangly accessories. He finished his conversation, stood up and peered into my booth. When he raised his arm, his T-shirt pulled out of his belt.

'Tough one?' he asked.

'Helen – I spoke to her last week. I was making progress but she hung up.'

'It's difficult not to feel some sort of expectation with the ones who call back,' he said.

I stood and the chair bounced into an upright position. In the lounge area Jane offered us her variety pack of biscuits and Christopher grabbed a handful of custard creams. We sat without talking. I listened to the clock and his munching and the distant traffic. It was dark outside. Wind knocked a branch against the window: six taps, pause; two taps, long pause. When the phone rang we all jumped up, but Jane got it.

'Do you ever hear phones in your sleep?' he asked.

I confessed that I heard the shriek of a phone in many sounds.

'Our actual phone rings all the time, too,' I said. 'My flatmate Fern won't give out her mobile number because that's just for text sex.'

'Text sex?' Christopher asked.

'Apparently it's the new phone sex.'

'Ah.' He smiled.

'Have you done it before?' I asked him.

'Text sex?' The tree knocked on the window.

'No, this, here,' I said.

'I was at Crisis Care for six years.' One of his trainer laces was undone.

'Really, when?'

'I left two years ago,' he said.

I didn't ask why; outside of crisis lines I rarely asked questions I couldn't answer myself. Instead, so he didn't feel obliged to explain, I picked up a book and read the blurb on the back.

'My wife left me,' Christopher said. 'I couldn't face doing it for a while.'

I put the book down. Jangly Jane asked a caller how it made them feel.

'Why did you volunteer?' Christopher looked at the Flood Crisis banner. It had to be the most asked question between volunteers.

'Why do *you*?' I fell back on the crisis-line technique to avoid answering.

Christopher awkwardly scratched his neck. I felt bad for passing it back to him and tried to think of a fake answer to save him. He said softly that his father had killed himself. The branch outside continued tapping its rhythm against the glass.

'I was twelve. No one was there for him. I like being there for people.'

Jane told the caller to take their time, her tone light and patronising. I wrapped my arms around my body even though the room was still ninety degrees. The phone rang; it was probably Christopher's turn.

'I'll go,' I offered.

'It's OK, I'll do it.'

I stood and insisted I would.

'I think you like being there for them too,' he said as I walked away.

I picked up the phone before sitting down. The Flood Crisis greeting came easily already and I clicked the pen and started a new page.

A male voice said, 'I wonder if I could speak to Katrina.'

I recognised the heavy, plodding effort behind the formation of the words. It was Sid, my first Flood Crisis caller.

'This is Katrina,' I said, as quietly as I could, aware that no one else knew this was a follow-up call.

When he asked if I remembered him I enjoyed saying that I did.

'I rang yesterday but the poor girl couldn't understand me like you did that time. Wasn't her fault. Maybe she was young and thought I was mad or something, which is understandable. I asked for you.'

I had to concentrate intensely; I heard eighty percent of his words and had to imagine the rest.

'Is it OK for me to ring again? Do I get a designated time allowance? Last week Crisis Care told me that I could only have one hour a week.'

I remembered that policy, implemented because they felt an hour was enough to explore feelings – and to make room for the many calls. I'd hated watching the clock, but I'd understood why such policies were in place: no time limit might result in a five-hour call that helped no one, and stopped others getting through. Such limitations hadn't been mentioned here though.

'You can ring again,' I said. 'Is something particular troubling you?'

'It is,' he said with a heavy sigh. 'But at least I found my glasses.'

I smiled.

'They were down the sofa.'

'Can you tell me what's bothering you?' I picked at the pencil end, hoping to reveal the lead tip.

'I don't feel quite right.'

'Quite right about discussing it?' I asked.

'No, not quite right in myself.'

'You mean to do with your stroke?'

Sid said it was something else, and coughed, then rasped that he needed water. I heard liquid running and him slurping, and waited for his return. When he did he apologised, and said it was a cold that wouldn't shift. Said he'd had a bad one last year, but the doctor struck him off and now he couldn't get another.

The word 'why?' nearly jumped out of my mouth, but I knew the important thing was today, now. Jane hung up in the next booth and returned to the lounge area.

'I know the stroke affected my coordination, and my memory will always be bad – I've got used to that. But I didn't have a cough until recently. The lift is broken at the flats so I've to use the stairs. Takes me ten minutes and I pant like an asthmatic afterwards.'

'Can you talk to anyone about the lift?' I felt frustrated that I could only ask about these things.

'The maintenance people are wrapped up in flood repairs. They forget the rain affected those who weren't flooded. I only moved back to this area from Spain seven years ago. It didn't flood there. But something drew me back.'

'What was it?'

He didn't answer.

'How does all this make you feel?' I asked.

The phone rang again in booth one; Christopher picked it up after three rings.

'Sad,' said Sid.

Sad – such an evocative word. I moved the blunt pencil in the shape of the letters an inch above the paper, writing the word in the air. 'Would you say you're depressed?'

'A little. My appetite is non-existent.'

'Try and eat small amounts.' I knew how lame I sounded.

'I do,' he said.

I'd felt a gush of affection that first time we spoke, thinking he was around the age my dad would have been. Now I thought of Christopher's long-gone father. Christopher's call must have been brief because he returned to the sofas.

'Talking tires me,' Sid said. 'Such effort for so little.'

'Take your time,' I said.

'I need to go,' he said. 'Need sleep. Goodbye, Katrina.'

I told him to take care and replaced the receiver.

Back in the lounge area, Jane talked about her night out on Saturday, recounting the three vodkas that had made her queasy and describing the guy who'd apparently tried to corner her near the men's toilets. I wondered what she'd have thought of my night on the town. Christopher laughed and said he could barely handle two beers anymore, let alone vodka. She suggested they share a bottle of wine and see who passed out first; he insisted he'd be the wuss. The phone rang and she got up and went to it, her skirt swishing against the chairs.

'I'm sorry about your dad,' I said. It sounded hollow and empty after the laughter, and out of context following my time away on the phone.

'So why do you volunteer?' he asked me again.

I wanted us to joke around, for him to look at me with one eyebrow raised, not discuss why we did or didn't do this. So I said I wanted to save the world.

'Is that what you said in your Crisis Care interview?'

I remembered the interview well. There were three staff members and me in armchairs around a table. One of them plonked a box of tissues down and said I'd not be judged for any dark secret I confessed. The violet-walled room had probably witnessed all manner of atrocities. I'd felt I should offer something intense but had nothing. Eyeing the tissues I'd merely said I felt compelled to listen to others and then regretted the word 'compelled', thinking it sounded like a bad book review.

'No,' I said now to Christopher. 'I told them I wanted to help people.'

'No one does it for such a simple reason – there's usually more to it.'

'And you have the answer, I suppose?' My hands blazed.

'Most of us have no idea why we come here. Sometimes we figure it out along the way. Sometimes we don't.'

'Does it matter?' I demanded.

He looked at me. 'Don't you think motivation is interesting?'

I thought about Helen and her acting lessons, how she'd been taught to analyse what drove a character to act a certain way.

'I couldn't give a crap.'

I picked up a book and opened it at chapter one. I knew how childish my response had been. Christopher picked up a magazine. I pretended to read but the words blurred.

Jangly Jane returned.

'Ten minutes to go,' she said. 'We can turn the phones off.'

She did it. I read a magazine article about a man who'd had his hand ripped off by a lion. Mine were tingling; I'd gladly have surrendered them to a hungry predator. I heard Jane get the logbook down and scribble notes into it. I felt Christopher move past me, smelt the washing powder he'd used.

When I heard the door shut and was sure I was alone, I looked up. His cup sat on the coffee table, surrounded by crumbs. I heard him unlock his bike; felt I should go and apologise for being silly but couldn't. Jane opened the door.

'You not going home?' she asked.

I grabbed my coat and scarf. When I got into the hallway, Christopher had gone. All I saw was his red bike light fading away and trees silhouetted against sky.

That night I slept for barely two hours.

I dreamt of the room.

I was alone in a derelict house. Every floorboard I walked on threatened to collapse and send me into a smoky void below. I knew the room was somewhere and wanted to avoid it. But every place I went led to the pulsating corridor and the fat, wet door at the end.

A bike had been chained to the banister and I thought I might use it to escape; but I couldn't undo the lock. Above the door an orange light flashed. On-off, on-off. Far away, at the end of the corridor, the shadow of a man. Bushy-haired. My heart sped up. Didn't he usually wait until I woke up? Wasn't he usually at the end of my bed?

Someone said I had to stop, and I cried, 'Yes, make it stop!'

When I opened my eyes, Fern was sitting at my feet, wrapped in a large checked shirt. It was dark. She told me I had to stop with the crisis lines. My leg was trapped in the sheet. I said I was fine. Fine – that pathetic word.

'Catherine,' she said, 'you had nightmares last week too, after your shift.'

She lifted hair from my face, but I pushed her hand away and insisted I *wanted* to do it.

'Then talk to someone,' she said. 'Your leader, *someone*.'

I told her I was the listener, not the talker. I wanted to be there.

'I'm here,' she said.

'I'm fine,' I repeated.

15

Not love unless it hurts

Fern got our smoke alarm free with her laptop. She often joked that she kept lipstick by the bed in case it ever went off at night and some gorgeous fireman had to rescue us. But when it woke me early, a few days after my second Flood Crisis shift, I wasn't laughing.

The shrill blast pierced the flat's stale air. Fern appeared in her bedroom doorway, dawn's weak light a halo about her head. The noise stopped as abruptly as it had started. Then *beeeeeep*, again.

And then nothing.

'What the hell *is* that?' she growled, and opened cupboards and drawers, slamming each one when it didn't reveal an answer. When she swore, I knew she'd tried the drawers that wouldn't open together.

'It's the smoke alarm.' I sat up and kicked off my duvet.

She peered at the white box above the sink, pink T-shirt barely covering her crotch. The alarm shrieked again as though to warn her away. 'Bastard,' she said. 'Why is it doing that?'

'Needs new batteries.' I got up.

'Do we have any?'

I explained that it would need one of those big, square things and said I doubted we had any. When the batteries for the remote control died we warmed them in the oven. We had many tricks for making a little go a long way.

'So how do we stop it?'

'Unscrew it and remove the dead batteries,' I said.

'Should I ring someone? Maybe Greg – yes, Greg. He'll know what to do.'

'We don't need him. We're modern, self-sufficient women and we can do it ourselves. Now – do you have a screwdriver?'

'Do I look like I possess a screwdriver?'

I laughed. 'Your column may be a total lie, but when it comes to you and DIY it's spot on. There's some truth in your bullshit.'

When Fern disappeared into the bedroom, I thought I'd offended her with my blunt words so was relieved when she reappeared with a large black hammer. 'I got it off Sean.'

'I'm not even going to ask why ... OK – why?'

Fern explained how, when she'd left him he'd taken her favourite CD and the blue mirror made of broken tiles. So she'd taken his hammer. He'd loved it, had built their bed with it and the shelf unit in the back room. Fern had used it to smash up his CDs and then left the wreckage under his duvet cover.

'If only your readers could see you now.' I shook my head.

'Will a hammer help us?' She dropped it onto the draining board with a rude clunk.

I pulled a wooden stool out of the cupboard. Fern wrapped herself about my legs to hold me in place, commenting on how spiky they were, and I reached for the offending smoke alarm.

Its screws had rusted and the test switch wouldn't move. It bleeped again. I winced. I always took these things as a sign. I'd panic if a black cat crossed my path but then walk boldly under a ladder. I had my own rules for signs. I couldn't explain these rules; I'd just feel them. And the shriek of alarm felt like a grim warning.

'Pass me a knife,' I said.

'No need to slit your wrists.'

'I'm going to unscrew it. I've changed every plug in here with a kitchen knife.'

She let go of me long enough to get a knife, then I carefully turned the tiny screws anticlockwise with the blade's tip. Clouds of rancid dust wafted out as I took the plastic drum down.

'Now what?' We stared at the disruptive creature in my hand.

'Now we get the battery out.'

Two beeps sounded – but it wasn't the alarm.

'That sounded like a phone,' said Fern and checked hers. She didn't have any messages.

The alarm screamed at us again, a long, ear-shattering sound. I grabbed two large cushions, squashed the smoke detector between them, and shoved the bundle in the back of the cupboard.

When the phone rang we both jumped. Fern answered; I listened to her subdued words until I knew it wasn't for me. The rush of water when I showered drowned out any further sounds. Afterwards I found Fern in her best, pinstriped skirt and ruffly cream blouse – her serious-occasion clothes.

'That was my editor.' She grabbed her coat from the back of the door. 'Got to see him now – sounds pretty important. Hilary Scott wrote a column about pigs and ended up with a whole page last year. Maybe they're giving me one.'

Fern's smile outdid the sun; I wanted to save her from being disappointed. I wasn't sure if it was the alarm that had made me anxious, or I was simply protective of my friend, but I couldn't bear the thought of her joy being ruined. I suggested she keep an open mind.

'Why else would they call me in?'

'I'm only saying wait until you hear what it is before celebrating.'

She whooped and said that when they gave her a regular, double-page spread we'd go out and celebrate *big* time. She left in a whirlwind of optimism and furry coat. I picked the shed fluff off the floor and put it in the bin.

I filled the day with trivialities, each punctuated randomly by the muffled shriek of the detector. I ignored the phone when I saw it was my mother's number. The smoke alarm mocked my cowardice. I coated my hands in steroid cream and put washing-up gloves on to help it work. The alarm mocked my effort. I checked my diary for upcoming shifts at the care home, pleased I'd some long-overdue days off. The alarm mocked my crappy job. I wondered about going and buying a battery for it.

Then I remembered my mobile phone had bleeped before. I took it from my coat pocket and my glove-and-cream-fattened fingers clumsily clicked the buttons; I didn't recognise the number.

The message said, 'Its Stan got yr number frm John, chekin u r ok. Hpe u dnt mind was worried. Wil u b out tonite.'

Stan? Ah, Robin, I realised. For days I'd managed to push all thoughts of him away, and now he existed again, on my phone in black-and-white text. Humiliation made me wish he wasn't working on my house for the next eight weeks, lurking in the shadows of my life. I associated his warm kiss, his hands, with that word; a word I wouldn't think of now.

The smoke alarm screamed at me.

I grabbed Fern's black hammer. The rubber glove squeaked against the handle. I pulled the alarm from its cosy bed between the cushions and brought the hammer down, enjoying the crunch of plastic and metal.

Silence; it was dead.

I dropped the hammer into the sink, gathered up the synthetic corpse and threw it in the bin. Free now of its shrill judgement I responded to Robin's text. An explanation might make things easier if I encountered him at the house. It took a few minutes to type because of the gloves.

'No need for concern, had too much to drink, wasn't well.' I wondered how to sign off. What would make it clear I wasn't interested without cruelty? I put 'Just got out of bad relationship' but deleted it and retyped 'Thanks for concern'. Then I deleted that too and sent the message without any afterthought. Now he could just write me off as unhinged and I didn't have to think about him.

I poured oat-flakes into a bowl and ate standing at the counter wearing the pink gloves.

Fern's heels clacked on the metal stairway. She kicked the door shut after her and I looked up, ready to make a caustic comment about door hinges. But her face erased my words. With a grunt, she threw the newspaper at me. It caught my cheek.

'Ow!' I cried. 'What was that for?'

'You rang them,' she said.

Confused, I thought of crisis lines. I hadn't called them, only taken calls. What did she mean?

'You rang the fucking paper,' she said.

I stared at her, not understanding at all.

'A woman called Catherine rang my editor and told him I'm not married. This Catherine said my column's bullshit and she can prove it because she knows my *situation*.' Fern glared at me.

'You think it was *me*?' I said the words as they came into my head, the question mark an afterthought. Cereal sank into my stomach like chewed bricks. I heard Victor drop a bag of rubbish in the garden.

'Was it you?' she asked.

'I can't believe you think so.'

'So why not answer the question. It's simple. Was it you?'

I wanted to say there were lots of Catherines, some with no *i*, to cause chaos. 'I won't answer,' I said instead. Why was I being so stubborn? Why didn't I just say that I hadn't called? Because I was so angry that she thought so. 'It's a ridiculous question,' I said.

'You're a jealous bitch.'

She stepped over the newspaper and swiped my bowl off the counter. It landed on the lino with a thick splat, painting soggy cereal up the wall. It looked how my walls had after the flood.

'I knew you were pissed off when I wrote that you had a new boyfriend,' she cried. '*That*'s a more absurd lie than me still being married. Who would tolerate *you*? And your comment this morning about the truth in my bullshit; exactly what you said when you rang them. How *could* you?'

'I can't believe you think...' I was unable to finish, and Fern wasn't listening.

Her eyes watered as she said she'd been sacked; mine did too, involuntarily. She got the newspaper, folded it lovingly and put it under her arm. My pink-gloved hand reached out in some sort of futile gesture, but she ignored it.

'He said the column was a slice of life readers could identify with, but it isn't fair to continue deceiving them. So now I've no income and I've lost the only job I ever loved. Writing is who I am. Back to care homes, now – like *you*.'

I insisted writing wasn't who she was, that she was *Fern*.

'Don't define me,' she said. 'Don't talk to me.'

'Did you suggest a column about single life?' My voice was husky.

'I *told* you Mick Mars does that on a Thursday – there's no room for me. Don't talk about my column ever again.'

I covered my mouth, tasting rubber.

'Isn't this what you hoped would happen?' she asked. 'You must've known they'd sack me; or did you just want them to give me a good talking to. I'll have to go back home or back to Sean maybe. Now that'd be irony, me ending up back with my husband but having no column to report it in.'

'Why do you have to go anywhere?' I couldn't imagine her leaving.

'You think I want to stay here with *you*?'

I tasted milk and acid. My hands burned inside their plastic coating. Fern headed for the bedroom.

'I didn't ring them,' I said softly; stubbornness gave way to desperation.

She turned and pointed a finger at me. 'You're the grumpiest bitch I've ever met. No wonder people get sick of you. But I never trusted anyone like I did you.'

'I didn't ring them,' I said, louder.

'In your words – bullshit. I'm just shocked you didn't give a fake name.'

She said I had so many she was surprised I knew who I was. I wanted to say I hadn't given any name because I hadn't called them. But she slammed the bedroom door. Outside, Victor told someone in the street that he'd chase them if they came near the windows with a brick again. I pulled off my gloves like a boxer having lost a fight. In the bedroom, I heard drawers opening and shutting.

The door opened and she glared at me. Her arms were full of plastic bags and she said she was leaving even if I stood in her way. I stepped aside and she went into the bathroom and grabbed bottles off shelves.

'You can have the bedroom now,' she said.

I didn't want it. She threw her key at me and opened the door.

Unwelcome air filled the room. Red hair flew away from her face like childish ribbons. She didn't look back.

I stood for ten minutes without closing the door. I couldn't; it was too absolute.

When I finally did it took all night for the flat to get warm again. Later, I turned all the lights off. I couldn't bear to look at the coffee table full of Fern's magazines, at Angelina Jolie's smiling face.

I turned on the TV – for company if nothing else.

On screen a man interviewed a woman in a cagoule, near a busy road. 'I was driving along the A63 and I thought, where's all this water going to go?' she said, wiping her eyes. Sunny skies contrasted with the subject, and I wondered why she wore a raincoat. 'I couldn't see through the wipers and thought the car would be swept into the river,' she continued. 'I hadn't even seen my house yet.'

The shot melted into another. Flies buzzed in swarms over armchairs and children's toys and rugs, the sky travel-brochure blue. 'It was the wettest summer on record,' said the voice-over. 'For many it was the most devastating, with a month's worth of rain in twenty-four hours and the largest civil emergency in the UK since World War II. Three thousand tons of rubbish was disposed of at this tip, all of it once furniture in homes across the region.'

The camera zoomed in on a child's doll with one eye missing. A woman's voice narrated. 'I come and look at this place. People wonder why, but I'm drawn here. It's a graveyard for all our memories.' 'Did you lose much?' the interviewer asked. 'Carpets and toys can be replaced, walls rebuilt,' she said. 'I lost my faith that day. What's the point in praying?'

I hurt so much.

It's not love unless it hurts.

I looked around, thinking Fern had returned, but after studying the kitchen counter where she often perched with marmite and toast, and searching the shadows for red hair, I realised she hadn't. So who had spoken?

It's not love unless it hurts.

Standing, I sent Fern's beauty magazines to the floor. Had the words come from the TV presenter? He was saying now that the biggest flood problems were the sewage and the rats that it attracted. I focused on his mouth. The words I'd heard weren't his; they were somehow inside my head.

No, they rose from the plughole. From the floor.

I didn't want to hear them.

It's not love un—

The telephone rescued me. I grabbed it from under the coffee table. 'Fern?'

'No, Christopher.'

'Oh.' I tried to adjust to the fact that it wasn't her.

'Are you OK?' he asked.

Would he stay on the phone if I said I was hearing voices? Could he help me understand why the word 'tiger' had my hands ablaze?

I said I was fine and that I'd just been asleep.

'It's seven-thirty,' he said.

'I'm tired.'

Neither of us spoke for a moment, and I wondered if he was assessing my background noise as I often did.

'Sorry to disturb you on a Saturday night,' he said. 'I wondered if you can cover a shift tomorrow. I know it's short notice and cheeky as it'll only be your third time, but we really need someone.'

They needed me. I smiled. Wanted him to say it again: *We need you.*

'I understand if you've plans,' he said.

I considered my plans; Sunday lunch with Sharleen and the gang, coming home to no Fern, and later a night shift at the care home. It was easy to say that I'd do it.

'Thanks. You've saved us from cancelling the shift. It's one until seven, OK?'

I could still do my night shift and get out of going to my mother's – always a bonus. I had saved them. Really, it felt like they had saved me.

'See you tomorrow then.'

'Christopher?'

'Yes?'

I wasn't sure what I intended to say. I only knew that talking to someone on the phone meant I wasn't alone. I was a crisis-line caller, the phone my lifeline. But there were no card prompts for a caller and I floundered.

'Thanks for asking me,' I eventually said.

'Thanks for saying yes,' Christopher said.

'See you tomorrow.'

'Tomorrow.'

After replacing the handset, I thought of a course leader at Crisis Care – Marg. She taught the Attachment & Dependency Core. Frizzy-haired and bespectacled, she'd loved discussion. A trainee volunteer had asked once why it was so wrong to get attached to callers. She'd explained that doing so would mean we took on responsibility for their wellbeing. Only the *caller* was responsible for that. Not us. So detachment protected not only them but us too.

I'd wanted to ask how she did it. I asked how we should turn off our emotions and remain objective, but some guy with a bolt through his nose asked about sexual harassment, and we moved onto that. Now I knew that disconnection only occurred with time. After hearing call after call, story after story, until there was no longer any room in your head for intimacy. But apathy also meant the end, Marg warned. What good would it do not to care at all?

When I lay down on the sofa it occurred to me that I had to connect so I could then disconnect. Answering helpline calls satisfied some urgent need in me. Never yet had a caller given an answer that meant I could stop. I wasn't even sure what the question was. What was I searching for?

It's not love unless it hurts.

Was that the answer?

16

Allergic to lemon meringue

Blazing eczema woke me in the middle of the night. I had only been asleep for half an hour. There is no lonelier time than four am. I read once that during bouts of insomnia Marilyn Monroe said she didn't know where the darkness ended and she began. And then she'd died. It had been so long since anyone I'd loved had died. The thought of losing Aunty Hairy to bowel cancer brought on the nausea I'd experienced after Nanny Eve's huge Catholic funeral, and the confusion when I'd not been allowed to attend Dad's.

I got up.

It was too early to start with today and too late to change yesterday. Fern's bedroom door was closed. Had I done that? Unable to open it and see that she wasn't there, I went to the bathroom and coated my fingers in thick lotion. It never worked. Not sure why I bothered. Aunty Hairy had been the first to take me to the doctor to see if they could cure my poor skin.

The memory came to me, sharp and exquisite. Though painful, the past that morning was more welcome than the present. I could escape there with my lovely Aunty Hairy and ignore that here – now – I was alone. I closed my eyes and let the memory in.

The two of us in a crowded doctor's surgery. Me nervous about what might be wrong with my body, my skin. Aunty Hairy reading an article about how apples slow down ageing and saying the doctor would soon have my skin lovely and peachy again. I was fourteen and Aunty Hairy had insisted they would finally discover what was making me itch so violently.

The night before, during dinner, I'd thrown hot tea over my mother's hands to let her see how it felt to burn day and night. It wasn't a nice thing to do. I knew this even as I did it. But it just happened, like when swearwords jumped out of my mouth.

'Bed,' she'd said to me, wrapping her hands around a cool glass of water like I had so many times.

'I'm fourteen,' I'd laughed.

'Well, behave that way!' she'd shrieked.

Aunty Hairy had persuaded me to give them a moment. I found out afterwards that she'd stuck up for me – as always – and said how awful it must be always to be raking sore skin. Shouldn't I have been taken to a doctor years ago? Perhaps feeling guilty at her negligence, my mother said Hairy could take me if she wanted to.

We got a last-minute appointment. I was glad to miss my chemistry lesson but nervous about being scrutinised. A boy of about nine sat next to me, covered in angry red spots. I wondered what had caused his disfiguration. The woman opposite us sneezed and studied my scarlet fingers. I lifted one in an obscene gesture, and she tutted and looked away.

My name was called: 'Catherine-Maria,' they said. With the name I was pure again. Perhaps they would cleanse my skin too. Stop my hands being clumsy and stupid.

The doctor was young and asked what was troubling me. Aunty Hairy, maybe seeing my furrowed brow, explained how my skin – mainly my hands but occasionally my knees and neck – flared up with hot welts, and cracked if I scratched.

'When did it start?' he wanted to know.

I wasn't sure. Aunty Hairy looked thoughtful. 'When she was about nine,' she said.

'Are you stressed?' he asked me.

I shrugged. Aunty Hairy said life was always stressful at fourteen. He didn't smile. He suggested an allergy test, which he'd book for next week, and said in the meantime he would prescribe some cream.

Afterwards Aunty Hairy took me for ice cream. She let me have the large one with all the flavours that my mother always said would make me fat. Then she bought me some new jeans and pink lip-gloss.

'I know you don't bother with make-up yet,' she said. 'But soon you will. Soon you'll not want to hang around your old aunt. You'll be interested in boys, and they'll be interested in you.'

I shook my head. 'I never want to get married,' I said.

'Of course you do!' laughed my aunt.

I shook my head, insistent; I was going to live with a friend or on my own.

It turned out I wasn't allergic to anything specific. Not grass or horses or cats or house mites. I said that they should have tested my reaction to my mother, and Aunty Hairy laughed and shook her head. I said I was allergic to Mother's awful lemon meringue. None of the creams worked. The stronger stuff eased the eczema for a while. Then it returned with a vengeance. There would be times it faded, like a suntan, but it always came back.

Aunty Hairy had hugged me after the allergy results. She had squeezed me so tight I thought I would suffocate. Her chin hair agitated my skin, but she reminded me of my dad, her brother, and so the attention was worth it. In the garden behind us, leaves began to fall.

'Your mother is trying,' she said. 'I know it must seem she's harsh, but it was hard when your dad died and she was left a single parent to a ... well, to a child she hadn't given birth to. That must have been very tough, you know.'

I said nothing.

'Everything will be OK,' Aunty Hairy said, suddenly sad. 'I'll always be here. No one will ever hurt you. *No one.*'

I opened my eyes now and my adult face stared back in the bathroom mirror. It was four-thirty. I'd been standing there half an hour. What had Aunty Hairy been talking about? Who would never hurt me? Was she just talking about the world; the unfairness of me being an orphan? Or something else?

What though?

My hands were sticky with cream. I'd scratched and raked them since I was nine. Nothing soothed me. Aunty Hairy had looked out for me. Tried to get me well. Stood up for me. I wanted to call her and ask, *What happened to me? Where the hell are my other memories?*

But she was ill. It wouldn't be fair. I wanted to look out for her now. Help her get well. Stand up for her. It would wait. She would live. She had to. She *had* to.

And then I would ask her what happened when I was nine.

17

Writing words in the air

'Flood Crisis, can I help you?'

The now-familiar syllables rolled off my tongue with ease. I shook a pen and scribbled on the pad; it refused to work. I knew remembering the words instead of writing them would prove difficult.

The caller had a Scottish accent and wanted to talk to a woman because men never understood him. They took the piss apparently, and he needed a sympathetic ear. Assuring him I could offer this, I knew I had no idea about what I was agreeing to understand. But then this was nearly always the case on a crisis line. If we knew beforehand, we'd never begin.

I asked what it was that men wouldn't understand, and he said 'his urge', the accent making his words a growl. I looked out into the lounge, where Christopher was separating tinsel into colour-coordinated piles, and Condom Kath knitted something that was yellow and matched none of the tinsel. The tea I'd forgotten to carry into booth two grew cold on top of an open *Woman* magazine.

The Scottish man continued with his growly urge, describing how when his wife was out he locked the door and put on her clothes. Apparently the feel of lacy undies, of the pressure of bra wire against his chest, was exhilarating. I didn't ask questions. I knew he just needed to talk about it.

But then he told me he was wearing them now. And was getting hard.

'Were you flooded?' I demanded.

'What? I thought you'd *understand* me,' he said.

'This isn't a sex line. There are numbers you can call where the women will understand you *perfectly*.'

'I can't afford those numbers!' he cried. 'You're free, and my wife won't know from the phone bill that I've called you.'

I hung up, glared at the blank page and the dry pen. In the lounge area, I threw it in the bin and replaced it with a Barbie pencil from the jar on Norman's desk.

'A man in women's undies on a Sunday afternoon,' I said to the room.

Christopher was standing on a chair, pinning threadbare gold tinsel to the ceiling; he paused to look at me. His mouth hung in an arc, like the decoration. Kath glanced up from her knitting for a moment but resumed the click-click-click of needles without demonstrating any curiosity. I wondered if she had given up on the silencing condom altogether, but wasn't about to ask.

I flopped onto the sofa and grimaced at my lukewarm tea. 'I didn't give up my Sunday for this.'

'But you did give it up to help me erect this Christmas tree.' Christopher climbed down from the chair and produced a thin twig with six branches, each poorly sprinkled with glitter, the whole thing listing to the left.

'I'm too tired,' I said.

I'd woken up at eight that morning, unable to go back to sleep. Fern's bedroom door had still been closed; it was easier to leave it that way. I couldn't look at her empty wardrobe and half-open curtains. It was painful enough seeing my solitary toothbrush in the blue pot in the bathroom.

'Sundays are usually quiet,' said Christopher. 'That's why Norman said to sort the festive trimmings out. It's rare one gets sexual stuff on the Sabbath.'

'Trust it to be me.'

'Wanna help me sort this lot out?' He plonked a second box on the table. I peered into it; the garish colours made it look like a Santa had been massacred.

'Isn't it a bit early for decorations?' I asked.

'It's the second of December,' said Kath, no pause in the click-click-click.

I glanced at the steam trains calendar above Norman's desk. Now the image was a black-and-white train – half light, half shade, like the Tennyson poem. November had gone. It had sucked me into volunteering, given Aunty Hairy bowel cancer, added another year to my life and snatched Fern from me. December promised no better.

'Three weeks until the big day,' said Kath. 'I've done my shopping. I've been doing buy-two-get-the-third-free in Boots, but it's a pain if you only need five things. I'll get some thermal socks to make up the amount.'

The phone rang, and Christopher abandoned a plastic Virgin Mary with overly exaggerated crimson lips and disappeared into booth one. I touched her carefully in case I broke her.

I made a second cup of tea and looked among the magazines for the article I'd started on Wednesday, curious about the man whose hand was eaten by a lion. It wasn't there, so I did a quiz in *Psychologies* magazine to see if I was a pessimist or an optimist. Turned out I was an optimist, which surprised me, since the thought of Fern returning or my house being completed filled me with hopelessness.

Kath's click-click-click monitored my growing headache like a stethoscope listening to a heart. I looked out of the window at the pinkish sky, which threatened more snow, and wondered what Fern was doing.

'I thought you would have made some sort of nativity by now,' said Christopher, back at the sofas.

He went to the kitchen, and I investigated the box of decorations. The phone rang in booth one and Kath picked up her wool and carried her knitting into the cubicle. She answered the phone, receiver wedged between shoulder and ear, and while talking she knitted very slowly and quietly. Christopher returned with two mugs and put one next to Kath.

'Finally tempted you into my box?' he said.

'This stuff is even older than my mother's crap.'

'Let's irritate everyone by bedecking every wall and surface with it.'

I shook a pine-cone garland and three fell off.

'Did you see yesterday's logbook?' asked Christopher.

'Shit, no.'

I knew I was supposed to read it; it had taken me months at Crisis Care to remember. Now I was forgetting all over again; we never forget how to forget.

'I wasn't having a go. A man called yesterday asking for you. Had a strange voice; Lindsey couldn't understand him. All she got was that he was called—'

'—Sid,' I finished. 'He's had a stroke.' I shook a snow globe with Rudolph inside, atop a frosty roof. 'I'm glad he called. I know we have to be impartial but...'

Christopher shook his head. 'Just be careful.'

'I know: we're not responsible for them.' I put the globe on the radiator shelf near the two booths and watched as the white flakes settled on Rudolph's crimson nose. 'I guess you like Christmas?'

'I throw myself into it to ignore it.'

'And how does that work?' I found a tiny baby Jesus underneath the tinsel, but he only had one eye, so I buried him at the bottom of the box.

'If you join in the card-sending and all the other crap, it passes quickly and no one questions your misery.'

He pulled a toy Father Christmas out of the box. Santa wore reindeer antlers on top of a traditional hat and a thick leatherette belt; his trousers fell down, revealing checked boxer shorts. Christopher wound up the lever in his back, stood him on the coffee table, and we watched him chant 'Jingle Bells' and thrust his pelvis pornographically four times before falling onto the floor.

'Where did this stuff come from?' I laughed.

'Volunteers have been bringing it in for weeks. I bet this came from Norman – it's very him.' He stood Santa back on the table.

'Why don't you like it?' I asked.

'I do. I might even take him home.' He smiled.

'No, why don't you like Christmas?'

Christopher didn't answer. He pulled at Santa's matted beard and left him posed ridiculously, hips permanently thrust forward.

'My wife left me on Christmas Eve,' he said eventually.

I touched Santa's rough felt boots and then fiddled with the plastic buckle because I didn't know what to say.

'I never liked this time of year anyway.' He glanced at me before looking at the floor. 'When Caroline decided she'd had enough and wanted to move in with a man from the gym, she chose the most cheerful day of them all to tell me: Christmas Eve. She'd loved Rick for three months apparently; I'd just thought she loved her new spinning class.' He paused. 'It was two years ago.'

'I'm sorry.' It was a phrase I hated.

'Me too,' he said. 'She was good enough to give me a Christmas gift before she left. Said she'd bought it weeks before, and I might as well have it. A watch. Shows how well she knew me – I'd never worn one in my life.' I looked at the watch on his wrist: red strap, black face, silver hands. He looked at the time; four-fifteen. 'But I wore it because I believed it would only be a matter of time before she realised she still wanted me and came back. Now I guess it's just habit.'

'Do you think some people come back?' I asked.

Fern had to. I searched through the remaining tinsel, not knowing what I hoped to find.

'Maybe,' he said.

I looked up; he was staring at me with slightly narrowed eyes.

'You're hoping someone will?' he asked.

'Not some man, if that's what you think.' I instantly regretted my harsh words.

'Who then?'

'My friend, Fern. We fell out. She left.' I fiddled with gold tinsel. 'If you say that she won't come back I might hang you with this.'

I thought Christopher was scratching his arm until I realised he'd undone his watch strap. Once free, he held it out. It curled up in his palm like a scarlet snake. He said he wanted it back when Fern returned.

'Don't be silly,' I said. 'It's yours.'

'It's not my colour – red plays havoc with my complexion.'

I thought of the red dress still waiting to be fixed and wanted to say that red gifts only brought me bad luck, and that, anyway, my mother frequently told me the colour aged me. But something about the spontaneous way he offered it made me wordlessly hold out my arm, palm down, in order to hide the raw skin.

'It's only a watch.' With warm fingers, he held my wrist and tried to turn my palm upwards so he could fasten the strap.

I resisted, embarrassed about its coarse appearance.

'What's wrong?' he asked.

I ignored him and silently displayed my wounds.

If he thought they were ugly he didn't show it; he secured the clasp and let me go. The telephone in booth two rang. We both looked towards the cubicle. Condom Kath was still in the other, knitting quietly with the telephone lodged between shoulder and ear.

'My turn,' I said.

'You sure? I can go.'

I handed him the gold tinsel and went into cubicle two.

'Flood Crisis, can I help?' I picked up the pencil – it was blunt. The blank page challenged me to find a way to record the call.

'I think this is Katrina. Am I right?'

It was Sid. My third call with him; already I found it so easy to decipher his words.

'Yes, it's Katrina,' I said.

'I lost my glasses again,' he said.

I smiled. 'And?'

'They were on my head.'

'How are you today?' I asked.

'I think it's a good day. Do people ring you about the good days?'

I should ignore the question, bring it around to him. 'Why is it a good one?'

Condom Kath returned to the sofas, her knitted creation trailing after her like a tail. A phone started up immediately and Christopher got to it in three rings.

'I finally slept,' said Sid. 'Well, for five hours. I think it's because...'

'Why?' I asked.

'Can I tell you something I remembered last night?' he said.

I was always interested in memories. 'Of course,' I said.

'I've forgotten a lot so I'm always delighted when a memory comes back to me.'

I was usually nervous about randomly returning memories. 'Tell me,' I said.

'It doesn't happen often,' he began. 'But last night I had this clear vision of my daughter. She was running in the garden, dancing around in circles in a checked green dress, with the leaves floating around her, all pretty, like. I lost her years ago, you see, and can hardly recall what she looked like. But last night I saw her vividly. Memory is cruel, isn't it? Just giving you snapshots of the past and nothing more.'

As Sid described the image his voice seemed to purify. I thought I'd imagined it and listened more intently; definitely his 't's were unmistakable, his 'o's more concise. I understood completely his frustration with memory. Mine teased me too – a pretty child who showed me her new Barbie and then ran away and hid before I could play with it.

'I can't see her clearly now,' he said, sadly. 'I could tell you her hair was mousy and her eyes were blue, but I can't actually see her.' He paused. 'I think I'll have soup for tea again. Were you flooded, Katrina?'

I could ignore the question, as trained, but I answered, as required.

'It must be annoying for you to sit and listen to others complain,' he said.

Christopher ended his call and returned to the lounge.

'I might take a sleeping pill tonight.' Sid's words slurred now he wasn't reminiscing. 'My friend Bill gave me some. He has a generous doctor – maybe I'll try and get on his books. This cough keeps me awake so anything would be good.'

'You should see someone about the cough.' I could hear a Crisis

Care trainer in my head – 'We're not here to give advice, we're here to *listen.*'

'I'll rest now, dear, if that's OK,' said Sid. 'Thanks for listening, Katrina.'

I returned to the lounge area after a while. Kath looked at the red watch and then at Christopher's bare wrist but just continued knitting. He was writing in the logbook.

I stood at the window. It had begun snowing while I was in the booth. The world could softly change while you were on the phone. I'd half forget that outside I was Catherine with a semi-built home and a dead-end job. It was very tempting to close the shutter on it all, leave Catherine in the snow and get lost in being Katrina, the woman people needed.

'You OK?' Christopher had put down the book.

'Do you think we'd even leave this building if the three-minute warning went off for a nuclear attack?' I let go of the shutter.

'Am I definitely going to die in this scenario?' he asked.

'They won't warn us,' said Kath, her yellow ball of wool tiny now. 'It'd be kinder to let us die without knowing.'

'I just don't know where else I'd be,' I said.

Christopher stared at me but I couldn't read his expression.

'Like, where else is there?' I continued.

He seemed to ponder this, but offered no answer.

'I wouldn't get to finish this cardigan,' said Kath, holding it up.

The phones rang only twice before the end of the shift, both calls from flood victims who wanted to rant about their inept builders and the local council. I checked my mobile twice for messages from Fern but had none.

It was dark when we shut off the phones, pulled the shutters closed, cranked down the heating and washed the cups. Christopher wheeled his bike down the frozen path and said he'd see me Wednesday, his smoky breath silver in the moonlight. Condom Kath hurried past to be picked up by her neighbour in a van.

Back at the flat I climbed the metal stairs, hoping Fern would be sitting on the sofa, full of sorry's and smiles. But the door was locked. The place was as I'd left it that morning: impossibly, pathetically tidy. I longed for her chaos and was tempted to smash the glass I'd carefully washed and turned upside down on the drainer. Instead I made a cup of tea and squashed the bag five times.

With only two hours until my nightshift I hunted for my overalls under Fern's bed. I saw Aunty Hairy's shoebox of pictures. I'd forgotten about them. Curious now, I carried it to the living room and took out the one of me sitting on the edge of a boat in Devon. Next I found one of Dad near an over-adorned Christmas tree; his smiling eyes were even brighter than the stars. Sitting cross-legged, I sipped tea and pulled out image after image. Pictures of me with missing teeth, of Dad hugging my mother, of relatives I didn't know. A faded one of my mum, perhaps a teenager, smiling shyly. She looked like me.

Halfway through was a picture of a rabbit. A black-and-white rabbit in my skinny child's arms. I had no idea whose it was and couldn't recall the white dress I wore. Though there was no menace in the photograph, and I grinned for whoever had taken the picture, my throat felt like I'd swallowed grit.

I picked up the phone.

'Mother,' I said over her customary civil greeting. 'There's a picture in Aunty Mary's box of me with a rabbit. Whose is it?'

'Catherine, I've got chicken soup on. I don't remember now.' I heard The Carpenters on her radio singing about birds suddenly appearing – but I wanted to know about rabbits.

'You must have some clue,' I snapped.

'You might have had one when you were nine or ten,' she sighed.

'So who got me it?'

'...Aunty Mary...' She didn't sound altogether sure.

'And was it a girl or a boy? What was it called?'

She thought about it. 'Geraldine.'

I looked at the picture and the word 'tiger' popped out of it and dissolved like a burst water bubble, splattering my nine-year-old face with tears.

'Did I ever call it "Tiger"?

'No. You called everything Geraldine – your dolls, your cups, your—'

'So what happened to her?' I demanded.

'You had one of your funny turns and set her free,' said Mother. 'You left the cage open and watched her escape under the fence. I told you I'd not buy another, but you were unapologetic; you even seemed to think it was funny. You just laughed when I sent you to bed early.'

'Mother, why don't I remember?'

I tried so hard; I willed my memory to bring the photograph to life for me. If only there was a password, some simple door-code, like the one for the Flood Crisis building. The word 'tiger' was merely a nausea-inducing clue.

'Catherine, I have no idea at all.'

'Why the fuck didn't you tell me about the rabbit?'

'Catherine, do not fuck on the phone please. How could I know you didn't remember? How could I know to tell you about it? You didn't ask.' She paused. 'While you're on the phone, Aunty Mary is having her operation on Monday afternoon, so we can see her on Tuesday. It'd be nice if you showed your face. And for goodness sake *please* don't swear on the ward.'

'I'll be there,' I said. 'I have a few days off work this week.'

'The soup's boiling, I have to go.' She hung up.

I still had so many questions. How long did I have Geraldine? Did I take care of her? Why had I set her free?

In the photograph, I held her cheek to cheek; but my smile was betrayed by sad eyes. The photographer's shadow cast darkness across my left side, blackening the white dress like I was Geraldine's mono-chrome twin. Who'd taken the picture? I recalled Dad touching my nose and promising me a rabbit when I was nine. His moustachy, fatherly scent wafted from the picture. But he couldn't have been there. Aunty Hairy must have honoured the promise, perhaps to cheer me up.

So *why* couldn't I remember?

I propped the photograph against the TV, and a flash of red watchstrap caught my eye. It chafed my skin. I loosened the fastener but wouldn't take it off. I started to put the lid back on the box to put it away, and an envelope corner appeared between two pictures. I pulled it free, frowned. It was yellow with age. Inside was a handwritten letter, the loopy letters familiar. I slowly read it.

'...The heart is the first organ that forms. It beats as early as two weeks after fertilisation. Some bodily functions continue after death, like nails growing and urination, but without the heart beating we're doomed. We die. We're supposed to listen to it. Follow it. Everything we need to know is in there. Mine was yours. Now, soon, you'll have to share it with...'

The paper was torn there. What was it all about? I was sure it was my dad's writing. Who was he writing to? My mother? My mum? Someone else? And why would she have to share his heart?

More mystery. More confusion. More questions I couldn't answer. I was so tired of them. On crisis-line calls we weren't allowed to respond to questions. We had to bring the conversation back to the caller and let them find their own answers. As Catherine, I constantly asked them. Night and day they begged for answers. I had no room for more.

I put the letter in my coat pocket. I would ask Aunty Hairy about it. I had to or I might go mad. There was only one thing I was sure of today. Only one thing I knew for certain.

I went to the sink, rummaged in the cupboard beneath. A candle. Just one. I turned on a gas ring on the hob and lit it, then carried it to the coffee table and let it dance there.

'Happy birthday, Nanny Eve,' I whispered. She would have been 101. 'Let's pretend there are another seventy candles.'

Because some things refuse to be forgotten.

18

A hospital visit

'The colostomy bag is only a temporary measure. I'll have it for a few months so everything heals fully, then they'll do surgery again to restore my normal, you know, *functions*. I think my bikini days are over.'

Propped up in a hospital bed, Aunty Hairy smiled like she was describing a trip to the garden centre. She whispered the word '*functions*'. That was the offensive one. She squeezed my mother's hand and added, 'It's not all doom and gloom you know, Jean.'

I stood at the end of the bed and pretended to read the jargon on her chart. The drugs they were pumping into my aunt via a long, spiralling drip must have been good. If she thought cancer and colostomy bags weren't too bad she must be high. I was glad; she didn't deserve to be miserable.

'You're in good spirits anyway,' said Graham.

He sat in the chair near her stiff NHS pillows, visibly uncomfortable but trying to be jolly. I wondered if anyone had ever proposed drugs for visitors so they could enjoy their time on the ward.

'Where's Martin?' My mother swivelled her head, unable to escape Aunty Hairy's consoling grip. He had gone to get cups of tea, saying that would make us all feel better. My mother looked with distaste at the grimy tiled floor and brown checked bed curtain and asked when Mary would be out.

'Perhaps ten days.' Aunty Hairy seemed to have lost half her weight in a week. Though she spoke with colour, her white skin emphasised her black, bristled chin. I'd kissed her cheek when we arrived; it smelt of antiseptic soap.

'Was it successful?' Mother pulled free from Mary's hand and took a wet-wipe out of her bag to clean her fingers. 'This hospital is filthy,' she said, not giving my aunt a chance to reply. 'Mary, you need to be careful when you go to the toilet.'

I wanted to remind my mother that Aunty Hairy had a colostomy bag so she wouldn't be spending much time in the lavatory but knew she'd consider such an observation worse than my swearing.

'It was a success, they got the entire tumour.' Aunty Hairy reached for any available hand to squeeze and found Graham's.

Mother wanted to know why she still had to endure chemotherapy, then; Mary explained that it was in case it had spread to the lymph glands. She said she'd likely lose her hair but would just get a wig or a jazzy headscarf.

In my pocket, I wrapped my fingers around the strange letter I'd found: *The heart is the first organ that forms. Mine was yours. Now you'll have to share it with...'*

'We'll do anything we can,' said Graham.

'I can stay here all day,' I offered.

'No, dear, you don't want to be in a place like this all day,' said Aunty Hairy. 'Your mother said you have to meet someone at your house.'

'I've already been,' I said.

I'd met Brian the plumber first thing that morning. He'd lectured me on the plumbing being the bowels of the house. 'If the waterworks are faulty,' he'd said, plonking a green flask on the stair, 'the whole house is at risk.'

I'd asked how long it would take to install a boiler, and he said you couldn't rush such things. I'd reminded him that I'd been out of my home five months. Surely single-span suspension bridges had been built faster.

'The electrician will say his work is more important,' Brian said. 'But is he here first? Plumbing is the priority. It'll be done when it's done.'

I said I'd call around at the end of the week and left him with his wrench, flask and yards of blue piping.

'How's the house?' asked Aunty Hairy.

'Just getting started,' I said. 'It may be February now before I'm back in.'

'It'll be February before I can lift anything,' she said.

'You can help Catherine move in then,' said Uncle Martin, putting a tray of drinks on the cabinet. He was as thin and bald as his wife was rotund and bushy, lightning to her slow, rolling thunder. Cancer would make them hairless twins, though.

'You not having a cup of tea?' my mother asked Aunty Hairy.

'I can't have anything until the doctor hears my stomach growling. That means the bowels are working. Even then it'll be water or juice and liquid food for a while. I'm going to be as thin as that lovely girl on TV.'

'Tess Daly,' grinned Martin.

I sipped my tea, but the milk was off so I put it back on the cabinet.

'It looks nice,' said Graham as I leaned over him.

'What?'

'The brooch.'

I touched the topaz-and-silver rabbit with its winking eye. I'd pinned it to my jumper, knowing Graham would be at the hospital. On the bathroom windowsill earlier it had it looked like a lone jigsaw piece, a key segment that might complete an unfinished picture somewhere. I understood now my fascination with rabbit images – I'd had my own as a child. But I still needed a few more pieces to complete the puzzle of my elusive memory.

Aunty Hairy touched my cheek with cold hands and said it was pretty. 'You shouldn't be here on a day off,' she said. 'You should be having fun with friends. Jean, tell her she shouldn't be here.'

'I think it's right that she's here,' snapped my mother.

'It's lunch time – why don't you go and eat. There's a cafeteria on the second floor. Martin will stay with me. He had a bacon sandwich there this morning, said it was a bit fatty, but at least it was hot, didn't you, dear?'

Graham stood, not needing much encouragement to escape the ward. Mother fussed and asked if Mary was sure.

'Go,' my aunt insisted. 'We'll finish this sudoku puzzle together.'

No matter how many floral cloths they put on the cafeteria's plastic tables it was still a hospital canteen, where weary customers took a break from cancer and heart disease, pale aliens in the harsh fluorescent lighting.

By the vending machine a Christmas tree looked even more tired than the pathetic twig in the Flood Crisis lounge. My mother chose a limp green salad and asked the till woman if they had de-caffeinated tea. I opted for a slimy burger in a roll, Graham the same. We found a table near the door, beside a group of doctors discussing a nurse called Suzanne.

While Mother checked the cleanliness of our cutlery Graham laughed and said Fern's column had been funny on Saturday. 'She said long-time partners grow to look like one another. I loved the line about Victoria Beckham looking more like David than he does. Does she think about writing something longer?'

My appetite died. I lifted the lid off my roll and poked the fatty meat.

'It was her last column,' I said, avoiding Graham's eyes. 'Someone told the paper she wasn't really married, and they sacked her.'

Graham dropped his burger on his plate. 'Why would anyone do that?'

'Perhaps readers realised what a phony she was,' sniffed my mother.

'Someone grassed her up,' I said. 'She thinks it was me.'

'Was it?' My mother opened a paper napkin and laid it on her lap.

'Jean, that's not fair.' Graham glared at her.

I shook my head. 'I thought whoever reported Fern must be a cowardly bastard, but people like you are worse. You judge and make snide comments but don't have the guts to actually do anything.'

'Catherine! You can't say "bastard" near doctors.' She shielded her face from them and pushed her lettuce away.

'You must have told her it wasn't you,' said Graham.

'I did – she still left.'

'I thought you looked pale today,' said Graham, 'but thought maybe it was the Flood Crisis stuff.'

'I love my volunteer work.' I took a bite of the burger and then gave up. It was when I *wasn't* at Flood Crisis that my life fell apart.

'Why don't you come home?' My mother cut cucumber into tiny pieces.

'Why the hell would I do that? I'm not going to slit my wrists or anything.' I stood and picked my plate up. The questions flowed. No wall prompt needed. 'How would that affect you, anyway? You've got Sharleen to shop with. You've got Graham to holiday with. And anyway, you'd have to endure all my swearing.'

'You're being childish,' she said.

I dumped my plate on the metal trolley and walked out.

In the lift, squashed between a wheelchair-bound man who stank of whisky and two gossiping nurses, I realised I'd no idea what floor Aunty Hairy was on.

With thirteen options I got out on the eighth and looked for familiar signs. Nothing marked this floor as different to any other. When I pressed the buzzer to a ward they let me in without asking who I was. I peered into the rooms, avoiding the wet patch where a cleaner had just washed the floor tiles.

I opened the door to what looked like a guest lounge and disturbed a sleeping girl. She'd been curled up with a fluffy rabbit and opened her eyes at the door handle's click.

'Are you here to see me?' she asked.

I said I was lost, and the word sagged.

'Who do you want?' She sat up, crumpling a blue pyjama top with the words 'I'm Trouble' on the front. Her bare arms were thin and bruised.

'Go back to sleep and I'll ask someone.'

'They never tell you anything,' she said.

No balloons floated above her bed. No flowers filled the nearby vase and no cards covered in juvenile images lined the window ledge.

'I forgot which floor my aunt is on. How silly is that?'

'Very silly,' she said.

I stood in the doorway, not going in, not turning to leave. I heard a children's TV show somewhere and wondered why no one slept at her side on a put-you-up-bed like I would if I had a child in the hospital. Rubbing a purple mark on her elbow she told me they didn't know what was wrong with her.

'This is where they can find out,' I said.

'I have an aunt too – Aunt Connie. I might be going to live with her.'

'I'd like to have lived with my aunt, too.' I glanced up the corridor.

'What's yours called?' she asked.

'Aunt Hairy.' I said it without thinking, and the girl laughed.

'Don't you like her?' she giggled.

'Yes, I do.'

'Why would you call her a mean name, then?'

I couldn't answer. Why *would* I do that?

She pushed back the covers and moved to the middle of the bed, where she crossed her pyjama-clad legs and asked what time it was. I looked at Christopher's watch beneath my fluffy jumper's overlong sleeve and told her it was twelve-twenty.

'I'm hungry,' she said. 'They bring dinner at about twelve-thirty, but I can't smell it yet. A girl called Rachel said the food is disgusting, but it's better than anything I've ever had. I love the tiny carrots. They cut them in circles like moons. Can you stay until my food comes?'

'Does no one visit you?' I asked, realising I'd been brusque.

Why couldn't I find Katrina when I needed her? As Catherine I spoke without thinking. The girl shook her head, and more gently, finally finding Katrina, I asked where her mum and dad were.

'Mum's away and Dad's not allowed to come here.'

I wondered how appropriate it was for a complete stranger to stay with a small girl until her favourite carrots arrived. I sensed a troubled background and had no idea if a nurse would call security. What a pathetic picture this child in the middle of a hospital bed made, her eyes huge with curiosity and faith. It formed a photograph in my mind. A print she might one day find in a shoebox, mixed with snaps of holidays and Christmas and rabbits. Might her mother give her half-lies when she asked about her origins? A half-lie only becomes a half-truth when the shadow finally moves.

'I like your brooch – it's Pinky.' She held up the toy and I stared at the un-pink rabbit. Maybe one day, in a few years, she'd ring a crisis line and Katrina might be there, asking how she felt, helping her find the answers, listening to the story of the rabbit that she hugged when she was alone and talked to the odd woman who disturbed her, who waited until the carrots arrived.

A nurse with a blood-pressure machine peered into the room. 'Are you Rebecca's aunt?' She looked me up and down.

'Oh, no, I got lost.'

She stared at me.

'She's looking for *her* aunt,' said the girl, Rebecca.

I thought of Rebecca Houghton, that day spent ice-skating, the day I forgot Nanny Eve. I wondered if classmates asked this girl out, or if she too hung around with boys and climbed trees.

'Which floor do I want if my aunt had cancer surgery?' I asked the nurse.

'The tenth, probably ward 130.'

'I hope you find her,' said Rebecca.

The nurse continued with her equipment to the next room, wheels squeaking as though crying.

'You have this.' I unpinned the brooch, and Rebecca stared at it in my hand. I was afraid to touch her.

'Put it on me,' she instructed. I pinned it above the word 'Trouble'. She smelt of clinical shampoo. 'I look cool. Will you come and see me again?'

'I won't be here,' I said.

Ring me in ten years, I thought. Ring me and tell me about this day. Tell me why you had no visitors, tell me your story, why you had no fear of a stranger, tell me you still wear the brooch she gave you.

Would she even remember?

I walked away but then looked back over my shoulder. Rebecca was watching me. The brooch winked.

In the crowded lift I pressed the button for floor ten, took the tube of cream from my pocket and coated my hot hands in gel. The many faces merged. Then in the mirror I saw the bushy-haired man. His face was disguised by a thick, bristled beard and moustache. My knees were jelly. Why was he *here*? He had only ever appeared as I awoke, there at the end of my bed, halfway between dreams and life.

I looked for him in the sea of faces. Not there. Did I know him? It felt like I did. From the mirror he smiled and mouthed 'tiger'. I shrunk back, nudging a pyjama-clad man who said, 'Hey!'

When the doors opened, I pushed my way out. Looked back. There was no bushy man. No bearded sort-of-stranger. My imagination? I sat for a moment in the corridor. Thought I might be sick, but it passed. Seeing him as I woke was unnerving but somehow explainable. He was some figment of a nightmare, maybe.

But now I was fully awake.

On ward 130 I recognised the Stoma Care Clinic poster and found the third room along. The curtain had been pulled around Aunty Hairy's bed; I wondered if she was being examined so I paused and listened for a nurse's voice. Hearing nothing, I peeped through the gap. Hairy was doing a puzzle, alone.

'Catherine, come and sit.' She patted the sheet. 'Martin's gone to get some stuff from home. Where are your mother and Graham?'

I sat on the bed near her legs, still trembling after seeing the bushy man, and said they must still be eating. Tea trollies jingled in the corridor and someone further along wailed. I scratched my fingers.

'You mustn't worry.' Aunty Hairy took my fidgety hand and patted it.

I began to consider that really I should call her Aunty Mary in my mind as well as in speech. She deserved her real name. Soon she might not even be bristled anymore. I insisted I wasn't worried about her. If anyone could send cancer packing with a pat on the hand, she could.

'You've enough on your plate with the house and your volunteering.'

'I'm sorry I called you Aunty Hairy.' I blurted it out in a messy jumble in case I changed my mind and didn't say it.

She laughed. 'Oh, Catherine, you funny girl. You mean that time at the dinner table? I laughed for days. Told Jean not to send you to bed.'

I was embarrassed to find myself crying and roughly wiped away the tears with my sleeve. I confessed that I'd called her it since then. 'There was a girl and I told her it was your name, and she thought I mustn't like you much.'

'Come now, don't get upset.' She pulled me to her chest and I wondered where her colostomy bag was and if I was leaning on it. 'It's not really about the name, is it?'

I wanted to argue that it was, that names mattered, but she hugged me tighter and said she'd fight this disease with everything she had. She stroked my hair and said, 'You know that, don't you?'

Now was the moment to ask. I took out the strange letter.

'This was in the box of photos you gave me,' I said. 'I hate to trouble you when ... you know...'

'Oh Catherine, distractions are good.' She unfolded the faded paper and read it. Then she closed it softly, tears shining in her eyes.

'What is it?' I asked. 'Do you know? Was my dad having an affair?'

'Oh, gosh, no,' said Mary. 'I've never seen it before and don't know how it got in the box, but I remember your dad telling me about it – about a gorgeous letter he had written for your real mum before you were born. About the heart. His heart. How she'd have to share it when you arrived. He had such a lovely way with words. Such a kind man.'

He didn't have to share his heart after all. She'd died and it was just the two of us.

'Wow, I'll really cherish this letter then.' I paused. 'What was my real mum like? *Really* like?'

'Sadly, we hardly got to know her,' said Aunty Mary. 'They weren't together long before you were born. You were quite the surprise. But we really liked her. She was kind ... gentle ... the good ones always go young, don't they?'

I nodded. 'Thank you for buying me my rabbit.'

'Oh – Geraldine.' She patted my damp cheek. 'You loved her. Used to brush her fur and walk her around the garden on a pink lead like she was a puppy.' She paused. 'I didn't buy her though, sweetie.'

'No? Who did?' Footsteps sounded and my mother opened the curtain.

'Who bought Geraldine?' Aunty Mary asked her.

'*You* did,' said my mother. 'Catherine, why are you bothering your aunt with this stuff? Didn't I answer enough questions about this the other night?'

Mary insisted it was OK, we were just reminiscing. Graham resumed his place in the bedside chair, the smell of cigarettes on his coat.

'*You* bought her.' My mother sat on the bed and glared at Mary, who seemed to rethink. I sensed a hidden message in my mother's look, in those three words. Something I couldn't hear or understand.

'I did.' Mary forced a giggle. 'How silly to forget. Must be the treatment.'

Her mannerisms were unnatural, and my mother chimed in with, 'Do you need anything from the hospital shop?'

I felt like the only one not in on a joke, though Graham seemed oblivious too. Female heels approached the curtain; I anticipated a nurse and was annoyed when Celine poked her head through the gap and said, 'Not disturbing you all, am I?'

'Not at all.' My mother smiled. 'Lovely of you to come.'

Celine wore a white jacket over a sequined vest-top, her sculpted breasts fighting for space inside it. New hair extensions swung down to her bottom. I could taste expensive perfume and needed air.

She flicked a strand of hair away. 'Dad, Jean, Mary, *Catherine*.'

I ignored her and said we should give Aunty Mary space. But Mary made room for Celine. She always had room at her dinner table, no matter how many turned up.

'What do you need at the hospital shop?' asked my mother.

Graham stood to leave, and Celine took his chair, looking with disdain at the catheter and other tubes that coiled from the sickbed. She kept her pink designer clutch bag on her knee. I glanced through Mary's puzzle book – she had attempted every one but completed none.

Aunty Mary handed a fiver to my mother and asked her to get a paper. Looking at me she said, 'Is tonight's the one your friend's in?'

'And what's the column about this week?' Celine looked down her expensive nose at me. '"Fern the devoted wife bakes sponge cake and makes a trifle and does voluntary work for the good women of the area"?'

I ignored her, adding the word *bitch* in answer to "female dog" in Aunty Mary's puzzle. Mary said she thought Fern's column was fun, that it was sad that she couldn't work it out with her husband. Maybe she wrote the column to cope with the sadness of losing him, she said.

'No, she sleeps with lots of people to do that,' said Celine.

'What's your Mark's excuse then?' I asked. 'Anyway, Fern won't be in the paper again. They found out she's not really married, so that's that.'

Aunty Mary said it was a shame. She only ever bought the Saturday paper to read Fern's column – and for the free magazine with the TV listings.

Celine teased a blonde lock into a curl around her finger. 'Maybe they'll get a proper writer instead.'

'You're a bitch,' I said.

'Catherine, enough of such words on a cancer ward.' My mother had returned from the shop and dropped the newspaper onto the bed.

'I don't understand,' said Aunty Mary, opening it. 'All my friends at the Post Office love Fern. How did they find out she was separated?'

'Somebody rang her editor. She thought I did it.' I was tired of saying it, of telling people she'd blamed me, having them possibly consider that it was. But mostly I was hurt that Fern had thought so. Aunty Mary said anyone who really knew me would know better.

'No smoke without fire.' Celine's eyelids were heavy with mauve paint.

I said that was what I'd thought when I'd heard about her husband Mark and the teenage girl.

'Why are you saying vile things?' asked my mother.

'Why am *I* vile? I'm only saying what's true. Mark's not vile for sleeping with girls half his age and she's not vile for dissing Fern? – But *I'm* vile. Everyone knows he slept with that sixteen-year-old girl. I'm going.'

'Don't leave, dear,' said Mary. 'This little madam should go.'

'Who are you calling a little madam?' demanded Celine.

My mother patted the pillows and said we should both go if we couldn't stop the bickering.

Celine stood, towering over me in her four inch stilettos, and tried to push past. But her heel got caught in the catheter drain and pulled it apart from the bag. Urine splattered like an orange firework, staining her trouser leg.

Mother pulled the buzzer cord. 'Nurse!' she called. 'Poor Mary! Poor Mary!' I heard: *Pure Mary, Pure Mary.*

'I'm covered in piss,' whined Celine.

Aunty Mary clapped her hands, put her head back and laughed.

'You really shouldn't say piss on a cancer ward,' I said.

I left Celine looking for paper towels, my mother shouting for help and Aunty Mary laughing, red-faced and delirious.

On the bus, I called Fern's mobile, but it was switched off. I rang her mother's home number. The phone rang and rang. When Fern's mother finally answered, she told me she'd gone, left that morning on a cheap, last-minute package holiday to Lanzarote.

'Who with?' The thought of someone else being with her made me scratch my hands.

'She went on her own. What happened between you girls?'

I was relieved that Fern hadn't told her mother; it meant she couldn't have fully believed it herself. Fern's mother said she'd be home on Sunday the ninth and asked if I had a message. I couldn't think of anything.

One of the Crisis Care wall prompts came to me: 'If you've already said it all suggest the caller repeats their story, and you might find a question you missed.' It occurred to me that I'd never messed with Fern's name. Perhaps its simplicity stopped me. But thinking over our story to find questions I'd missed, I realised it was because I'd had no need. I'd trusted Fern enough not to.

That night I slept for three-and-a-half hours.

I dreamt of the room.

There was a metal bed in the corner. Little Rebecca slept there with all manner of tubes transporting thick, dark blood into her veins and extracting stained mucus from others. The sheet was soiled. My father's letter was pinned to the wall.

'The heart is the first organ that forms. Everything we need to know is in there.'

I approached the bed; Rebecca opened her eyes with an audible click.

There's another room, she whispered, without opening her mouth.

A door appeared behind her, the wood breathing, up and down, up and down. *Everything you need to know is in there.*

In the room or in my heart?

You must see it, Rebecca whispered, soundless. *You must face it or I'll die.*

She pulled the tubes from her arm and fat droplets of blood hit the floor. Drip, drip, drip.

I'll die if you don't see.

Drip, drip, drip.

See. Everything you need to know is in there.

I woke to the leaking tap. Drip-drip-drip. I'd forgotten to wrap a tea towel around it, or to put one underneath to absorb the noise. My heart mimicked the sound. No Nanny Eve on the bed singing. No Fern at my feet. I recalled her words the last time I'd woken from a dream: 'That place is giving you nightmares.'

But today I hadn't been to Flood Crisis. And when I had gone on Sunday I'd not dreamed at all. The realisation pleased me; helplines and callers and their stories were not the source of my anguish. But then relief gave way to a question that I saw flashing eerily in the DVD player's green digits.

If crisis centres weren't causing the dreams – what was?

19

Two sixes at Santa's feet

'I won't play unless I'm the shoe.' Christopher picked up the tiny metal boot, waited for dispute, and when no one argued he placed it on the Monopoly board.

The Flood Crisis coffee table had been cleared – magazines shoved under the sofa, mugs of tea in hand or by feet, and the singing, thrusting Father Christmas relegated to the corner, from where he watched in silence. Jangly Jane had commented on Santa's inappropriate underwear and tried to cover the offending shorts.

'This is the most-played board game in the world,' said Christopher. 'It's also a game of luck, so I'm doomed before we begin.'

I picked up the silver Scottie dog; I had no preference of ornament, no reason to choose the animal, so really he picked me. Jane, after trying to resist the game and arguing that we should do some role-play practice, surrendered. She picked the car charm out of the box.

'Skill is required more than luck.' She shook the two dice and threw them onto the board. One dropped off the table and revealed a three; the other was a one. 'Skilled players win more often than unskilled.'

'I'm also doomed, then,' I sighed. 'Can we just play snap instead?'

'The dice decide who goes first,' said Christopher. 'Going last is a significant disadvantage, because you're more likely to land on property that has already been bought and therefore be forced to pay rent instead of having an opportunity to buy an unowned property. And don't buy Park Lane; according to the laws of probability seven is the most likely roll of two dice, with a one in six chance, so Park Lane is one of the least landed-on squares because Go to Jail is seven places behind it'

'You need to get out more.' I threw the dice – two fives landed in the middle of the board with a satisfying clatter.

Christopher picked them up, shook his cupped hands for ages, expression serious, and cast them onto the board. He wore a black shirt. One vertical crease up the left arm ruined the otherwise smooth material. I wondered if he'd been to an interview before our shift and not ironed his clearly just-taken-out-of-a-packet top. 'Eleven!'

'How do we play around the phones?' Jane glanced at the booths.

'We'll each assign someone to fill in for us,' said Christopher. 'Obviously, if two people are away we'll pause the game. I'll cover your turns, Katrina.'

'I'm not sure that will work,' said Jangly.

Having appointed herself the banker, she organised the money piles and straightened the Chance and Community Chest cards. Christopher arranged his play-money into piles according to denomination and imparted words of wisdom.

'Did you know,' he said, 'that though dogged by bad luck in real life, King's Cross Station has the fortune of having both a Go To dedicated card and one that advances the player to the nearest railroad. So it's a lucky spot.'

'So those unlucky in life fare better in this game of chance?' Jane sipped tea.

'I was merely observing,' said Christopher. 'Consider me the bearer of information from which one can draw great inspiration.' He grinned.

'Or consider you an arsehole,' I said. 'Shall we?'

I handed Christopher the dice. I added that if the phones got busy it would be the longest game ever played, and on cue the telephone in booth one chimed.

'I'll go.' Jane stood and headed for the cubicle, calling over her shoulder, 'We should pause the game. You two might cheat.'

I finished my tea and put it under the chair, away from feet that might fidget or jump with anticipation. With a deliberate flourish,

Christopher threw the dice and moved his boot five places to King's Cross Station. He bought it. I threw a seven and landed on Chance.

Picking the card from the top of the pile, I read it aloud, 'Drunk in Charge; Fine £20,' and threw it down in mock rage. I dropped a twenty in the bank pile.

'Do I need my watch back yet?' Christopher looked at the red strap as I reached over the board.

'Not yet,' I said softly.

I was tired of unexpectedly finding Fern's remnants in the flat. I was tired of missing her, of being angry that she'd misjudged me. That morning I'd opened the drawer that could only pull out when the other was shut, searching for thread to repair the red dress, and I found the white silk napkins she'd stolen from the fancy restaurant. Folded beneath our tenancy agreement, they had reminded me I should tell Victor she'd gone and arrange to pay the full monthly sum – cold, monetary details that only added to my torment. I'd held the napkins to my cheek. When I saw my reflection in the cracked mirror I felt stupid and put them back in the drawer.

She'd only been gone four days.

Jane jingle-jangled into the room. 'Just someone wanting the number for a nightclub in Birmingham,' she said. 'Do we sound like a telephone directory?' She looked at the board. 'You played on?'

She threw a nine and each of us had another go before the phone rang again. I got it on the third ring and said, 'Flood Crisis, can I help you?' while scribbling on the pad and adjusting the chair from its too-reclined position.

'Is that Katrina?'

I touched my chest. 'Yes, it is.'

'It's Helen. Do you remember?'

Of course I did. Acting-lessons Helen. Never-about-the-trees Helen.

'How are you?' I asked and tried to forget game-playing and dice and numbers, and concentrated on breathing and tuning out the world.

'I'm good.' She sounded it. I recalled her sometimes-childish-sometimes-sad voice and barely recognised her. 'I've been remembering,' she said. 'You helped me so much last week. I got off the phone and cried for three hours. Then I stayed in bed for two days. I shut the curtains, locked the door and ignored the phone.'

'But you're up today,' I observed. 'And you feel better?'

'Yes, I do.'

I wrote 'better' on the pad.

'Marcus – remember him? – was worried. He called fifteen times while I was in bed, left message after message. I kind of liked that: stressing him out. Then I saw him. I gave in and let him into the house when he wouldn't leave and ... well ... and...'

'Can you tell me what happened?'

I drew a tree on the pad, leafless and solitary. She was silent for a moment. Silence during a call is unnerving until you learn to decipher it. In my early days of volunteering I'd filled the silent gaps with questions and encouragement. I'd pour my words into their void, worried the caller might hang up or think me uninterested. I learned with time to be patient. Just because the caller can't speak doesn't mean they don't want to. A breath can be a second, a minute, an hour.

'Marcus pinned me to the wall,' said Helen eventually. 'He held my arms over my head like I was a tree, pinned me ... between my legs ... with his knee.' I visualised her as a tree with stretched-out branches. 'I told him to stop. I didn't like it. He said I did and I screamed at him to stop, said, "Stop Mr Westerly!" He let go then, asked me who the fuck Mr Westerly was, and I cried.'

Helen sobbed as she spoke. When she stopped to inhale, I didn't push – I waited for her to breathe.

'I'm OK,' she reminded me. 'I just need to cry while I'm telling you, but I'm OK. I told Marcus it was over. He was gentle then and said he'd thought I enjoyed his passion. It's not his fault. He's not Mr Westerly.'

'Tell me about Mr Westerly,' I said.

I had a feeling in my heart – like when you watch a film and you know a scary scene is coming; you know the girl is going to be ripped apart, you've seen it before and you know it's coming, but you can't turn it off or look away.

'Mr Westerly was my acting teacher,' she said. 'He took the whole class but he told me I was one of his best students, along with a girl called Joyce. He said whoever behaved best, whoever played the finest role, would receive extra lessons. He said I was a beautiful tree. My mother was proud when I played Juliet – she sat in the front row and applauded the loudest when I stabbed myself with Romeo's dagger. "Helen Boyce, you'll be someone, now!" she cried. Mr Westerly helped me die so well.'

I drew my chafed hand into a fist and pressed it to my closed mouth.

'He used to touch me.' Helen's voice was angry. 'Not like he should have done. You know how I mean, don't you? I was eleven. How should you touch an eleven-year-old? Not on her chest when you're showing her how to be a willow tree or at the top of her leg when you're holding her. Not in her underwear when she's changing into her costume, not on her back, her thighs, her mouth. I asked my mother if I could stop the acting lessons, but she begged me to carry on. She said I could be somebody one day. I didn't think to ask if I could just swap teachers. Eventually Mr Westerly moved away, but I had no interest in the theatre after that. I still can't bear to watch *Romeo and Juliet*.'

'You're so brave.' That was all I could think to say. I felt like I'd eaten something hot; acid moved from my stomach up to my throat. 'It must have been difficult telling me this. Does it feel good to talk?'

'Yes,' she said. 'It wasn't my fault. It really wasn't. God, I was eleven. I thought that by accepting his lessons I had given him permission to do those things. And now I've left Marcus. I'm not pathetic after all. I thought a relationship had to be about, you know, surrender. I told Marcus that, and he hasn't harassed me since. He was something I had to do to see that.'

'How does it feel to remember this?' The question came from Catherine not Katrina.

'I'd never forgotten,' she said. 'We forget nothing – memories are always there. We're just afraid to look. But why? Fear is just fear. All we have to do is look, and we won't be afraid.'

'Will you take a different class?' I asked.

'Maybe,' she said. 'Maybe I'll avoid classes. Perhaps I'll train to be a teacher. I think I'd be good at it.'

'You sound optimistic,' I said.

'I am. Thank you, Katrina. I know we only spoke a few times, but you have no idea how it's helped.'

She hung up and I exhaled; my breath was slow and unremembering.

Back in the lounge area I wasn't in the mood for the game anymore. I asked Christopher to take my turn and went to the kitchen. The Sex Addicts R Us poster caught my eye as I made tea. Beneath a glitter-covered pine-cone garland, the advertisement depicted a group of people sitting on chairs in a circle, the words 'You are not alone' above them. I'd looked at it maybe twenty times but never noticed the image.

Was the circle supposed to comfort the addicts? Perhaps link them in an eternal ring in which each guest faced another, never alone. I preferred the idea of the phones. Only anonymity would help me remember. Helen had said we're only afraid to look, but I disagreed. I *wanted* to look. I wanted to remember my rabbit Geraldine and my ninth year and people in photographs who smiled with me.

I drank my tea at the sink because I hadn't made one for the others and went back into the lounge. Christopher was in booth two.

'It's your turn.' Jane sat at the Monopoly board, eating a KitKat and polishing one of her bracelets on her sleeve.

'I can't remember where I was.'

'You're here.' She pointed to Park Lane. 'Christopher said it's the unluckiest street.'

'Wonder if it was flooded.'

'Doubt it,' snapped Jane. 'It didn't rain in London.'

I wondered if Christopher would have chosen to buy it if I'd been on the phone and he'd assumed my place. Did he think the whole world was unlucky or just him? Jane and I circled the board a couple more times, her buying property for Christopher until his pile of money diminished. When he returned from the booth we managed a few more turns before the phone took her away.

'Norman's coming in later to see you.' Christopher counted his boot ten places and landed on Park Lane.

'I own it!' I cried. 'You owe me thirty-five quid.'

'You bought it? You *are* an optimist.'

'Why is Norman coming to see me?' I put the money in my pile.

'To see how you're getting on.'

Jane flopped into her cushion. 'A man about anal ulcers,' she said.

'So are we going to play the game until someone is bankrupt or until the end of the shift?' I threw the dice and moved my dog seven along.

'Whichever comes first,' said Christopher. 'And when I reign supreme you can buy drinks at the Christmas do. You coming, Katrina?'

'I don't know. When is it?'

'This Saturday night. We're all meeting in Sharky's bar.'

'Will you bring your date?' Jangly looked at Christopher, who fiddled with his shirt cuff. 'Did he mention he has a hot date tonight? He's such a dark horse. He was telling me while you were on the phone.'

I shuffled my money and put it back on the board.

'It's not a date, it's a favour,' said Christopher. 'My sister set me up with her friend – we're all going out. She thinks I should socialise more.'

'That's a date,' said Jane. 'And you're wearing such a nice shirt.'

I stood, intending to go back to the kitchen and make tea for everyone, and caught the board's corner, tipping it up, sending money fluttering to the ground as if from a speeding getaway car, scattering trinkets and cards, and tossing the dice, which resulted in two sixes landing at Santa's feet.

'Katrina!' Jane held her face.

I felt stupid, apologised and blushed and left the room.

'And you were winning,' said Christopher.

I went into the kitchen. The phone rang in one of the booths and I knew it was my turn but didn't care. Clumsy Catherine my mother often called me – clothes I wore got torn, steps I climbed tripped me up, drinks I poured got spilt, games I played got ruined. My stupid hands looked like fire, my hair was frizzy from the damp weather, and my ill-chosen pink bra showed through my white shirt.

In the privacy of the kitchen I swore four times and clattered cups to hide my tantrum. After enough words I returned to the lounge.

'Shall we play cards instead?' I suggested to Jane. Christopher was on the phone.

'I think it's time we took our roles seriously,' she snapped.

'Guess that's a no then.'

I picked up a *Woman & Home* magazine and flicked through pages about how to cook and how to be assertive and how to fold napkins and how to seduce a man, and decided they should write an article on how to remember. I'd done research on the library computer on it. I'd read tips like 'visualise it'. How could I if I didn't know *what* to picture? I'd read tips like 'pay attention', and 'eat more fish', and 'convert words into pictures', and 'use rhymes'. These were all ways to remember people's names or masses of notes for an exam. But how to remember what happened long ago?

Outside a half-moon hid behind the fir trees at the end of the garden. The flat would be cold. I had a frozen meal to look forward to and reality TV and, hopefully, oblivion.

When Christopher came back from the phones he sat opposite me. A piece of tinsel pinned to the Flood Crisis banner fell behind him, landing with a gentle swish on the floor. We looked at it and one another and shrugged.

Jane took the next call.

'What's she like?' I asked.

'Who?' said Christopher.

'Your date.'

'It's really not a date. My sister likes to interfere. I think we're going to the new Italian place up the road. I'm really not bothered about it.'

'No one would make me go if I didn't want to.' I opened another magazine.

The phone rang; my turn. It was a silent caller. He or she just breathed softly and I heard a TV teatime discussion show in the background. At Crisis Care we had to give such callers twenty minutes before hanging up. They might just need to hear a voice. Some had perhaps taken pills and were waiting for them to work, wanting another human to witness their passing.

I said, 'Take your time,' to the caller and I waited.

I understood how it felt to not find words. I listened to the breaths and waited. After a while I said, 'I'm still here.' In the end, all you can do is tell them to call back if they need and hang up, which I did with the despondency I always felt at not having helped.

Christopher was looking through one of Norman's drawers; Jane was on the phone. I dropped into the big cushion and Christopher opened the logbook he'd found. He slammed it shut after a moment.

'Do you think I should go tonight?' He held my gaze.

'Do you think I should go on Saturday?' I asked him.

Jane returned to the lounge. 'Poor woman,' she said. 'She was four months pregnant when she was flooded and lost the baby. The stress of all the upheaval. She's pregnant again now and terrified.'

The Singing Santa burst into song, giving us one warped chorus of 'Jingle Bells' and three improper thrusts, then he died again. Christopher laughed but he was the only one. The phone rang and I watched him walk into the cubicle, his shirt now creased at the back, too. A moment later I picked the other one up after four rings and said, 'Flood Crisis, how can I help?'

'It's Sid,' he said. 'This sounds like Katrina.'

I smiled. 'Yes, Sid, how are you today?'

'I rang yesterday and chatted to a man for five minutes, but he couldn't understand me like you do.'

I wrote 'Sid' on the pad and underlined it twice. I didn't care if I was getting attached; I was just pleased to have made a connection with a caller. Why else would anyone do this if not in the hope that they touched someone and made a difference?

'How's your cough today?'

'Still bad.' He coughed as though to prove it. 'I ended up in Casualty on Monday. My mate Boris was over from Doncaster. We had a game of cards and I was coughing up blood, so he took me straight down there. Didn't want to go. Hate hospitals. They've done some tests, and I'm waiting on the results. I was sent to the ward, but the nurse wouldn't let me help myself to tea so I discharged myself. Nothing they could do about that.'

'Will you go back if you need to?' I asked.

'Rather not. I'll wait for my test results and take whatever they give to cure me and stay here in my flat. I hate having a card game interrupted like that. I was winning, too. One card away from a royal flush. Not had one of those since 1983. Nearly lost my house in a game in Prague once.'

I laughed. 'Nearly? Must have been scary.'

'I loved those moments. I was living then. What am I doing now? Playing poker with cherry boiled sweets and an eighty-nine-year-old mate who's almost blind.'

'You're still playing,' I said.

He coughed. 'Glad I remember how. Funny that I remember over a hundred card games but I don't know where I've left my glasses or what happened three years ago. A stroke is a cruel thing – wouldn't wish it on anyone.'

Sid's memory had been stolen by the stroke; I wondered if I'd had a mini-stroke, one with no symptoms other than memory loss and perhaps clumsiness. Or had I been this way all my life? It was difficult to know with such a bad memory.

The chair squeaked as I reclined and I felt a twinge in my back. Christopher had returned to the lounge area. I could hear him talking to Jane about his faulty motherboard.

'When did you have the stroke?' I asked Sid.

'Just after the floods.' He'd told me the same the first time we spoke. 'It may have been stress-related, except I wasn't flooded.'

'Your friends moved away and you're alone. And we were all nervous about whether there would be more rain.'

'I wish the stroke would make me forget all that, but it only took my good memories. I remember all the crap but I can't remember my daughter's face.'

'What do you remember about her?'

'How she smelt.' He sighed.

'Can you tell me what happened to her?'

After a long silence Sid said, 'I lost her. Though I can't remember the details of her face, I remember her voice.'

I was curious what he meant but also didn't want to know. It wasn't important. The *why* wasn't as important as how one felt; always the feelings at crisis lines.

'Tell me about that,' I said. He could define the question however he wished.

He chose not to respond.

I scribbled out the word 'daughter' on the pad and said we could talk about something else.

'What else is there?' asked Sid. 'I've been thinking about my life. It's all I do – think. I wonder if we think about our lives the nearer we get to the end of them.'

'But how can we know when we're near the end?'

'I sense it.' He had gone from 'we' to 'I'. He wasn't musing on an idea; he was talking about himself. 'I'm not saying I'll drop dead tomorrow or next year, but I can feel my mind closing down. I have regrets. Oh, I can remember the regrets. We can't go back though, can we?'

'Would you like to talk about them – the regrets?'

I wondered if that was why he'd called us. The flood, the stroke, the cough, the loneliness, they were all incidental. It was never about those things. Never about the trees. Callers often talked of symptoms but they needed to discuss the cause, and that was never so obvious.

'I don't want the results,' he said.

'The hospital results?'

'What's the point?' Sid coughed, and I could tell he was covering his mouth so I didn't hear its full extent.

'They'll be able to make you better,' I said.

In my head, I heard Roger from Crisis Care: 'We're not Citizen's Advice, we're here to listen. We're here for the heart not the head.' My dad had written that everything we needed to know was in there – in the heart.

'I'm tired now,' said Sid. 'Do you mind if go? I might sleep.'

'That's OK.' I wanted to cry. I knew I wouldn't. It would serve no purpose. Sometimes the wanting was better than the doing because the doing didn't bring the relief hoped for.

'Thank you, Katrina.'

The phone clicked and he was gone. I held the receiver to my ear, not wanting the call to end. When I replaced it, I stared at its black surface for a while. Then the door to the hall opened and I let Sid go. Norman had arrived for my catch-up.

'Hey Katrina,' he said, as I returned to the sofas.

Christopher looked at me over his newspaper. Jane was in the kitchen; I heard cups clattering.

'Just here to find out how it's going. Shall we go and chat in the kitchen?'

I followed Norman to the door. He wore a black T-shirt with Green Day's last tour dates down the back. Jane passed with drinks.

'Cover the phones for a bit, will you?' Norman asked her.

In the kitchen, he pulled two stools out from under the worktop and motioned for me to sit on one. He placed his opposite mine and sat, like Chris Tarrant facing a *Who Wants to be a Millionaire?* contestant.

'How's it going, Katrina?'

I was tempted to ask if I could go for the fifty/fifty option or phone a friend. 'I feel like I've been here forever.'

He laughed. 'Is that a good or bad thing?'

'Good, I think. I'm enjoying it, if "enjoying" is the right word.'

Having just spoken to Sid, I thought again of that first call with him, the call I should never have answered. Should I tell Norman about it now? I decided not to; it was already long enough ago that surely it wouldn't matter?

Norman reached for the kettle, displaying damp armpits. 'Tea?'

'No, thanks.'

'Christopher said you're a natural on the phones.'

'He did?'

'He said you're an asset to the team and you fit in well and take on your share of calls. So now that you've done four full shifts you don't have to be on with your buddy.'

'My buddy?'

'Christopher – your buddy.'

I remembered the buddy thing, him supposedly mentoring me and working the same shift until I was confident. I had forgotten that we were only together until I became accustomed to the phones.

'I think you'll be fine on your own now.' Norman hunted for a clean spoon, wiping the one he'd acquired on his T-shirt. 'So, you can stick with Wednesday and I'll let Christopher know he doesn't have to do them. He already said he'd prefer not to – unless of course you'd rather change to a different day? I can't remember if you specifically picked it?'

'He wants to do a different day?' I asked.

'He can be someone else's buddy now.' Norman stirred black coffee.

'Of course. Are we done?'

'Yes, if there are no issues?'

I stood and said I was fine, that I should get back to the phones. I heard one ringing on cue and returned to the lounge.

It was seven-thirty – in fifteen minutes we could switch them off. Christopher was in a booth; Jane reclined in the armchair, eyes closed.

I went to the window and looked out into the night but could only see my reflection. My tired face, my dirty hair, the room behind. Whenever I tried to look beyond the glass I could see only the room. I placed my hot palms on the cool surface of the window, my breath marking the spot just above. In the reflection, I saw Christopher return to the lounge area, glance at my back and watch me for a second before turning off the phones.

'We're done,' he told Jane.

Norman came into the lounge, said he was leaving and we shouldn't forget to lock up. I pulled the shutter across the window with a violent clatter. Jane helped Christopher carry the cups to the kitchen and asked if he was nervous about his date. I followed them. Saying he might cancel it after all, he dropped the cups into murky water.

'When are you meeting her?' she asked.

'Eight-thirty.'

'You can't cancel a date half an hour before you meet her,' chided Jane.

I dried my mug, put it in the cupboard and went into the hall. When I was halfway down the steps Christopher called, 'Katrina.'

I held the wall for support while he grabbed his coat from the banister and followed me.

'No bike?' I asked.

'I'm only going up the road.'

I paused at the gate, looking left, the direction of my bus stop.

'Wait,' he said. 'I have to go this way.' He looked right. 'I should go this way but I don't have to. Shall I go this way?'

'Why are you asking me?'

Where he stood – awkward, one hand in his pocket – a streetlamp shone on his head like a spotlight. I was reminded of a game show whose title I couldn't recall, in which a clock ticked while the stage was spot-lit and contestants had sixty seconds in its glare to answer the questions.

'You've done all you're supposed to,' I said.

'I don't understand – "all I'm supposed to"?'

'Norman said you swapped shift to accommodate me.' A car whizzed past, splashing slush onto the path. 'You must have juggled your schedule to be with me while I got the hang of things. But you're not obliged to anymore.' I paused. 'Your date will be waiting, and I don't think you're the kind of man to let anyone down.'

He looked up the road towards the restaurant, and then at me.

'Go,' I said.

And he walked away.

When I got home I didn't turn on the lights. I was too tired to eat, to think, to feel. Dropping my clothes on the floor near the door, I slipped between the sheets on the sofa, pulling the covers up to my neck, and stared straight at the photograph propped against the TV.

I sat up again, picked up the photo and studied the image of me with Geraldine once more.

Tell me where my memory is, I willed her.

For a second her nose twitched. Whiskers scratched my cheek. I was in a dark place, a place where Geraldine snuggled against me.

There was someone else.

I tried to see who it was, but the memory died, as if I'd reached into water and made ripples that broke up the reflection. I threw the photo onto the coffee table and closed my eyes.

I decided that if I dreamt of the room, I was going in. I was going to grab the pulsating handle and open the fat, wet door and *see*. Helen had said fear is only fear. It was just a dream room and I could face it. I *could*. The not knowing was driving me madder than any answer could. I was ready.

I was ready, but when sleep came after four restless hours, it was dreamless.

20

Knowing all the words

The tap dripped.

Fat droplets hit the bottom of the stained sink every five seconds; two days earlier they'd been falling every seven. I knew because I'd lain awake, counting and timing and cursing. Nights of drip-drip-drip. I'd even given up on the tea-towel trick.

Early morning, on the day of the Flood Crisis Christmas night out, I got up at seven and hit the tap's spout with Fern's hammer. A long pause, and I prepared to celebrate. Then drip-drip-drip again, every four seconds. I wasn't just annoyed with the tap. Part of me wanted to go on the night out, hoping Christopher would be there. Part of me thought, *Let whoever his new buddy is go.* Part of me thought, *Get a grip, why do you even care about what he does?*

Drip-drip-drip went the tap.

When the phone rang, disturbing the beat, I half hoped it would be Christopher saying he wanted me to go to the party, and he'd only go if I did.

'Just letting you know how Aunty Mary is.' My mother's tone suggested I hadn't cared enough to find out for myself.

'And how *is* she?'

I took off Christopher's watch and put it on the worktop. It had been rubbing my wrist. I was beginning to hope Fern didn't come back. Anger at her leaving me when I'd done nothing grew each day.

'She's doing amazingly well,' said my mother. 'Especially as she's had an infection. Strong antibiotics will sort that out. The doctor said it'll take time for her to get back to normal, and she may have the odd setback, but she should be home from hospital next week.'

Aunty Mary's slow progress mirrored the work in my house. Brian the plumber had called the previous day to say he'd need another week to complete my heating system. Like intestines or bowels, if pipes didn't work properly the house would be in trouble. I felt I'd never get back home, but it was good that Aunty Mary might do soon.

'Give her my love,' I said to my mother.

'You're not visiting her today, Catherine?'

'I have to do a shift at Flood Crisis,' I lied.

I wasn't any more in the mood for the hospital than for a night out. I saw my pale face in the cracked mirror; I was exhausted and looked it. Since I'd felt ready to open the pulsating door in my nightmare and face whatever horror lay beyond, in the room, I'd not dreamt of it. I'd searched and searched hazy dreams without reward, my footsteps punctuated by the drip-drip-drip that repeatedly woke me.

'You pick the troubles of those faceless strangers over your family,' said my mother.

'I don't. I just offered to cover for them when they're desperate.'

'Are you coming for Sunday lunch tomorrow or are you covering then too?'

'I'll be there,' I said.

Life outside crisis lines was what happened in between Sunday lunches at my mother's; her roast beef or stuffed chicken was a marker that began and ended each week. Last Sunday I'd escaped it when I covered the shift with Christopher and Jangly Jane. Now I listened to my mother describe Aunty Mary's latest stool sample and wondered whether it was normal to find answering the phones to the depressed and suicidal less stressful than her company.

'At least ring Aunty Mary today,' she snapped.

'I'll see her tomorrow,' I sighed. 'Look, I have to go.'

'Go then, Catherine. Go and help your callers. Go and do that strange thing you're compelled to do. I'll never understand it!'

She hung up.

The tap continued to taunt me. I rummaged in the drawer for another tea towel. It made little difference. The sound of the plops only thickened, as though they'd grown larger. Victor would have to fix it, but I doubted he'd rush to do so at my request. I wished for a moment that Fern were there to flutter her eyelashes and have him repair it in an instant. Instead I bashed the spout one more time with the hammer and threw it in the sink.

Drip-drip-drip.

I was in no mood to go out tonight. No mood to be affable or jolly. No mood for anything or anyone. No mood for taps.

I took the rest of my tea to the window and looked out. Grey sky, grey mood. Christopher's watch glared at me from the worktop. Its ticking hands added up my misery and counted drips. Suddenly I was sure I *didn't* want Fern to come back. The girl whose name I'd never messed with had believed I could go behind her back. She didn't know me. Not really. No, I would be fine on my own. When you have nothing, you can't lose anything. Without my home, my friend, a partner, or my memory, what else could possibly hurt me?

I left the watch where it was and booked a taxi for seven-forty. I would go out.

It was no fun getting ready alone. I had no heart to listen to music or drink vodka. In silence broken only by drips, I applied pink eye shadow and pulled on a silver vest-top, not caring whether they complemented one another. The red dress Fern bought me hung in the bathroom window like a holiday towel from a balcony, fluttering back and forth. I'd sewn the frill up and reattached the strap but had no desire to wear it again. It attracted attention I didn't want and reminded me of things I'd rather forget. If I had to go out I would dress down, not up. So I carried it into Fern's bedroom and put it in the empty wardrobe. I imagined her suddenly in the doorway, half dressed and offering to style my hair. 'Fuck you,' I whispered. I had never felt more alone.

Victor whistled merrily and dropped bin bags in the back garden as seven-forty approached. At the taxi's horn I grabbed a jacket and bag, glad to escape drips, watches and women I no longer needed.

The car hurtled past flashy bars full of festive partiers. The driver – an identity card on the dashboard said BOB FRACKLEHURST – sang merrily along to the radio.

'Christmas work do?' he asked after a while. He reminded me a little of my dad, and my heart squeezed.

'Yeah, kind of,' I said. 'The place I volunteer. Annual night out.'

'My Trish volunteers,' he said. 'Wonderful thing to do. Blessed are the ones who give so generously, especially at this time of year. When you give like that, you deserve whatever makes your heart whole.'

I was tempted to belittle his words with a flippant comment, but resisted.

I decided I wasn't going to drink, a resolve that faltered as we pulled up at Sharky's and I faced going in alone.

'OK?' asked Bob.

'Yeah,' I said, paying the fare.

'Have a great evening,' he smiled.

I waited ten minutes on the pavement and then made my way inside. A Christmassy Mariah Carey song blasted out of speakers. The floor was sticky with spilled drinks. Bare-chested and full-bearded barmen wore Santa hats over white wigs. I hate walking into pubs on my own. I always imagine I'll never find whoever I'm meeting and have to wander around before pretending I've somewhere more important to be and going home. The multi-mirrored, flashing space was hot; after the sub-zero street, I felt as if my make-up was melting. I loosened my jacket while scanning the many heads and pushed through the tightly packed bodies.

Then I saw Christopher.

He hadn't seen me yet, which gave me a chance to study him. Under a neon 'Cocktails' sign he frowned at something on his phone. Even though he wore the usual Flood Crisis apparel, he seemed different; he had jeans on and the black shirt he wore on our last shift; his hair was as unkempt as any day on the phones, but somehow he was sharper, more real. One hand on his chest and the other holding his phone, he fidgeted, so unlike the relaxed crisis-line man.

When he suddenly looked up I sought another face to study. Jangly Jane was talking to a man in a fake-leather jacket, nodding like one of those toys on the back shelf of a car. Nearby, Norman leaned on the bar wearing an England T-shirt and laughing too much at a blonde woman. I saw Condom Kath with an old man in a string vest, and Lindsey, who waved vigorously. When I looked back at the 'Cocktails' sign Christopher had gone. The neon flickered, went out for a moment and came back on; the letter C was missing.

'We didn't know if you'd come.' Lindsey grabbed my arm. Her hair was teased into a dramatic sweep and gold glitter highlighted her cheeks. 'You can save me from Norman – he's hammered! What are you drinking? I know the barman; I'll get you one for nowt.'

I thought of Fern but instantly pushed her image away. 'Gin sling,' I said. 'Large. With ice.'

Reflected in every mirror, it appeared that multiple Lindseys made for the bar, all gold-highlighted. While waiting for her, a draught tickled my neck, like a ghostly kiss.

Like breath.

In the festive song I heard the word 'sweets': Will's pet name for me.

The breathy draught on my neck had me expecting him to say it. Expecting him to move my hair from my shoulder, which I'd automatically pull back again. Had he returned from Scotland to see if I'd let him affectionately reposition my hair? Let him call me sweets without protest?

No, he loved Miranda. And I didn't want him.

Maybe Robin had returned to haunt me, to nuzzle my neck. Had he seen my solitude exaggerated by the mirrors and sought me out? I heard again that word in the climax of the song, the word he'd called me while his hands climbed. 'Tiger'. Shame and regret warmed my cheeks.

Goosebumps rippled my skin's surface.

Maybe Fern had come home and her smile had caused the whisper of breath. A sorry ghost to go home with, to be at my feet when I woke. I frowned.

Then a heavy hand touched my shoulder and I thought it must be that fourth ghost, like the evil godmother at Sleeping Beauty's christening. The ghost whose face I could never fully see but whose imagined presence sent my hand to hold my chest, my stomach. I didn't know this ghost's name only that he would be tall and hairy and would call me all the names I hated.

It wasn't him.

No, this ghost said the name I liked. The one I'd chosen: 'Katrina.'

I turned.

'You don't have a drink, Katrina.' Christopher looked at my empty hands.

'You don't have your date,' I said.

'She stood me up last week.'

'Lindsey's getting me one. She didn't show up?'

'I was relieved.' He laughed and took a sip from his beer bottle, seemingly less anxious now than earlier. 'I just got hammered on cheap wine with my sister and her husband. Apparently Emma – the non-date – had a family emergency. I think her fish died or maybe the neighbour's cat.'

I laughed.

'I just texted you,' he said.

I found my phone and read the message: 'I hope you come out tonight, Christopher.'

'My fish died,' I said. 'So you're very lucky I did.'

Lindsey appeared with my gin sling and an ostentatious blue cocktail in her other hand. 'I think it's called a "blue sextini"', she said. 'Hey Christopher, how was your date?' Everyone seemed to know about it.

'Not good,' he said.

'Well, I think Kath's single,' she smiled. 'I'm off to dance.'

She disappeared in a flash of gold and black. The music intensified and the hordes cheered when a DJ took to a small podium with silver tinsel twined around it. I drank. The ice tinkled in my glass like anchor chains in a port.

'You look really n—' began Christopher at the same time as I said, 'Will you be—'

'You go first,' he insisted.

'No, you...'

Norman joined us. Sweaty hair stuck to his neck; his eyes shone wildly. 'Can you believe this place?' he said. I caught Christopher's eye and he raised an eyebrow. 'I love it. Nice to see you, Katrina. Didn't think you liked any of us enough to come out. What are you drinking?'

'I want whatever he's on,' I whispered to Christopher as we followed Norman to the rest of the Flood Crisis party in the corner.

Christopher touched my arm, leaned close and whispered, 'I think Norman's on another planet, so we should maybe stick with beer.'

I said hi to Jangly Jane but she ignored me, even when fake-leather-jacket guy looked at my chest and asked for an introduction. Kath drank red wine and introduced me to Nigel, the string-vest man, and then I chatted for a while to Lindsey about a sex call she'd taken the previous day where the man asked her to pretend she was a headmistress called Myrtle.

Norman dragged me to meet Chris who was really Chris, Al who wasn't Al, and Ed who was Ed everywhere. I couldn't remember who was who. Names dripped like a broken tap. Holding my third gin, I called Norman Paul and Kath Nigel and laughed along to conversations I couldn't hear. The music grew louder as my glass became emptier.

Then I saw the bushy-faced man.

He watched me from the other side of the room. Black eyes studied me from beneath his bristled brow. His name rose in my throat with the gin. But I couldn't remember it; I just couldn't *remember*.

You don't belong here, I thought. *You're in my head.*

When I looked back he'd gone.

Where had I seen him before? Before, he was the phantom when I woke. There were so many mirrors and so many people, I could barely focus. Why had he moved from my bed-end when I was half conscious into the real world – to a hospital lift, and now here, on a night out?

Christopher handed me another drink; I spilt some as I pulled away. I was confused when I couldn't detach from him. My bracelet had caught on his cuff, the tiny fastener tangled in a loose thread. We were tied together.

'Hold still.' He fiddled with the clasp. 'Guess this is the only way I can get you to stay here and talk to me, eh?'

I shrugged, nodded toward the Flood Crisis gang. 'I don't even know any of their names so how can I talk to them?' He freed the bracelet and I rubbed my wrist. 'So who are you when you're not here?' I asked him.

'Not here?' He looked around the bar, which was suddenly full of boisterous women in pink T-shirts with 'Chantelle's Getting Married' across the chest. I hardly dared look, afraid I'd see the bushy man again.

'I mean not at Flood Crisis. What do people call you?'

'Chris.'

I wouldn't say it.

'And who are you, Katrina?'

I wasn't sure how to answer, but Norman saved me when he came over, silver Bride-To-Be sash wrapped like a tie around his neck.

'Who's the lucky man?' I asked.

'A gang of hens accosted me. It's Chantelle's wedding tomorrow.' He swilled beer everywhere. 'Man, I love this song!'

Another Christmas anthem filled the air. Bride-To-Be-Chantelle pulled him onto the dance floor near the DJ's box, stripped him of his sash and gyrated against his body while the masses cheered.

Christopher said something, but I couldn't hear over the racket. Faces blurred. I'd had too much to drink, too fast. The chanting for Chantelle to dance sounded like 'tiger, tiger, *tiger*'. I'd no idea what they really sang. Among the spectators I saw the bushy man again. All eyes were on the performance except his; and through the wiry beard and black moustache, he smiled.

'Just going to the bar!' yelled Christopher.

I wanted to say *no, don't leave me*, but resisted, not sure why I was so afraid. When I looked back into the crowd, the bushy man had gone. Norman had fallen to his knees and Chantelle wrapped her sash about his neck, tugging on it and rubbing her backside against his rapturous face. My hands began to burn and I scratched my palm vigorously.

'You'll make it worse,' said Christopher.

I pressed my palms against the cool of the glass he handed me. Chantelle had abandoned Norman for her pals, and he staggered back to us, topless now.

'She stole my shirt,' he slurred.

Chantelle snaked past, waving Norman's red T-shirt like a trophy. She shouted the name of the club they were going to. It was the one I'd been to with Fern.

'I'm going,' said Norman, with a wild grin. 'You should. I bet Kath will. She said she's not had such a great night since Hector's funeral.'

He bounced back to the others, his back scratched like Jesus heading for the crucifixion.

'We can't ruin Kath's best night since Hector's funeral.' Christopher finished his beer. 'And we should take photos of Norman for blackmail purposes.'

'I don't know.' I thought of the night of my birthday; all the ghosts I might encounter if I returned to that club.

'You don't know whether you want to watch Norman strip completely?'

'Sorry. You go, don't let me ruin your night.'

'It won't be much fun without you,' he said gently.

Once, a hundred years ago, Will had woken up and stared at me like I was the only person in the world. When I'd asked him what was wrong, whether I had some mark or other on my face, he'd said he was seeing me for the first time. He'd said his dad felt like that about his mother all the time. It was what kept them together. I'd always been scared to see someone that way. But Christopher looked different now. I'd thought it was that he'd stepped out of the crisis-line shadow, emerged into the glitzy glare of this over-lit bar. But this wasn't new light – it was just light. This was seeing him for the first time, fully lit.

'Not fun, with Norman?' I asked him.

The Flood Crisis gang headed in a single chain for the doors and I grabbed Lindsey's arm and told her I wasn't going to the club.

'Are you coming, Christopher?' she asked him.

He looked at me. 'Go,' I told him. 'I'll be fine.'

'You'll stay here on your own?'

'No. Yes. I don't know.'

He left me and followed Lindsey. When he spoke into her ear and I couldn't hear the words I felt like I had when my mother and Graham shared all the hugs and secrets. I prepared to wander around as though looking for a friend, act like I'd lost someone. Then I would go home alone. Checking in my purse for the taxi fare I fought the sudden urge to cry.

I found a fiver and looked up; Christopher was still there.

'You really think I'd leave you on your own, Katrina?' he said.

I smiled and couldn't think of any name to call him.

'Another drink?' he asked.

'Can we go somewhere quiet? My head's going to explode in here.'

'Quiet? Two-and-a-half weeks before Christmas?'

'I can't stay here,' I insisted.

He nodded and we put our empty glasses on the shelf and headed for the doors. I looked back and thought I saw the bushy man. But it was just a girl with tangled, eighties hair.

Outside, wetness. Water coated cars and road surface and roofs, silvery as cake frosting. My thin jacket served no purpose other than decoration. We ran across the road. Christopher took my hand and held it close to his body. I wondered if he'd let go once we'd dodged the speeding cars, but he didn't.

Up a cobbled backstreet we found a dingy pub that stank of poorly maintained toilets and stale beer. Elderly men gathered at the bar and older couples made use of the shadowy corners. No music and no Norman.

'Same again?'

Christopher let go of my hand and I fiddled with my buttons. He handed me a drink and we headed for the pub's gloomy rear, where we found a stained but empty sofa facing another, where a couple were chatting. We sat, our knees only inches apart. This was perhaps my seventh drink. My eyelids sagged and my tongue fell asleep.

'I'm sorry I dragged you away from the gang,' I managed to say.

'I'm not,' said Christopher.

The couple opposite were both maybe fifty, and I guessed it was a second or third date. They held hands and looked at one another, the way lovers do when they are yet to see each other call the toaster a bitch for burning bread or smash glasses during a tantrum.

'I didn't think you'd come tonight,' said Christopher.

'I came because...' I couldn't find the answer.

'Why?'

'Because I had nothing better to do.'

Finishing my drink, I plonked the glass on the table between the sofas. The words in my head fell apart, as if a Scrabble board had been knocked over. I couldn't remember if he'd said he was Chris or Christopher to people in the real world. Had I told him my real name? I was barely even sure what it was. Katrina or Catherine? Catherine-Maria? And I wasn't sure if I'd imagined the bushy man or if he'd been real. Yet I could hear the conversation I'd had with Norman three days before – about my progress and the future of my shifts – like it was playing on a radio nearby.

'So you're changing your Wednesday shift.' My voice sounded like a record on the wrong speed.

'Am I?' Christopher frowned; I studied the lines.

'Norman said Wednesdays are awkward and you'd prefer not to do them.'

'Norman said that?' He shook his head. 'No, I just didn't want you to feel *you* had to swap.'

'You'll be a buddy for someone else now.'

'I'm sure you don't want to see my ugly face every time you come to Flood Crisis.' He scratched his stubble.

I shrugged.

'Glad you're enjoying it enough to stay,' he said.

'Enjoying it might not be the best phrase.' I paused. 'Do you enjoy it? Go on, give me your usual all-knowing answer.' I bit my tongue too late: I'd fallen into my bitch role again.

'Like you say, enjoy is an odd word,' he said. 'My father killed himself when I was twelve.' He had told me before; I'd forgotten that too and I felt terrible. 'He was depressed. Clinically depressed, not just angsty, poor-me depressed.' Christopher swirled his drink around the glass. 'Probably would have been on lithium for the rest of his life. One day he took them all and some paracetamol and a litre of vodka. He swallowed the lot in a deserted warehouse near the river. A dog-walker found him, still alive, but he didn't make it to the hospital.'

'I'm sorry,' I said.

'Don't be. He was a pretty lousy father: beat my mother up; sired different kids by many different women while married to her; stole from his sister.'

'No, I'm sorry for being a bitch.'

He didn't say anything.

'My father died when I was eight,' I said. 'Not by his own hand – heart attack.'

Christopher said maybe loss at a young age made us search harder for answers. That didn't mean we were better at finding them than the next person, but we craved them that much harder.

The speaker nearby suddenly crackled and music drifted into our space – a rock song from long ago. Christopher seemed closer to me on the sofa but I wasn't sure if the drink had blurred my perception, made distance appear smaller. His thigh touched mine when he moved. I was acutely aware of his nearness.

Christopher looked at me with deliberation as though he was a card-player considering his next move, and I knew he would kiss me. I didn't know if it would be in a moment or later but I knew. I smiled and he asked, 'What?' but I just shook my head. Then he put his hand on my cheek. I didn't brush it away. His fingers were soft but definite. I put my hand over them, saying without words that I accepted the affection.

'I came tonight because I hoped you'd be here,' I said.

He leaned closer and paused to look at me. Then he pressed his slightly parted mouth to mine. For a moment, we didn't even move. I saw the couple opposite smile and whisper before closing my eyes and savouring his warm, beery taste, his breath, his understanding, his pause.

When he opened my mouth with his, I kissed back. It seemed as if the song slowed with us, bass line intense, words unimportant. Christopher kissed me harder; I scratched his arm's skin until he bit my lower lip with a groan. It was just us, just warmth and song.

Then an image of Robin and running rabbits and unwelcome words jumped into my head. I squeezed my eyes more tightly shut but the sinister syllables opened them again. Someone whispered 'tiger' in my ear. Christopher played with the strap of my top and pressed his thigh against mine.

I pulled away, shaking my head. 'I'm not, I can't. I just can't.'

'Did I do something wrong?'

'No, you did nothing.'

His hand hovered near my face as though assessing where to land and his eyes studied me, not invasive but concerned.

'I like you too much,' I said.

He smiled. 'You like me too much to kiss me?'

'Yes.' I thought of Will, of Robin, of the bushy stranger, of all the ghosts and of words that might explode if I let Christopher touch me or whisper in my ear. 'If we do this we'll end up at your house, or mine, in bed probably – if not tonight, another time. And then we'll end up shagging in a chair at the Flood Crisis place because I'm a freak and have to be tied up or have death or trauma to distract me. And then we'll want it more, and I can only do it if you argue with me and tie my hands, and I don't want that, and you won't think that I'm worth being with, and I'll have to end it and then you won't even want to be my friend, and that's terrible.'

He smiled. 'I kind of like your prediction – except for the parts about ending it. We can imagine that a different way. Tell me more about this chair.'

'I'm not being playful.' I shook my head. 'I can't do this.'

'We don't have to do anything.' He was serious. 'We can just talk.'

I stood, picked up my bag and knocked my glass over. Clumsy Catherine. The couple opposite tore their eyes from one another.

'I just can't,' I said.

Disorientated by the dark and the throbbing song beat, I looked for a door, any door. Everywhere I turned people grinned, eyes glowing orange, faces hairy, bristled, waving huge hands, mouthing words. I finally found the exit and burst through it. I leaned against the wall, breathing hard. A taxi pulled up to the kerb and I opened its door.

'Katrina, wait.' Christopher emerged from the pub. 'Don't run away. Tell me what's wrong.'

'There was a man.' The words came out before I'd realised it.

'A man?'

'Yes. He used to just be *there* ... when I woke up ... Now...'

'Now what?' asked Christopher carefully.

'He's been everywhere, following me, watching me.'

'In the pub?'

'No, not in there, in the other one.' I shivered. 'I'm scared he's just in my head – but even more scared he's not.'

'Katrina, I'm not leaving you like this. I'm not just after a shag. You should know me well enough by now to realise that...'

'Are you OK?' asked the driver. It was the one who'd dropped me off earlier. What was his name? I couldn't recall.

'She will be,' said Christopher.

We got in the taxi and I moved to the other side, wrapping my flimsy jacket around me.

'Where do you live, Katrina?' asked Christopher.

'I know,' said the driver, concern apparent in his eyes. He headed for the west of the city.

'Don't say any words, will you?' I asked Christopher.

'I'll not talk if you don't want me to.'

'No, I mean strange words, names.' I'd never done LSD but imagined this was how it must feel. In my mind colourful words danced with one another: it was a mocking performance, and the colours were bloody. Large and small letters joined hands but I would not read what they created. 'I think I'm going mad. I'm drunk but it's not that.'

'It's OK, Katrina, I don't have to talk.'

I watched the lights fly past, my view blurred like a ruined painting. 'I think I know the man,' I said.

'Who is he?'

'I don't know.'

'Did you really see him?'

'I don't know.'

'Do you like him?'

'No. God, no.'

'What's his name?'

'Please don't ask me.'

We were at the flat. Christopher got out and paid the driver through the window. As I was about to follow him, I remembered: Bob Fracklehurst. That was the driver's name. He'd said earlier, 'When you give like that, you deserve whatever makes your heart whole.'

I leaned towards him between the seats and said, 'My heart's all smashed up.'

Bob Fracklehurst must have remembered our conversation. 'But if it's the kind that makes you volunteer,' he said, 'it's the best kind.'

Inside, the flat was cold. I put my bag on the counter and said I'd turn the heating back on. The tap still dripped, faster than earlier. Drip-drip-drip. I removed the soaked tea towel and put another beneath the gush.

'It's broken,' I told Christopher. 'Been getting worse all week.'

He looked at it, touched the handle. 'Maybe I could fix it for you?'

I turned the kettle on and listened to the water bubbling inside it. He looked around the flat, at the pictures, at my things, touching the photo of me with Geraldine the rabbit and saying it was cute. I looked at the shadow over my small body and couldn't stand up anymore. Christopher put the picture back near the plant pot and came to me.

I sat on the sofa, held my face. 'My head's spinning.'

'I'll make us something,' he said. 'Stay there. You need a hot, sweet drink.'

I heard cups tinkling as he found them in the cupboard and thought of us at Flood Crisis. If only I could call a memory helpline and get the answers I wanted. But what would I do then? What if the knowledge was worse than the questions?

'You have drawers like mine,' said Christopher.

'What?'

'I can only open one when the other is closed. I always think it's like someone with Alzheimer's – some part of the brain is always closed. To have them both open together you'd have to tear out the kitchen and rebuild the whole thing. God, I should shut up.'

In the corner the tap continued to drip. The water's plop echoed; every sound but that one was muted. Drip-drip-drip.

I looked at Christopher and his lips moved slowly but the words drowned. In the disharmony, I heard my name, each letter a droplet. But it was not Katrina or Catherine that it spelled. I heard the name no one called me anymore. The name no one sang, no one wrote, no one loved anymore. I squeezed my head.

Christopher touched my arm gently, gave me a coffee and sat at my side on the sofa.

'She's here,' I whispered.

'Who?' The word was slow, eerie.

'Catherine-Maria.'

'Who's she?' No judgement clouded his tone, and he didn't move away in fear.

'Me,' I said. 'She's me.'

I didn't know how to explain it when I barely understood myself. I could hear a child. The tap spelled her name. I heard her laugh. She opened the flat door and came in. She was nine. She began to cry. She was me. I cried.

'What is it?' Christopher touched my cheek in a way that suggested nothing more than kindness; I leaned into it. He didn't wipe away my tears, just let them fall over his hands.

I was scared but not of him. Not of her either but of what she would tell me. She was full of words and names, and I knew if I listened and let her into my heart they would be black and many. 'Everything we need to know is in there', my dad had written of the heart. 'When you give like that, you deserve whatever makes your heart whole', Bob Fracklehurst had said.

'She's going to tell me.' I covered my ears, knocking Christopher's hands away. 'She knows all the words,' I said.

'Don't be scared; words can't touch you.'

'They can,' I said.

'Maybe you should listen to her, Katrina. What if you listen to her and I sit here with you? I'll sit just here and I won't leave you.'

The tap dripped. I thought I heard footsteps and pictured the bushy man on the metal stairs outside, mounting them in time with the water's rhythm. It was like being flooded all over again. Drip-drip-drip. I wanted to pick up the sofa and the TV and carry them to safety. Drip-drip-drip.

'Don't let anyone in.' I looked at the door.

'It's locked,' he said. 'No one's coming in.'

'They're already here.'

'I'm here,' said Christopher. 'Don't be scared.'

'You can't just sit here. It's the middle of the night. You must have somewhere to go.'

'Katrina, I can stay.'

'I'm not Katrina,' I whispered.

'Who are you?'

'I'm Catherine-Maria.'

I couldn't see Christopher anymore. I knew he was there and was glad but I no longer heard his gentle words. The room melted away like snow and my raw hands softened into smaller ones and my hair untangled like thin snakes. My heart grew big and full, and my head bounced with new words and my heart with questions. And I knew buried under the weight of those heavy words was something terrible that would answer all those questions. Something grave that would shatter my nine-year-old heart.

There was something else – some*one* else. Like a cold spider, the memory stirred in my head and spun an icy web about my brain. Someone else crawled in.

It was him. It was the bushy-haired man.

I remembered.

21

Maria in the moon

Nanny Eve chose my name: Catherine-Maria. When she calls it in her sing-song voice I am as beautiful as the sparkling Virgin Mary statue in her hallway. Virgin Mary is always there when I go for Sunday tea; she smiles sweetly, palms out as though she wants one-pound pocket money. She stands on the tall table next to a candle and I'm not allowed to touch her.

Nanny Eve would let me, she says, but Mother says Virgin Mary is too precious and I'm only nine and too clumsy.

I broke the flower pot in the garden last month. It was waiting for soil and seeds and I had to stay in my room until teatime. When Mother tucked me in I told her it wasn't on purpose and she said my hands are little accidents waiting to happen.

I used to touch Virgin Mary when no one was looking, stroke her blue dress and kiss her stony feet. But now I'm scared my accident fingers will crack her smooth face. I wouldn't like to break her.

Nanny Eve says virgin means pure. Pure Mary. I think it would be nice to be pure. To be precious and not have fingers that mess up pretty things.

My English teacher, Mrs Willis, said Catherine-Maria is an ostentatious name. So I asked Mother what ostentatious meant and she said pretentious and that Mrs Willis was embittered. I asked what embittered meant and Mother told me to go play on the swing. She said I ask too many questions.

Mother is busy. She likes flowers and baking and cleaning. She wears a pink apron with palm trees and sunshine on the front, and rolls pastry and cuts shapes and sprinkles sugar. All day long.

She's in the kitchen when I go to school and in the kitchen when I come home. When I've had my tea she tells me to go and play on the swing, but it's no fun because Dad hung it too high, so my feet don't reach the ground and I can't push myself off. I call her to help me, but she says she's busy. I want to ask her why – why she is busy, what she is doing, why don't her cakes taste sweet even with sugar? but I know she will say I ask too many questions.

My dad liked questions. He said that it's good to ask them, that it's how we learn, alongside watching and living. He died last year when I was eight. I miss him. My heart feels like a hand is squeezing all the love out of it when I think about him. He answered every question I asked, and I had lots and lots.

He told me about my mum, who I've never met because she died having me. He told me that the moon is about 250,000 miles away from us and that the dark patches are called *maria*, which is Latin for seas. So my name is in the sky, right by the stars. Maria in the moon.

Dad showed me how to tell if the allotment tomatoes are ready for picking; he said that they ripen from the bottom to the top, and are heavy and even when done. He gave me a book about rabbits when I asked if I could have a pet, and he said he'd buy me one when I was nine. He helped me learn my spellings every Thursday night and so I always got ten out of ten on Fridays.

But I'm not in the top English group anymore. I never get full marks now. Mrs Willis said she is disappointed and she will be having a word with my mother. I don't think they'll be words that I like.

I like to sit in Dad's green chair in the study, hugging his cushion and talking to him. But it's difficult because I can think of millions of questions and none of the answers. I try to say his answers but they sound stupid. Mother asks who I'm talking to, but I don't tell her because she'll be cross and I'll probably have to go to my room again.

So I whisper his words but they're not really him. Not really his.

Then I wander into the living room and sit at Nanny Eve's feet and she sings, and I know it's because I make her happy. She pats my head and calls me Catherine-Maria and knits hats for her friends and coats for my dolls and tells me about Poorly Patsy who hasn't got long left, and she sings and I don't ask any questions.

I don't like Uncle Henry.

I haven't told anyone I don't like him because I think they all do and because Nanny Eve says God said we should love our neighbours. But since he doesn't live next door and I've never seen God, I think it's OK not to like Uncle Henry.

Uncle Henry has been visiting a lot since Dad died. He is my dad's brother, Aunty Mary's brother too. He has a bushy black beard that I think birds could live in and matching eyebrows and hair. He says he will cut it soon, that he's experimenting with it. I whisper to Dad, *What does experimenting mean?* They all laugh when Uncle Henry is here. He has a booming voice, not like Dad's, who spoke softly about numbers and the moon and musical notes. Mother makes beef casserole and gets out the blue swirly plates, and Aunty Mary with a hairy chin comes for tea and brings a homemade cake and Uncle Martin comes too.

Uncle Henry always gets a second portion and the sugar gets stuck in his beard as he talks about his *travels* – about sunny places and deep rivers and craggy mountains. Mother says she wishes she were free to escape and go to the sun. She always acts silly and smiley when he's here. Aunty Mary says Uncle Henry brings the sun here.

He is very nice to me and gives me a pound every time he visits, so I have lots. My friend Anna says I'm lucky because her uncle just gives her toffees that are so old the shiny wrapping won't come off and she can't even eat them. And then he falls asleep in the chair and snores. I say she could have some of my pound coins because they are just sitting in a jar on my windowsill. In the morning, they shine golden in the light and I wonder if maybe Uncle Henry did bring the sun from his travels and he coated them in it.

He brings laughter into our house. He makes Aunty Mary giggle. He makes Mother clap her hands. She says I'm grumpy for ignoring him, and she doesn't let me have any cake. Aunty Mary sneaks me some under the table, but my throat always seems to close up and the crumbs make me gag and the sun burns me through the window. I don't think it likes me.

Uncle Henry bought me a rabbit.

I love my rabbit, but I wish Dad had given her to me instead. I pretend that he did and hold her to my cheek so I can hear her squidgy nose sniffing and feel the tickle of whiskers on my chin. She's called Geraldine and she is black and white. She lives in a hutch in the shed. Uncle Henry said that having the hutch in the shed would keep her safe from cats and foxes. I give her carrots and cabbage and ask her questions, but she just wiggles her nose.

Is she the one you would have chosen? I ask Dad.

My friend Anna comes to see Geraldine, and we take turns brushing her long fur. I'm better at it. I'm not scared when Geraldine wriggles and scratches because I know how to calm her down. Her heart beats really fast under the fur and I hold her until it slows down. Dad told me how. They had rabbits when he was little and they ran all over the place, mating and making millions more. Anna says I'm lucky, that she wants Henry to be her uncle.

I'd happily have her uncle instead.

Sometimes Uncle Henry visits when it is just me in the house. My mother puts keys and tissues in her bag, wipes the kitchen counter and says she'll be back at four. I look at the heart-shaped clock on the wall near the oven and it's always twelve. I'm good at maths and so I know how much time we have.

Uncle Henry tells her not to hurry, that we'll be fine, we shall have fun, just him and me. I don't want her to go. I asked her not to go the first time and she told me not to *resent* her for escaping the house. That if I loved her I'd want her to live. She put on her furry coat and looked cross. I do love her. I do want her to live. I don't want her to die, like Dad or my real mum. She kisses my forehead when she goes, but her lips don't touch my skin.

She smells safe.

Uncle Henry smells of hair and calls me 'Tiger'. He tickles my chin and says, 'Tiger, let's go and see Geraldine.'

In the shed Uncle Henry puts his scratchy face near my ear and blows into it. I laugh because it must be a game but it's one I have never played and I'm not sure what I have to do. Leaning into the cage, I touch Geraldine, but he says that we can have more fun.

Just us.

And he whispers to me, 'If you tell anyone about this game they won't believe you because it's in your head, Catherine. Listen to me, Tiger. Listen to me; it's in your head. This special thing we'll do, it's magical, it's all up here, and no one will believe you anyway.' Then he taps his head and I hear his black thoughts moving around.

I want my name back. Tiger isn't my name; neither is plain Catherine. Tiger isn't in the sky; Catherine isn't in the sky. Catherine-*Maria* is in the sky.

I think about the sky when he puts his hairy mouth on mine. He doesn't kiss me like Uncle Martin does or like my dad used to. He doesn't just brush my lips with his. He holds my face and pulls my hair and pushes my mouth open with his and then puts his tongue into my mouth. It's hot and wet and I don't like it. I squirm and wriggle like Geraldine does in any hands but mine, and he stops and tells me I'll get used to it.

'If your dad was still here, it's what he would do with you.'

I shouted the first time he said that. I said, 'No, no, no, my dad would never make me hurt.'

But Uncle Henry said that it's time to grow up, that I am a big girl. He shushes me with his finger now, but he doesn't need to. I am used to it. I don't argue. I am a big girl. He bought me a rabbit and it's all in my head. I think about the sky and about being in the moon when he kisses me and puts his hand inside my dress, and I don't know what it's called but I don't like it.

So I whisper in my head.

Maria in the moon, Maria in the moon, Maria in the moon.

He squeezes the top of my leg so hard I cry. He digs nails into my skin. He says, 'It's not love unless it hurts,' and kisses my tears.

His fingers move into my underwear and I kick because no one touches me there. Not even my mother when I had chickenpox all over and she had to cover me in cream. It hurts so much I think I will die. His fingers have broken me, reached inside my tummy, pushing, ripping, hurting, tearing.

Then he undoes his belt and drops it to the floor and Geraldine runs to the back of her cage. Uncle Henry is cross because I bite him. But I don't want to see and squeeze my eyes shut. I feel spiky hair and hot skin and something hard and warm but I don't open my eyes.

'That's my Tiger,' says Uncle Henry. 'That's my Catherine.'

He squeezes my hand inside his and moves it, and he is breathing hard. After he stops, a long time after, I open my eyes and there is blood and something else on my dress. Something warm and sticky like chickenpox cream. Uncle Henry says he will sort it out; he will wash it before my mother comes back and he will say it was an accident. That I fell in the mud.

'You are beautiful,' he tells me. 'My beautiful Catherine. My Tiger.'

I think that maybe his hands are the accidents waiting to happen.

Mother says they will call me Catherine now. We have lasagne for tea and she lets me have extra cake for being quiet at the table. She says I'm not a baby anymore so I need a grown-up name. I will soon be ten.

Nanny Eve says that my full name, the name she chose, is beautiful. She says that Catherine means pure and Maria is the Latin form of Mary. Pure Mary. She says that I should still be called Catherine-Maria if I want to be. But I don't know what I want or who I am.

Mother shouts at me for ignoring Nanny Eve's question. I can't eat the cake. My throat feels like the sawdust in Geraldine's cage. Mother says I'm never grateful and don't deserve a lovely name. Nanny Eve tries to pat my hands, but I don't want her touching them. Mother throws the cake in the bin and says they will all call me Catherine and that is that, no questions.

I don't like questions anymore anyway.

It is Sunday now. After church. Nanny Eve asks why I knocked the Virgin Mary over and smashed her face into sharp bits and won't say sorry. I don't have an answer. I can't remember. Mother asks why I'm so moody. I don't have an answer. But I know I am Catherine. No questions. Even Nanny Eve calls me Catherine now, and her voice is never quite as sing-song.

When I'm with Uncle Henry I'm Tiger. We stroke Geraldine, his big hand on mine, and he reminds me that she might die if I tell anyone about our special time in the shed.

'You're a big girl now,' he says. 'You're very special to me.'

Geraldine is a rabbit and she is part of me. She is in the hutch and she is between my legs, hairless there, smooth but bleeding, sore and hurting. Uncle Henry sits me on his knee. The shark belt buckle cuts into my bottom.

Until he takes it off.

Geraldine never stays. She covers her head with her black paw, one ear flopping over her eye. I don't stay either. My body is here. His hands stroke up my dress and push inside me and his beard rubs my cheek and leg. But my mind is in the moon. I learn my spellings for school but can't find the words. I spell *m-a-r-i-a* and *m-o-o-n* and Uncle Henry shushes me and shushes me and shushes me. Before we go back to the house he tidies my hair and wipes me with a tissue. There is no blood any more. No pain. *Because it's all in my head.*

Uncle Henry strokes my hair and says he'd like to take me when he goes away. When I grow up I'm going to have my own house with a red roof, white bricks and a painted wall. On it I'll draw a beautiful face. But not Virgin Mary, someone *truly* pure. And I'm not going to have people in my house. I won't let anyone in. I'll let my friend Anna stay because she likes the same things as me – except Uncle Henry. We like to dress up and play card games and sleep side by side. We'll make cakes and style each other's hair and laugh. We'll borrow each other's clothes and stay up late and talk.

We won't have boyfriends or uncles, just each other.

It is snowing today. The sky is grey. It's going to be Christmas soon and Mother has chosen a silver tree. It's bare in the corner, waiting to be prettied. I'm in trouble for losing clothes again. I can't tell Mother my dresses are in the bin, that they're messed up and torn, because it's only in my head.

She hangs baubles on the new tree and says that Uncle Henry has gone and he won't be coming back. Not ever.

The table is set for three and there is no cake. Nanny Eve knits a long pink scarf in the chair by the window. She looks like she lost something and hasn't a clue where to look for it. Mother says Uncle Henry has gone back on his travels, that I should forget him because he'll never be visiting again.

Aunty Mary took down the picture of him holding a set of shark's teeth. She cries in the bathroom when she visits us and she won't let Uncle Martin in and he tells her through the door that he loves her and hates to see her sad. I wonder if she is crying because Uncle Henry took her sun.

Or because there is a hand around her heart.

When she comes out she pats my head and hugs me really tight. 'Forget him,' she says. 'Forget him, forget him.'

I think Uncle Henry was never here. I think we all made him up. It's easy to forget a story. You just close the pages and all the words suffocate. The pictures take longer to dissolve.

But they do after a while.

I open the shed door and then Geraldine's wire hutch flap and call her name. I can hear Mother talking on the telephone to someone inside the house. My footprints are deep in the snow and my hands itch and burn even though it's cold. I whisper for Geraldine to go, to run, to escape. But she sits at the back of the cage, wiggling her black nose at me. I love her so much. My heart feels like a hand is squeezing all the hate out of it.

Run rabbit, run rabbit, run run run, I whisper.

She comes to my sore hand and licks it and sniffs the air. Then she leaps onto the wooden floor and lollops into the garden. She twists and leaps across the white and I laugh.

Mother is coming now. I can't stop laughing because Geraldine is free. She will not die. Mother shouts at me and chases Geraldine and tries to catch her. But she squeezes under the fence and snow flies away from her feet like that stuff they throw at weddings.

Mother shouts and shakes her head and shouts again. I have to go to my room. She pulls me upstairs, saying I'm reprehensible, and I don't even care what it means. I tell her she's not my real mum anyway. Tell her she's a bastard and I never liked her. My heart feels like a hand is squeezing all the love out of it. But I can't stop laughing. I know that it's not love unless it hurts. But I can't stop laughing.

My mother calls me Catherine, and I cry.

22

Nothing's unfixable

Christopher turned the tap full on and allowed it to spurt an angry waterfall for a few seconds, then twisted it off with a squeak. He looked at me; we waited. It didn't drip. I stared, expecting it to defy him, but no more water escaped the rusting spout.

He had fixed it.

'What did you do to it?' I asked.

He shrugged. 'I just fiddled about with the pipe, tightened it here and there.'

'But it was completely broken.'

'Nothing's unfixable. Did I disturb you?'

I sat up, pulling the duvet with me. The sofa seemed to sag under the weight of my full memory. I emerged from its warmth enough to look around the room.

Everything seemed different. Not only because Christopher stood in the kitchen, looking like he needed a shave and some sleep. It was different like it had been rebuilt after a flood. Like someone had polished it. Edges appeared sharp, colours defined, and the light coming through the half-open curtains bright.

Dangling from a hook on the door, I could make out the individual fibres of my scarf; flecks of rich orange within brown, fat strands with thin. The picture of me with Geraldine the rabbit lay on the coffee table where Christopher had abandoned it. I knew now who had taken the picture and this knowledge enhanced its colours. It should have darkened them, but I saw sun not just shadow over the dress.

'Katrina?'

I looked at Christopher, awkwardly leaning against the kitchen worktop, jeans creased. Our dirty cups from last night sat on the draining board. His face was full of a million questions.

'Where did you sleep?' I asked. 'Did I fall asleep before you?'

He came to the sofa and sat at my feet as Fern had done so many times, as Nanny Eve used to. He held the watch. Looking at it I remembered the strap chafing my wrist. I liked the memory; it was a reminder of pain being necessary. He glanced at the cushion on the floor, dented where his head must have rested, and said he'd slept there.

'You must have been cold,' I said.

'You left the heating on. It clunked on and off all night. I was fine. I used to go camping all the time, so this was bliss to me. I can sleep on a washing line.'

'We don't have one or I'd have offered you it.'

'You took off the watch,' he said.

I didn't want to talk about Fern. I looked at the radiator as it chugged into life again. Two black bras and a pair of pink socks hung on it. They had been there three days – *I should put them away*, I thought. I looked back at Christopher. I couldn't remember turning the heating on last night.

'You remember what you told me?' he asked gently.

'I remember,' I said, and glanced at the tap, expecting it to drip. But its tears had finally dried up.

Christopher watched me and I couldn't interpret the frown lines.

'Does this change who I am?' I asked. 'Are you repulsed by me?'

'God, no.' He put his hand on the duvet near mine. Not over it; perhaps he *was* revolted, despite his denial. 'Why would I be? You were nine – a *child*. That man was ... he was ... inexcusable.'

I pushed disorderly hair behind my ears and shrugged. They were my thoughts too, but I had to be sure how he felt. I longed for a bath but feared the water might wash away my newfound memory, strip it away as the flood water had Marilyn from my living-room wall.

'Inexcusable,' he said again.

'So why didn't you touch my hand?' I asked.

'I'm afraid,' he admitted.

'So you *do* see me differently.'

'I'm just afraid of hurting you. Afraid I'll seem pushy, presumptive. I don't know what to say. I have no idea how you must feel, what you must want me to say.'

I put a hand over his. My palms flaked but didn't itch. The fire that had kept me awake, driven me to endlessly scratch, had now cooled. Christopher turned his hand palm-upwards to meet it, wrapping his fingers around mine, warm and safe.

'Don't be afraid, I'm tough,' I said.

'You are.'

No intrusive tap dripping or radiator clunking or sound from the Sunday street broke our silence; it was wonderfully quiet.

'What do you want to do?' he asked after a while.

'Today? Now? Or with my life?' I'd never known the answer to that question and today was no different.

'Will you talk to anyone?'

I looked at him. 'I have to tell my mother.'

'Surely you don't have to do anything yet. Wait and see how you feel.'

'I'll never be ready but I *need* to.'

She was the first person I'd thought of when I opened my eyes. Her image brought more questions. Had she known? No. She couldn't have. It was impossible that she could have carried that knowledge all these years and been so frequently insensitive to me. Had she maybe known afterwards and just not found a way to talk about it? I doubted that too; she always spoke her mind. But could I be sure?

'I want her to understand me – like I now do,' I told Christopher. 'I want her to know why I was such a difficult child ... and adult.'

'There's no rush, Katrina.' Christopher squeezed my hand. 'You're still dealing with it yourself.'

'Maybe she'll care.' My voice was barely audible.

Outside, a car screeched to a halt. Heels scraped on path, a girl said her head hurt, a door slammed and it pulled away. Christopher asked if I'd seen my uncle since I was nine, whether he had come back at all.

'No. I'm pretty sure not, anyway. I don't know why he left. It was all very sudden and odd. I'm still getting used to remembering it all. I think one morning he was gone, and everyone was obscure about why. Naturally I didn't ask much – I was more than happy to forget him.' I paused. 'And how well I did *that*...'

Christopher asked if I thought my mother had known – or Aunty Mary, being his sister; and maybe *that* was why Uncle Henry went away. I shook my head. But was I sure?

We sat in silence again. Then after a while he asked if I was OK and looked at me as though I might sprout horns or turn green like the Hulk.

'It was such an intense way to remember,' he said. 'It was like you were there, like it was happening now. I was scared you might never come back. I've heard so many stories on the phones; I've listened to people die; but I've never heard anything like that, Katrina. It was like *you* were dying.'

'I'm not dead.' I squeezed his hand. 'Not knowing why my memory was so vague or why I couldn't recall chunks of the past was worse than last night was. Now I know; and oddly it doesn't feel like a surprise. Maybe I always knew – it doesn't feel like I ever didn't. I might not be fine later or next week, but I'll deal with that then.'

The phone rang. I looked at the time: eleven. Probably my mother. The thought of her unsettled me. I knew what our next conversation might be and wondered if I would be capable of it. I let the phone ring.

'Do you know who it is?' Christopher asked.

'I just don't feel like talking to anyone yet.'

He nodded. We were both accustomed to the phones, had been united by them. It was strange to ignore one together. The last call I'd answered in his presence was from Sid. He'd hung up tired and I'd wandered back into the lounge where Norman waited to have a chat and Christopher had watched me over his paper. I'd watched him too. I'd watched him so often. He had tied a tea towel around my leg's bloody cut that first shift and he hadn't want to swap Wednesdays because of me and he'd fixed my tap. Now he held my hand as a man might his pregnant wife's.

'What are you thinking?' he asked.

'That I'm hungry,' I said. I felt like I hadn't eaten for days.

'Shall I make something – go and get a hot sandwich from somewhere?'

'Toast will be fine.'

'I'll do it.'

I said I could do it and started to get up, but he insisted. In the kitchen, he found bread and dropped two pieces in the toaster, turned on the kettle and rinsed out the cups we'd used the previous night. I pointed to the cupboard and said he'd find marmalade there.

'You need Christmas decorations in here.' He squashed the tea bag in each cup three times. 'There's spare stuff at Flood Crisis – all the volunteers have been fighting to get their hands on that Singing Santa.'

I remembered us sorting through the box of festive trimmings, the confession that his wife had left him on Christmas Eve, giving him the red watch as a parting gift. People don't come back, he'd said.

He was wrong. I had.

The toast popped up and Christopher smeared it with marmalade and brought it and the drinks to where I lounged, still wearing clothes from our night out. For simple food, it tasted incredible. I'd often had marmalade with my dad. It was a quick and easy breakfast when we were going off on some adventure. The orangey taste always filled my mouth with good memories.

'I haven't put a tree up either,' Christopher said.

I thought of that long-ago tree, bare, waiting to be prettied, the year Uncle Henry left. The marmalade soured and I drank tea instead.

'I didn't bother last year,' Christopher continued. 'What's the point? They should do a "tree for one" – like those sad "meals for one". A small tree that fits in the alcove near your freezer full of TV dinners.'

'I don't want one,' I said. 'But I might find a Virgin Mary.'

'I saw one in a junk shop whose eyes lit up red.'

'Just my kind of Mary,' I said.

I loved talking with him like it was a normal Sunday morning, one that any couple anywhere might have. We did not make small talk to avoid bigger talk; instead it augmented our heavier words. But it would have to end. He'd have to leave at some point, and the thought made my chest feel like four bibles were piled on it. I also knew I could not yet take our relationship further, so it was futile fantasising about future cosy breakfasts.

He got up and took the plates and mugs to the sink. I watched him wash and dry them, putting them away in the wrong cupboard.

I tried to describe my concerns. 'You know ... I might not be able to ... you know ... give you anything ... What I mean is...' I paused and tried to put my words into a logical order, but they wanted out, like a woman's baby in the transition of labour, when she cannot go back, only push.

Christopher put the tea towel down and looked at me.

'Remembering is immense,' I said. 'The word isn't even enough to describe it. It's like I had an infected wound and now it's been cleaned. It hurt like hell but I feel better. It still stings but I'll cope and I guess I have to let it scab over. I'll have to live with the scar. I'm terrified of telling my mother. But it just isn't an option not to. And I'm not sure why – whether it's for my sake or hers.' I held my head. 'So I can't get into a like a proper relationship or anything with you. Not yet. I know you're not asking for that; I'm just saying.'

'I know.'

I felt like he did and yet I wanted him to argue, to insist that I was selfish.

'But I do like you,' I said.

'I know.' He smiled. 'I like you too.'

'If I were in a normal place right now, I would.'

'I doubt you'll ever be in a normal place, Katrina.' He paused. 'Are you Katrina? Should I call you Catherine now?'

'I like Katrina,' I said. 'It's who I am with you.'

He looked at the clock, fidgeted, said, 'I don't want to go but I'm supposed to be at Flood Crisis in an hour.' He came back to the sofa and I pushed the duvet back and got up too.

'I've been keeping you. You should go.'

'Do you want me to call in sick?' He glanced at the phone.

'No,' I insisted. 'They need you more than I do. You've listened to me for long enough. Go, listen to them.'

'You're sure?'

I nodded; I was. Much as I enjoyed being with him, I understood that when you call in sick at a crisis line you let real people down, not some faceless organisation or office. It wasn't merely a job. The heating clicked back on and the pipes filled with water, the trapped air juddering through the system.

Christopher insisted he shouldn't leave me so soon after my remembering.

'If you don't go I'll throw you down the stairs. Don't make me.'

'OK, I'd like to stay intact.' He paused. 'I guess I'll see you soon, then.' He picked up his coat and looked at it like he'd never seen it before, and then at me, and then went to the door.

I moved to where he stood and kissed his stubbly cheek. He touched mine. Then he turned the key with an unwelcome click.

Downstairs I heard Victor taking rubbish around the back and plonking it in one of the bins. One hand still on the key, Christopher didn't move. I recalled how I'd wet his hand with my tears last night and wondered how it would feel to have those hands on my body.

I put my mouth to his. He didn't resist or respond. I pulled away after some time and we looked at one another. Still he did nothing. I liked him all the more for his restraint – because I knew why.

'I want you.'

I leaned into him and knew he wanted me too; I felt his arousal against my stomach. I pushed him back and kissed his neck.

He said against my ear, 'The key's digging into me.'

'Wuss,' I said.

He fidgeted and moved so he was flat against the door and I knew he feared hurting me, but that had never felt less possible. Nothing else could. When I kissed him again he put a hand in my hair and returned the urgent exploration of my mouth.

'It's been a while,' he admitted.

'Shhh,' I said.

'Two years. More.'

'I'll be gentle,' I smiled.

'No, *I'll* be.' He was serious.

I wanted to know that I was normal. Had to know if I'd been permanently spoilt by my returned memory. Had I been fixed and reborn? I needed to know how it might feel to have someone without needing to be forced or verbally abused. To be with someone who wasn't a stranger I'd send home. To be with someone away from the suicide of a crisis-line caller.

I pulled Christopher by his collar towards the sofa, and we fell in a tangle of sheet and leg and coat, groins crashing together. Yes, I still liked the tumble. His shin hit the coffee table and he mumbled 'damn' into my hair, said it would bruise. I laughed and called him a wuss again. The sofa sagged under our bodies and the duvet bound us. I threw it down and knocked the bin over, spilling a half-empty coke can onto the rug. He murmured 'the rug' into my mouth and I said, 'Fuck the rug'. My silvery vest fell away, I took off his T-shirt, skin met skin, hot, real, unclean, pure. His chest hair tickled my breasts. Then he stopped and sat up. Said surely it was too soon and we should wait. So I undid his zip. He shivered.

He said, '*Katrina.*'

I said yes, that was my name.

Then I pulled him close and guided him into me, pausing, savouring. He waited, understanding the pause, his words swallowed, and the can of over-turned coke still fizzing nearby.

Katrina, Katrina, Katrina. And I was; I was. The radiators filled slowly with liquid. I was Katrina. I was Catherine-Maria. I was all of them.

He said afterwards, 'You should have been a rugby player.'

We disentangled and I felt as bare as a tree waiting to be decorated. Sadness rushed into the gap. The heat died. Had I done this too fast? He studied me without being invasive, a gift he seemed to possess naturally. The coke can had long stopped fizzing and a brown stain had settled into the rug.

'You're quite persuasive,' he said.

'You're very persuadable,' I said.

'Is the rug yours or your flat-mate's?'

I said it had been there when we moved in so it must be Victor's and that I'd pass him Christopher's telephone number for the cleaning bill. I paused and then asked if he preferred Chris to Christopher.

'I suppose I kind of like Christopher now you say it.'

I thought of all the names I'd given people. Derogatory ones. Affectionate ones. I thought of all the names I'd been. The one I'd had stolen. The one that had replaced it. And the one I'd chosen.

I told Christopher I didn't want to give him a name he didn't like, that I'd been a real pain for doing that.

'Call me Christopher then.' He paused. 'I never wanted to go on that other date, you know. I was kind of hoping you'd insist I didn't go in a fit of jealous temper. I don't mean that I arranged it for that – my sister really did set me up – but I kind of hoped you'd be bothered.'

'I *was* jealous – I went to the kitchen and swore four times.'

Christopher laughed and laughed. He shook his head and laughed some more. I told him he'd better stop laughing because he had fifteen minutes to get to Flood Crisis.

'That's what all the women say to get rid of me,' he said.

'I'm not saying I want you to go, just that I know you don't take Flood Crisis lightly. You wouldn't let them down, and I'd feel kind of responsible if I made you stay.' I covered myself with the sheet and blushed.

'Now she's coy,' he said. 'I should go or I never will, what with you semi-naked like that.' He sat up and reached for his shorts and trousers, examining his shin for injury.

'Go like that,' I said. 'Do a Norman.'

'I couldn't compete with him.'

'Yeah, you'd lose.'

When he had dressed in clothes now wrinkled and buttoned wrong, he mock-hobbled to the door; I followed with the sheet around my body.

'You look like a Greek goddess or something.' He fingered the key that he'd already turned once. 'Now you've remembered, will you continue at Flood Crisis?'

'Look what it's done for me. I think I might enjoy it more now, be better at it perhaps.' I wondered what he was thinking.

'You're a natural on the phones, Katrina.'

He opened the door. Coldness invaded our intimacy. Snow blew up through the gaps in the metal stairwell, like the world had been turned upside down. How easy it would have been to go with him. How much I *wanted* to.

But I wanted to see my mother, go home and tell her. It occurred to me that I could tell Aunty Mary instead. She was my blood relation. She loved me more. Perhaps we'd snuggle under the duvet and watch *Gone with the Wind*, like we had when I was a child. Or maybe I could even talk to Graham, who might offer me a cigarette and tell me how proud he was that I'd survived it.

No. I needed my mother's response. I needed her to know, whatever that meant.

'Will you be there on Wednesday?' I asked him.

'Would you like me to be?' His insecurity touched me.

I nodded – I couldn't picture the place without him in it, making tea and suggesting games to play and responding to my digs. There when I hung up the phone; there when I couldn't help callers; there when I could; there when I wasn't sure.

'I wonder how Norman got on with Chantelle last night.' Christopher didn't seem to want to leave either.

'He'll have a headache today,' I said.

'I wonder if she'll go to her wedding with Norman on her mind.'

Christopher fiddled with his coat. His hair flared in the wind, reminding me of how I'd messed it only half an hour before. He said he'd see me on Wednesday, and it sounded like a question, and I understood that he was asking whether he would see me before then.

'Wednesday,' I answered and he nodded.

I had so much to think about. Wednesday seemed a lifetime away. It was our day. Sunday was my mother's day and I'd promised to go. And memory's obligation tugged at me like a hungry child pulling at its mother's coat.

'If you need me, call me.' He lifted his hand like he might touch my cheek but then didn't. 'Will you really tell your mum today?' he asked.

I almost corrected him, said she was my mother not my mum, but resisted. 'I have to do what I have to do.'

'Yes, you're right.'

He shrugged and studied me for a moment and then turned and began down the stairs, holding the rail.

A fist squeezed my neck. I wanted to shout 'Thank you!' to delay him. Wanted to detain him with a witty remark. Wanted to kiss him again, but instead I closed the door and returned to the warmth. I remembered longing to leave my flood-wrecked home, but also wanting to stay because I loved it, couldn't bear to abandon it. I was as torn now. I wanted him but knew I wasn't fully repaired enough yet to be able to make it work.

When he'd been gone a while – when I'd locked the door and leaned on it and said 'anyway' out loud, and curled up on the sofa and held to my face the sheets we'd shared – I cried for a full hour.

23

Footprints in the snow

'Same old tree, year in, year out,' I said. 'Don't you feel like cutting it into pieces and burning it with all the other ancient ornaments?'

I touched the silver branch weighed down with crimson baubles and matching tinsel, with scratched wooden reindeer and plastic angels. Only its position changed: some years it resided by the hearth in the dining room and some years, like now, it got relegated to a corner in the hall.

Graham closed the front door after letting me in, the eternal guest in my childhood home. 'Your mother said she'll get a new one next year.'

He took my coat and hung it on the banister next to a fake holly garland that twined round the dark wood spindles. The mention of my mother brought the first tingle of an itch to my palm; I squeezed my hand into a fist.

'She says that every year.' My words were not as harsh as they might have been any other Sunday. Any other Sunday, before I arrived, picturing her bending down to retrieve something from the oven or patting her hair into shape, I would dread hurting her with my words. But once I'd walked through the door, I could not keep them in.

'You OK?' Graham looked at me. He was concerned but something else caused the frown, something more than worry at my dishevelled appearance. He assessed me and I wasn't sure why.

I shook my head, my throat tight. 'Where's Mother then?'

'In the kitchen,' he said, and I should have known. Where else would she be on a Sunday before we ate? What other thing would she be doing? Her predictability only amplified what I was about to do, what I was about to share, how I might upset her carefully organised routine, her peace.

'You look white as a sheet, Catherine. What is it?'

'Is Celine here?'

'Why do you ask?' He was defensive, touching his chest. I wasn't sure what was going on but had too much to think about to question it now. 'She's coming later.'

'Graham.' I spoke quietly so my voice did not echo in the cavernous, wood-panelled hallway. 'When I go in there could you give us some time? I have to talk to her about something, privately. If Celine arrives, can you tell her to give us space too?'

'Of course.' He nodded and rubbed his neck, as fidgety as a witness on the stand. 'You're OK though? Is it serious?'

Was it serious? A question I'd never asked a crisis-line caller. Nothing is less serious than something that makes a person pick up the phone and call a stranger to share their darkest, most intimate, most shameful secrets. But Graham was only concerned; we ask all manner of mindless questions when we're confronted by something we don't understand. And now *I* was going into a room to share my darkest, most intimate, most shameful secret with a stranger.

I touched his arm and said, 'It's pretty serious but I'm OK.'

The bell sounded and since I was closest I opened the door. Celine stamped snow from her booted feet and held her face with her pink fur gloves. She eyed me sheepishly; such an expression on her brazen face was unfamiliar to me.

'What's with you?' I watched her put her heavy wool coat over mine. She glanced at her dad and back at me. He shook his head, responding to a question I'd missed.

'Nothing's with me,' she said, brilliantly pleasant.

'Why don't you two go and play your game in the other room.' Back home I was the child again – irritable, sulky, ignored. 'I'm not interested in it today.'

'You should talk to her, Celine,' said Graham. The hallway was still cold from the opened door but it was better than the heat that awaited me in the kitchen. 'If you don't, sweetie, I'm going to.'

I shook my head at them. 'Shit, I have more important things to—'

In my bag the phone vibrated with the jazzy ringtone Fern had installed, a tune that I recognised, though I couldn't remember the singer. I rummaged through tissues and bus tickets for it, irritated now by all the delays and obstacles that were stopping me going into the kitchen to begin reluctantly ruining my mother's life. Not recognising the number, I flipped it open.

'It's Brian the plumber, love.' He said it like I was expecting the call, but I'd barely thought of the house recently and realised that it was a week since I'd checked on the status of work. 'Just letting you know my job's done. Your heating system is in place; your new boiler is a real beauty, it's one of th—'

'Brian,' I snapped, because he'd started the first-name-basis relationship. 'It's Sunday afternoon. Can we do this tomorrow?'

He insisted I needed to know about the high pressure, which was apparently a common problem and didn't mean my toilet wasn't normal.

'Brian, we'll talk tomorrow. I'll come to the house then.' I held the phone away from my ear thinking I was going to swear but the word stayed in my throat.

Graham looked at me with unease, patted my arm, and followed Celine into the lounge. She avoided my gaze and knocked a plastic angel to the floor as she passed the tree.

'I'll not be there, love, I'm done. The electrician's going to call you Tuesday about starting his work. I just like to conclude a job properly and give you all the facts before I leave. You have long hair, don't you?'

I looked at my disorderly curls in the hall mirror, my expression perfect for the 'before' shot in a Botox advertisement.

Why the hell was he asking about my hair?

'Most clogged sinks are caused by long hair – pubes and men's shavings generally go down OK, but long hair tangles in the pipes. So you should always brush or style your hair in the bedroom and n—'

I hung up and threw the phone in my bag. The calm I'd felt after crying for an hour died. The resolve as I'd then walked two miles in brisk air was wavering. And the heat I'd felt at Christopher's suggestion that there was no rush to speak to my mother now barely simmered in the chilly hallway. Nevertheless, I uncurled my fists and swallowed dread-flavoured saliva.

And went into the kitchen.

My mother looked small. Like the kitchen had eaten her. The smell of chicken roasting was both familiar and foreign; perhaps the bird was doused in lemon rather than stuffed with the customary herbs. Vegetables bubbled on the hob and an open tub of margarine stood next to the potato masher. Though ajar, the window had steamed up and obscured the trees, the sky – the world beyond the imminent revelation. My mother stood at the sink – the small heart of my claustrophobia, pink plastic gloves on and pearl earrings in place. I closed the door and she turned.

'Have you been to see Aunty Mary?' she demanded.

'No, I needed to talk t—'

'Catherine, why not? She'll be very hurt.' She wrung a cloth out into the sink. It stank of bleach. 'You promised me yesterday that you'd go. I understood you had to do your voluntary stuff. I was very tolerant, but there's no excuse today. She was sad when I spoke to her this morning.'

'Mother,' I said. She no longer looked small. 'Listen, I have to talk to you. That's why I didn't go to the hospital first.'

She started scrubbing at a yellow stain on the side of the fridge, one that had been there for as long as I could remember. A strand of immaculate hair fell out of the black Alice band; she pushed it behind her ear. I smelt the potted African violet on the windowsill: sweet, sickly. Next to it sat a picture of us all at Christmas: Graham, Celine, me, smiling in front of the tree.

It occurred to me that it was the tree my mother bought the year Uncle Henry left, the silver one that had awaited decorations as I let

Geraldine out of her cage and into the snow. I realised suddenly that Geraldine would have died. Unless rescued by neighbours, a rabbit wouldn't survive a winter night. I had only freed her from my trauma; I had probably begun hers. If I told my mother about Uncle Henry, I would begin hers too.

'I'm tired of looking at this mark,' she said. 'I need a new fridge really.'

'Mother.' I opened and closed my fists.

'I'm getting a new tree first though – I've seen one in Argos. Green, like a real tree. Maybe I'll buy white tinsel to mimic snow.'

'Mother.' When she ignored me still I said, '*Mum*,' and she stopped scrubbing for a moment but didn't turn to query my alien salutation. We both knew who my mum was. 'I have to tell you something.' I had no idea how I was going to do it, what words I could possibly find.

'Is this about Celine?' She put the cloth in the bin and pulled off the gloves with a wet slap.

'No, it's not about Celine.'

'You called her Celine,' she observed, suspicious now. 'You finally quit with the Sharleen nonsense. I'm surprised, especially with ... well ... you know.' I didn't know. I hadn't even realised my use of her real name. 'I don't condone it but I'm not going to slate her. She's my step-daughter as much as you are. It wouldn't be fair to Graham.'

'I don't know what you're talking about.' I was sick of her name now.

'Oh.' She stared at me. 'Graham didn't...?'

'I don't give a shit about Celine. Just let me talk.'

She tutted and started to say, 'Catherine, do we have to have a shit on—'

But I cut in with, 'I'm sorry for swearing but you're not listening to me. Sit down, *please*.'

'I don't want to sit; I've got to prepare the gravy.' She dragged the metal tray from the cupboard, dropping spoons and ladles with a disharmonious clatter. The potatoes bubbled gently. 'Tell me while I do this.'

I watched her hunt for the gravy mix; I tried to find a word and only found his name.

'What is it Catherine?' she demanded, shaking granules into the tin. 'Don't be so mysterious.'

I didn't want to hurt her. 'It's about Uncle Henry.'

'Uncle Henry?' Crumbs of powder fell onto the counter like brown, soiled snow. 'Uncle *Henry*? He's been gone years. I wasn't even sure you remembered him. Have you seen him? Around here?'

She finally looked at me.

'I haven't seen him since I was a child ... It's about when he used to come to the house.'

'That's so long ago, Catherine. Why do we have to talk about him now? It's nearly Christmas. Let's not ruin it.'

His name was possibly worse than fuck or shit but it had to be said; it had to ruin Sunday lunch.

'Just listen to me, *please*.'

She put the tub of gravy granules on the worktop and faced me. I moved nearer to her, holding the sink. She looked at my hand; it was red and scaly again, only white where I gripped the edge. Then she looked at my face, curious rather than concerned now.

'Uncle Henry ... I've been thinking ... remembering ... I remember.'

'What do you mean, you remember?' She shook her head like it might revoke the words. 'What did you forget?'

'I remember *him*,' I said.

'Is that it? He came here a lot after your dad died.' She reached for the tea towel, expecting to resume her cooking.

'I remember what he did,' I said.

Her hand froze mid-air inches from the towel. 'What he did?'

I nodded, studying the tiled floor. The one to the left of my right foot had cracked in the shape of an H, his initial. He was the H-word; far worse than any C-word I could mention in the stifling kitchen.

'What he did? What did he do?'

The question was weightier than any I'd asked at a crisis line. If it fell it would break the tile to the right of my foot, matching the other and leaving a crack in the shape of a C. A caller on a crisis line could decline from answering, though. I wished at that moment to be merely a caller who could hang up, end the conversation and change her mind.

But I was here; there was no going back now.

'Mother, he...' I inhaled and moved away from the sink's support.

Why had I begun this? What did I really hope to achieve? Was Christopher right to be concerned? Was I setting myself up for more pain in the rush to unburden some of the weight?

'Uncle Henry did things to me. He put his hands on me. He put them ... *in* me. He touched me. He put his ... you know ... he ... He made me touch him. He ... That's what he did.'

She blinked twice and her hand fluttered near her throat. Her pearl earrings trembled like tiny snowdrops and a range of expressions crossed her face: horror, confusion, disbelief, belief. The belief stayed – dark grey. Her half-moon mouth hung open, but nothing came out.

'Remember my rabbit, Geraldine? He'd take me to see her and do it then. He said he'd kill her if I told anyone. Once he described how he would skin her and remove all that lovely fur with his knife. Said no one would believe me. That it was all in my head. And I thought it was. I thought we all made him up – you, me, Aunty Mary.'

'No, it can't be.' She sank into a chair without looking at me.

'It was ... It is.' I knew she believed me. Her denial was simply shock; her face said she believed me. 'I remembered it last night. It came to me in a waking dream. It's been coming for a while. I know why you all stopped calling me Catherine-Maria and I remember Nanny Eve's Virgin Mary statue that I broke and the new tree, and I know now why I've always found it so difficult in this house.'

'But we sent him away!' She glared at me now, a red, slap-shaped blotch staining her cheek. 'He can't have done that to you: we sent him away!'

'What?'

'We made him leave; he can't have done those things!'

'What do you mean, "he can't have done"?' I felt like she was squeezing my windpipe. 'He *did*.' I paused. 'You sent him away?

Why did you send him away? I don't understand.' I didn't want to be asking the questions. I had all the answers now and I didn't want any more.

She looked at me, her face full first of shame, then of panic, and then, strangest of all, guilt. 'That bastard,' she said. 'That bastard. Coming into this house, invited into this house, violating this house. I should have killed him.'

'Stop, Mother. I don't want you to shout or swear. I want you to understand. He hurt me.' I knelt at her feet, the tiles cold against my legs. Something burned in the oven. 'Look at me. He hurt *me*. Don't be angry at him or at yourself; be sad for me. Be a mother. Just be my mother – even if you didn't give birth to me, you signed up to be my mother. You're not a stand-in.'

She stood up and brushed past me, knocking my arm.

That'll bruise, I thought, and they were Christopher's words. 'That'll bruise,' he'd said of his shin. His words, so right. I had confessed for the wrong reasons. I wanted her love. I should have waited.

'Wait until I tell your aunt Mary.' She held her head. 'Wait until I tell her we were too late.'

'Mother, no, I don't want you to.' I got up and grabbed her arm; it was hot – she was fire. The burning oven was contagious. 'You can't burden Aunty Mary with this when she's ill. You're scaring me. Sit, have a drink, talk to me.'

'Graham!' she called, trying to pull out of my grip.

'Mother!' I cried. 'Stop! I don't care about Aunty Mary right now and who knows and who doesn't and him going and your anger. This is about me. It's always *you*. If you love me, you'll sit with me.' Tears tickled the corners of my eye, warm, tempting.

Graham came in. 'Are you OK?' He looked at her, then me.

'That animal,' my mother snarled.

'What animal?' he asked.

'Henry. Her uncle Henry.'

Graham went to her and wrapped her hot body in his arms and she flopped there, the fire finally fading. My knees were stiff from the cold floor. I turned all the cooker's knobs to off to save whatever was crisping and stop the vegetables bubbling.

Mother whispered into the folds of Graham's Rudolph jumper that they had been too late.

'I don't understand.' He looked at me, but I was all out of answers.

'Remember,' she said to him.

Remember, I thought. Come on, Graham, it's not that difficult.

'I told you years ago about what we found.'

'Oh. Yes. But why were you too late?'

'He'd already been...'

'Been what?'

'Abusing Catherine.'

Graham looked at me, and I felt ashamed, like a naughty child.

His eyes filled with tears. 'Catherine,' he whispered. 'No.' He let go of my mother and told her she should hold me, not him.

'I can't deal with this, I just can't,' she said, not moving.

'What did you find?' I asked her.

'Disgusting,' she mumbled.

'What the fuck was it?' I yelled.

'I just can't deal with it.' She pulled away from Graham and ran from the kitchen.

'Someone had better tell me what you found.' I shivered. Graham approached me, but I held up my hand. 'Don't. I don't want your affection right now, Graham; I wanted hers. Just tell me what you found before I leave.'

He looked at his feet. 'Mary and your mother found some ... pictures.'

'Of what? Where?'

'In the room Henry had. They found pictures of children.'

'What do you mean? Whose children?' I shook my head.

'No one's children. Just children. Posing. You know ... pornographic images.'

'No one's children,' I said.

'I'm sorry. I meant children of no one we *know*. Your mother was trying to hide a Tiny Tears doll she'd bought you for Christmas. There was a walk-in cupboard that locked in the room where Henry slept. They were there. Your mother was sick on his bed. She and Mary made him leave that day. They threw his things in the drive and told him that he was never again to come back or contact them. Your mother said she was glad they found out before … before he … acted upon his … perversion.'

'I'm someone's child,' I said.

'I know.' Graham's voice was a croak. 'Catherine, all this time carrying that. Why didn't you tell someone?'

'Because I've only just remembered,' I said. 'And now I wish I hadn't.' I pushed past him. 'Where did she go?'

'Let me talk to her,' he said.

'What good has *that* ever done?'

I slammed the door and looked in the lounge. Celine was reading a copy of *Vogue* near the smaller gold tree. The gifts beneath it had been arranged according to size so they appeared as steps leading up to the branches.

'Shit.' She closed the pages. 'He told you? I didn't realise it would upset you *this* much. I was wrong, OK? I should never have done it. I didn't think they'd fire her. I just thought it would be funny to have her come clean in the column. That's all I thought would happen.'

'*What?*'

'Didn't Graham tell you?' Mauve eye shadow had smudged near her left eyebrow.

It dawned on me; it might have done sooner if I hadn't been working for a crisis line and didn't have a derelict house and a friend who had deserted me and if I hadn't been dealing with a childhood memory that had taken twenty-two years to emerge. '*You* were the one who rang Fern's editor,' I said.

The tree's string of multi-coloured lights was set to flash. Though the flashing seemed random it had a pattern if you were patient enough to figure it out. Flash, flash, not; flash, flash, flash, not; flash, not.

My head pounded.

'So you admitted it to your dad. Pretty big of you, Celine. I'm surprised.'

'Um, no ... Not really. He overheard me the on the phone, telling Stephen about it. I'm sorry.' Celine folded and unfolded the corner of the cover page.

'You're not,' I said. 'You're just embarrassed you got caught, but that's fine. I only wish I'd figured it out sooner.'

She stared at me. 'So what's up with your mother?' She looked through the French doors and I followed her gaze – Mother stood on the lawn, by the shed.

I went outside. Fresh, untouched snow covered the garden. The only footprints led to her. I followed them and remembered the verse Nanny Eve had on her kitchen wall about there only being one set of footprints because Jesus carries you in your darkest hour. I tried to stay within my mother's imprint but my feet are bigger and I ruined the shape. She must have heard the crunching grass but she didn't turn. I stood behind her, cold. Her cardigan was grey, bobbled where her elbows had rubbed.

'When your dad died,' she said, without looking round, 'I asked Uncle Henry to come and stay. I knew you'd taken the death hard. I knew you loved him more than you did me; it's understandable. He was your blood. So I wanted to have another kind of father figure in the house for you. Who better than your dad's brother? And he was great with you. He gave you all the attention I thought you missed; he even kept your dad's promise by buying you that damned rabbit.' She glanced over her shoulder. 'So can you imagine how I feel right now?'

'Of course,' I said gently. 'I've imagined it all morning. I've dreaded this, and I wasn't sure why I wanted to tell you. I suppose I just wanted you to understand why I've been so difficult all these years.'

'I wish you hadn't told me. I don't know what to do with it.'

'Me neither,' I said.

Snow began to fall again. Soon it would cover our footsteps.

'I need time,' she said, still giving me only her back. 'I can't deal with it.'

I walked around in front of her, disturbing the undisturbed snow. 'Mother, my uncle assaulted me. Not you: *me*. In that shed. Look at it – look at *me*.'

She did both, but her eyes were full of resistance, and her breath hung in the air.

'Don't you care how *I* feel?' I asked.

'I'm in pain,' she said. 'Physical pain. Couldn't you have just told your crisis people?'

'They're for people who have no one else.'

'They'd know what to do.' She began to shiver.

'You might feel guilty that it happened, but you don't have to.' I thought about touching her arm but she was too distant. 'How could you have known? This isn't your fault; I don't hold you responsible. At all. I know about the photographs, Graham told me – how sick they made you, that you did what you felt best. I came here with no judgement, only sadness for the pain I was bringing.' The tears that had teased earlier now streamed a hot trail down my cheeks. 'But you're guilty of failing me *today*,' I said. 'Guilty of turning your back on me *now*, when I've come to you. You ask me if I can imagine how you feel but you're not considering how *I* feel. How do you think *I* feel? You're not the victim. *I* was. I came to you as a daughter today, but you're no mother.'

My hand rose before I knew it, and I saw it in front of me. Felt the jolt through my arm as it made contact with her cheek. I had slapped her. But I knew instantly that it hurt me more. I remembered her cliff-top slap. I was as bad now. We were equal.

'You're a cunt,' I said. 'When you're not, come and say sorry to me.'

I left her in the ruined snow by the shed. Soon my footprints would not even be there either. I went inside, up the stairs, to the room at the back where Uncle Henry had slept.

Now it was a storage room with unlabelled boxes stacked against the wall and a single bed without covers. It held no particular memory; Henry had never taken me into the place where he ogled no one's children.

I opened the door in the wall, half expecting piles of faded images to spill out. But those nameless children were no longer in the cupboard. It housed only Graham's fishing magazines and old towels and Christmas wrapping paper. The nameless children were long gone. I only hoped they were free now. Had their true names.

As I finally did.

Learning from Fern

After climbing the flat's metal stairwell, shutting the door behind me and closing my eyes to block out that solitary line of footprints leading through the snow to my mother, the words 'You look like total shit' surprised me into reality. My eyes snapped open and 'Huh?' jumped out of my mouth: a verbal sneeze.

I scanned the room for the voice.

Fern sat on our sofa, a golden creature with olive skin and freckles and sun-lightened hair. A red suitcase spilled multi-coloured bikinis and sarongs all over the coffee table, and duty-free bags covered the floor. That corner of the room shone brighter than the kitchen's fluorescent bulb. She wore new shoes.

She was home.

I waited for the joy to fill me.

'How'd you get in?' I had her keys; they hung from a cup hook, awaiting her claim.

'Victor.'

'Why are you here?' I asked.

'What kind of a hello is that, woman?'

She uncrossed her tanned legs and waited for me to respond, but I couldn't. Anger burned away any joy at seeing her; her quick judgement of me darkened that too-light corner.

'I knew as soon as I got to the airport,' she said, and paused as though I might ask what she'd known.

But I didn't. I wanted her to leave again. I was still trembling from the exchange with my mother. I couldn't deal with this too.

'Once I'd calmed down I knew that you'd never do a thing like that,' she said. 'I never even *really* thought so. I was just pissed off. Blinded by the bad news and desperate to blame someone. And there you were. Your name.'

She looked at me. I held that gaze without a smile.

'There's no excuse,' Fern admitted.

Still I couldn't say anything. Why should she have it easy? Why should she hurt me and go away and expect to walk in here like nothing had happened in between?

'So I sat on the plane with my double vodka,' she said. 'Some guy called Leonard paid for it. And I realised how ridiculous even the idea that you'd ring my editor was. Like, you'd *never* do it. I tried to call you as soon as I landed but I couldn't find my bloody phone. I think Leonard stole it. I was flinging stuff all over the airport, searching my case, my bags, my pockets...'

I hung my coat on the door but I didn't go over to the sofa. She watched me with watery eyes, gauging my response to her explanation. I didn't feel she deserved my words. The radiator clicked into bubbly action; some things never changed.

'I was cursing at the airport officials about bloody thieves,' she went on, her waterfall of words fast and invigorating, willing me into forgiveness, 'and I couldn't understand a thing they were saying, though I reckon I could have got with one of them – slicked hair and tight trousers. I desperately wanted to ring you, but all my numbers were in that phone. You know numbers and me. I never even remember my own date of birth. May ... fifth?'

'Sixth,' I grunted.

She nodded. 'What would I do without you?'

If she wanted an answer I couldn't give it. What *would* she do without me? What had I done without her? I'd hurt. I'd been lonely. I'd worn a stupid watch until it chafed my wrist.

'It was no holiday,' she went on. 'I was forever turning to tell you something – every day. There was this guy on the beach wearing a leopard-skin thong, must have been eighty, and I actually said aloud,

"Would you do him for a thousand quid?" I was so frustrated I couldn't call you. I rang my mum every day to get her to pass on a message to you, but she never picks up when it's an international number. Thinks it's those people selling stair-lifts. But I thought, *Catherine will know. She knows how temperamental I am, and she'll realise that deep down I didn't think she'd done it. She'll know I'm stupid and wrong and that I'm coming home.* You knew, right?'

'That you're a stupid cow?'

'Yeah, that too.'

But too much truth filled the room; I couldn't lie and say I'd known. It was just like with Celine's deception, I thought: if I'd had less going on I might have guessed.

'Sit with me,' said Fern.

'No,' I said.

So, she came and hugged me, smelling of a hundred different fragrances. Her body was warm, so unlike how my mother's had been. I was desperate to give in and have the simplicity of our relationship again, but I couldn't. I pulled away.

'It's good to be back,' she said, uncomfortable. 'I could murder a proper cup of tea; that stuff in Spain tastes like piss.' She looked at my face, at my dirty hair. 'Been arguing with your mother, as usual?'

My heart ached. I ignored her and put the kettle on. I didn't want to tell her about my memory, my past. She hadn't been here while I'd gone through the ordeal of remembering; that was what hurt most of all.

'Nothing changes, does it?' she said, clearly trying to fill our awkward silence. 'It's Sunday, so you've been at your mother's. I should be hungover in bed, ignoring texts from some guy and never learning my lesson with drink. I could go away for a year and come back and nothing would really change.'

'Things do change,' I said gruffly. 'The tap's fixed.'

'Is it?' She glanced over at the sink as though willing it to leak.

'Listen, I...' I tried to find the right words. 'Right now, I need to be alone. I just can't be all fine and normal with you, because things aren't fine and normal. You hurt me, and I can't just get over it because you're here again. I believe you're sorry, I do. But a lot happened while you were gone. Stuff I could have ... well ... used a friend for.'

Fern's eyes filled with tears. She nodded. 'You're right. It's wrong of me to expect anything. Look, I have stuff to do, so I can make myself scarce. I can stay the night at my mum's. We can, you know, catch up soon, when you're ready.'

'Sleep here,' I said. 'It's fine.'

She put on her coat. 'OK. Well, I need to see my mum so I can give you space and come back later.'

When she left, I had never felt more alone.

I must have fallen asleep on the sofa because when I opened my eyes it was dark. Fern sat at my feet, her head on the sheet that had tangled around Christopher and I only that morning.

'What time is it?' I asked her.

'Time you got a watch.' She paused. 'Only seven pm.'

I sat up. At least Fern seemed sorry. My mother had only been cruel, given me the cold shoulder. Maybe I should be kinder to my friend.

'I know I hurt you,' she said, as though hearing my thoughts. 'And I'm sorry. It sounds so lame, but I am.'

I shrugged.

'You had a man here, didn't you?' she said, and I could just make out her smile in the dimness. 'And not just because the tap is fixed. I can tell. I turn my back for one week, and you have the whole British army over. How many? Come on, give me the juicy details.'

'There *are* none,' I said.

'Who is it?' She leaned closer, further creasing the sheet. Had Christopher been here only hours ago? I felt sure Fern would smell us, what we had shared. I blushed.

'Just someone from Flood Crisis,' I admitted.

'I'm so happy; you so deserve it. Does he have a name, then?' She clapped her hands like I'd won the jackpot on a game show.

'Christopher,' I said. 'And it was only...'

'Only what?'

'Well, it's nothing, really.'

'You're blushing,' smiled Fern. 'And you don't want to talk about him. That means you like him. Come on, what's he like?'

'Never mind,' I said coolly. 'I'll make tea and you can tell me about your holiday romances.'

I went to the kitchen and switched on the kettle. She rummaged through a carrier bag. I needed her light and fluffy tales.

She called over the rustling of the bag that a man called Jake might call. Except for my hurt, it was as though she'd never been gone. She came to the counter and sat on it as she had done many times, yellow plastic bag in hand. 'I met him by the pool,' she said. 'His shorts were the same pink as my bikini and he reckoned we were meant to be.'

I laughed, perhaps too hard, and Fern looked at me.

'Catherine,' she said.

'Yes?' I put the dirty teaspoons in the sink.

'I'm sorry with all my heart that I called you grumpy and moody and that I said you were a jealous bitch. You're not. I was so pissed off at losing my column. And I nearly lost you too.'

'I *am* moody though.' I pulled the drawer open and rummaged for a cloth to mop up some tea I'd spilt. When there weren't any I shoved it shut and dragged out the other one.

'I didn't miss those drawers,' she grinned.

'I like them.' I did.

'This is for you.' She handed me the carrier bag, a yellow gift. I was glad it wasn't red, did not signal danger. Perhaps optimistic yellow signalled a new start. Inside was perfume.

'You shouldn't have. You don't have a job now.' I paused. 'It's a shame about your column.'

I considered telling her about Celine, but it would only make things worse. Such a revelation would make Fern angry now, take away from us working things out. Maybe later. Maybe when I had forgotten it and remembered again.

'What will you do now?' I asked Fern.

'I haven't told you.' She clapped her hands. 'My mum told me this afternoon that apparently my editor John rang Sean while I was away; funny really since they know I'm not even with him now. Anyway, they want me to write a sexy single column after all.'

'What about whatshisname who does one on a Thursday?'

Fern shook her head, her streaked hair flowing. 'Mick Mars got married to some woman called Cassie and discovered Jesus so he doesn't want to write about humping everything that moves anymore.' She sipped her tea. 'Think what I can write about – you and me and *our* relationships. I'm going to have to start remembering names, though, or at least develop your skill for making them up.'

'Always find out the real names,' I said.

Downstairs Victor and his Happy Housers began their late-afternoon ritual, clattering implements and playing the radio loud.

Fern looked sad. 'What happened while I was away, Cath?'

'I'm not ready,' I said. 'Let's just talk about you.'

'You're sure?'

I nodded.

'But my stuff is so trivial. And you seem so...'

'I need trivial,' I insisted.

'OK. Well, my editor wants to call the column "Learn from Fern", but I think that's pathetic – what does that have to do with sex and the modern world? He said he'd have a sub-heading underneath like, "The World of Dating with Fern Fielding". What do you think? It's bad, isn't it?'

'I like it.' I put my empty cup on the worktop and whispered it aloud. 'It's poetic and simple. Means it doesn't just have to be about men – it can be about *you*. Keep the title but tell him his sub-heading sucks.'

She sprayed my perfume on her wrist and smelt it with a hearty sniff, nodding at her great taste in scent. Its heady fragrance barely concealed the smell of chicken and spices that emanated from below.

'What would I do without you?' she asked.

'You'd have a crap sub-heading,' I said.

Fern laughed. 'How come *you* don't have a column?'

'Because I don't have anything to write about,' I said softly.

'You'll have to help me think of a sub-heading. How about we do it now and I'll start the first piece? I've already got some great ideas.'

I didn't like the idea of creating stories; I was just coming to terms with truths. I was suddenly exhausted, despite my nap.

'Not now,' I said. 'I need to sleep.'

'But we're OK?' said Fern, softly.

I paused. 'We will be,' I said.

The next morning Fern gave me space. That she did touched me. I knew how hard it was for her not to talk every five minutes. So later that night we chatted until almost morning. I admitted I was still angry with her and that it might take time to trust again. She listened. We created one-and-a-half articles for her column, and Fern finally disappeared into her room. I looked at Christopher's red watch on the coffee table. Thinking of him made me smile. People did come back, but things were not quite the same as if they'd never gone.

I fell asleep without difficulty and dreamt of the room.

Its door was smooth and painted pale blue. I opened the silver handle with ease and entered. Inside, snow covered the floor, the windowsill and the rabbit hutch in the corner. Geraldine sniffed at my ankles, so I picked her up and held her close and let her whiskers tickle my skin. We left one set of footprints: mine. The ball of familiar fur fidgeted to be let down. I relented and watched her run in circles, tiny imprints marking the white powder. Ring after ring of dots. But I knew she had to run, make her own way and return to me only when she chose.

It was cold but I wasn't. It was the room not me. I was not the room.

I sensed someone there. A ghost. I was not afraid. Ghosts cannot hurt us. Only humans do. I turned. By the smooth, pale-blue door was my mum. Mum. She was not faded or out-of-focus. Gentle waves of golden hair framed her face. Eyes the same as mine shone. She smiled and closed the door behind her.

I was not the room. I was not Katrina. I was Catherine-Maria.

Maria in the Moon.

Editing out the wrong words

Jangly Jane dropped onto the Flood Crisis lounge sofa, her colliding bracelets almost tuneful. She said she'd read a theory in a magazine that we write our own lives before we're even born; like some sort of futuristic blueprint. I still could not help but call her Jangly Jane in my head, though I was careful never to say it aloud.

'Which magazine was it in?' asked Christopher, half closing his book but leaving a thumb inside to mark where he was.

'Why does that matter?' She raked through the pile of newspapers.

'If it was in *OK!* I might be sceptical.'

Christopher put his book on the coffee table. Someone had perched the all-singing-all-thrusting Santa on top of a Ford Escort manual. For now, he was silent, his battery likely dead.

'It was *Psychologies* magazine,' said Jane, unable to find one.

'So what exactly did it say?' I asked.

She looked at me like she'd only just realised my existence, her left earring dangling lower than the right as she cocked her head. 'It suggested that we're on a path that we alone have created and so we can only blame ourselves for everything that happens to us. We've written everything we do and everything we are.'

I was surprised at her poetry; Jangly Jane the stickler for rules, the lover of authority. I considered asking her if we got a spellchecker when we wrote this life, but knew I'd sound sarcastic. She opened a newspaper with a dismissive crunch, her earrings even again.

'It's an interesting theory,' said Christopher. 'I like it better than the idea of a God. We write ourselves. Wish I'd given myself big biceps and a washboard stomach; perhaps a French accent. Can we go back and edit?'

I smiled and Christopher mouthed 'What?' at me, but I wasn't about to say that I thought his biceps and stomach were fine, so I shook my head. The phone in booth two pealed and I stood, but it stopped after one ring. The caller had perhaps lost their courage. It takes so much to dial, I imagined that hearing it ring might frighten many away.

'Maybe he forgot to write what he'd say,' I mused, resuming the sofa.

'You're mocking me,' said Jane.

'I'm not, I'm serious,' I said. 'You have to consider that some people might mess around with their words. Maybe forget them occasionally or even regret the ones they chose. And what if we outlive what we wrote?'

'You can't do that,' said Jane, her bracelets clashing.

'So we write our deaths?'

'According to the article, we write ourselves seven exits and then pick one as we see fit.'

'Just think,' I said, unable to resist a little teasing. 'If the spellchecker wasn't activated, you might end up being hit by a speeding brain.'

'Spellchecker wouldn't correct that,' sneered Jane. 'It isn't spelt wrong; it's just the wrong word. You're such a smart-arse, Katrina.'

'So there *is* a spell-checker then.' I licked my lower lip.

'I won't rise to it,' she said.

'So what kind of writer would you say Norman is?' Christopher grabbed the pack of photos from the shelf under the magazines and took out one from Saturday night. Norman was topless, red-faced and being supported by Chantelle and her friends. One of them brandished an empty champagne bottle, the contents of which Norman clearly wore in his hair and down his almost-hairless white chest. 'In this one I'd say he writes great fantasy.' Christopher held up another of Norman reclined on a sofa in some club with Chantelle sitting astride him, her skirt hiked up so far she showed her pink knickers.

'Definitely a self-indulgent writer.' I squinted at the image. 'Wouldn't it be good if we could misbehave and make mistakes and just go back and edit it so we never did?'

'Like, edit out all the wrong words,' said Christopher.

'Give me a red pen. I could be here all day.'

'I'm making tea,' said Jane, abandoning the paper. 'You two can mock me. I simply won't rise to it.'

'Jane, don't be so sensitive,' said Christopher. 'We're only playing.'

When she had gone, I asked him, 'Do you think when she wrote her life that the pen ran out halfway?'

He laughed and said, 'I bet it was a pen with a dangly toy hanging from the lid.' Then he put a picture of Norman burying his face in Chantelle's chest between the pages of his book and looked at me and asked, 'How are you doing, Katrina?'

I considered my answer with the deliberation such an honest question deserved. I thought how angry I'd felt when Fern first returned. But, like spring sun on the last snow, she'd slowly melted those feelings. The previous three mornings had been less dark, and I'd smiled when I woke to the sound of fingers tapping on a keyboard or Fern swearing at the two drawers.

Then, each morning, I'd remember my mother. My breath suspended every time our phone rang, then escaped in a gasp when it wasn't her. Graham had called to say Aunty Mary was home from hospital, but I was yet to visit her. Since remembering Uncle Henry I'd avoided her. I didn't want to take the same pain to her that I had given my mother; I couldn't bear her also wishing I'd taken my confession to a crisis line.

My hands no longer itched and the nightmares had stopped.

But ... how *was* I?

I was breathing and not scratching and I could remember and I didn't dread sleeping and I had Fern. But though I had all these lights the street remained half lit. The darkness had not all gone.

'I'm fine,' I said to Christopher, settling on that feeble word I knew belied my search for more.

'How did it go with your mum?' he asked.

I didn't correct him; I looked away. Someone had propped a neon star on top of a booth; it flashed so infrequently you could count the seconds in between. You might think it had finally packed up and then ping, it flashed. Every gadget in the Flood Crisis lounge was either faulty or worn or broken: the grotesque Santa, the fickle star, the stark tree, and the hideous, cracked Virgin Mary.

'You were right,' I said. 'I should never have told her.'

I didn't tell him about slapping her. I couldn't bear his harsh judgement of my violence. I still heard the ringing sound as my skin met hers, sharp in the cold air.

'Katrina, I never thought you *shouldn't*. I was just concerned because you were so vulnerable that morning. I felt bad leaving you.' He paused. 'You didn't ring me this week.'

'You never rang me either,' I snapped.

He shrugged. 'I didn't want to push you.'

I nodded. 'No, you're right. I haven't made any of this easy for you.'

He touched my wrist with his warm, familiar fingers. 'You're not wearing the watch.'

'No.' I wanted to take his hand and hold it in mine, like I had on Sunday, but couldn't. I just couldn't. Why couldn't I? I didn't know. Eventually he took it away. 'Fern came back. I meant to bring your watch today.'

'Keep it,' he said. 'I'm really glad she's home. You must be happy.'

'But you said that you wanted it back when she returned.'

'Did I?'

'You did.' I frowned. 'We were sorting through the decorations, and I was laughing at that Santa and you...' He smiled and slowly I smiled too, realising his game. 'You tease,' I said. 'You remember.'

He sat forward in his seat and the cushion squeaked resistance. He put one hand on my knee where I'd cut it that first day, just below the hem of my skirt. His face grew serious. 'Katrina—'

The door opened and Jane came in with drinks. I held Christopher's look for a second more, wondering how tired and messy I must appear, but enjoying his gaze. A second is only as long as the things you fill it with.

'The milk might be off,' she said, plonking a drink next to me.

The phone rang so I picked up my sour tea and stood, my leg briefly touching Christopher's knee.

I headed for the booth and answered on the fourth ring, saying, 'Flood Crisis, can I help you?' I grabbed the pen and scribbled, but it wouldn't work. I would not write this caller's life today.

A shrill woman squeaked that she didn't think she'd spoken to me before and I thought momentarily of Helen: Helen's acting lessons, Helen's tree, it never being about the trees. I felt sad that she would not call again. It was selfish; she was happy and no longer needed a crisis line. I'd done my duty. So, I thought of Sid and wondered if he'd ring. I'd helped Helen and myself and it would be good to help him too. Perhaps he was the final light that would illuminate the whole street.

The ones you get attached to on a crisis line – against all better judgment and against all training – are the ones who keep you there. I wanted to make sure he was OK; he'd been my first caller here, after all.

The woman on the phone demanded if we were the suicide place and asked for Ben. I could hear Fern Britton talking about masturbation on *This Morning*. The woman grumbled that she missed Richard and Judy. She said that Judy had always had such beautiful, coiffed hair, and that she wanted to talk to Ben because he'd understand.

I hadn't written anything on the pad. What was she *really* saying? How could I define her? When I opened my mouth to ask what was troubling her, she hung up. Dissatisfied, I went back into the lounge area.

'No one seems to be able to remember what they wrote.' I squeezed between the cushion and the sofa. 'That woman must have forgotten her blueprint. Let's just go home, shall we? A day in bed – that's what I'll write for today.'

Christopher looked at me, his expression giving little away.

'Anyway,' Jane said, continuing whatever conversation they'd been having as though I'd never interrupted. 'It was only pre-1991 that suicide rates in women were higher. Since then men kill themselves far more frequently; I think three-quarters of suicides are committed by men.'

'Maybe they're better at it.' I sat down opposite Christopher. I'd left my half-drunk tea in the booth but couldn't be bothered to go back. 'What are the statistics on people who try but fail?'

'It's not suicide if they fail,' sneered Jane.

'Perhaps that's worse,' I said. 'How must they feel when they come around? They failed at living and then they failed at dying, too.'

'Have you ever wanted to die?' Christopher asked us, though he looked at me.

'Not me,' said Jane, shaking her head vigorously.

I thought about it. 'No,' I said. 'How about you?'

Suddenly the Santa on the table thrust twice and sang half of 'Jingle Bells' in a voice that sounded like it came from *The Exorcist* before falling backwards onto the floor. Christopher stood him up and seemed to consider his life while smoothing Santa's beard.

'I've wanted to not be here,' he said finally. 'But that's not same as wanting to die, is it? I've never wanted to be dead, but there have been times I wished I didn't exist.' He shook his head, then got up and left the room.

I stared at the door, still seeing his shape in my mind. The room without him in it was empty. I followed him into the hallway.

'You can't leave just one of us in here for the phones,' said Jangly Jane.

I let the door close on her voice. In the kitchen Christopher rinsed out cups. I watched him for a moment, picturing those hands on me, but it only made the last streetlight I was looking for seem to flicker more.

'I did think about ringing you,' I said.

He dropped the cup into the bowl of water and fished about in the suds for it. 'I thought about ringing you too,' he admitted, wiping wet hands on jeans. 'I even picked up the phone a few times and started dialling. But then I hoped you'd find your way to me when you were ready.'

'I'm just a bit nervous about a relationship,' I said.

'I know.' He smoothed his hair.

'Not cos of you.'

He nodded.

I moved towards him and pressed my mouth to his; I tried to mute my confusion about what I wanted. I wanted to be able to just have a normal relationship. To turn on that last streetlight. He spun me around and pushed me into the cabinet, banging my head against the top cupboard. Gripping my upper arm, he kissed back. We fought to be close.

I stopped, suddenly afraid. Not of him or even of me, but of being happy. It was such a risk to take. What if I got used to it and then something happened? That was why I'd always ruined relationships. Why I'd hurt people. I had to get in there first. Had to hurt before I got hurt. But I didn't want to do that to Christopher. He held my face and kissed me more, but I pulled free, still holding his hands, not wanting to break from him altogether.

'Katrina,' he said into my hair.

'I don't know,' I whispered. 'It's so soon after...'

'I understand. I was with you when you remembered. I'd do anything to make it easier. Maybe it's best I let you be. I can't do the kissing and then not kissing.' He pulled away, unable to look me in the eye. 'I've no right to expect anything from you. I've no right to complain about you kissing me and pushing me away. But I'm afraid I might get hurt again. Selfish, I know.'

I wanted to say that we were both scared, but I didn't interrupt.

'I can't help but imagine a relationship with you. I know we've never even gone out or anything, but some of our shifts have sort of felt like a date. Like when we've talked about nothing and everything. When we've analysed theories and talked about TV shows. Small talk. First- and second-date talk, I suppose. I love kissing you and I loved when you had your epiphany at the flat on Sunday, saying how afraid you are but that you do like me.' He paused and fiddled with the drawer handle; I knew he wasn't done, so I still didn't interrupt. I let him have his Wednesday-afternoon epiphany as I'd had my Sunday one.

'I'm afraid too,' he said. 'I'm not saying that to pressure you or compete. I think about what it was like when my wife left and I didn't get out of bed for a week and I didn't wash or eat, and my sister said I was pathetic, that life should go on. It was the same when my father died. I couldn't function. I felt abandoned. I don't cope well with that.

So, I feel foolish that I might let a woman I've slept with once and never even taken out for dinner do that again.'

I couldn't think of a single word to say; he had used them all.

'Did you write that before you were born?' I asked, referring to Jangly Jane's theory. Then I worried I'd been too flippant after his emotional admission. I tried to correct myself. 'Because it was really honest.'

'You were honest on Sunday,' he said.

'I wonder about a future too – a relationship. But do we have to write it *now*? Can't we just *see*? I'm not going anywhere. I'll just be at the flat unless my house gets finished early.'

A phone rang. It was Jane's turn. It stopped after three rings.

'Christopher...' I had no idea what I was going to say, and then, before I could even work it out, Jane opened the door with an intrusive crash of jewellery.

'That guy with the funny voice wants you,' she said to me, glaring. 'You two should just get a room or something.'

'Fuck you, Jane,' I said.

'You can't talk to me like that.' She leaned against the doorframe, arms crossed, bangles squashed together like a car pile-up. 'And you can't keep a caller waiting.'

'I should get that,' I said to Christopher, and he said, 'I know.'

The phone receiver waited for me, black and needy. I picked it up and switched gears. I was Katrina.

'Hello Sid, how are you?' I said.

'Hello Katrina.' His voice was clumsier than I remembered and yet somehow more understandable; his tongue sounded heavy but his tone was light. 'I worried you'd have the day off.'

'I'm here.'

I picked up the pen. This one worked. Today I would write Sid's life in blue with my right hand, my white, non-itchy hand. I watched Jane come back into the lounge area, eyeing me through blue lashes like millions of tiny pen tips. Christopher didn't follow.

Someone had tacked a plastic baby Jesus by his foot to the prompt board; he dangled perilously above the 'How do you feel?' question. I wrote the date at the top of a fresh page; it smudged, staining the end of my thumb.

'Sid isn't my name,' he said.

I'd always known this. I couldn't blame him for giving a false name. I considered asking what his real name was but didn't – not because it was the wrong question for a crisis line but because it didn't matter. Our name is not who we are. I recalled that he'd once said names often evaded him, that he would call people 'thingy'.

'Katrina isn't my name, either,' I admitted.

This went against all I'd been taught in training, but I liked that we had in common our pen names. I looked out into the lounge area: Christopher had returned and had resumed reading his book. He looked up and then at me, his eyes kind of sad and his mouth curled slightly.

Of course he was sad.

'I want to be honest today,' said Sid, slowly.

I wrote 'honest'.

'Why do you feel like being honest today?' I asked.

Finally, I understood how significant the right question was. Perhaps in the past I'd been too aggressive, too impatient, when trying to tap into my own memory. Only when I was ready to open the door in my dream had the handle turned of its own accord, quietly, effortlessly, permitting me to see the whole room. The wrong questions led me to a locked door, to a false room, so now I fully understood their importance on the phones. Some answers need more than a gentle tone or non-judgmental silence. They require the right words, maybe the right person.

'I got my test results back,' he said.

I recorded the sentence in blue and read it twice. But I didn't want to ask the inevitable question.

'I have lung cancer, Katrina,' he said.

Some answers we never want.

I thought of Aunty Mary. 'They can do stuff for cancer,' I said. 'I know people who get better. They can remove it. They can cure you. You can be home after—'

'Not from lung cancer. Not this far along. The doctor said I'd be lucky if I have a month. Showed me a scan-picture thing. God, what a mess. He said I've probably had it a while, that I should have gone sooner about my cough. But I hate doctors and hospitals. I'm weak anyway. What a mess, eh? A stroke, the floods, and now this. But none of it matters.'

'Of course it matters,' I said, tears pricking my eyelashes.

'No, it doesn't. You mustn't feel sad for me, really you mustn't. Getting the results helped me. I'm no spring chicken and I'm lonely. I have no one. Who'll miss me?' He paused. 'So I've made a decision.'

'Well, that's good,' I enthused.

'Maybe.'

'Tell me about your decision,' I said, gently.

Christopher left the lounge again and the door slammed on its fire safety hinges. The steam-trains calendar above Norman's desk fell down. Jane looked up, at the door and then me. In the other booth, the phone rang and she went to it, her expression stony. The star on top of her cubicle paused between flashes.

'I know I can tell you, Katrina. I know you good souls on these lines deal with this all the time.' I counted his words; the pause in between each was half a second, his syllables flat.

'You can tell me anything,' I said.

'I have decided that I'm going to die today,' he said.

'I don't understand.' The pen was warm in my hand, the paper waiting for words.

'I will die today. This afternoon. Here, now.'

'You can't,' I said.

'Katrina, it's too late. I took them all.'

'Took all what?'

'Paracetamol, sleeping pills, ibuprofen, some pills from a bottle with no label. Everything I have.'

The slow voice, the clear voice, the heaviness, the lightness, the difference – I knew now. I shook my head and looked out into the lounge, but it was empty. I thought of Christopher's father, of Christopher saying he'd felt abandoned when he killed himself. I had been angry for a time after my dad went. It was how I felt now. Abandoned and angry. But I had no right. Sid was not my father. He was not my anyone.

'No.' I put my hand over my mouth. 'No, you can't.'

'Katrina, this isn't how I want you to be. Aren't you supposed to respect our choices? I'm going to die, I want to. I don't want to be here anymore. And I need you to talk to me until I go. You've been here for me these few weeks and you have to finish this with me.'

'I can't.'

Tears fell onto the pad and wet the word 'honest'. I looked out into the lounge area; Christopher was back but no longer reading. He held his head in his hands. Though I tried I couldn't catch his eye. In the next cubicle Jane asked the caller whether they wanted to explore the reasons further.

'You must,' mumbled Sid. 'If you don't I'll have to die alone in this armchair with only a view of an empty courtyard and the back of the supermarket.'

My father had died in his chair. His heart gave out in the chair by the study window, as mine was threatening to now in this fake leather thing.

'Let me ring an ambulance,' I suggested. 'Let me talk to you until they come. You might have another month – two or three, even. Isn't it worth having that?'

'I'm not going to die in some hospital bed, coughing, and shitting my innards out, nurses full of pity and the doctors indifferent. This is my choice. You have to accept it.'

He sounded calm and ready. Who was I to question him? Didn't he deserve acceptance? Didn't he deserve to choose his death, to have another human witness it, to die in his own way? My training and my head said the answer to all these question was 'yes'. But my heart couldn't get on board so easily.

'Tell me your address,' I persisted. 'I won't call an ambulance; I'll just have it, in case.'

'There is something.' His voice was a deathly whisper.

'Something?'

'Something I need to tell you.'

'Tell me your address,' I whispered.

'There's something I've carried for all these years,' he said. 'Something I can't carry anymore.' He coughed for a while. 'It eats away at me. I've bottled it up, but I have to share it with someone before I go. Do you know how old I am? Sixty-eight. And I look eighty. Let me tell you...'

If I listened to his confession, I was agreeing to his death. The flashing star reflected bloody in Jane's sleek, red hair. Again, Christopher was not in the room. I was not in it either.

'You have to hear me, Katrina,' whispered Sid. 'Yesterday, last Tuesday, last month is vague, but this memory never leaves me. I take it to sleep and wake up with it. I swallow it with my morning coffee and my late-night brandy. You have to hear me.'

'Share it with me.'

A lump of familiarity stuck in my throat like indigestible food.

'I think you'll judge me,' he said, his voice slow and heavy now.

'You know I'm not here to judge,' I said.

'I know you're not supposed to, but you will. *I* do. I've done a terrible thing. What you won't understand is that though I regret the hurt I caused, I also don't. I can't. Because I loved her. But my love hurt her.'

'We all make mistakes,' I said softly. 'We hurt people we love all the time.'

'I think if I tell you, Katrina, you'll hang up and leave me to die here without ever sharing it with anyone.' Sid's pain hung on the tapering of the last word. 'But I have to take that chance.'

I said I wouldn't hang up.

I thought about the hundreds of calls I'd taken, the nine active suicides I'd been witness to and how this might be my tenth. I thought about going against all I was supposed to do and trying to obtain his address so I could get Christopher to call an ambulance. I thought about how I'd been abused by my own uncle, how I was still here in this leatherette chair, still able to go on despite it, perhaps even because of it, and I was angry that Sid would not do the same. There was nothing he could tell me that I would judge. But I didn't want him to die, because then I would have failed as a crisis-line volunteer. Failed the one person I'd become attached to. My first caller here. And yet I had to accept how he had written his end.

'Are you still there?' Sid sounded as though he might fall asleep.

I nodded, said, 'Yes, I'm here,' and knew I might have little time.

Pills could take minutes or hours to dissolve; it depended on type and quantity, on resistance and mixture, what they had been swallowed with, how empty or full the stomach was, or how large or small the victim. I glanced at the Flood Crisis banner and the stickman with no head. Whoever had drawn that must have just finished a call with someone they were attached to and lost.

'Don't write it down,' he slurred. 'I know you probably write notes but I don't want anyone but you to know.'

I lay down the pen. Baby Jesus fell off the wall and onto my pad with a loud clump. Picking him up, I studied his cracked face. I dropped him in the wire basket under the desk.

'I'm not writing,' I said. 'Just give me your home address so I can send someone. Someone here will call an ambulance while you tell me. You have options; you don't have to do it this way. Tell me what you want to say, but don't die.'

'Don't ask me that, Katrina. I'm tired now ... very tired. Let me tell you ... I must...'

'But I don't want you to die!' I cried.

Jane had ended her call and poked her head in my booth. 'You can't tell a caller that,' she hissed. 'If they've chosen to die, you have to accept it.'

I covered the mouthpiece. 'Go fuck yourself, Jane,' I said.

'You can't talk to a co-volunteer that way. You're not in a fit state to take this call. Give me the phone, now.' She reached for it, purple nails glinting.

'If you touch me, I'll bite you,' I hissed.

It was a threat I'd often used as a child. I remembered it well and now I knew why. If a person invaded my space, or tried to pull me from where I'd hidden, I'd threaten to bite them.

'Katrina, I have to tell you this,' murmured Sid.

'I'm calling Norman,' snapped Jane, marching back into the lounge.

'It was a long time ago,' sighed Sid. 'It was snowing. White flakes. Lots of them.'

I looked at the darkening sky outside; it threatened to snow but for now it remained contained.

'It was snowing when I left her. I've never loved anyone since I loved her. My precious girl.'

I realised he was going to tell me about his daughter, the one he'd once mentioned. This dying man, a father, who surely should be with that daughter, sharing his final moments with her, not with a faceless crisis-line volunteer.

'Where is she?' I asked him. 'Can we call her?'

'No, she won't want me.' The gap between the words grew longer than the words themselves.

Christopher appeared at the booth, his expression everything I needed to see in a face. He crouched at my feet. 'Are you OK?' he whispered. 'Jane said it's an active suicide.'

'It's Sid.' I held Sid in one hand and reached out to Christopher's face with the other. I placed the handset against my body and whispered back: 'He took paracetamol and sleeping pills and shit knows what else. I don't want him to die. I know I'm wrong to.'

'You're not wrong,' said Christopher.

I put the handset to my ear again. Sid was coughing. I told him I was still here; I was waiting.

'But here,' insisted Christopher, 'we have to let them make their own choices.'

'What if this was your father all that time ago?' I said, covering the handset again. 'Wouldn't you want me to try and stop him?'

'It's not my father, Katrina.'

'He's someone's father,' I said, and listened to Sid once more.

His coughing had subsided. 'My daughter won't want me near her,' he mumbled in my ear, words light as snow.

'Tell me why not, Sid,' I urged him.

Christopher remained at my feet.

'I did a terrible thing – did I tell you that? I'm tired. I can hardly remember now. Maybe I don't want to go. Maybe I just want to sleep. I'm scared ... of going to ... hell ... going to hell ... I'm a coward ... I just want to go to sleep for a long time and wake up and I'm young again ... and I'm with her ... and I won't hurt her ... I'll just love her.'

'Give me your address, Sid,' I begged.

Christopher watched me but said nothing.

'I don't know ... can ... you ... forgive me?' Sid was floundering now; I could hear him flapping at the water.

'We're not here to forgive.' I repeated the crisis-line mantra.

'Forgive me,' he begged. 'I need ... someone ... to know ... that I just loved her ... and I'm sorry...'

'Give me your address.'

'*Forgive me.*'

'Your address.'

'*Forgive...*'

I shook my head. Held my head. Tried to keep my head. 'I forgive you, Sid.'

He gave me his address, and I wrote it on the pad, the only record of his confession. 'Ring them,' I told Christopher. 'He gave it to us so we can.'

He took the address and looked at it. I knew he was thinking of his own father.

I watched him pick up the other phone and heard him speak to the emergency services. Jane marched up to him and demanded what was going on and he showed her the address.

'She coerced him,' she spat. 'Norman's on his way.'

'I'm sleepy,' said Sid.

'Stay with me,' I said. 'Someone will come. Tell me your memory. I won't judge you.'

'She was just a child...'

'Your daughter?' My heart counted the seconds. I imagined they went faster than real seconds, faster than a wailing ambulance.

'Not really … not *really*…'

'But you loved her.'

'My little…'

'Your little what, Sid?'

The star flashed again. It lit the adjacent booth and the top of Christopher's head like an intermittent halo. He sat on the chair with the phone in there off its hook to show that he was only with me, not the world.

'That's not my name.' Sid's breathing rattled.

'Who are you?' I asked him.

Be you, I thought. If you must die, be you when you do. Be the name you were given at birth, the name that will one day be recorded as your death, even if it must be today.

'I'm Henry,' he said. 'And she was … my tiger … my Catherine…'

I was no longer in the sticky leatherette chair but curled up in the faded one in my father's study. I held Dad's cushion to my cheek and wore a yellow-and-white-flowered party dress. I was ten. It was my party. Everyone was looking for me. I could hear them in the hallway. Uncle Henry suggested to the guests that I might be in the shed, that it was my favourite place. When they went looking for me, he came into the study. He towered over me. He wore my 'I'm Ten Today!' badge on his checked lapel. He smiled. He wanted me to sit on his knee and kiss him for my birthday, but I wouldn't. Not in my father's chair. There was too much sadness there already, too much pain. I couldn't bear the weight. It pulled me and pressed me into the chair. Into my dad's chair.

Into the chair in the crisis-line booth.

'Just a kiss from my tiger,' he was saying. 'Just a birthday kiss.'

'No,' I said now. 'You're Sid. You're not Henry. I like *Sid*; I forgave *Sid*.'

'I'm … Henry … that's … my name … Catherine … was … my tiger.'

'No,' I said.

I was in my father's chair and there was snow sticking to the lattice window. Henry had gone. He did not come looking for kisses in the study or take me to see Geraldine in the shed because she was gone too. They had both gone, and Catherine-Maria as well. They were all gone.

The snow had covered all the footprints.

'Honest ... today ... my name ... Henry...'

'You left,' I whispered. 'I don't want you to be back.'

Why would I have written it this way? I was no poet or artist. I could not have chosen these words and I would not read them now. Would not accept them.

'I ... loved ... her...'

I retched spoiled milk and half-chewed biscuit all over the desk's surface. The pen slid through the slime. The word 'honest' on the pad drowned under the waterfall. Christopher touched my forehead and said something I couldn't hear. He tried to take the phone from me, but I snatched it back, held it to my chest and shook my head, spit flying from my mouth. Jane's face appeared. She was large, fuzzy at the edges, and her words tumbled over words, none recognisable to me.

'You took my name!' I screamed into the receiver.

I sank to the floor beneath the vomit-covered desk. Milk dripped over the edge, fat, rancid tears on the leather chair.

'I know who you are! I know all about the pictures you had!'

'Katrina ... what ... are...?'

'I know you,' I whispered, kneeling, curled.

'I ... don't ... understand...'

'Don't you dare pass out! Don't stop talking. Live, you bastard. You wait for them to come and revive you. Talk to me in your stupid, pathetic voice! Live with it like I have had to!'

'Katrina...' The word was faint.

'I'm not Katrina, I'm Catherine-Maria. That's who I am. Remember? And I'm not your daughter, and I'm not your love or your tiger. I was Catherine-Maria. Don't say my fucking name ever again.'

I thought he was laughing or coughing or maybe retching until I realised he was crying. Slow, pathetic gasps of breath. Slower, slower, slower.

'Why the fuck are *you* crying?' I demanded.

Christopher touched my arm and sank to the floor next to me, my vomit on his sleeve.

'It's him,' I said.

'Give me the phone, Katrina,' said Christopher.

'Forgive … me….' begged the man I'd called Sid and let in.

'Oh God oh God oh God oh God.' I held my head, rocked on my knees.

'Katrina.' Christopher prised the phone from my hands and put it to his ear. He put his other hand on my back. 'I can't hear him breathing anymore,' he said after a while. 'I think he's gone.'

'No. Call him, check, shout for him.' I had forgotten how to breathe.

'What should I call him?'

'You know his name,' I said.

'Henry,' said Christopher into the phone. 'Are you still with us?' He looked at me. 'I think I can hear breath. Henry…'

I grabbed the receiver. 'Are you there? Are you still there, you bastard?'

The man I'd called Sid and let into my heart moaned. He was trying to talk but the noise was all 's's and 'e's, and I didn't want to know. I didn't want to know. I remembered how easy it had been to pretend he'd never existed. How I'd rewritten him, edited him out of my life, scratched him out altogether with a child's red crayon, helped by my mother's removal of all his pictures, his belongings, by her telling me to forget him and then never uttering his name again.

But I could not delete him.

'I think he's going, Katrina.' Christopher dropped the phone between us and held my face with both hands. 'How do you want this to end? You have to live with it – not him. You have to do whatever you must to cope with this after today.'

How was I supposed to do that? How could I find any peace? I had to stop erasing, stop editing, and let the words find their own way in. It was his story. I only had to decide if I could get through it to the last page. Deal with what was written there. The man who had stolen my name, who had sneaked into my trust with his own fictional one, could now barely say anyone's name. Only that he was sorry.

A knock sounded at his end and then muffled voices.

'Sid,' I called because I couldn't say that other name.

A single, laboured breath. Banging on the door. Another breath. The voices on the other side of the door stopped. It wasn't Sid who had asked for forgiveness. There was no more breath. It wasn't Sid who was dying. No more breath. It wasn't Sid. A crash. A door banging against a wall. Tramping feet. Christopher held my hand.

'Henry,' I whispered.

No breath. Voices. Other voices.

'Henry, I forgive you.'

Christopher opened my fingers and removed the phone. I surrendered to the words of the paramedic telling me Henry had gone. I staggered past Norman and Jane into the whiteness. There was a sudden bleeping in my pocket. It was my phone. I pulled it out.

It was a text. My mother.

It said, simply, 'I'm sorry.'

26

Keeping the ghosts away

Another dream that was a memory:

Anna, my childhood friend, lay at my side. For a moment, we were on the sofa together, entwined in my sheets, the DVD digits colouring our breath in the icy living room ghostly green. I closed my eyes and snuggled up to her. She thawed my toes and fingers.

Then we were no longer in the post-flood flat. My sheets dissolved, became a daisy-covered duvet. The wallpaper melted, as mine had done in the rain, and turned into soft lilac paint. We were in my childhood bed. It was warm. The darkness safely cocooned us. The rest of the house was quiet.

'Are you asleep?' Anna asked.

'No,' I whispered. 'You?'

'Of course not,' she giggled. 'How could I ask if *you* were?'

I smiled. 'I knew that.'

'Let's tell ghost stories,' she said.

I paused. 'I can't be bothered.'

'You mean you're scared.' Anna shoved me. 'Big scaredy-cat. Go on. Let's make up the creepiest stories we can. Imagine if ... I know! We're lying here and we hear the door handle rattling. Dead soft at first, and then super loud. And then the door opens! And—'

'No,' I cried.

'What?' Anna's voice was confused in the dark.

'I don't want to do ghost stories.' I hated them. Always had. I was never sure how real they were.

'OK, OK. Don't know why you're scared, though. I always feel dead safe in your house.'

'Do you?' I was surprised. I didn't. I had done, once upon a time, but now it seemed a different place, and I wasn't sure why.

'Yes,' said Anna. 'But that's probably cos of you.'

I smiled.

'I still miss Geraldine,' she said.

My throat felt tight.

'Tell me again how she got away?'

I buried my face in the duvet. I couldn't remember. There was just a feeling. A feeling that churned my stomach and heated my cheeks. I knew it had been last Christmas. What had I told Anna? She probably knew more than I did. She had my memories. She was the teller of stories.

'Can't be bothered,' I said.

'There are no ghosts here, you know,' said Anna.

I wasn't sure.

'Are you asleep?' Anna asked after a while.

I pretended to be.

'I know you're still sad about Geraldine,' she whispered, her breath on my cheek. 'I think that's why you don't talk about her.' She paused. 'When we're older we'll get a house together. Just me and you. That's what friends do. No one else. And we can have a rabbit if you want. It's dead weird, but I had a dream the other night that we did have a house. But it got washed away like Noah's Ark. And we were dead sad. But it didn't matter cos we had each other.' Anna's voice slowed as sleep took her over. 'Anyway, I don't think it matters where you live, as long as you've got the right people with you. *That's* what keeps the ghosts away.'

I woke up and I was on the sofa. Alone. The DVD digits said 4.56. Fern was sleeping quietly in her room. I wanted to go home. I just wasn't quite sure where that was. The flood hadn't washed it away; the ghosts had.

But I wasn't afraid. Anna was right. The right people keep the ghosts away. And the blackest ghost of all had finally gone.

27

A snowy funeral

Fern poked her head around the bathroom door and, speaking around a pink toothbrush, white froth dribbling down her chin, asked who Uncle Henry was.

She spat into the sink and shouted over the water that I'd never mentioned him before. I heard the toothbrush drop into the mosaic jar where it had always belonged. She came back into the lounge for my answer.

I didn't have one.

In the cracked mirror above the oven, black clothes drained all colour from my face. I patted my cheeks to add pink. Not even Fern's gold beads tied in a stylish knot above my chest lessened the pallor. The dress was hers, too: Prada, exquisite and rich ebony. She'd received it during a two-month relationship with a much older man, on a trip to Paris.

'So who was he?' she repeated.

'Just a distant relative,' I finally answered. The word 'just' was as feeble as the words 'I'm fine'. 'I've not seen him for a long time. I'll tell you about it one day, when this one is done.'

When he's buried, I thought.

'Was he one of those uncles no one talks to? The kind who gropes you at family events and wears too-tight slacks and always dances to "The Birdie Song"?' Fern wrinkled her nose. 'Like my Uncle Nick – or Uncle Tit as we call him; he kept pawing me at a wedding, saying he was adjusting my sash.'

'Yes,' I said, sadly. 'One of those uncles.'

'So why go to the funeral?' Fern stood beside me. Her bathrobe was tied with the gold belt that had accompanied last night's outfit for the newspaper Christmas party. She moved my hair behind my ear. She was white fluff to my black satin. Light to shadow, yin to yang. We were opposites that fit perfectly together, despite our fall-out. If I could forgive my mother, I could certainly forgive Fern.

'And why are you so sad if you didn't know him?' she asked.

I leaned into her hand. 'It's always sad when someone dies.'

I wondered if it was. This certainly didn't feel like when my father had died or when I saw Nanny Eve in her coffin on the lounge table. Nanny Eve had always said that death was the great equaliser. She used to polish Pure Mary and say we all had to face it, whoever we were, whatever we'd done.

'I suppose.' Fern kissed my cheek and switched on the kettle.

I flattened the disobedient hairs of my left eyebrow. 'Aunt Mary will be sad,' I said.

Cut into warped segments, my face in the broken mirror looked curiously like hers. In my sadness, I became her. Time and pain twinned us. The fourteen-year-old Catherine who had enjoyed her comfort must now offer it. Henry was her brother. She would need me today.

And I'd have to see my mother.

We'd not seen one another since Henry's suicide, and I dreaded it. We had spoken on Wednesday after her texted apology. In the street outside Flood Crisis I'd rung her. Running away from that last phone call, passing through the light and dark created by the streetlamps, realising now how that very first call from the man I thought was Sid had broken the seal on my locked-away memory, I'd sobbed to her. She hadn't cried. She hadn't said sorry, not in words, but she'd promised to try to be some sort of a mother.

When we talked again on Thursday, I told her how I'd spoken to Henry, thinking of him as Sid, several times at Flood Crisis. Told her that must be why the hidden memory had finally broken out

– something about the sound and cadence of his voice that my unconscious mind recognised, allowing those events of my ninth year to reveal themselves once again.

I told her, too, that not only had I been witness to Henry's passing, but I had forgiven him. She had fallen silent. I wasn't even sure I *had* forgiven him. With my returned memory came the realisation that my mother had liked Henry. I recalled how she had flirted with him when he came to stay after my father's death. Whatever she had loved about my dad, she must have seen in Henry, despite how very different they were. Perhaps she had needed his affection, his attention, and inviting him for my sake had been merely an excuse.

My mother told me that, despite being his only remaining immediate relative, Aunt Mary wouldn't claim Henry's body or accept any responsibility for him. So the funeral would be arranged by whoever did so in such circumstances.

'He doesn't even deserve that' said my mother.

An official contacted them on Friday and suggested that, since no one had come forwards the council would incur the costs of a basic funeral. If they were not paying for the funeral, they would get no say in how it was arranged.

'I only ask that you make it as soon as possible,' Aunt Mary had apparently said.

My mother stated that she could endure the funeral and acknowledge his death, if I would *please* not say fuck in the cemetery. In those words, I saw our future; it would be difficult, sometimes impossible, always intense, but we would be OK.

'Be sad then,' said Fern now, on this Tuesday a week before Christmas. On the morning of Henry's cheap funeral, six days after his self-written but unrecorded passing. 'But don't torture yourself. There are happy things, like that Christopher at Flood Crisis.'

'I'm not going back there.' I rubbed concealer under my eyes to hide the dark rings.

'To Flood Crisis?'

'I'm done with crisis lines. I'll call Norman tonight and tell him

I'm not going in tomorrow. I'm tired of death and trauma and abuse. I should join the living now. *I* didn't die last week, did I?'

'But you've always said you want to help people.'

I sighed. 'I *do*. But maybe I need to … I don't know.'

Fern made us tea and handed me the black MENSA mug that I could never remember the origin of. 'What the hell happened last Wednesday, Cath? You said there was a bad call. You've been avoiding talking about it all week.'

'I was sick. There's a nasty bug going around. Volunteers are sick of Christmas.' I put two spoonfuls of sugar in my tea, needing sweetness to negate the sour day.

'I *know* that's not it,' said Fern gently.

'Another time,' I said.

When I tell you about Henry, I thought.

'You should've spoken to Christopher.' Fern smiled. 'He called again last night. Why don't you talk to him? He sounds worried about you.'

The tea was too hot and burned my throat. 'Look, some stuff *did* happen while you were away, you're right. And sometime I'll tell you. But I have to get this funeral over first. OK?'

'I know what it is,' said Fern, dipping a digestive biscuit into her drink.

'What?' My throat constricted.

'Does this Christopher wear stone-washed denim?'

I laughed. 'I wish that's all it was.' I emptied my undrunk tea in the sink. The steam misted the cracked mirror, obliterating my image. 'Right, do I look presentable for a funeral?'

She stood back, cocked her head and nodded. 'You look gorgeous.'

I wrapped my arms around my chest. 'I don't want to look gorgeous. There's a corpse no one likes.'

'You should keep the dress; you fill it better than me.'

I wondered if I had time to put on my blue suit instead. 'I can hardly walk in this skirt. It's all wrong.'

Fern smoothed it flat, her red nails like ladybirds. 'Did you know funerals are one of the best places to pick up a date? Remember that Neil guy with the huge hair? I met him at Scott Smith's funeral.'

I shook my head and put on last year's dark-grey coat, fastening the buttons up to the collar. I realised there was little point in the black dress when it was minus two outside and no one would even see it beneath the coat.

'There'll probably be only me, Mother, Graham, Mary and Martin. Don't think Celine will come to this one.'

'Don't mention that bitch's name to me,' said Fern.

In a bleak mood on Thursday morning I'd let slip that Celine had told the paper about Fern's column. Perhaps I'd wanted to cause trouble. Perhaps I'd thought Fern deserved to know. Fern had stormed into her bedroom and made some changes to the column she was about to submit.

On Saturday I saw the amendments.

'I'm surprised your editor ran it,' I'd told Fern as I read the piece over muffins, trying not to choke. Perhaps he'd felt bad over his hasty treatment of Fern and allowed her a little creative freedom in compensation. 'But I'm glad they did,' I added. *Celine won't be,* I'd thought.

'You want me to come today?' asked Fern now.

'I doubt there'll be any single men,' I said.

'I'll go back to bed then.' She kissed me and softly said, 'Call me if you need me afterwards, OK? I'll get wine if you think we'll need it tonight.'

I picked up the box from the sideboard.

'What's in there?' asked Fern.

'Pictures.' I took out the ones I needed and put them in my coat pocket.

☾

When I got to my mother's she was in the kitchen by the sink. Perhaps if we do write our own blueprint we make sure that when a catastrophe is predicted in bold italics someone always stays in the kitchen and makes tea and food. Even during the flood, I imagined the first thing people struggled to rebuild or create in whatever temporary home they found was a kitchen. Something must remain constant; a safe theme when the plot tests us.

Graham wore the smoke-grey suit he'd worn at every wedding for the last decade. He hugged me, answering my unspoken question with a nod towards the kitchen door. I hung my coat on the banister and returned to the kitchen I'd stormed out of a lifetime ago.

My mother wore a black skirt and jacket with the customary string of pearls, her hair in an upward sweep. She had baked bread and ham and broccoli quiches. The yellow stain on the fridge was still half scrubbed. The floor was spotless.

'How are you?' I asked her.

She took a tray of fresh bread from the oven. Its heat warmed my frozen legs.

'I don't know if I can do this,' she said. 'I don't think I can put on any sort of face.' She looked at me, briefly. 'But you're right to think we should. You're brave, Catherine.'

'No, I'm selfish,' I said. 'I'm doing this so I can move on.'

'I already said goodbye to him once.' She turned the tray upside down and let the bread drop with a heavy thud onto the wire rack. 'I told him twenty years ago that I never wanted to see him again and I still don't want to see him. Even in a grave. He doesn't deserve for us to go to his funeral. I'm only doing it because he's your dad's brother; Mary's brother. It's what you do for the dead.'

'Death doesn't excuse him.' I fingered my dress's thin, shiny belt. 'It doesn't cancel what he was. So, don't go today for him or even for me – do it for you. He was what he was. He fu ... sorry ... he *messed* with our past, and if we don't go he could mess with our futures too. You've put on your black suit, so part of you wants to go. Part of you wants to say goodbye. That's all we're doing.'

'I'm wearing black because it's the right colour,' she said, and I nodded. 'Why did you forgive him?' She slammed a drawer closed, held up a bread knife and glared at me. 'How *can* you? I just don't understand.'

'Because he was sorry.' I spoke quietly. I was cold and wished she'd left the oven door open.

'No, he wasn't. He was dying. A scared, desperate coward.'

'I think he was sorry.' My voice was barely louder than the oven fan.

'How can you *defend* that monster?'

'I'm not!' I cried. 'You have no idea! I *have* to believe he was sorry! I have to or I can't...' I wiped my running nose on the back of my coat sleeve. 'It isn't about him, it's about *me*. About living with what happened.'

'Your dad would never have forgiven him,' she said.

That hurt. It hurt in places my body had never been hurt. I knew my dad would likely have killed him. That it would have destroyed him.

'But Dad doesn't *need* to forgive him,' I said. 'He doesn't have to live with it.'

'I do miss your dad sometimes.' Mother stared out of the window at the trees covered with fresh snow, their branches bowing under the weight.

'I miss him all the time,' I said.

'I'm glad Henry's dead.' She turned, her arms crossed, her pearls askew. 'If he wasn't I might have killed him.'

I nodded and said, 'I'd love to bury what he did, but that doesn't work; I already tried it. So, I've forgiven him. I'll see him in the ground and go on.' I paused. Took a breath. 'When you found that ... those *pictures* ... didn't you wonder about me? Didn't you, even for a second, think he might have ... you know...?'

She shook her head. 'No. We got rid of him and I shut him out of my mind. Have done ever since.'

'But my behaviour. My moods. You must have wondered why I was such a pain.'

'I thought it was because of your dad's death. You were never the same after he went. I should have been ... *kinder*. But I was hurting too. Maybe I was resentful that I was left with it all. With you. Wrong, but ... well...'

I didn't mind. I liked her honesty. We knew where we stood with one another.

Graham came into the kitchen.

'If we're going, we should go,' he said. 'We have to pick up Mary and Martin and Celine, then be at Hen ... at *his* house for twelve.'

'At *his* house?' I asked. 'We go from his *house*?'

'It's OK, Catherine.' Graham put his arm around my shoulders. I didn't think I would ever get warm or want to eat homemade bread again. 'We don't have to go inside or anything, and we're all here with you. They just bring out the coffin and we follow the hearse to the church.'

'They're letting him in a church?' My thoughts were ridiculous. No one knew what he was; they only knew him as a tragic old man who'd taken too many pills and died in his chair.

'It's a public-health funeral,' said my mother, putting three quiches on the windowsill to cool. Her heels clacked on the tiles. She avoided the H-shaped crack. 'Just the basic necessities: collection of the body, church service, hearse, coffin and the committal at the grave. The intention is that anyone looking couldn't tell the difference between this and any other funeral.'

'Except there's a monster in the coffin,' I said.

My mother glanced at me but said nothing. I guessed the word 'monster' was allowed. Maybe she'd ignore the odd necessary 'fuck', too. And yet today of all the days I had no pressing urge to say it.

'We don't have to go,' said Graham.

'We'll go,' I said.

White flakes stuck to the kitchen window. It always seemed to snow when I hurt. Mother sniffed a ham quiche and wondered aloud if three was enough; Graham assured her it was more than enough for six.

In the hallway, I put on my coat and prepared for the cold. Mother opened the door. Snow blew in, disturbing the tiny bells on the Christmas tree so they chimed our departure.

She held the door open as we stepped onto the drive, and as I passed her, she softly said, 'Catherine...' she kissed my cheek '...you look nice in that dress.'

I looked down at the fabric, tempted to irritate her by telling her it was Fern's. But I resisted. This was maybe the closest I'd ever get to an apology, and I didn't want to slap her again. So, I kissed her powdered cheek and got in the car.

'Does Celine know?' I asked Graham as we approached her street.

'We just said he's a distant relative.'

'Why is she coming?'

Graham pulled onto the kerb and pressed the horn. 'I said she should.'

'Why?' I demanded.

'I just thought she should. She owes you, in light of what she did.'

Celine emerged from her ostentatious detached house wearing a furry brown jacket and suede trousers, her styled curls bobbing in the wind. When she got into the back of the car her perfume outdid the cold, making me sneeze twice.

'Mark not coming?' I asked, without my usual sarcasm.

'He's away.' She fluffed her hair and said 'Hi' to my mother and Graham. 'He should be home for Christmas. Sorry about your uncle.'

'I'm not,' I said. 'But thanks.'

Aunty Mary was waiting on her doorstep as we crawled up her drive, grit spitting away from the tyres like tears. Martin stood at her side. She scanned the car windows, and I knew she was looking for me. So I leaned forward and caught her eye. She touched her cheek. Slamming the door, I ran over to her. She wrapped me in her arms and pulled my face to her chest and said, 'Oh, Catherine, you should have come to me. Oh, *Catherine.*' The name I'd endured for twenty years surrounded me as much as her warmth. Then she whispered, 'Don't press me too hard, dear; I'm not quite accustomed to my colostomy bag yet.'

'Oh.' I pulled back, suppressing a smile.

'I've never been to a funeral with a colostomy bag,' she said behind her hand, cheeks pink. 'I didn't think I had a black dress with enough room to feel comfortable, but I got this one in the Epilepsy Charity Shop yesterday.'

Martin patted my arm and headed for the car.

Mary kissed me, chafing my chin, and I realised she was almost as scratchy as Uncle Henry had been. Gagging, I ran to her sculpted hedge and threw up into the snow. I heard her saying 'Catherine' again, over and over, asking if I was OK, saying we could go inside and have a cup of tea and cake instead like when I'd stayed home from school.

'Don't go,' she said. 'You don't have to. I'll explain to the others.'

My mother was watching from the car. I saw her starting to open the door, but Graham touched her shoulder and she remained where she was. I held up my hand; the universal sign for 'I'm fine'.

I said the same to Mary: 'I'll be fine. It just comes over me. It will only get worse if I don't go today.'

'You're sure?' Flakes of snow landed on her shoulder, making her a bride.

Of all the words I looked for only 'fine' resurfaced.

'Catherine, I'm not going to say what I think of my brother. You don't need to hear that.' Aunty Mary shivered and pulled her grey shawl a little tighter. 'But I will say that I'm sorry we didn't see what he did. I can't believe it. I do, I mean, I do, but back then I never in a million years thought he'd have done that to you. I thought he just liked to look at those ... at those ... awful pictures. It's no excuse, but I thought your eczema and your moodiness was because your dad had gone. How stupid I was! I'm sorry we let you down.'

'No, you don't have to b—'

She put her finger on my lips. 'I am. I understand why you're doing this and I'm with you; I'm at your side today and in whatever you must do. I can't imagine your hurt but I can at least try and lessen it. Come on.'

She held my hand and we went to the car. We climbed in the back, everyone shuffling along to make room until we were packed in like a bridal party wearing too-big dresses.

'Mind my bag,' said Aunty Mary to Martin, and I wasn't sure whether she meant her leather clutch or the one attached to her abdomen.

It took half an hour to get to the house. I couldn't help but think of it as Sid's home because *he* had died there, looking out onto a car park and the back of a supermarket while holding a phone and talking to me. For me, until I saw him buried, Henry was still alive.

The building he'd lived in was unremarkable: three floors of drab, small-windowed flats near a bingo hall, supermarket and burnt-out factory. Renovation work was going on downstairs, the flood damage still apparent in the salt-streaked walls and crumbling plaster. But there were no clues that a man had killed himself here. That a man who had tormented his nine-year-old niece had lived within its walls, fooling people into befriending him and a crisis-line worker into affection.

'Here's the hearse,' said my mother. 'Graham, will you?'

Graham got out and spoke to the pallbearers, and they went into the building.

'I feel sick,' I said.

'Don't say that,' said Celine. 'Now I do too. I hate funerals.'

'Why'd you come, then?' I demanded, hand over my mouth.

'You're my sort-of stepsister,' she said.

I laughed and the nausea passed.

'Oh God, here's the coffin.' Aunty Mary put a fist to her mouth.

It was dark wood, significantly simple and utterly flowerless. Graham followed the pallbearers to the hearse with his head bowed and waited until they had loaded it into the back before returning to us.

I wondered what Henry looked like inside it. My memory gave me a virile, laughing man: bearded, tanned, strong, insistent, cruel. But Sid had been weak, ill, pathetic, *kind*. Who had really died? Could the spirit of a powerful man go on? I wanted to lift the lid and see the face I was bidding goodbye.

'No one loved him enough for flowers?' asked Celine.

'A council funeral doesn't include them,' said my mother.

The hearse pulled away, and we followed at the same respectful speed. Aunty Mary cried and tried to hide it, her face in Martin's waistcoated chest.

I didn't mind if she was sad; he was her brother. I said to her, 'It doesn't hurt me if you cry.'

My mother stared at the back of the hearse. The wipers swished back and forth to brush away the snow.

'I thought he was just a distant relative,' said Celine, looking uncomfortably at Mary.

'Even blood can be distant,' I said.

The church was one that would have been pretty rising behind a blushing bride and her enamoured husband in wedding pictures. Partially hidden by evergreen trees, the spire tapered off into a rusted weather vane. Doors formed a perfect archway to frame newlyweds.

We followed the coffin down the aisle in pairs, me with Celine, our shoes clacking. Every sound was magnified in the lofty space. By the altar was a life-sized twig stable and inside were stone statues of Jesus, Mary and Joseph. Joseph held a lantern that glowed orange, lighting the Holy Virgin's face. I saw the one in Nanny Eve's house; my namesake smashed on the floor. Broken at my hand. Now she smiled at me, pure and encouraging and forgiving.

'God knows how Mary styled her hair without heated curlers,' said Celine.

There were other people already sitting in the church: three older men in worn suits and a woman with a cherry-adorned hat perched on a frizzy wig. I couldn't hide my surprise and stared at them as we found our places at the front.

'Who the hell are they?' I asked my mother.

She sighed, resigned more than cross. 'I have no idea.'

The pallbearers placed the coffin on a waiting stand with expert precision, and the priest made the sign of the cross. Martin had once joked that it was the sign for put it down and sod off. Father Colahan (named in the ceremony pamphlet) looked like a drunken Hugh Hefner going to a Halloween party dressed as a vicar.

He said, 'I am the resurrection and the life;' and the ceremony began. When he talked of our hope for eternal life, I asked Mother what my dad's funeral had been like.

She looked at her hands, folded neatly in her lap and said, 'The church was full. He was loved.'

I'd not been allowed to go; everyone had decided that I was too young at eight to witness such a thing, which was ironic considering what I would experience only a year later. So I never got to say goodbye or see my dad in the ground. Mother blew now into her cupped hands, even though big radiators blasted dry heat across the pews. Looking at the Virgin Mary's motherly face I decided that if I ever had children they would witness every death, say goodbye to everyone who left. How badly written was my life that I'd be at this funeral but had missed my father's? Suddenly too warm, I undid my coat and let it fall open. Celine looked at the dress and I knew she would not resist a comment.

'Where did you get *that*?' she hissed. 'It must have cost a fortune.'

Father Colahan said we were to entrust Henry to the love and mercy of God.

'It did, but I slept with the Prada shop assistant,' I lied.

'Catherine, please,' whispered my mother. 'Can we not have sex in a church?'

Father Colahan asked God to give comfort to those who mourned here today. He suggested that, since no one wanted to speak about Henry, he would read a passage from Isaiah 40:20-31, and the old woman in the fruity hat put her hand up and asked, 'May I speak, Mister?'

He nodded and she joined him at the podium, her hat dropping two cherries as she walked.

'I'm not family or nothing,' said the woman. 'But I'm sitting here thinking it's a shame no one wants to talk about Henry.'

I jerked at the name; I'd imagined she'd say 'Sid'. Mother touched my knee, and the wedding ring my father gave her glinted in the multi-coloured light from the stained-glass window.

'Henry lived two floors above me,' Cherry Hat continued. She wore a fake fur coat and had a gold bag across her chest. 'He took me in when I was flooded until I got me another place to stay. We played cards when the water was washing over me new carpets – council ones but still new. Me mother's chaise longue that we couldn't move got ruined. But he let me win the game to cheer me up. He pretended he had nothing of value, but I saw his cards when we got done. He didn't know. He had three kings and I'd had nowt.'

I remembered going on the bus to my first Flood Crisis shift and seeing Will with his new girlfriend, Miranda; he'd said that I played the worst game with the best hand of anyone he'd known. That I could have four aces and still lose. Uncle Henry had played that game too, but he'd faked it.

'So I just wanted to say,' said Cherry Hat, 'that Henry was a good sort. Liked his brandy of an evening. Kept himself to himself but wasn't rude. Always said "good morning" on the stairs. He missed travel and not having family, but I guess he had 'em cos I see 'em here today, and I guess that's what matters: that they're here now.' She looked at the coffin and said, 'Rest in peace, Henry,' then resumed her place behind us.

Before we left for the burial, I sneaked back into the church and lit a candle. Not for Henry. But for my dad. And for my mum. While the few mourners were getting into the cars, I struck a match for the woman I should have seen blessed and spoken about by her grief-stricken family. For the woman I'd been too young to know. In the draught from the open door my flame flickered. But it stayed alight. Mary – the most famous mother on earth – watched me leave.

As the car crawled through the cemetery's iron gates, I scanned the gravestones for my dad's plot.

'Henry won't be near Dad, will he?' I said.

'No, sweetheart.' Aunty Mary squeezed my cold hand within her fat one. 'He died too long ago. Henry will be in the new bit where it's fresh.'

My father and Henry, though joined by blood, were separated by time, by rows of uneven monuments and a line of gaunt trees and a sloping hill. I was glad.

The cemetery was white. Shifting shades of black, we stood around an open grave awash with snow. I imagined we looked like a negative strip of photograph yet to be developed. The trees were reversed too – adorned with transparent slush instead of green leaves. To observers the scene must have looked like any other burial, but for the lack of flowers and the pitifully few mourners.

But other guests came – guests only I could see.

The priest announced that he would commit the body to the ground. Aunt Mary suppressed a sob. And I saw Flood Crisis Helen by the trees. Among the bare branches I pictured her as I had while talking to her on the phone: tall and willowy with flowing hair about her shoulders. She bent with the wind, not against it, unbreakable. She waved at me, and I smiled back.

Father Colahan whispered about 'ashes to ashes' and 'dust to dust', and I saw Will with Miranda. He held her hand but he watched me, eyes full of understanding. Before they disappeared behind a stone angel with snow gathered at her feet like worship, he smiled and whispered, *Be happy, Cath*.

Father Colahan's voice narrated my life with words about 'in the sure and certain hope of resurrection to eternal life' as Geraldine lolloped between the crosses and cherubs, leaving tiny marks in the snow. She circled for a while. Sniffed this grave and that. Then she vanished into the bushes, like the rabbit in *Alice in Wonderland*.

My mother and Aunty Mary picked frozen earth from the pile near the gaping hole and threw it onto the coffin. By the trees I saw Sid. The Sid I'd pictured and grown fond of. The Sid I'd imagined, with grey-streaked hair and strong hands and tired eyes. Sid, who had never existed but who now waved at me and walked into shadows cast by the falling sun.

For a moment, the sun blinded me. I blinked.

And there was Nanny Eve. Nanny Eve in her many layers of clothes to ward off the cold, with a bag of knitting and mint sweets. She sang. I heard her melody across the space. Now I knew why she'd stopped singing all those years ago. It hadn't been me. Or the broken Virgin Mary. But the moment she had learned what her son Henry was.

I opened my pocket and took out three pictures. The one Henry had taken of me in a summer dress holding Geraldine. One of me sitting on the garden steps looking as sad as a child possibly can. One where Henry held up a huge fish, grinning, his teeth as bared as the fish's. I threw them on the coffin. They scattered like cards abandoned by a resigned loser.

I said goodbye to Henry.

I could because in his death's aftermath all the ghosts died. I could put my sadness into that yawning grave on top of his cheap coffin, next to the photos and the earth. I'd not have to carry it around anymore. Only those standing with me would move into the future: my mother in her dark suit; Aunty Mary in her charity frock; and me in my borrowed Prada. I could forgive. I could forgive him and my mother and Celine. And most of all myself.

'Let's go home,' said my mother. 'We're done.'

As we left. I looked back. Two more ghosts.

My mum and dad.

They stood in the middle of the path and watched the car pull away. Dad's hair, so like mine, shone with life in the dying sun. Mum's eyes twinkled. They held hands. He said my name and it bounced as it had when Nanny Eve sang it. It jumped and leapt and lolloped, like a freed rabbit. All the way to the moon that suddenly appeared opposite the sun.

Go and be happy, Catherine-Maria. Maria in the moon. The heart is the first organ that forms. Everything we need to know is in there. Mine was yours. Maria in the moon.

Driving home, we fell quiet. The windows steamed up so I couldn't see the moon anymore. Aunty Mary held my hand. I put the other inside an empty pocket. I felt empty too but in a good way, as though I'd surrendered the weight of something and now I could breathe.

The quiches on the windowsill had gone cold so my mother warmed them in the oven for ten minutes. Graham lit a cigarette in the garden, and smoke curled past the window like a sensual spectre. Aunty Mary turned on the Christmas lights and we all sat in the dining room and drank tea, silent. Outside, more snow fell, burying the day. In the hallway, the old clock marked another hour closer to tomorrow. After a while Celine picked up the Saturday newspaper, flicked through it, read something and tutted.

'What's wrong with you?' I put my cup on the table.

'I should sue your friend,' she hissed.

'I guess you're referring to Fern's column?'

'How *dare* she call me a slag?'

I smiled. 'I believe she called you a cliché but if you want to interpret that as slag...'

'Oh, good,' enthused Aunty Mary. 'I'm so glad they reinstated her.'

'What does she mean "not really married"?' demanded Celine, skim-reading. 'I *am* married.'

'I think she's just observing the irony that someone with a marriage like yours revealed the sham of hers.' I leant across and looked at the picture of Fern wearing her favourite silver, I-have-class blouse.

'What's that supposed to mean?' Celine snatched the paper away, crumpling Fern's face.

Graham came into the room with a tray of egg mayonnaise sandwiches, and Celine whined to him that the column was slanderous.

'For God's sake, shut up, Celine.' He placed the tray on the table. 'What do you expect? Now give it a rest and have a bit of respect.'

I could have argued that she meant 'libellous' since slander is the spoken word, but couldn't be bothered. I just wanted to put the day to rest.

I endured quiche and egg mayonnaise until the hallway clock struck six and I could go home. Not to where the walls had been rebuilt, or to some place 'where the heart is' but somewhere I could feel safe; where I could truly be myself. Where Fern was.

My mother was in the kitchen, her predictability a comfort. Life would go on. I broke my storming-off-after-Sunday-lunch routine and went to say goodbye to her. She was methodically loading the dishwasher. She had taken off her black jacket, revealing a blouse of a surprisingly fresh green.

'I'm going,' I said.

'OK.' She straightened up, closed the dishwasher door and clicked the button. It whirred into life. 'Are you coming for lunch on Sunday?'

'You have to ask?' I leant forwards and kissed her cheek, stiff, not accustomed to being so close to her face. 'Where else would I be on Sunday?'

She got some Mr Muscle out of the cupboard under the sink. On my way out into the snow I turned and watched her starting to scrub the work surfaces. Her immaculate hair shimmied in time with the action. It occurred to me that we are all perfect in our imperfections, unique in our failings. She might not be my biological mother and she might have made many mistakes, but I knew that I loved her despite this; because she had stayed, and because of her realness and her shortcomings.

And that was the most flawless love of all.

Choosing the best words

I was back at my house. The one that would soon be my home again. The wreckage didn't look quite so bad now. Perhaps it was because I felt more optimistic about its future. Robin was waiting while John went to the van to fetch whatever implements were required for the day's building task. He leaned against the fireplace he'd once eyed me from, toying with the strap of his overall. I had floor now: new and barely scuffed wood that hid the dry soil and wires beneath.

'Do you fancy going out sometime?' he asked.

I felt for a moment like the boards had come loose. He buried the pretty hands that once made me nauseous deep into his pockets and hunched over as though preparing for the onslaught of my answer. I'd thought of him as Robin and now couldn't recall his real name.

I considered the clichéd 'It's not you, it's me' reply. It was true, but surely I could find better words than that for this man who'd done nothing wrong. Though I no longer feared strange names or adverse reactions to my words, I had no desire to go out with him. It wasn't him; it really was me. I was a cliché. A not-interested cliché. But I didn't say that.

'I'm with someone now,' I lied. 'Robin—'

'Who's Robin? I'm Stan.' His too-soft hair flopped in indignation. Of course he was. That was his name.

'I'm sorry. See – what kind of girlfriend would I be?' I laughed. 'I can't even get your name right. Imagine trying to reserve a table? We'd get to a restaurant and not even know who we are.'

Robin stared at me like I'd just lifted my skirt or something. Outside I heard John rummaging in the van, a clatter of heavy tools against metal, and then, despite the weather, an ice cream van's cheery tune. The draught from the open door kissed my bare ankles.

Robin blushed and said he felt stupid for asking. 'I wasn't going to,' he said. 'But then I thought I might not see you and I'm going home for Christmas. Now I wish I hadn't.'

'Don't be sorry,' I insisted.

I admired his willingness to reveal more than I did with my naked ankles. I could never have asked anyone out. I'd never risk the rejection. But he was willing to put himself in a vulnerable position.

He shrugged. 'You met someone. It happens. It's fine.'

'Ro ... um, *Stan*, I'm sorry about what happened that night in the taxi.' I pulled my bag up my shoulder little, looked at the new floor and then at his youthful, not-yet-lived-in face. 'I was a mess then. I just wanted you to know that it wasn't anything you did.'

'I'm glad,' he said. 'You scared me.'

'I'm fine,' I said; and it was no cliché, only the truth.

John clomped back into the house, spreading mud all over my new floorboards. He dropped a bag of tools near the fireplace.

'We're only working until lunchtime,' he said. 'We'll never get back to Manchester tonight if we don't leave then.'

'I didn't even think you'd be here today,' I said.

It was Christmas Eve. I had worked the nightshift at the care home until five and then decided only to nap for an hour or two so I would sleep deeply that night. I'd be having Christmas dinner at my mother's the next day, and the familiar feeling of not wanting to go was a welcome one.

'Why are you here?' John asked. 'Not got shopping to do?'

'Just seeing if there was any last post,' I lied.

Really, I'd wanted to see the house. Wanted to stand on the new floors and see the foundations before they disappeared forever beneath fresh wallpaper and gloss paint. The place had survived floods, been stripped to brick. Soon you'd not even know what had happened here. Its inner workings – the plumbing and wiring – were done, and now the exterior would be repaired. Without strong foundations, no external beauty can survive. Paint can only hide so much before the memories crawl out of the woodwork.

'When will you be done?' I asked.

'At about noon,' said John.

'No, when will it be finished?'

'Maybe four weeks,' he said. 'Close enough?'

I couldn't quite imagine it completed; living there again. And even when it was done, it wouldn't be finished, I thought. I asked them to make it beautiful. Said I was putting my house in their hands.

I looked at Robin's but they were still in his pockets.

'We're good builders.' John puffed up his chest at the suggestion that they might be anything else. 'Me and matey-boy here will do you proud.'

'Thank you.' I fastened up my coat. 'Have a great Christmas.'

John opened a huge plan and laid it across the floor: the map of my future. Robin looked at me, maybe seeking a different answer to the one I'd given. I admired his childlike optimism and wondered why I couldn't just say 'yes' and go on a date with him. But instead I left knowing I might never see either of them again.

That evening – our first Christmas Eve together – Fern prepared extra spicy chilli and rice in a wok she'd acquired from Victor. While the mince simmered and Fern chopped red peppers, I sat on the worktop and watched her, a plastic cup of wine in my hand. Our tiny gold tree stood on the coffee table; Fern had adorned it with multi-coloured condom wrappers.

Two days ago, in its yellow light, I'd told her about Uncle Henry. She had cried; I hadn't, because I'd done all my crying. The light had made her tears into icy drops on her cheek. Then we'd fallen asleep on the sofa, my head on her feet and her arm across my ankles, tummies together, the way Anna and I had shared a bed once upon a time.

'I saw that builder Robin at the house,' I said now. 'He asked me out.'

Fern poured some wine into the wok and it hissed. 'What did you say?'

'No.'

'Why?' She dropped the empty bottle in the bin. 'Cath, you have to get back in the saddle. I know it's harsh but I get up again and again all the time. You're over Will. You're the bravest person I know with what you've been through. So why not give some poor man a chance? What's the worst that could happen? You get your heart broken? You'll live.'

'It's easier to be alone.' My words hung in the air, disrupted only by the bubbling chilli and Fern popping the cork of another bottle.

During the week following the funeral I hadn't felt like talking to anyone other than Fern. I'd had to call Norman to say I was leaving Flood Crisis. He understood. He'd called me the morning after my last shift to suggest I go in and talk about the whole experience; but I hadn't wanted to. I couldn't imagine walking up those steps again, looking for a handrail in case I fell and not finding one. Now I knew I was done with crisis work.

I thought often of Christopher during that week; of when he'd taken the phone from me at Flood Crisis, of how he'd helped me do what was best while Henry died. In the middle of the night I wondered about calling him, but I was afraid. He hadn't rung for a while now so he must have decided I was too difficult after all. Maybe he couldn't deal with what he'd seen; with my running away from him that last day at Flood Crisis. With my past. Me.

I swallowed more wine to bury the hurt that rose in my throat.

'Take a risk,' said Fern. 'Turn up at Robin's door in nothing but a raincoat.'

'I don't have one. And he goes home today. Anyway, I don't want him.'

I watched the chilli sauce bubble like sizzling tears. I told Fern about when I was nine and dreamt of having a house with a red roof and white bricks and a beautiful face on a wall that wasn't the Virgin Mary. I bit into a piece of red pepper. 'I used to imagine I'd never let anyone except my friend Anna in, and we'd share clothes and stay up late and talk. But no men were allowed.'

Fern ground black pepper into the chilli and nodded and asked if shutting people out had made me happy. I couldn't answer her.

'You can't be sad,' she said. 'It's Christmas tomorrow. Next year is going to be our best. Your house will be finished and my column will be made into a number-one book; that's what I'm hoping for anyway.' She paused and looked at me. 'Why are you so sad tonight?'

I didn't know. 'Maybe I'm just tired.' I stared at my wine until I couldn't see anymore.

'You've had a hellish few weeks. But it's time to relax and overindulge and be full of festive joy.'

Christmas was the worst time to be sad. I kicked against the drawer that only opened when the other was shut. 'Do you know how many calls crisis lines receive at Christmas?' I asked Fern. 'How many more people attempt suicide? How many people are alone tonight?'

'Quit thinking about crisis lines. You're done with them.'

'I am,' I said. 'But not with helping people. I'm thinking ... maybe...'

'What?'

'I should retrain or something. I like the idea of counselling. But I'd have to study, wouldn't I?'

'You so could, especially with all your experience – the volunteering, and what's happened to you.'

'Maybe I'll look into it in the new year.'

'You'd better.'

Fern poured more wine. 'I can't believe we're both single. The happiest night and no chance of a Christmas shag. Well, I suppose no one can dump us. Imagine that? On Christmas Eve?'

I could; I remembered that Christopher's wife had done that. Left him with only a useless gift and gone. How must he feel tonight?

The radiator filled up, its frantic bubbling competing with the bubbling food. I stared at our gold tree and saw something poking out of the magazines piled beneath like gifts. The watch; his watch. I put down my wine with a clatter.

'What's wrong now?' Fern turned on the radio and Cliff Richard started singing about the saviour. 'You want more wine?'

'Did you put it under the tree?' I asked, jumping down from the counter.

'Did I put what under the tree?' she called after me, while Cliff reminded us to open our eyes, that we shouldn't look back or turn away.

I rummaged under the magazines, pulling at the pages like a child with glittery wrapping paper on Christmas morning. I retrieved the watch and held it up. Fern looked at it and said she'd seen it lying around and wasn't sure where it came from so she'd thought it would do as a gift for someone.

'It's Christopher's,' I said.

Fern put her hand over her mouth.

'What?' I asked.

'He rang,' said Fern.

'What?'

She looked at me. 'Last night. I forgot to tell you! Damn! You were in the shower and then I got busy writing my column and it just slipped my mind.'

'*Slipped* your mind?' I gripped the red strap. 'What did he say?'

Fern looked sheepish. 'He said he wondered why you hadn't returned his call ... asked if you were OK, I think.' She turned back to stir the chilli; I could see she was blushing. 'I think I said you weren't too good but I was sure you'd ring at some point.'

'Return *what* call?'

The chilli popped and spat a drop of scalding liquid onto Fern's arm, making her swear. 'Didn't you get my note?' she asked, dabbing the spot with a damp cloth.

'Shit, Fern, *what* note?' I burnt hot but my hands felt cold.

'I wrote a note and left it on your pillow. He called the other night when you were at your mother's. I put it here – just *here*.' She went to the sofa and pulled away the duvet and cushions, searching in the cracks and gaps and eventually pulling out a yellow square of paper with 'Christopher rang. Call him' scrawled across it. 'I thought you'd seen it and just weren't interested – you never said anything.'

'Shit, I didn't see it.'

I stared at her scribbled words, imagining how warm they'd have made me feel if I'd seen them with the ink still wet. Now they were dry and I hadn't responded. Christopher *had* rung.

I pulled on my coat, grabbed my scarf, and said I wouldn't be long.

'Where are you going now? The food's nearly ready.' Fern followed me, wine spilling from her glass. Her mouth hung open like a thirsty dog. 'It's freezing and nowhere's open.'

'I'll be back for dinner.' I kissed her cheek. 'I promise.'

'Are you going to his? Have you got your best underwear on?'

I closed the door on her string of excited questions, without giving her a single answer.

Victor was smoking a cigarette on the doorstep; he watched me descend the metal stairs, gripping the railing. 'Happy Christmas,' he called, and said he hoped Santa had a bulging sack tonight.

I laughed and wished him the joys of the season.

Frozen black puddles reflected strings of lights and flashing angels. Gardens had been decorated with silly Santas and smiling snowmen. I walked on the grass verge so I wouldn't fall, holding onto walls when I had to endure the path. Tonight I wouldn't cut my knee as I had on that first Flood Crisis shift.

Tonight there'd be no hurt.

A group of carol singers hurried past me, practising their high notes, warbling in unison. Festive hats covered their heads, and tins of money rattled in their hands. Though I'd never visited the place, I remembered Christopher's address from the sheet Claudia gave me at our training session. No star guided me, only three drunken girls in feather boas, who gave me shrieked directions. But I *was* bearing a gift that was part gold.

The street when I found it was quiet. Christopher's house was at the end of a cul-de-sac, near a huge field glistening with patches of ice. Far away, someone sang 'Silent Night'. Pure words carried on the air. I wrapped my hand around the watch and counted the house numbers as I had so many times on the approach to my own flood-ruined place; one, three, five, seven, nine, eleven.

I stopped at thirteen and stared at the brown door with a rusted brass knocker. No light shone to signal that someone was at home; my heart dropped. Still, I walked up the path, slipping and stopping to hold the fence to stop myself toppling over.

At the red step I almost turned and left, fearing what this door might reveal. But I banged the knocker twice then stood back and waited. Eleven intakes of frosty breath and I prepared to leave. Then Christopher opened the door. White-faced, he blinked in the unwelcome light. His T-shirt was creased.

'Katrina?' The word was a sleepy question.

Katrina. Was I her?

'Were you asleep?' I tried to look past the half-closed door and see what I'd never heard in the background on the phone, what I had tried to visualise some nights when I couldn't sleep. But he blocked my view.

'I think so. I was watching TV.' He scratched his hair. 'Might have been something with that woman off *Building Fabulous Houses* in it.'

'It's only eight-thirty,' I said. 'But if you were watching her, I understand.'

'I'm tired.' His hair was flat on one side but stuck up on the other.

'I just woke up too,' I said.

'You were asleep in my street?' Though he joked, he didn't smile.

'No, I mean, I *realised*. I remembered something.' My breath hung in the air; his feet were bravely bare.

He shivered, wrapped his arms across his chest. 'You remembered more?'

'Not things about me; about you. I remembered that day we were sorting through those hideous decorations at Flood Crisis and what you told me.'

Across the street a group of teenage carol singers discussed which houses were likely to cough up the most money for a rap version of 'Jingle Bells'.

'What did I tell you?' Christopher asked.

The rapping teens called out to us and asked if we'd give them a fiver for a song; we both shook our heads.

'About your wife: you told me she gave you the watch and left you tonight – on Christmas Eve. So, I was talking to Fern about suicide calls and how they increase this time of year and how depression is—'

'And you thought of me?' Christopher laughed, but it sounded more like a cough and he seemed to withdraw further into his hallway. 'That'd make a great obituary: "He reminded me of crisis lines and depression."'

I tried to explain that that wasn't what I'd meant at all and tried to describe how sad it made me when I imagined his wife leaving. That it made me sadder than anything I'd ever felt for anyone. Sadder than for any calls I'd taken. Sadder than when I'd broken up with Will. And not sad in a bad or pathetic way, I tried to explain, but sad in a raw and true way.

'I don't know what it means,' I said and held out the red watch. 'But you're right – people come back.'

He stared at it, then put out his hand and touched it like he'd never seen it before, reluctantly reclaiming it. He shrugged. 'Yes, your friend came home.'

'I was thinking the other night, that people have to go away to come back. But some people never leave. They do emotionally but they're never actually gone.' Now it was empty I put my hand back in my pocket. Nothing I was saying made sense. 'But that's not why I've come here. I wanted to ask you something.'

'I've got a question too,' he said. I could make out the sound of the TV inside his house, perhaps the theme-tune to *CSI*. 'Why did you leave Flood Crisis? Was it because of that awful shift? I'd totally get it if it was. Or was it because you didn't want to see me anymore?'

'No, it wasn't because of you. People will be going home soon and their houses will be repaired and they won't need us, will they?'

'Katrina, they—'

'I'm not sure I'm Katrina anymore,' I said. 'I have to be Catherine, don't I? At some point, I have to be Catherine.'

'I knew you as Katrina.'

The teens rapped in harmony further up the street, 'Jingle Bells' Kanye West style.

'She's gone,' I said softly.

'Is that your way of saying I liked a ghost?' He leaned his head against the doorframe and studied me. 'Did you come to remind me that my wife left two years ago tonight? And to tell me Katrina has gone? I *know* those things.'

I shook my head. It started to snow. Soft flakes fell soundlessly on top of the ice, softening the sharp edges.

'I'm sorry if I messed you about. I know I ruined everything. I should've just been brave enough to call you. But people make mistakes. Your wife made one when she left you. I did when I didn't call you last week. I wanted to. I was going to. So many times. But I was scared you'd reject me, which is silly. You've only been good to me. And then tonight I just found out you'd called me and I felt worse. But kind of happy too.'

'You didn't know I'd called?' He blinked.

'No.'

'I rang *twice*.'

'I know that *now* – I found out twenty minutes ago. Bloody Fern left me a note the first time and I never got it. Then she only just told me that you called last night.' Snow was settling on my shoulders now and on the step. 'I would've been so happy if I'd seen that note on my pillow. I'd have called you back.'

'I thought you just weren't interested.' He shook his head. 'It hurt.'

'I'm sorry,' I said. 'I was ... I *am*.'

'You had a question.' He let the door fall open some more, granting me a view of his hallway, of letters and newspapers on a small table, of blue-carpeted stairs, perhaps a bedroom beyond. 'Just to avoid confusion, who's asking?'

'Catherine. Me. I am.'

I held my face in my hands, not sure if it was to hide or warm it.

The snow made everything new.

I'd spent my life asking questions. I'd asked millions, over and over and over. At crisis lines I'd asked people if they were sure about dying. I'd asked if they were still there and about an acting teacher called Mr Westerly. I'd asked what a man with a strange voice could remember about his daughter, and then who he was as he died. I'd heard answers that had made me cry, ones that had surprised and angered me, ones that had revealed my own truth as much as the caller's.

Snow continued to fall.

None of the questions I'd asked felt as heavy as the one I opened my mouth to ask now. I tried to form the words.

Glancing at the avenue blanketed in new snow, I realised two street-lamps were out, either stubborn or broken. But there was still enough light to see. Even half lit the path was visible. I could see trees and faithful carol singers. Not all lights are needed to dispel the dark.

Maybe I could have used other words, less oft-used ones. Maybe I could have phrased my question more eloquently. Maybe I could have picked one that did not sound like a prompt and that had not been asked so many times before, perhaps on a doorstep such as this.

But I think I chose the only words there were.

'Christopher,' I said, 'do you fancy going out sometime?'

'Maria in the Moon'
– an original song by Carrie Martin

'Little girls made of sugar and spice,
and all things nice;
we should keep them safe in jars,
upon a shelf.'

Something a little bit magic happened when Louise told singer, Carrie Martin, about her latest novel's themes and storyline. A soul-stirring tune Carrie already had in her head finally found its words, and the song was born – quickly, in a matter of days.

With its stunning video, haunting melody, and emotive lyrics, it's going to be a sure-fire winner. Wherever Carrie plays it – at gigs and festivals – it brings the house down. She has already garnered much love with her fantastic album *What If* and for her captivating performances, but Carrie feels this song is something special. And it really is.

Visit Carrie's website – www.carriemartin.co.uk – to find out more about the creation of the song, about Carrie and Louise's friendship, and how you can download the track and see the video.

Acknowledgements

I want first to acknowledge all the Hull and East Yorkshire folks who flooded in 2007. Hopefully, this book is a tribute to your bravery.

As always, thank you to Karen Sullivan for everything. For the passion. For the belief. For the friendship. Thanks to West Camel for the always thoughtful, always helpful, always perfect edits. And to Kid Ethic for the stunning cover design.

Thanks to my pal Jess Addinall, who squealed at me at every twist and turn of *The Mountain in My Shoe*, and demanded Maria in the Moon early! Hope you enjoy it now it's here. Thank you to Chris Miller for the helpful advice when this novel was in its infancy, just after the floods.

I must thank the following for their incredible support – Rosie Canning, Jeanette Hewitt, Janet Harrison, Cassandra Parkin, Tracey Scott-Townsend, Hayley at RatherTooFondOfBooks, Joanne Robertson, Anne Williams, Ellen Devonport, Tracy Shephard, Tracey Fenton, Sophie at Reviewed The Book, Jane Isaac, Victoria Goldman, Lorraine at The Book Review Café, Clair at Have Books Will Read, The Book Trail, Anne Cater, ShotsMag, NorthernCrime, Tony at MumblingAbout.com, Louise Wykes, Sumaira Wilson, Annie at The Misstery, Steph at StephBookBlog, Lucy V Hay, The Quiet Knitterer, Sheila Rawlings, ThisCrimeBook.com, GrabThisBook.net, Lisa Adamson (Segnalibro), Jen at Jen Med's Book Reviews, Sue Bond, Kate Furnival, Katherine at Bibliomaniac, ChillersKillersAndThrillers, Steph Broadribb CrimeThrillerGirl, Books Underground, Portabello-BookBlog, Liz at LizLovesBooks, BlueBookBalloon, NeverImitate @ followthehens, Lauren Allen, Rebecca Boof at The Book Whisperer,

Carol Lovekin, Emma The Little Bookworm, bloominbrillientbooks, Janet Emson, LiveManyLives, The Last Word, Damppebbles.com, Claire Knight, Jules at LittleMissNoSleepDaydreams, The WelshLibrarian, Sarah Hardy, Karen at My Reading Corner, Chelsea Humphrey, Louisa Tregar, Gill Paul, Melissa Bailey, Kerry Fisher, Merith @bookfairiecymru, Nicola Smith at Short Book & Scribes, If Only I Could Read Faster, the Fudge Book Club, Donna Roussel, Annie de Bahl, and Richard Littledale.

Huge thanks to Helen Cadbury for sharing my York book launch. You are hugely loved and missed by the book community. Also to Russ Litten for hosting the Hull one, and to Michael J Malone for the magical London one.

I was profoundly moved when Claire McAlpine got in touch because *How To Be Brave* helped her though a tough period with her beloved daughter. It connected us (and Grandad Colin). Thank you.

Also, to Melanie Hewitt, who said I'd 'opened the door to reading again' for her. I'm honoured to have done so.

Thank you to the Prime Writers for all the writing encouragement; I won't name you all for fear of leaving someone out, but you're an endless support.

Thank you to The Facebook Book Club (TBC) led by Tracy Fenton – again too many to name, but you're a cracking group, where I have such fun.

Also to Book Connectors – a place that's such a haven for bloggers and authors.

Thanks to the Women of Words gang – you know who you are!

Thank you #BeechsBitches – Helen Boyce, Ellen Devonport, Gail Shaw, Frances Pearson, Donna Young, Donna Moran, and Barbara Beswick.

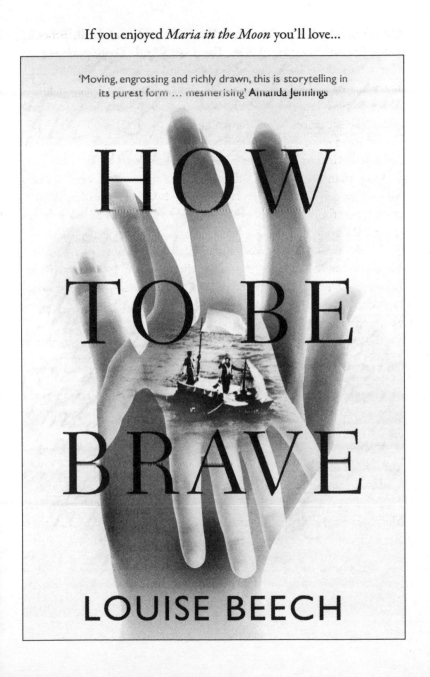

'Moving, engrossing and richly drawn, this is storytelling in
its purest form ... mesmerising' **Amanda Jennings**

HOW
TO BE
BRAVE

LOUISE BEECH

the

mountain

in my

shoe

LOUISE BEECH